We are not the only ones watching.

The umpires, as they shall come to be known stand apart from the servants who bring delicate foods and sweet drinks from some unseen kitchen. They watch, their faces masked, and they guard the silver door.

—Where does this door go? we ask.

—To the higher league.

—What is the higher league?

—It is a place for games.

—So is this place, so is this entire house. What is different about the higher league?

—The games are different.

—Can I join?

—Have you been invited?

—No.

—Then you cannot join.

—How do I get an invitation?

—We watch. You play.

And so the door remains shut. For now.

Praise for

THE NOVELS OF CLAIRE NORTH

84K

"An eerily plausible dystopian masterpiece, as harrowing as it is brilliant."

—Emily St. John Mandel

"An extraordinary novel that stands with the best of dystopian fiction, with dashes of *The Handmaid's Tale*."

—Cory Doctorow

"[A] captivating novel from one of the most intriguing and genre-bending novelists currently working in the intersection between thriller and science fiction."

—*Booklist* (starred review)

The End of the Day

"A beautiful, if occasionally uncomfortable, read that resists being labeled with any particular genre."

—*Library Journal* (starred review)

"Wholly original and hauntingly beautiful. North is a writer to watch."

—*Kirkus*

"North is an exciting voice in contemporary fantasy, and *The End of the Day* should be a welcome calling card from her to many new readers."

—*San Francisco Chronicle*

The Sudden Appearance of Hope

"North...has established a reputation for tense, dense, science fiction/fantasy–inflected thrillers that defy facile expectations.... Simultaneously a tense conspiracy caper, a haunting meditation on loneliness and a brutally cynical examination of modern media.... Well-paced, brilliant and balanced."

—*New York Times*

"Remarkably powerful and deeply memorable, the latest in a string of terrific books from this newly emerged star in the genre-blending universe."

—*Booklist* (starred review)

"It's intricate, but somehow, once again Claire North makes it all work.... A fantastic read featuring a unique protagonist with a unique problem."

—*Kirkus*

THE GAMES HOUSE

CLAIRE NORTH

www.orbitbooks.net

Omnibus copyright © 2019 by Claire North
The Serpent copyright © 2015 by Claire North
The Thief copyright © 2015 by Claire North
The Master copyright © 2015 by Claire North
Excerpt from *Someone Like Me* copyright © 2018 by Mike Carey
Excerpt from *The Ten Thousand Doors of January* copyright © 2019 by Alix E. Harrow

Author photograph by Siobhan Watts
Cover design by Lisa Marie Pompilio
Cover images by Arcangel Images
Cover copyright © 2019 by Hachette Book Group, Inc.

Orbit
Hachette Book Group
1290 Avenue of the Americas
New York, NY 10104
orbitbooks.net

Simultaneously published in Great Britain and in the U.S. by Orbit in 2019
First Edition: May 2019

Orbit is an imprint of Hachette Book Group.
The Orbit name and logo are trademarks of Little, Brown Book Group Limited.

The publisher is not responsible for websites (or their content) that are not owned by the publisher.

The Hachette Speakers Bureau provides a wide range of authors for speaking events. To find out more, go to www.hachettespeakersbureau.com or call (866) 376-6591.

Library of Congress Control Number: 2018962987

ISBNs: 978-0-316-49156-3 (trade paperback), 978-0-316-49157-0 (ebook)

Printed in the United States of America

LSC-C

10 9 8 7 6 5 4 3 2 1

THE SERPENT

Chapter 1

She is gone, she is gone. The coin turns, and she is gone.

Chapter 2

Come.

Let us watch together, you and I.

We pull back the mists.

We step onto the board, make our entrance with a flourish; we are here, we have arrived; let the musicians fall silent, let those who know turn their faces away at our approach. We are the umpires of this little event; we sit in judgement, outside the game but part of it still, trapped by the flow of the board, the snap of the card, the fall of the pieces. Did you think you were free of it? Do you think yourself something more in the eyes of the player? Do you fancy that it is not you who are moved, but is moving?

How naïve we have become.

Let's choose a place and call it Venice. Let us say it is 1610, six years since the Pope last declared this place heretic, barred from the blessings of his divine office. And what was this to the people of the city? Why, it was no more than what it was: a piece of paper stamped with wax. No Bishop of Rome could shake this sinking city. Instead the black rats will come, they will come with fleas and plague, and the city will rue its impiety then.

But we run ahead of ourselves. Time, to those of us who play in the Gameshouse, stretches like kneaded dough; fibres split and tear away but we persist, and the game goes on.

She will be called Thene.

She was born at the close of the sixteenth century to a cloth merchant who made a fortune buying from the Egyptians and selling to the Dutch, and her mother was a Jew who married for love, and her father fed her pork from infancy and made her swear never to reveal this terrible secret to the great men of the city.

—What will I be when I am old? she asked her father.—Can I be both my mother's daughter, and yours?

To which her father answered,—No, neither. I do not know who you will be, but you will be all yourself, and that will be enough.

Later, after her mother dies, her father remembers himself speaking these words and weeps. His brother, who never approved of the match and dislikes the child as a symbol of it, paces up and down, rasping:

—Stop crying! Be a man! I'm ashamed to look at you!

She, the child, eight years old, watches this exchange through the door and swears with her fists clenched and eyes hot that she will never be caught crying again.

And a few years later, Thene, dressed in blue and grey, a silver crucifix about her neck, leather gloves upon her hands, is informed that she shall be married.

Her father sits, silent and ashamed, while her uncle rattles off the details of the match.

Her dowry is greater than her name, and it has purchased Jacamo de Orcelo, of ancient title and new-found poverty.

—He is adequate, potentially a fine husband given your degree, her uncle explains. Thene keeps her fingers spread loose across her lap. The act of keeping them so, of preventing from them locking tight, requires a great deal of concentration, and at fifteen years old, Thene has not cried for seven years, and will not cry now.

—Is this your wish? she asks her father.

He turns his face away, and on the night before her wedding day she sits down with him before the fire, takes his hand in hers and says,—You do not need my forgiveness, for you have done

5

nothing wrong. But as you want it, know that it is yours, and when I am gone I will only remember the best of you; only the very best.

For the first time since her mother died, he cries again, and she does not.

Jacamo de Orcelo was not a fine husband.

For the sake of Thene's dowry, this thirty-eight-year-old man of the city swore he would endure the snickering of his peers who laughed to see his fifteen-year-old bride, whispering that he had married the merchant's daughter, and murmuring that beneath her skirts there was only cloth and more cloth, no womanly parts at all for a man to grapple with.

The first night they were alone together, she held his hands, as she had seen her mother do when she was young, and stroked the hair back from behind his ear, but he said this was womanly rot and pushed her down.

His aged mother told her that he loved fresh shrimp cooked over a smoky flame, the spices just so, the sweetness just right, and she learned the secrets of this dish and presented him a platter for his supper, which he ate without thanks, not noticing the efforts she had gone to.

—Did you like the meal? she asked.

—I had better as a boy, he replied.

She sang when first she came to this house, but he said her voice gave him a headache. Then one night, when she was walking alone, she sang one of her mother's songs, and he came downstairs and hit her, screaming,—Jew! Jew! Whore and Jew! and she did not sing again.

Her wealth bought him some redemption from his debts, but money dwindles, and the laughter persisted. Was it this, we wonder, that made their marriage so cold? Or was it the fumbling of the old man in the sheets with his teenage bride, his love of wine, his affection for cards and, as she failed to produce

6

an heir, his growing fondness for whores? Which piece of all of this, shall we say, was it that most defined their home?

We watch their house, proud and tall in the heart of San Polo, hear the servants whisper behind their hands, see the wife withdraw into her duties, witness the husband spend more on less, see the coffers empty, and as the years roll by and Jacamo grows ever more reckless in the destruction of himself, what do we see in her? Why, nothing at all, for it seems that against the buffets of fortune she is stone, her features carved into a mask of perfect white.

Thene, beautiful Thene, grown to a woman now, manages the accounts when her husband is gone, works with the servants and hides in the lining of her skirts those ducats that she can best secure before he finds them and spends them on whatever—or whoever—it is that today has best taken his fancy. And as he grows loud, so she grows quiet, until even the whispers against her character cease, for it seems to the gossipy wives of Venice that there is nothing there—no merchant's daughter or gambler's wife, no woman and no Jew, not even Thene herself—but only ice against which they can whisper, and who has any joy in scheming against winter herself?

All this might persist, but then this is Venice, beloved of plague, reviled by popes, the trading heart of Europe, and even here, all things must change.

Chapter 3

There is a house.

You will not find it now—no, not even its gate with the lion-headed knocker that roars silently out at the night, nor its open courtyards hung with silk, or hot kitchens bursting with steam, no, none of it, nothing to see—but then it stood in one of those little streets that have no name near San Pantaleone, just north of a short stone bridge guarded over by three brothers, for there are only two things that Venetians value more than family, and those are their bridges and their wells.

How did we come to be here?

You—why, you have come with Thene, you have followed Jacamo, who is for ever looking for new ways to lose his wealth and heard rumour of a place where he might do so in most extravagant style. You have come with them both to the door, for Jacamo is angry with his wife, angry at her coldness, her constant politeness and failure to scream, and so he takes her with him now, that she might witness all he does and suffer in him. Follow them as they knock on the door and step into a hall hung with silk and velvet, pressed with the smell of incense and the soft sound of music, past two women clad all in white, their faces obscured by nun's veils though they are of no such order, who whisper,—Welcome, welcome, please—won't you come in?

Follow them inside to the first courtyard, where torches burnt about the pillars of the walls and the sad faces of martyred saints, mosaicked in the Eastern style, sadly look on from their hollows above the arches of the doors.

Like Jacamo, perhaps you spot the prostitutes, hair pulled up high and dresses hitched about their knees, cooing in darkened corners at their clients. The sound of music, the smell of meat, the soft chatter of voices, the roll of dice, the slap of cards—why, they all call to him, sweetest nectar.

But more.

Perhaps, like Thene, you see too the boys and men who coo at the wealthy ladies gathered here, their faces hidden by long-nosed masks or silver-woven veils. Perhaps you observe the other doors leading to other places, from which different voices and different smells drift like the reflected spread of candlelight.

As her gaze falls around this place, and ours follows, we too now perceive that of all the games being played in this courtyard and the halls that surround it, there are more than the mere casual tumblings of chance from the gambler's cup. For now we see chess, checkers, Nine Men's Morris and many we alone can now name as toguz kumalak, baduk, shogi, mah-jong, sugoroku and shatranj—all the games of the world, it seems, have come here, and all the people too. Is he not a Mogul prince, a diamond larger than her fist in his hat, who now moves a piece against the Jewish physician, yellow scarf wound about his neck? Is she in red, rosaries slung around her wrist, not a Frenchwoman who now places her bet against a Ragusan pirate freshly come from plunder? And more—more exotic still! For it seems to us, as we inspect the room, that a Muscovite nobleman, who spits and curses at the foulness of Venice, now turns over a card which is beaten by a Bantu prince, who smiles faintly and says,—Another try? Is that not Chinese silk draped across the white sleeve of the veiled woman who brings drinks to the table, and is there not a hint of Mayan gold in the brooch of the man who stands guard before a silver door to a place that is, at this time, to us unknown?

Thene sees it all, and though she cannot so precisely pinpoint the origins of all these sights as we can, she has wisdom enough to perceive its meaning.

Chapter 4

Jacamo plays.

He loses as he plays.

He is a man who is played upon by players, and poor ones at that. We shall not bother much with him.

Thene watches. He keeps her close so that she can watch him lose twenty, thirty, a hundred ducats. When she does not react, he pulls her closer, one arm around her waist, so that she can watch him lose on the next hand, his father's ring, his estate near Forli.

When even this does not cause a flicker in her brow, he grabs the nearest girl by the thigh, kisses her neck.

Thene says,—Shall I fetch wine?

And rises and walks away. Her hands, folded one on top of the other across her belly, are perfectly relaxed. Jacamo knows the meaning of this, though others do not, and is satisfied.

He swears tomorrow they shall return.

Chapter 5

We are not the only ones watching.

The umpires, as they shall come to be known stand apart from the servants who bring delicate foods and sweet drinks from some unseen kitchen. They watch, their faces masked, and they guard the silver door.

—Where does this door go? we ask.

—To the higher league.

—What is the higher league?

—It is a place for games.

—So is this place, so is this entire house. What is different about the higher league?

—The games are different.

—Can I join?

—Have you been invited?

—No.

—Then you cannot join.

—How do I get an invitation?

—We watch. You play.

And so the door remains shut. For now.

Thene watches too.

She watches her husband, his fortune steadily obliterated by men of meagre skill and poor strategy. She watches the lucky and the poor, the calculating and the giddy, as they move through the room, daring each other to greater odds. She spots a member of the Council of Seven, and two from the Council of Ten. She sees judges and merchants, lords and priests, and more—she sees women. Wives and daughters, mothers and ladies of the night: some play, some watch and there are some who are let through the silver doors to the unknown place without a whisper, without a sound, their faces hidden by the masks of carnival, their eyes watching her watching them.

Then there is the man.

Let us call him Silver in honour of the tracery of thorns that runs in that colour so softly, a thread wide, along his sleeves. He approaches her, and it is testimony to how innocuous he appears in all other senses that she does not mark him doing so, and as she turns at the sound of breath he says:

—Do you play?

No, she does not.

He smiles, half shaking his head.

—Forgive me, he says.—I misspoke. *Will* you play?

She looks at her husband's back, the empty glasses at his side, the coins on the table, and realises that there is anger on her lips, a tempest in her belly and her hands hurt—they burn from not clenching—and with the softness of winter mist in her voice says simply,—Yes.

They play chess.

He wins the first.

She wins the second.

They do not speak more than a few words as they play. The wager is information, for there must be a wager.

—Is it not enough to play for joy? she asks.

At this, terror flickers across his face.—You would wager your *happiness*? You would gamble with your self-esteem? Good God, don't play for joy, not yet; not when there are so many lesser things you could invest in!

This sentiment should have felt strange, and yet it settles over her as sure as the altar cloth across cold stone.—For information then, she says.—For answers.

When he wins the first game, he asks her even before the king has hit the deck,—Do you love your husband?

—No, she replies, and is surprised at the candour of her words.

When she wins she thinks a long time, and asks then,—What do you want of me?

And he replies,—One day I shall need a favour from a stranger, and I am curious to learn whether that stranger could be you.

Then Jacamo is up and drunk, and she takes him home.

The next day she dismisses another servant who they cannot afford to pay, and two nights later, they return to the house.

Again, Jacamo, the cards, the drink, the losses.

We are delicate watchers; we do not stare every night, but we have come here enough and seen him in this state before, and can surmise that there have been many more times that we were not privy to when this pattern played out.

We tut, perhaps, but say no more. Who are we to judge?

This night, however, we observe an alteration in events. Tonight he falls asleep after three hands, spittle falling from his lips onto the tabletop. Thene would feel ashamed at her husband's display, but regret, like the sound of her mother's songs, was lost a long time ago. Then Silver is by her side and says,— Will you play?

They play.

She moves too quickly on the first game, barely glancing at the board. When her final piece falls, he asks his question, and it is,—What do you fear?

She thinks a long time before answering.

—The things I might do, she says.—The woman I have become.

Their second game is slower, harder, and three moves before he's checkmated he says,—I should probably resign, but that would sully an otherwise superb win. So he plays through and she wins, and asks even before his king has toppled,—Did you poison my husband tonight?

—Yes, he replies.—How did you know?

—I saw you watch him play, stand close to his elbow. You have never watched him before, nor shown any interest in his playing as it is so poor. You smiled and laughed and sounded like one of them, the men with their cards, but you are not. I can only assume you have some other intention, and now he is asleep and nothing stirs him.

—He will live, I'm afraid. I won a knowledge of alchemy from an Alexandrian once. I wagered my knowledge of gunpowder against his skills. By chance, he played his pikemen badly and I captured the castle.

—You talk in riddles.

—You must learn my language.

—Or you mine.

—But you want a thing I have, my lady.

—And what is that?

—You want to know what is beyond the silver door.

—Perhaps I do.

—Let us not be coy.

—Then I do. I want to know.

—Then we should play.

They play.

Chapter 6

On the day she has to take a loan from a moneylender in the ghetto who knew her mother and whispers that for her, he will find a special rate, the umpires come to her.

That night, as with many others, Silver is not to be seen, but she has grown confident now; she plays many people as she moves around the room, and loses some but wins more. Jacamo is too drunk to care, and so carefully she acquires wealth won on board and table, with cards and stones, pieces and dice, building up her own small stash of coin for the day, which must come soon, when he drowns himself and the household in that drink too far.

At first people played her out of pity, and lost. Then they played out of curiosity in the wife of this husband who plays so much better than the man who is meant to be her master. Now they play for the purest cause, and in the purest way, for now the Gameshouse works upon their souls and they play for the only thing which matters—for the win. And certainly, there are some players in some forms who will beat her on a certain day, but a great many more who lose, and still they try and try again.

Then the umpires come.

The voice is female, but beneath her white robes who could tell until the moment in which she spoke?

—Come with me, she says.—We have watched you play.

—Come where?

—You would like to meet the Gamesmaster.

It is not a question, nor does it need to be.

Thene follows to the silver door. Like Thene, perhaps we

15

pause here to inspect the four carved panels which are mounted there. They depict the fall of empires. Proud Rome, overcome by the barbarians of the north. Noble Constantinople, its people screaming as the Ottoman pushes them from the walls. Two cities she cannot name, and as the door opens it occurs to her that, to another pair of eyes, the images carved there are not tragic laments at all, but celebrations of the new empire that slays the old.

Then the doors close and we are alone with Thene in a corridor, too long, the path obscured by silks hung like ancient spider-webs, the sound of music muffled, the smell of wax and candlelight sweet in our senses.

She is briefly afraid, but to go back is impossible, so on, on she goes until a pair of wooden doors opens to a new place, a hall of soft voices, of low couches and bunches of grapes in copper bowls, of the old and the young, the beautiful and the strange. In the courtyard of the lower league, she thought she had seen some great variation in the peoples of the world, but now she looks and sees faces that, to her eyes, seem barely human, and yet now we might name for her as there the high historian of the court of Nanjing; there, the wife of a samurai slain in battle, her obi tight about her waist. Here, the Maori chief who glowers at the fur-clad woman of the steppe, and here is there not some clue to the nature of the house? For even Thene, who knows nothing of the camel-herders of the east or the canoe-builders of the south, can look and know that these people are alien to her world, and that their garb is not fitted for Venice. Not merely is it absurd to think that they could have passed without comment, but the very weather itself is set against them, for surely she who wears such white furs about her throat would swelter in the autumn warmth, while he who wore—and even she turned her face away from the sight—little but animal hides about his midriff, was surely too scantily clad to endure the Venetian night?

How then did all these people come to be here? A great many doors lead in and out, and of a great many different designs, for the one she came through is of a classical Roman bent, but over there are paper panels that slide back and forth, and there a great metal barrier that must be winched back to permit the passage of people through its maw.

All this she considers, and again feels fear, though it is a fear which cannot be named, and is greater for the ignorance which spawns it. Then an umpire is there and says,—Come, please, come.

She follows.

A small black door, tiny next to the vastness of the space, leads up a narrow flight of stairs.

At the top of the stairs is a windowless room.

Cushions have been set on the floor, and three men are gathered there already. Two of the men wear masks. The other she recognises: a player from the courtyard like herself, whose record stood on a par with her own.

Before them all, sitting cross-legged on a heaped mess of cushions, a silver goblet at her side and veiled all in white, is a woman. Like the umpires, her face is hidden, but her robes are greater in volume and length than any other, swathing her entirely so that only where her wrist protrudes from her long winding sleeves, and when she speaks, could any sense of her form or sex be discerned.

For a long while they are silent, the four strangers and this gowned woman, until at last the latter seems to rouse herself from some manner of meditation and, raising her head, says to them,

—You have all been chosen.

She stops a moment and considers this remark, which came so easily to her lips. How many times has she spoken it before, and to how many players? Too many—too many.

—There exists in this house two leagues in which players may compete. The lower league you have all experienced, and there is gold and pride aplenty to be won from those who seek such material things. The higher league I now invite you all to join. Here we do not play for merely earthly things. You can wager diamonds if the glint of those gems amuses you, or rubies, or bodies,

17

or gold, or slaves. These are all objects that others may covet. But here you are invited to wager something more. We invite you to wager some part of yourselves. Your skill with language, perhaps. Your love of colour. Your understanding of mathematics. Your sharp sight. Your excellent hearing. Years of your life—you may wager so much, if you choose, and those who wager unwisely and lose the game will find themselves growing old before their time, and those who play and win may live a thousand years, and become in their playing more than what they were. Nor, with the stakes so high, do we play petty games of chance or symbolic objects. If your objective is to capture a King, then we shall name that King, and to his court you shall go to win your prize. If you wish to compete, as our young boys do, for the ownership of a flag or other symbol of your power, then rest assured it shall be the flag of the mightiest general in the land, and your troops shall be legion, and with cannon and powder shall you make your claim. Our games are played for amusement and the increase of our minds, but they are played with flesh and blood and guts and pain as surely as any monarch of the world.

—You may decry such things as impossible or witchcraft but they are neither, and were you considered of such narrow-minded sort as to reject the veracity of what I am saying, you would not have been invited to participate. A great many people have heard rumours of this league and our house, and many lives have been lost and confidences betrayed in seeking to reach it. You are, in many ways, blessed to have been chosen, but if my words cause you fear, then you may leave now and the game will go on. Be aware that you shall not be invited to return to this league, nor shall you be permitted to speak of it to any other. This is a term inviolable.

She finishes speaking, and waits.

No one rises, no one leaves.

—Very well, she says.—I accept your consent. Yet as this is the Gameshouse, you cannot simply walk into the higher league without some venturing first. Four of you have been judged suitable—one will join the higher league. The rest shall leave this place, never to return. A game is proposed to determine a winner. Please—take the boxes.

We watch now as four boxes, each in silver, are presented by the umpires to the players, whose fingers itch to open but who keep themselves perfectly still, locked perhaps in fear of she who sits before them.

—The game, she continues,—is one of Kings. Within these boxes are pieces that you may deploy. Each piece is a person, somewhere in this city, who has through rash venture, wager, debt or misplaced ambition come to owe a certain something to this house. Their debt we now transfer to you to be deployed as you may. You will also find within these boxes the details of your king. There is a vacancy emerging in the Supreme Tribunal for an inquisitor in black. Four candidates of some equal strength will compete for it. Each one of you has been assigned one of these candidates—one of these Kings. The winner is he or she whose king takes the throne. The rules of the game are also laid down within your boxes. Anyone who violates them will be punished most severely by the umpires and, friends, please do not doubt that the umpires will know. They will know.

So she finishes, and so she rises, and so the players rise too, and for a second all stand, stiff and silent in the room, waiting for something more.

Do we imagine a smile behind the hidden face of the Gamesmaster? Do we think we can hear humour in her voice?

We dare not speculate, not tonight, not with a silver box in our hand and the terror of the unknown beating in our breasts.

She leaves, and so do we, the room dissolving like memory.

Chapter 7

We are in a most private place.

Thene and her husband do not share a room, and he, for all he dares, does not dare enter this place, her place, the highest room in the house, a place usually reserved for servants though they are now nearly all gone. In it are some little things, for only in little things will Thene invest, knowing that when they are stolen, destroyed or taken from her, the material loss is nothing, and as for the emotion, the history and the time she has put into them…why, let it go. Let it go.

We are bold, you and I, to be here at all, watching unseen. Yet here we must come, voyeurs to another's story, for here it is that Thene removes her bodice and her heavy outer skirt, unpins her hair, lights another candle from the stubby end of the first, sets it down beside her bed and, sitting cross-legged on top of the mattress like a child with a secret enthralling book, opens the silver box.

Dawn is rising outside through the streets of Venice, the grey light seeping in over the islands of the lagoon, through the slumbering workshops of Murano, across Piazza San Marco, that proud place built in defiance of Byzantine ambition, along the still waters of the Grand Canal and towards San Polo, where Thene's treasures are revealed.

A piece of paper outlines the rules.

Do not harm the other players.
The winner is the player whose king is crowned.

There was nothing more.

She turns it over a few times, then laughs out loud and stops herself at once lest the sound be heard in the house.

She looks into her box.

A silver figure, a statuette, showing a man in flowing robes and flat cap. His name, engraved on the bottom, is Angelo Seluda, though she little needs to be told. Everyone knows the Seluda family, who have for these twenty-five years fought running battles with the Belligno family in the streets of Cannaregio. The Seludas wear blue; the Bellignos wear green. The Seludas trade glass; the Bellignos trade fish. Everyone knew why the feud had started, though no one knew the same thing. Some said a woman...others said a boat. It was whispered that Belligno's favourite son was betrayed to a rival from Milan by a Seluda captain. The boy loved a woman (in as much as a seventeen-year-old boy knows how to love with anything but a blazing passion that dies like candles in rain) but that woman had a brother, and the brother was jealous, and two years ago the child vanished. Belligno is too powerful for any one house to openly murder his kin, but not powerful enough, it seems, that even his mighty word can keep the wandering children alive. Then again, who is to say what really happens in matters of the seas and war? We trust only the uncertain men, for they are the ones who hear everything and believe nothing, reporting rumour as rumour, and in their doubts they stumble on a truth, and the truth is that no one knows anything and people like to talk for a long hour or two in the sun.

In three hours' time, word will spread through the city that Stephano Barbaro is dead, there will be elections for a new inquisitor to the Supreme Tribunal, and both Angelo Seluda and his arch-rival, Marco Belligno, will leap from their beds to fight for the post.

How, we wonder, did the Gamesmaster know that Barbaro would die?

We wonder, and then we do not. To wonder too deeply seems unwise, and will not aid our goal.

21

Her king, then, a sixty-one-year-old head of a merchant house, member of the Collegio, rival for the throne. She wonders who the other players have been given as their piece. Venice is a republic, a democracy even, in as much as a great many wealthy men of the city may vote for the Doge in the following manner: thirty members of the Great Council are chosen by lot. Another lot then reduced this thirty to nine. These nine members then chose forty members of their kin, who took another lot, and by this were reduced to twelve. These twelve then chose twenty-five, who were reduced by lot to nine, and these nine then elect forty-five. Of these forty-five, a lot again reduces their number to eleven, and these eleven then elect the forty-one who elect the Doge.

Is this democracy?

Why, certainly, it is democracy, if democracy is the machinations of a small handful of great and powerful men who by bribery and marriage own the others. Chance is not welcome when lots are drawn in Venice; votes are only worthwhile when the electors know that the votes will be cast the proper way. But who would be Doge? A worthless, ceremonial position; a man in a hat, living in a gilded cage. The Supreme Tribunal, to be a Tribune, there is where the power lies! This every Venetian knows. Even the silent; even the women.

A letter unsealed. A ribbon with a ring attached invites her to read, then seal at her own leisure. She opens it.

Dear Sir, the bearer of this note will assist you in your enterprise. Please accord her full courtesies. Your Friend.

She examines the ring with which this note should be sealed. It bears the head of a lion, roaring as do the knockers to the Gameshouse gates. She seals the note with wax and puts it aside.

More objects from the box. A white mask, which, unlike many of the masks made for females, does not require the wearer

22

to bite a handle between her lips to keep it in place. She may speak, strange liberation, though her face is unknown.

Tarot cards. The Fool. The Three of Coins. The Knave of Swords. The Queen of Cups. The Seven of Staves. The Tower. The Priestess. The King of Coins. On the back of each card is written a name and a place of residence.

A promissory note for five thousand ducats.

A single golden coin. The face carved on it was none she knew, and the inscription is Latin. We know it now—how we know it!—a coin from ancient Rome, but with it no note nor an explanation. What is its purpose? Perhaps it will only become apparent when other tasks have been completed? Games, unlike life, have a structure, a pattern, an order to unlock. Play, and all mysteries shall be revealed.

She laid it aside, sealed her box, blew out the candle and lay down to sleep.

Chapter 8

She placed one thousand ducats on the table.

Jacamo de Orcelo watches it. What does he see in that purse? Ships? Chests of cloth, barrels of fish, precious spices from the East, slaves, grains? Or does he merely see casks of wine rolled across the pantry floor?

For a while they stand there, husband and wife, on the opposite side of the gold, and their faces speak, rage in the arguments that their voices have no courage to express, until at last Thene says:

—I'm going into a convent for three months to pray. You will find all things have been arranged. Goodbye.

He screams then,—Whore, hussy, harlot, where did you get the gold? Where can you get more? and tries to grab her by the hair, but she punches him. It is not the open-palmed slap of a lady of house Orcelo, but rather it is her, herself, the Jew's daughter, who hits him full in the face, and as he falls back bloodied, she gathers herself together and says,—If you want more, you will have to wait until I return.

He sits on the floor, legs splayed, rump down, and for a moment is too shocked to move. Then the little boy within him comes out, and he weeps, and crawls on his belly to her feet, and kisses her shoe and says,—I love you, I love you, don't go, I love you, where's the money? I love you.

She turns away.

Chapter 9

The house of Angelo Seluda is by a canal. Its lower floors are—
in traditional fashion—a place of business, its middle floors for
the family and its topmost reaches crawl with servants, clerks
and men of trade, humbly appreciative of their post from a man
so great as the master of this house. It has its own well, the surest
mark of status, and there is something of the Byzantine in the
patterns above the windows, the carvings on the wall, scratched
to the tiniest detail, which tell of an old home for an ancient
name.

Thene examines it from across its private bridge and sees
the statues raised to guard the entrance: Ares and Venus, hands
clasped together in an arch above the gate. She feels a cat brush
against her legs, curious at her curiosity; hears the push of oar
through water, another supplicant coming up the canal to do
homage to Angelo Seluda.

She is afraid, but has already come too far.

She loosens her fingers in their grey gloves and finds herself
humming half a tune, a song she thought she had forgotten on
the edge of her lips. She wears her mask, and coming to the door
is stopped, challenged and when she speaks, surprise and distrust
grow deeper on the faces of the lazy boys armed with clubs who
accost her.

—My letter, she says.—I can wait.

She waits outside, five, ten, twenty minutes. In the time she
stands there, we do not see her feet move, her back bend, her

fingers ripple with impatience. Ares and Venus sweat in the face of her composure.

A boy returns, his face humbler now, and says,—Please come in.

She follows inside.

The door shuts her from our view.

Chapter 10

Snatches of a conversation overheard through an open window.

He is Angelo Seluda, and we have observed him before in the streets of Venice on his way to prayer, arguing with merchants fresh come to port, inspecting timber and glass, giving censure at the Doge's palace, watching his rivals from between the cracks of the door. His family long ago discovered some secret sand, or some hidden colour, or mystic tincture—like all things in Venice, the detail is unclear—and took a great interest in glass. War has sometimes been unkind to this trade, but after every war there is always a great sighing of peace and, more importantly, a great many cracked windows to repair. And so on Murano his name is worth more than gold, and in the little islands that pepper the edge of the lagoon where twenty, thirty men at most inhabit and labour, Angelo Seluda is uncrowned king, Doge in all but name, commander of the workshops across the water. For too long he has laboured in the Senate, seeking advancement, but alas! He has always been a little too wealthy to escape envy, and thus his rivals have barred his advancement; yet he has never been quite wealthy enough to buy his way through this conundrum.

His hair is grey, his beard is long and, as only the old and the great do, he wears a gown even in summer which reaches to his ankles, and a chain of gold about his neck, and a purple cap upon his skull, and his most prized possession is a brooch of golden fleece given to him, so the rumour says, by a Spanish king for some service against the Turk in a battle long since fought, long since forgotten.

27

Or perhaps he bought it second-hand. Who can say, with a man like Seluda?

His voice now, meeting hers.

—I did not expect a woman, he says.

—Nevertheless.

—Can you play?

—I would not have been chosen if I couldn't.

—The notion of putting my fate in the hand of a woman disquiets me. I was promised assistance from the Gameshouse in exchange for some...services. When I agreed to these terms, I had imagined more than this.

—You will find I am very suited to the task.

—May I see your face at least?

—No.

—Or know your name?

—Not that either.

—I am fighting for election to the Supreme Tribune. If I should win, I will command the Council of Forty in all but name, and what's in a name when so much power is at stake? If I command the Council of Forty, I will rule the city beyond the power of any mere Doge. I know what my rewards are and how much is staked. What do you get and why do you care?

—I win the game.

—This isn't a game.

—Isn't it? There are rules, boundaries, constraints on your action. Clear goals, tools to achieve them, a set table of rivals who must obey the same rules that you do if they wish to reach the same end. The only difference between these events now unfolding and any other game is the scale of the board.

—Games should be enjoyable.

—Levity and sincerity are not antonyms. We take pleasure in playing chess, but that does not mean we make wasteful moves. You have invested things of great weight into these coming events. Your honour, your prestige, your finances, the welfare of your family, your business, your servants, your future. Such

28

matters can weigh heavy on a mind and cloud it to wisest judgement. I suggest that having the assistance and resources I offer, untainted as they are, will be of service to you.

Seluda is silent a while. Then

—What do you need?

Chapter 11

She takes a room in the top of his palazzo.

The mask will not leave her face now, save for in those few, few moments when she is alone, high above the waters of the city.

She needs pen, paper.

The rest she can do for herself.

A servant of Seluda is sent to the Doge's palace with orders to wait and not move a muscle until he has heard who else will stand for the Supreme Tribunal. In all, seven names are called. She studies them, trawling through memories and faces, esteemed gentlemen half known from prayers at church or whispers on the wharves. Who of these seven are serious contenders, has something to gain? She draws circles around four names, including Seluda's, but nothing is to be taken for granted yet. Each party must be assessed, their business known, for even a minor rival who cannot win the prize on his own part may yet disrupt her activities in bidding for it.

She expects Belligno to run, and indeed his name is one of the first that reaches her ears. Whether Belligno has decided to campaign for his own gain or because he hears Seluda too seeks the prize, she is not certain, but she pays a beggar and his daughter to observe all that Belligno does and report on those he is seen with, rumours that are uttered about his name. For two days they watch, and at the end of the second day there is still no sign that anyone plays Belligno, save himself.

Faliere—jovial, smiling Faliere, who it is said prepared the poison himself that killed three of his guests at a feast some seven years ago, though equally it could have been a bad fish or a rotten egg. How can a man who smiles so boldly and laughs with such hearty appreciation of others be a poisoner? And then she looks a little closer and thinks perhaps he laughs as he prepares the brew? Perhaps, like a child making mud pies, he chuckles to himself as he stirs belladonna into his enemy's wine, chortling at the thought of their eyes widening, their hearts racing, their minds clouded and tongues hysterical? Perhaps this same thought keeps him merry as he serves drink, and people mistake this continual self-entertainment with being a more generous spirit and think his humour is at their wit rather than his own?

Or perhaps he never poisoned anyone and knows that it is good to be both loved and feared, and so laughs and is generous to his friends and lets the rumours persist of what he may do to his enemies?

Paolo Tiapolo and Andrea Contarini are not only both strong candidates, but have the gall to attend mass together. She sits at the back of the church and observes them, on opposite sides of the aisle. They smile at each other, embrace as old friends:— Paolo, Paolo, so good to see you;—Andrea, your wife looks beautiful and I hear all is well with you?—and when the other's back is turned they bend down and whisper to their wives and their secret companions,—*There goes that bastard. Watch him—he's a snake...*

Tiapolo has three daughters whom he has kept virginal and unmarried for an unfashionably long period of time. The eldest is nearly twenty-four and people are already questioning if the old maid is even capable of bearing children but now! Ah—clever now, clever Tiapolo, we understand! You were waiting for Brabano to die; you were waiting for the time as well as the place when each child might be most helpfully deployed in your cause. Well prepared, Tiapolo, well did you play the game, even before the game was begun.

And Contarini? He has quarries on both this and the other side of the Adriatic Sea; his business is mortar, stone, brick, clay and those judicious men who have mastered all of the above. His children are long since married to wagon masters and marble merchants, so barely a building can be raised in the city now without the Contarinis' mark etched above the door. Foolish men mistake the master for his trade, call Contarini "Old Man Stone" and say his wit is dull and heavy as the slabs of the coffin—yet how they change their tune, these laughing men, when they want an extension added to the top of their palazzos or repairs done to the inside of their wells! How then they flock to him, our master Contarini, and laugh at his jokes which are, we will concede, exceptionally dull and surprisingly crude, made only marginally funny by the hope of discounts gained through humour shared.

These two—smiling Tiapolo and leaden Contarini—are rivals indeed, though each in their different way, and as she watches them bow before the bishops, she wonders what they make of her piece, or if they think of him at all.

A flash of colour in the church, a smile caught in the corner of her eye. She looks, and then looks harder, astonished by what she sees. Puffed sleeves of cyan-blue, rings of silver and gold, and features familiar, manner known. Whoever is playing Tiapolo as their piece doesn't bother to hide. He sits, proud as Zeus, directly behind his piece, his pawn, his king—whatever it is you may call these would-be masters of all they survey. He does not wear his mask in church, for to do so would be an offence to the Lord and the great servants of the Lord gathered there, but step outside and he wears it, a badge of prestige and power. It is not he himself who hides behind that carved smile and gold-rimmed eyes; no, rather it is *he*—himself, the great man, the player—that he wears instead of his face: lord of his dominion, master of the game.

She watches him; she watches Tiapolo. She fears the piece more than the player.

Though he has appeared at Mass, he vanishes by private barge, and for two days after she cannot find Contarini. He has moved, he is hidden, but let that not be seen as a sign of weakness, for when he needs to appear in the Doge's palace, he is there, shaking hands, and when he leaves he does so by two private boats, one which turns left, the other right into the bay, and no man can know which of the hooded men that sit within it is the man himself. Contarini fears the blade of an assassin and his fear perhaps tells us the direction in which he too shall take this game. She makes no effort to track either of his gondolas. Assassins are crude tools and should only be played when the board has coalesced into something more coherent. Contarini will wait.

At night, she lines the pieces up on her table. Faliere, Tiapolo, Contarini, Seluda. Do the other players study these as she does? Are they sitting alone with a single half-burned candle considering their enemies, their friends?

(And now we see! Three unnamed rivals spread across the Venetian night. He, the one who is proud, so proud of his cleverness and his power, so rich on the satisfaction of his game, so aloof from humanity—he drinks at the high table with Tiapolo, and will go to bed drunk and wake late, and tell strangers that he has slept with Tiapolo's wife, knowing no one will question him, and thinking it is because they are afraid.

And he, who plays for Contarini, or on Contarini, depending how you look at the matter, watches the house of Seluda where even now Thene resides, and knows that his piece is a powerful man, and will not be happy until this rival is removed, and he feels the weight of a silver box given to him in the Gameshouse, and knows the power therein and wonders whether soon is too late to strike.

And for the last?

Why, like Thene herself, he sits alone in the shadows and considers his move.)

33

Faliere, Tiapolo, Contarini, Seluda.

And beneath them, a question. Why was Belligno not chosen as a piece? Why is she not playing him in this game of power and politics? His claim to the position on the Supreme Tribunal is strong, perhaps stronger than Seluda's own. Why is he not being deployed and moreover, will he be a threat, though he is neither player nor played?

Questions in the night. We shall leave her with them for her bedside company.

Chapter 12

Let us consider a card.

Its frontage shows the Seven of Staves, but who is he?

A man who has struggled to the top, perhaps, and now fights to hold his position? A middling functionary, not a king, but neither is he a pawn, but rather he is Alvise Muna, who at fifty-seven years of age has lived longer than most who serve within the Doge's court and yet, for all that he has wandered these halls for decades and heard the secret mutterings at midnight, there is a sense about him that he will rise no higher, but remain for ever as he is: a councillor, reliable, solid, unremarkable, a little prone to bribery but not at unreasonable cost which, in Venice, is as high an honour as may be given to a man, and going nowhere more than where he stands now.

She meets him in the Piazza San Marco. He walks alone, a roll of documents under one arm, a velvet cap pulled down upon his grey, bent head, a great mole upon his chin, utterly devoid of colour, paler almost than the skin from which it grows, and when she steps before him, he moves to pass without looking, for there is nothing in these streets save business to be administered, and he would rather administer it from his office than in the presence of the people themselves.

—Signor Muna, she says, and he half turns at his name, slowing his pace.—I hold your card.

Now he stops, now he looks all around, now he grabs her by the arm and whispers,—In some other place.

They enter the basilica separately, and for a while he prays and

35

so does she, though he is on bended knee at the front of the aisle while she sits behind, beneath gold and the eyes of Christ. Quiet is amplified in this place more than noise, for every whisper echoes and every hush that falls is deepened, deepened by the depth it has to plummet. When he has finished at his devotions, they meet beneath the gaze of St. John, a lamb at his feet, a book in his hand, his eyes sorrowful at the deeds that men will bring.

—I owe some favours, he whispers.—I acquired some debts. A woman dressed all in white offered me a chance. She said you would one day come.

—What kind of debts?

—That's my business. They are forgiven when the game is done.

—You are positioned in the palace?

—If you call it that. I do all the work that everyone else is too busy arguing about. I worry about the waterways, about silt and mud. I consider the price of crab, the quality of fish, the depth of new wells dug in old squares, the paving materials and safety of rooftops. Other men should do this but they have their eyes on a bigger prize.

—Your work sounds difficult.

—I will never be more than a slave to other men's ambitions.

—I believe now the favours you owe to others have devolved to me. That is the meaning of this card, is it not?

—It is, though I am no pawn to be moved across a board. My debts are my debts, but when they are paid I will risk my neck no more in any man's business.

—I do not ask you to take risks.

—Then what do you want?

—A sounding of the Senate chambers. In less than a month a Tribune will be chosen to replace the deceased Barbaro. For now, I wish to know the disposition of the electors, what influences them and what they desire. These things will not be won on principal but on the greatest gain for the largest sum of people. It is only information I need now, which a man of your qualities will have well disposed. Information is not a great burden to acquire.

—And in a month?

—The game will end, and so will your obligation to it.

—And my debts?

—All debts end with the game.

—I shall do as you ask.

He does not see her smile.

And who is this?

The Queen of Cups.

La Bella, beautiful lady Pisana, queen of the night. She is a poetess and a good one, though her words will be burned by a vengeful bishop-turned-lover who will call her heretic and whore. She has read the works of Julian of Norwich, and calls God "mother" and Jesus "sister", and proclaims that the word of Christ is compassion and love, and that man who would deny it is no more holy than the droppings of a donkey. Is this heresy?—No, she will say, when they put her before the judge.—For the divine is neither man nor woman, and being so I choose the name that is most kind, most loving, most giving to the goodly of earth, and say that in heaven I shall find my sisterhood.

Now she sits, ankles showing, knees showing, one leg draped across another, skirt pulled high, and turns the card that is presented to her between her fingers and smiles.

—I used to be a player, she says.—I know your game. What sad times that I am now a piece.

—Sad indeed, Thene replies, barely wetting her lips with the fine wine that was offered.—How did you come to this pass?

—I wagered more than I had to give. I gambled the life of my child against fifteen years of a woman's youth. But my child died before the game was completed, and there being no mercy in the house, I lost my place. I am not angry now—those are the rules, this is the game. The game is greater than I comprehended, and has been played longer and on boards far wider than this you play now. Had I known that, I might not have laid any wager at all. Yet here we are.

—Here we are.

—You want something from me, no doubt. I am a powerful card in your hand, yes? The Queen of Cups, no less! It is apt, I suppose, and good to see that the Gamesmaster has not lost her sense of humour.

—I hear your women sometimes are about the house of Orio Faliere.

—You hear correctly, but they never attend the old man himself. He has interest in neither women nor girls—not even pretty boys seem to arouse his icy flesh.

—Who then do your ladies sport with?

—His sons. His servants. His men-who-hang-about-hopefully. The vast majority of the great houses of Venice are peopled with this sort, and they all seek an outlet for their disappointments sooner or later.

—They are of some use to me, but not so much use as Faliere himself.

—You are playing a game for...what? The Supreme Tribunal—is that your prize? It is, isn't it?! I had wondered if the Gameshouse would intervene. Which player do you play? Belligno? Tiapolo?

—I do not think I should say.

—Perhaps not, though the card you hold binds me to you for the duration of the game, and there is much discretion in my business. Let me ask you this then: how many players do you know of?

—Four.

—Four! And of those four, I can assure you, luck will have been uneven in her favours. Ask yourself, why has the Gamesmaster—or mistress I should say—singled out only four? The house has its purposes, and you must never forget that if you desire to win.

—Perhaps when I have won, I will enquire further.

—When you win, you will not enquire at all. The victory— the victory is all! Should you win, you may not wish to jeopardise your new status with reckless questioning. So it is that comfortable people settle into a deceiving life, finding truth somewhat unpleasant. But I like you, my lady. I am glad that you hold my card. If you wish to deploy me most advantageously, I would not suggest Faliere. He is too cold, too aloof, too dead-to-the-skin. Seluda now, he is fiery for every kind of flesh, though you would hardly think it to look at him; Belligno and Contarini both have wagging tongues, and other parts besides.

—They also have other weaknesses which I might explore. There is a rumour that Belligno had a son...

—Ah yes, the foolish boy who went to Milan!

—You know something of this?

—I know that he was reckless with his love and wrote ballads and odes for nearly every lady of Venice. The husbands of these ladies doubtless would have had something to say on the matter, but in this city Belligno protected his boy from their ire and so he became more love-struck and even more foolish.

—And vanished?

—Not in Venice: in Milan.

—Why did he go to Milan?

—His father was a little embarrassed, I believe, at the son's activities.

—A little embarrassed?

—Even Bellignos feel shame when the boy is too drunk to tell the difference between pretty girls and pretty boys, and takes all equally.

—So sent the boy to Milan?

—This was two years ago, maybe more.

—He never returned.

—No. He never did.

—And what does the father make of all this?

—He believes his boy is dead.

—Do you believe that?

The Queen of Cups hesitates, lips curling into her mouth, tongue running along the inside, head turning a little to one side.

—Why do you play, my lady? she asks at last.

Thene hesitates.

—Come, come, chides the other.—We are sisters, and I am in your hand. I was a player; I may be of some greater use to you than you first perceived. Why do you play?

—To be free.

—Of what?

—My husband. My family. My blood. My name. All of it. To be…powerful. Nor do I say "power" for its own sake, but rather I would say for power-as-strength. Power as the strength to be known for myself, to live for myself, to be—in a manner that has until now been denied to me—myself. That is why I play.

At this, Pisana tuts.—That is a very bad thing for a player.

—How so? Surely a good player has cause greater than themselves to play?

—Not at all. A cause will corrupt your perception of the board, lead to decisions made in sentiment which should have been made in thought. There is only one reason, only one, why you should embark on this game. Would you like to know it?

—Yes. I would.

The Queen of Cups leans in closer, whispers, her lips brushing the ridges of Thene's ear.—You play to win, she breathes.—That is all.

So saying, she sits back, smiles a pleasing smile, giggles like a girl and says,—We were discussing Belligno?

Thene takes a moment. Relaxes her hands. Looks a little to the left, a little to the right, then meets Pisana's eye again. The moment that was might never have been.—Do you believe Belligno's son to be dead?

—Yes. I do. They say he was unwise in his affections in that city. Those husbands, fathers, brothers who in this city might have permitted him to have his amorous adventures in fear of the father, in Milan felt no such concern. Belligno could not protect his boy once he had crossed the lagoon, but both father and son were, I think, too foolish to consider this.

—So the son died?

—Vanished, rather. Though what the difference is, save for

40

one of suspended hope, who can say? Do you want me to make enquiries? I have some friends in Milan.

—No. Thank you. I think it perhaps best that I use other resources for that enquiry, and employ you on matters more conducive to your trade. Faliere—

Here the Queen of Cups huffs indignantly; Faliere, Faliere, what good is he to her, or she to him? Yet Thene will not be swayed.

—…keeps himself isolated from all things, is never seen beyond his own four walls, is guarded constantly, confides in no one. He is the piece that must be broken first, for he will be the hardest to break.

—I do not think female tenderness is your most likely tool to achieve this.

—A man may be approached by many means. Money, servants, spies, traitors—but Faliere is cold to them all. However, as you point out, his household is not. He cannot win without calling upon the resources of all he now possesses, and he cannot defend every part of his kingdom at once. An unlikely assault from an unexpected source, targeting his pieces and not him, seems one of the few viable options available, and while I have enough money to bribe some in this regard, you are the Queen of Cups. You would not have been given this title were you not something greater than the usual sort.

—What do you know of the "usual sort"?

—More than the men, Thene replies.—Unlike men, I look at what is, rather than what I wish to perceive. Tell me—if Faliere is so cold to women, then what is the condition of his wife?

At this, Pisana smiles.

—There, she murmurs,—*is* an interesting question.

Chapter 13

A strategy.

Every player needs a strategy, but plan too precisely, commit too closely to only one path, and what danger there lurks! For you are not alone in this game—others will act against you as you act against them—and so softly, softly on.

Many words trouble her, the laughter of the Queen of Cups echoes in her mind.

I was a player once.

Play to win. That is all.

She shakes her head a little, pushing the memory of Pisana's breath from her thoughts. A plan is forming now in Thene's mind, but she is wary. First information, then the kill.

The Knave of Swords sits, one leg upon the table, his hands folded behind his head. Is it possible to swagger while sitting? If so, he succeeds.

His beard is black, darker than his brown hair. His nose and eyes are little hollows between the roaring mass of hair that shadows his face. He dresses in an extraordinary patchwork of fabrics, French and Bavarian, Flemish and Portuguese, his tailor a drunkard who loves to travel.

He says,—I fought a duel. My sword broke, and I lost. My sword never breaks. And here we are.

—I hold your card.

His arms open as if he would bow from where he sits.—My lady, he says, though he does not stand, does not remove his foot from her table, does not alter the fixed smile that waits without laughter behind his facial hair.

—Would you like me to kill someone? he asks.

—No.

—Why not? I am good at killing.

—Assassination is a crude move. Kill a piece too soon and the other players are made stronger in its absence. While there are four players there is balance, forces pulling every which way, resources stretched. My piece seems...perhaps weaker than I would like, but this could be an advantage. Let other players expend cards on battling each other, the strong tearing each other down, until they are weak enough that I may strike. An assassination now would destroy that balance, and though one day the balance must break, it is too soon for that.

—I'm better at fighting than I am sitting around composing Greek verse.

—Contarini has been behaving in an extraordinary manner. He does not sleep in the same places more than two nights in a row, sends decoys to hide his every move, writes letters in code and generally speaking behaves in a manner more suited to a criminal in the night than a candidate. I know that this is to protect against any interference from players such as myself, but I believe that in doing so, he has created a weakness. Being constantly on the move and with security so high, he must of necessity devolve some of the everyday running of his affairs to lower men of his household. It is this that I wish to explore. Speak to his stewards. Buy them drinks, share tales of adventure, walk drunkenly home with them through the night. Find out from them not where Contarini is, but where his wealth is. Like the rest of us, his position depends on finance—if we can empty his chests before the election, he will be no threat.

—Drink and politics?

—I would have thought some of that would appeal.

—You hold my card, he replied with a shrug.—Not my decision how you play it.

*

And as she walks through the streets in the night
…a sense.

A suspicion.

A question?

Is she being followed?

The thought, made sharp by circumstance, runs with her all the way to the Grand Canal.

The rules have promised her safety, but what does that mean now? Nothing, perhaps. Everything. Something. A question she cannot answer, a fear she cannot know, she picks up her pace, not running, not that, but moving in search of light, people, alleys too tight, buildings too high, a church ahead—to this she flees, slamming the door behind her, candles, the smell of incense, her heart too fast, too fast in her ears, in her eyes, in the pulsing of her throat. A church is not safety, though it may be stillness for a while. She stops. She slows her breath. Slows her fingers, her eyes, her thoughts.

She is a player.

She is a player.

She is *the* player.

Victory will be hers.

She turns to the doors and steps out into the dark.

Examines the shadows—see her there, so proud, so straight! Thene, Thene, there is no fear now: there is only the player. She watches and defies the dark to do her harm; it is *her* dark, her night, her city; to her will it shall bend, if it bends to anything at all.

We watch her depart.

We watch.

Chapter 14

Alvise Muna, the Seven of Staves.

—Tiapolo bribes everyone, he whispers.—He has promised his daughters in marriage to nine people already—nine! They say he has pledged over ten thousand ducats to the election so far, with a promise of land, glory, wealth—anything—to anyone who supports his cause.

—And does he succeed?

—A great many men have accepted his gifts, but no one says his name out loud.

—And why do you think that is?

—He makes promises he cannot possibly keep. His spending is unsustainable; it is... *crude.*

Muna's lips curl in disdain at the word. He says,—His people threaten those who do not speak in his support. It is not how we play the game. A man who receives the precise sum of gold that will discharge his debt to a clawing physician is more grateful and more personally bound than he who receives some greater, larger sum paid without consideration.

—But if the election were today?

—Tiapolo would win because no one else has yet made their move, and because the Council of Forty knows the value of a weak leader too, one who might be easily lead.

—And if it is tomorrow?

—That depends on what you do next. A loyalty that is purchased for coin lasts only as long as the next offer.

—You say he has people.

—A man in court that I know for certain.

—Do you know who?

—Someone powerful, high. Yesterday Belligno's man was denied access to the Council of Seven. That has never happened before.

—Someone on the Council itself?

—I imagine so.

—I need to know who.

—How do you suggest I find out? Ask in the palace, "Is anyone else sworn to serve a stranger with a card, a house with no name?" I don't think so.

—Extraordinary behaviours stand out, breaks in pattern. I must know what cards the others are playing if I am to counter them. But if you think so little of Tiapolo's efforts to win support, who would you consider next in the running?

—Yesterday it would have been Belligno, but he lost votes this morning when word came of a ship of his floundering at sea. We do not like people who lose vessels.

—So today?

—After Tiapolo...Contarini is the most spoken of, and with the greatest respect. The bishops have declared for him, and their coffers carry as great a sway as any word of the Lord.

—Contarini, not Faliere?

—Faliere is still unknown, as is Seluda. Both seem to be waiting to make a move.

—Faliere trades with Constantinople, does he not?

—Indeed. He was one of the very first to speak to the infidel when peace was declared. At the time he was derided for this, called a traitor and a heathen. But those unwise councillors who mocked him then come begging to his door now for passage to Egypt or a bar of Syrian soap.

—It does not affect his standing?

—Honour is easily bought, and Faliere is very rich.

—The bishops, you say, are for Contarini?

—Yes.

—Thank you.

—Are you winning? he asks as she turns away.

—Not yet, she answers.—Not yet.

Contarini, Contarini, how infuriatingly hard it is to find information on Contarini! What is his game? What does he do with the bishops, this stone merchant, this man of stone? She looks and she cannot yet see it, though at least now she has some idea of the direction in which it turns. She pens a note to the Knave of Swords saying,—The bishops. See what it is Contarini does for the bishops.

Then there is Faliere: his fingers touch only paper and steel, nothing warmer, and it seems that his soul is made of the same stern stuff. The Queen of Cups is about her work but then again, there is nothing in the rules of the game that says Thene herself may not make some enquiries. Not at the top—no, the heads of the Faliere house are too afraid of their master, too tightly knit to him, to ever betray his trust.

To the bottom then, to those quiet people with flapping ears who everyone ignores, the necessary souls who are no more and no less than a piece of floating furniture.

A gondolier, his legs upon the prow of his boat, his hands behind his resting grey head, who laments—how he laments!—that his day is spent waiting for Orio Faliere to summon him to his trade, how days sometimes go by and no, he does not set forth, he does not do his duty but rather waits and waits and waits, forbidden from leaving this place on the chance that someone in the house needs his services, but he could be elsewhere, he could be fishing...

—But are you not paid to wait? she asks.

—Yes, I'm paid to waste my youth in this place, waiting on whims, but I could be paid *and* fishing, instead of paid and waiting!

—...see.

This unfortunate gondolier, so tragically trapped by wealth into waiting on his master, tells her that almost nothing has changed in Orio Faliere's house since the death of Barbaro and you would not think that his master was competing for the post at all, save for in one matter—that last night a masked stranger, a man, came down to the boat and requested that he was shipped to the Doge's palace where he stayed for some twenty minutes before returning and being returned again to these halls. The masked stranger said no more than the place to go to and the command to wait, and on his return didn't even tip.

—How much are you paid to wait? she asks.

—Not enough, he grumbles.

—How would you like to earn a little more?

These streets, these streets!

Is she afraid to walk them?

(Yes. She is. We know this; we know it in the deep beating of our hearts; she looks and she is afraid.)

They are her streets, they are the streets which gave her life, and it is not fear of the shadows nor fear of the dark that walks beside her but rather more, worse, greater—a fear of the past, which does not leave her.

But she has a card in her hand, the King of Coins, and it must be played soon if results are to come in time for the election, and to play it she must cross the bridge into the ghetto while enough daylight shines so she can still get out.

The ghetto is in Cannaregio and there is, architecturally speaking, nothing much to the casual eye to set it apart from its surroundings. Like so much of the city, it has absorbed the styles of both east and west: a large square at its centre, tiny alleys all around, sloping cupolas and sharp corners, clothes drying from lines strung between every window. And yet look, look a little closer, for here there are no crucifixes but rather candles burning in the menorah, and there are those who live a little too close together in space that should have been expanded many years ago, but instead the floors have been lowered so that each room feels a little compressed, and where only five storeys might have inhabited the warehouse by the water, here there are seven. Now listen, listen, and you may hear not merely Venetian spoken, but the Spanish of the Sephardic Jews expelled by a Christian queen, or the prayers of those who fled from the Holy Roman Empire when Protestants mistook them for friends of the Catholics, Catholics for friends of the Protestants. They do not pray together, the east and the west, but rather each turns to their own synagogue, whispering that though they are all of one family, one blood, yet *he* does not practise to the same rules as *she*, and it is bad form to shake the hand of a man who has shaken the hand of a man who is a Christian.

So though compressed together, yet even in the ghetto—or perhaps especially—it is easy to be a brotherhood divided.

Of these people, one at least is universally known, and if not loved, then certainly no one dares speak of him with anything less than admiration. He is called Saloman. They stand together by the gates to the ghetto, watching the Jews and Jewesses of Venice busy about their daylight business, while the day permits them to work. His card is apt, she thinks, for he is the King of Coins to more than simply herself. Only four professions are permitted to the Jews of Venice, and one of them is moneylender, in which part they are derided, cursed, spat upon and envied.

—There is a cycle of humiliation, he explains. The Christian, to do himself up, humiliates the Jew, calls him dog, beast, devil, imprisons us at night, bids us wear yellow on our sleeves, tells us to eat pork and sleep in the sewer. But we fight with all that we have to become greater than our surroundings, and so we lend money and cure diseases and practise those philosophies that the Christian in his decadence does not. So they come to us for help, and then what is their predicament if they need the service of a dog and a devil? Does this not make them lower than us? And shall they not therefore pull us down in seeking to feel great again?

—How contrary it all is, he whispers as if she is not there.—How easily wisdom buckles before pride.

49

—Is it money you want? he asks, all business now: business, business, business.—Though I am your card, I can only lend cheaply, not gratis. Players usually want money.

—Not money.

—What do you want?

—I need to win Belligno to my cause. Though no player moves him, yet he is too powerful a piece to be ignored.

—You want to bribe him?

—No. I want you to make some enquiries in Milan.

—Ah, you are listening to rumours! The story about the Belligno boy, yes? They say that he went with a woman whose brother, it transpired, was not of a kindly disposition in these regards. Some say Seluda sold the boy out; others say he was just stupid. Me, I think he was probably stupid. Most boys are.

—I am told you have connections across all of Europe.

—And most of Africa too, but even I cannot find a dead man.

—Is he dead?

—He has been gone for two years and his father made many enquiries.

—I heard that the Milanese were vengeful people.

—Death is vengeful.

—I think we both know that death is a lesser evil in Milan. You can find answers?

—You wish me to speak to my cousins, rather than spend my coin?

—A bit of both, perhaps.

Then he turns to her, surprise on his face.—Do I know you? he asks.—Your voice...there is something familiar in you. When players are dealt my card, they see only the Jew, the Jew who lends money, the dog to be hounded by other dogs. You— you play me in a different way. It is unexpected.

—Can you do it?

—I can try.

—That is all I ask.

And as she turns to go:

50

—I know you, he breaths.—You hide your face but I know your voice. I knew your mother. She was a wonderful singer.

—I am a player, she replies.—The rest is nothing.

She is gone.

At night, we sit beside her, unseen, warmth from the candle. She considers Andrea Tiapolo, remembers him in the basilica, his player sat behind, puffed up and proud. He is moving too fast, playing his pieces too fast. He bribes too many, not realising that the key to success is to learn who the few great men are whose minds must be swayed, and focus resources on them rather than expend largely on the lesser loud men of the Doge's palace. He has shown his pieces too soon, but here is the question: does she deliver the killing blow to Tiapolo's campaign, or wait for another player to do so? Faliere bides his time; Contarini is moving slowly and carefully, but move he does. And what of Belligno, Angelo Seluda's greatest rival? He acts alone, is not a piece supported by a player but rather moves independently, and again the question—*why* is he not a piece? His moves are strong, he would be an excellent piece to be played, yet the Gamesmaster did not choose him for the game.

Yet, like the Queen of Spades as she emerges from within the shuffled pack, though he is not played, yet he still is a player.

She waits and hums her mother's lullaby under her breath, barely noticing the sound.

Chapter 15

The day that Thene spots—absolutely spots—another player's piece, she is delighted. Less delighted when she sees what he is: Abbot Padova, dear friend of the Patriarch of Venice, dearer friend yet of the Doge himself, for it is said that when the Doge's wife was sick, the abbot laid hands upon her and within a day—nay, perhaps within an hour!—she was up again, about her business.

This Abbot Padova she sees now at prayers, whispering when the liturgy is done in the Patriarch's ear, and as he whispers, Contarini watches him and smiles, and she knows that Padova is his man.

And why not? she muses.

If she had a piece like the abbot to play, she would deploy him to the very hilt.

She flicks through her cards, looking for the answer.

The Priestess.

She says:—Perhaps you do not consider it appropriate that a nun should be a piece in your game?

—I have no thoughts of appropriateness or rank, or any matter other than victory, Thene replies as the two of them walk side by side through the little chapel of the nunnery where the Priestess resides. It is not on the mainland of Venice itself, but on an island where the dead are taken to be buried, a steep little protrusion of green from the blue waters of the lagoon where the funeral barges wait in silence at the water's edge for the priests

52

and diggers of that place to carry their shrouded cargo into black soil. Dark-spined trees hang overhead, gravel crunches beneath their feet and birds sing between the branches, oblivious to the solemnity of this ground.

—Quite right, murmurs the Priestess.—A piece is a piece; the game is the game. It is the separation of humanity from the enterprise that will permit you to win it. That being so, what do you desire of me?

—I hear that the Church supports Contarini's candidature for the Supreme Tribunal.

—The Church doesn't concern itself with such matters.

—Come, you and I both know that isn't true. Abbot Padova is very much Contarini's man, and I have no doubt that he is being played.

—Indeed? Well, there are more than some of us, perhaps, who made...arrangements with the Gameshouse we might someday regret.

Thene hears the thoughts in the Priestess's voice, feels the sorrow, sees her eyes drift towards the still waters of the lagoon, and though the offer is sweet and her curiosity blazes, she does not ask the question, but rather swiftly moves through it, for she has business to attend and is beginning to learn that a piece in this game is not as simple as a counter on the board, for these pieces have secrets and prides, and though they are hers by the rules of the game, yet they too must be shaped into something more.

—I need to know what it is that Contarini has offered the bishops to sway them, and what it would take to change their minds.

—And you expect me to find out?

—I do, Sister. I think you are trustworthy. I think your honesty and piety are written in your face. I think you are regarded as spiritually notable but politically insignificant. I think you will be able to find out these truths very easily indeed.

—I hope you have been dealt better cards than me, she replies.—Though I will, of course, do as you ask.

—Thank you, Sister.

And then, as she makes to go:

—May I ask—how did you come to know of the Gameshouse?

Thene hates that she cannot stop herself from asking, then forgives herself at once, concluding that the value of the question perhaps—but no, it cannot be—but *perhaps* even outweighs the glory of the prize for which she plays.

The Priestess stands still, considering this question, considering her answer, whether it is apt to reply at all. At last she says,—I have seen four or five players set upon different matches who have asked me that question. The first time I was played, I was the Two of Cups, a novice in the order in Rome. The player asked me to perform a task which I could not achieve and I was nearly expelled, and he, having played me badly, lost the use of me as a piece and eventually the match. Then, the game was one of cardinals, and though I was not a player, I could see the pattern of moves well enough to know what the prize was. Ask yourself this, my lady: you play now to crown a king in Venice, and this is, I think, your very first game. Imagine the stakes that more experienced players must work for. Imagine the scale of their ambition. Though I am only a piece in your hand, I am powerful enough to take some interest in these matters, and of enough curiosity to wish to know how the Gameshouse makes its moves. I think anyone who considers themselves wise would do the same.

—You are not tempted to play?

—And risk losing? No. It is enough for me to know the board and see the direction that the pieces flow. I will not wager on it.

As her ship pulls from the island, she sees another, taller, greater, a pennant proud on its mast, heading out towards the open sea. It is a ship of Faliere, though where it is going, riding so high in the water, she cannot tell. Her lips thin ever so slightly behind her mask—her ignorance frightens her more than any certainty of Faliere's schemes. What does this man plot, who is so aloof from the machinations of the city, so far beyond the reaching of the game? She does not know, and is for a moment terrified.

*

And as she returns to shore she sees black fires rising from the harbours.

Men run, buckets, buckets, the buildings fall, the smoke rises up in a plume then spreads out into the sky at a certain point, as if passing some invisible barrier between the compressed, buffeting world of man and the expanse of heaven. If we stand close—too close!—the heat tears at our faces, at our skins, our lips crack, the blood pulses in our toes; retreat, nothing can save this now, and let us stand with the children who gape at the timbers cracking, the walls coming down, who watch the sparks of this blaze spin and flick towards heaven and say,—Mummy, it's pretty—can we see another one?

Onshore, the messenger confirms what she already knows: the warehouse was one of Tiapolo's. It was supposed to be empty, all goods shipped out three days ago but look, there is the old man on his knees, weeping, weeping, all is lost and it seems that the rumours were a lie. The warehouse was not empty at all, but rather filled with a secret stash of pepper for sale to an Englishman who had promised five times its weight in gold and now—now!—all lost in a sweet-smelling smoke. Tiapolo will be ruined, some say, but no, he'll come back, his kind always do.

Thene does not stay to witness the old man on his knees, or to observe the masked man who stands behind him, a silver box empty in his hands, who turns at last and walks away.

—Of course he can't win, tuts Alvise Muna as they walk together beneath the low arches of San Marco at the setting sun.—Tiapolo's entire strategy consisted of bribery and intimidation; it was already suspected that he couldn't pay his debts and now he definitely cannot enforce his threats. One day he might be a competitor, but not today.

Not today.

There are only three contenders now: Seluda, Contarini, Faliere. Belligno still moves on the margins, but she cannot think he will last long.

Which of Tiapolo's rivals delivered the blow? What cards did they play?

(Ah, the King of Swords! Char still clinging to his fingers, the smell of oil about his clothes; his card played, his debt discharged, he turns away from the blaze—until the next game.)

She has bided her time long enough.

Time to move.

Chapter 16

When they first invite Pietro Zanzano and his wife to dine, a message comes back pleading a headache.

When the next day they propose the same again, the messenger returns that alas, they have prior commitments.

On the third day, she visits the house and will not leave until she has seen the master personally.

He is busy, irritated, his grey hair sticking out beneath his black cap. He is something of a rarity in Venetian politics—not only does he have a great name, but the wealth which bought that name has grown, grown over the centuries where so many others have declined. If there was ever a quality close to godliness in Venetian eyes, it is this, for how rarely do economics and honour collide?

—Madam, he says, barely bothering to look at her,—I cannot visit your master's house. My wife is ill-disposed.

—Sir, she replies,—my master is most sad to hear that, but nevertheless some private conference will be of great use for us all.

—Doubtless he wishes me to do some favours for him; I cannot of course interfere in this process.

Hearing this, she smiles beneath her mask. It is the first time we have felt this, and it is so unexpected that we want to freeze this moment, capture it like a portrait, a second that was, and shall never be again.

Then—then!

She removes her mask.

So long we have seen her in this guise, we have almost forgotten that she is human. Shall we use the word "beautiful"? Beauty is a thing that changes with the eye that sees it, but any woman, any living creature, is surely more beautiful than a mask which hides her and so yes, we shall now declare that from the moment that was to the moment that is, she is alive, is living and is beautiful.

Zanzano looks up and perhaps he is not as impressed as we are by this sight. Or perhaps he is like the mask that now she holds in her hand, a face without a heart.

—You have already been made an offer, she muses out loud.— Very well. I will not do you that disservice to suggest that my master can beat the proposal that is already before you from Faliere—it *is* Faliere, I assume, who has approached you?

He does not move, and she is correct.

—It is a good move on the part of Faliere, as doubtless your voice holds great sway over these matters and you have power enough to decide, if not the vote, then a deal of it which is undecided until you speak. I will not do you any great dishonour to press you in this regard. You are a man of integrity; I wish you good luck.

So saying, she leaves.

And when she returns home, what of the mask shrouding her features?

Do we detect anger in her voice, or is it merely the intensity of a plan that now must fall as she demands, else all is lost?

We cannot tell. Our judgement here would be too subjective.

Yet here she speaks, and what she says is:

—*Faliere.*

And it is a statement, and a challenge, and a move that is yet to be made.

Chapter 17

The birds are still singing on the island of the dead, the sun still shines as fresh coffins are lowered into the crowded earth. Thene walks by the Priestess's side as the other says:

—Contarini has a relic in his possession. The elbow of St. Simon.

—Surely there are at least twenty elbows of St. Simon in Venice already?

—The bishops seem to believe that this one is genuine—or rather...

Thene smiles to see the Priestess smile, for it is such a rare expression across her features that it reminds Thene, in a way she cannot describe, of herself.

—...I do not know where Contarini found it: he did not have it three weeks ago and no vessel has come into port with any such thing about it. Indeed, the whole thing is being kept very close.

—I can make a few guesses as to where this relic came from, murmurs Thene as they walk together by the water, watching the clouds, the water, the city, the woman and the nun, the player and the played.

—Contarini has offered not only to hand over this relic, but to build the bishops a sacred place to house it. Doubtless the contracts for this exploit would be...very lucrative...to many individuals in the city.

—Ah—I see! He wins the bishops' vote by offering a little theological temptation in a golden box, then wins over the support of half the Senate by proposing building works which will keep them in coin for fifteen years yet to come. But by securing the Church's support for this venture, he doesn't even have to pay for more than the initial gilding himself if he can convince Rome to contribute to the construction of a reliquary while turning a profit on the contracts to construct! It is wonderful!

—You are pleased at this?

—I enjoy how so simple a move can trap so many pieces. Bishops, builders, men of faith, men of money. No wonder they have declared this sacred elbow or whatever it is to be the genuine matter, no doubt curing all manner of diseases. It is in the interest of everyone to find it so. Where is the relic now?

—No one knows.

—The bishops are committed?

—This enterprise will bring them wealth and prestige, which to the greatest in this church are of vastly more interest than salvation, sad to say.

—And for the same reason, much of the Senate will follow. Then we must see to its failure as quickly as possible, for the sake of their souls as much as our enterprise. Thank you, sister, for your assistance.

Chapter 18

And together in the dark, their voices hushed in secrecy, a veil across one woman's face, a mask across the other's, firelight in the heart and the sound of men, drunk, in the street outside, the Queen of Cups, Pisana, lady of letters and lady of the night says:

—Faliere is so cold I begin to question whether he is even a man, even human, or just some animated statue that sometimes shits and sometimes spits and shows no more that those human functions.

—I take it you have had little success infiltrating his house, murmurs Thene.

—He has doubled his guard, thrown out anyone he doesn't trust, sent his children away from the city.

—How prudent of him. But his wife?

—Ah—his wife. (And here, through her veil, we feel rather than see our Lady Pisana smile, for she learned long ago to find joy in those few joys that life can give, whatever their calling, whatever their form.)—Poor Lady Faliere: with a husband made of clay, what can she do?

And then, her enthusiasm for the thing itself breaking through her delight at the game of hiding it, she leans forward, the veil stirring around her lips at her breath, and whispers:

—She has taken a lover. A lady in San Marco; a very beautiful lady at that.

—Does Faliere know?

—If he does, he has done nothing.

—Tell no one. Protect the wife and her lover. I need their

relationship to continue until election day. Do not let anyone find out.

—I like you, lady. You have a romantic bent.

—Do not believe it.

—Be careful not to lose yourself too deeply to the game. Emotion is a weakness, but players are still human; so are pieces. If you forget the meanings of love or fear, you will not be able to see the board clearly.

—I know the meaning of fear.

—And love?

Thene didn't answer. Pisana nodded to herself and said,—You are the player I hoped you would be. She told me you were good.

—Who?

—The Gamesmaster.

—The Gamesmaster spoke to you?

—Yes. When she gave me my card, told me the conditions of my arrangement. You do not think I was ever just a piece, did you?

—What did the Gamesmaster say?

—What is it worth to you to know?

—You have a request.

—Rather a favour, let us say. If you win this game—and I think you shall—you will become a great player in the higher league. That could be of use to me. We could reach some understanding, you and I.

She thinks about it for a moment, then says,—No. Not yet. This is the game; I am the player. You are a piece, and I must win. Perhaps, when that victory is won, we can talk again of other things.

—As you wish, my lady. As you wish.

And so the Queen of Cups is gone, as are we.

Chapter 19

The coin.

Thene turns it over in her fingers.

There are only three cards in her pack left to be played. The Fool, the Three of Coins, the Tower and this strange Roman coin, old yet not old, no reason, no great value—what is the purpose of this? How is it to be played?

She lays it aside and goes to the Gameshouse.

The warmth of fire, the distant sound of music, the taste of drink, fine food, the watching umpires all in white, faces hidden, hands clasped, welcome, welcome, welcome to the Gameshouse, all things are possible here.

How is this house standing in this place? How can it be here, where it was not a few months ago? It is as if the street itself shuffled ungainly to the side to make room for it, buildings all around squeezing a little tighter, and yet she has wracked her brains and she cannot remember any building works or hearing any rumours of this place until the day she came to its lion-headed door.

She has questions, but knows the answers are not yet hers; not until victory.

Games.

They focus her.

Thoughts sharpen.

The complexities of the world are simpler here.

Black, white.

Forward, back.

Win, lose.

She plays, her mask still on her face, and she wins without thought, without passion, without enthusiasm for the victory, but with an intensity that speaks of another game, another Thene, working behind the mask.

We watch her, and she does not see us, so intensely her mind turns to the game, until...

...another player sits opposite her at the chess set.

He wears a mask that is nearly the twin of hers: white, soulless.

She looks and starts—a huge reaction for her—towers topple, earth shakes, she starts in surprise but hides it at once and perhaps it was not even seen, save by us who have so long been in her company.

The other, the player, says:

—Shall we?

She gestures her acceptance.

They play.

A while they are silent.

Pawns fall, knights scuttle, bishops are swapped for bishops, queens break from cover, kings cower by the castles, quick moves and silent periods of contemplation, until at last, without very much business about it, the other, the man, says:

—You will lose, my lady.

—She looks up from the board into his empty face, then back down at the board and is silent a while.—The position is balanced, she replies.

—No, he answers.—It is not.

Again she raises her head, and his eyes are blue, so very blue where they meet her own. Who is this man? She can recognise, even behind the mask, the face of he who played Tiapolo, and knows that player to be no threat. Is this stranger now Contarini's man, the player who pulls his elusive puppet's strings? But no.

No.

She knew at the moment he sat, she knew without the need of words what he is, who he is, his purpose tonight.

He plays Faliere, and though the board between them is even, the board that matters is not.

She knows, as she has known for a while, that he is winning. He has won Zanzano, and though as matters presently stand, she thinks the Senate is for Contarini, yet Faliere has many cards yet to play, and he is waiting to make a great move.

—What would you do? she asks, almost surprised to hear herself speak.—To win, what would you do?

He doesn't pause to think about the question.

—Anything, he replies.—Anything.

—So would I, she says, leaning away from the board.

Then,—We should stop this, she says, gesturing at the game between them.

—You said it was evenly balanced.

—The game before us is, but we are now playing another by different rules. I dislike the asymmetry of it.

—No one said the game was simple. If you don't feel ready for the challenge...?

—Do you ask that because of my actions, or my sex?

—I merely ask.

—You are wrong.

—Am I?

—In one regard. You say that I am losing, but you are mistaken. At this point in time, you and perhaps Contarini are ahead in the count, winning the election. I am not. But, sir, my time has not yet come. Do not assume that you have won until every player has made their move.

—I assume nothing. And yet here you are, my lady, alone in the Gameshouse while your drunken husband whores and gambles alone in the house you wish to leave behind. You assume every air and speak the speech as if it were doctrine, but you are still only the Jew's daughter. As for the game between us...shall we call it a draw or would you like to test your mettle tonight in preparation for tomorrow?

Her hands are soft in her lap. Her voice is light as breath. She has mastered both these things from a long time ago.

—Let us call it a draw, she replies.—I think the joy may have gone from it for now.

Alone.
    In the dark.
    Walking.
    She is
    angry.
    So long she has been angry, and so long she has bitten it down, becoming nothing at all but tonight
    there!
    It rises.
    It rises.
    She
    rages!
    Rage!
    Rage.
    Until it goes.
    And then she is alone again, and with the buoyancy of anger spent, she feels small and lost in this world.

Chapter 20

A moment in which we look inward.

Let us make an inventory together as Thene walks through the palazzo of Angelo Seluda, her piece, her king-in-waiting. We count up servants, slaves, nieces, nephews, cousins from the countryside, wife, two daughters, a son, physician, nurse, accountant, couriers, sailors, merchants and knaves. Dozens of people flitter in and out of the house of Seluda every day, and no one seems to keep an account of their activities.

She asks herself a question:
What wouldn't I do?
To win.
Nothing. There is nothing.

In the evening she stands before Seluda at his table weighed with messages and papers and says:
—The prostitutes must stop.
He splutters some denial.
—I have spoken with certain ladies who make little effort to disguise their purposes in this place. They are a risk to the security of this endeavour. I have other requests.
—Requests?
—Suggestions you would be wise to consider. Too many unknown people come in and out of this place; too many letters are sent by too many men; too few precautions are taken. I have spent the last few days gathering information on your rivals,

positioning pieces to be of service in your cause, and I have no doubt that others are doing the same. You are a threat to them as they are to you; therefore they will be acting against you. From now on, greater care with security must be taken.

—This seems…

—…do you want to win?

—Yes.

—…then as I say, I have some suggestions. We must guard your warehouses, protect your ships. Your power is money, prestige, the friends you have, the contacts you've made. We secure your wealth, remove it from anyone or anything which might be a risk. If you have supported gambling nephews, that support now ceases. If you have loans in play, recall them now. You have men-at-arms who you trust? They secure this house, your family, your gold. And no one captain works alone: two captains together, that they might watch each other, guarantee the other's loyalty. No messages are sent unnecessarily, and when you do dispatch a note, your messengers do not wear house colours, decoys are sent and secrecy is maintained. In the Doge's palace, we must look who to bribe and who is a lost cause already; this election will be won with money. Do not trust people who are too easily swayed; they may be swayed by another's cause. Every night tonight you will dine with groups of your dearest friends and your more questionable allies—but if you have eating habits, you will now change them. Simple dishes, you must eat foods you dislike, drink modestly, commit few indiscretions. Anyone who you do not fully trust, send away for the coming two weeks. Anyone or anything which could be used as leverage against you, we also retire. A castle is as strong as its weakest point—I cannot win the game for you if you are defeated from within.

—You talk like a general, like Tacitus himself! he says.

—I am a player, she replies.—I know the value of a good defence.

—What you propose is very costly.

—Do you wish to win?

—Of course.

—Then invest in victory.

Chapter 21

A letter from the King of Coins arrives at last! We have checked for messengers every day, never running, never in a hurry—we would never be caught being so undignified—but at last, *at last* it is here, on the cusp of that moment which would have been almost too late.

She forces herself to open it slowly. Splits the wax. Unfolds the paper. Holds it close to the flame. There is strength in being slow; intelligence in never rushing. She must be strong.

The King of Coins says that he has a cousin who has a cousin who has a sister whose husband's brother was married to...

...you know how it goes...

Someone whose word he trusts—this is the heart of it— helped wipe up blood from a cellar floor in Milan some two and a half years ago. The boy who bled was a Venetian who had made an unwise accord with a woman whose brother was not of good humour in this regard. The boy died; the sister sent to a convent. They say the boy's remains were thrown into the river, but that is not the whole story, for the water in Milan is sluggish and no sooner were the remains dumped than they were pulled out again and the unknown corpse was buried in a patch of unsanctified ground where now wild garlic grows.—Now I know a man who knows a man who has a cousin who has been known of a quiet night to dig up corpses from their fresh graves and carry them to the scholars of the city, who all in secret dig through guts in search of mysteries, and prophecy a new age of blood and bone. Upon hearing some tale of your lost boy, I asked this friend to make a little enquiry, and he pulled a corpse from the earth that had upon its flesh, a most terrible tale to tell.

Yet they say that the body wore a ring upon its finger that bears a seal.

Would you like to guess to whom that ring belonged?

And then Seluda says—no, *roars*:

—*Never!*

She stands before his ire, hands clasped in front of her, shoulders pulled back, and says simply,—If we are to win this battle, we will need the support of Marco Belligno.

—He is my bitterest enemy, a whoreson, an eater of dung...

—He is also an important piece in this game, one which has been sorely neglected by the other players. I do not think he can win by himself, but he commands a significant faction which, if it can be swayed to our side, will help secure the day.

—I will never work with that man. I will never—

—You need not speak to him; I will handle that. The important consideration here is what you are willing to agree.

—Nothing. Nothing. Nothing!

—Then, sir, I do not think you shall ever be a Tribune.

—You are a player! You are supposed to make this happen!

—I am only as good as the cards that are dealt me.

—A player should be able to win off any hand.

—We both know that is not always the case. There are those in Venice who consider you an outside candidate, and marvel that your name is even considered. I have a great deal of work to do to put you in a position where you can win this. Belligno is the ignored partner in this—I can use him.

—What about Zanzano? He's a friend, he's a good man...

—...he has been bought by Faliere.

—Then buy him for more!

—I do not think that will solve the problem. He is, as you say, a good man. The definition of "good" is such that it is best encapsulated by the terms of being a man who, having taken a bribe, will not take another that runs contrary to his original

70

contract. Nor can I believe that it was purely wealth that was offered him, since he has such an abundance of his own, but rather something more subtle we have yet to determine. Other players have cards they have played as well as I.

—We need Zanzano's support…

—And we will get it, but not by flattery or bribery. Rather, if we are to secure the support of Zanzano we must demonstrate that Faliere's tenure, profitable though it might appear, will do greater harm than good to interests other than the lining of his purse. The only thing which Zanzano prizes more than money is honour—that therefore is what we must target and the tool we must use. Securing the support of Belligno is honourable if done correctly, and the policy I wish to pursue.

—I will not speak to that man.

She considers, a question which she does not want to ask, has no interest in yet which rears its head and will not leave her until it is uttered.—Did you betray Belligno's son? she asks at last.—Did you betray him to Milan?

He is silent a while, and in that silence is a great answer and a great deceit that, just this once, has the good grace not to be uttered.—You're a player, he says at last.—You must know something of grief, if you would use the grief of my enemy to make him my friend. Tell me then, my queen of stone, do you know something of anger? Of rage and jealousy? Or are they merely tools, as the chisel is, which you use to carve your victory like a mathematician, all lines and no heart?

—I know grief, she replied,—and rage. I know them so well that I think they have burnt a part of me to ash, leaving only the shape of what they were inside me, and not the feeling itself. I do not care if you betrayed Belligno's child to his death. I care that you cannot be caught at it.

—There is no proof that I did anything, he replied.—There never was.

—Then that is enough.

Chapter 22

And then she stands before Marco Belligno and says:

—I need you to cast your lot in with Angelo Seluda.

Belligno, the fish merchant's son, who has married his daughters off nearly well enough that people no longer dare mention his origin (at least, not to his face) cannot hide his astonishment.

—Are you mad?! he exclaims.—Are you looking to die? Do not think that because you are a woman I will not split you in two where you stand, *are you mad*? Now I know the old man cannot have sent you unless he despises you and hopes that I will do his dirty work, destroy you where you stand, in which case you are betrayed, or you are not and he is mad, you are mad, all things are madness!

—You are not going to reach the Supreme Tribunal, she says simply.—Faliere and Condarini have the election too closely held. The most you can hope to do is push your support one way or the other for a suitable consideration. Faliere and Condarini will not bother to bribe you because they assume that Seluda, being your enemy, will take action against you instead. Either way, and however you view the argument, your support—your considerable yet insufficient support—is something that must be either won round or destroyed. I wish to win you round.

—I would *never*...

—I believe you lost a son?

Silence now. He is silent, though whether he will burst or whether he will stumble, who can say? She pushes on.

—The rumour is that Seluda sold him to a Milanese man who

72

believed your son had violated the honour of his sister. I do not believe that Angelo Seluda had the opportunity, though doubtless he had some motive in this. Regardless, no one would confess to having kidnapped and murdered your child, and so you must persist in ignorance. Ignorance can be worse than knowing, can it not? I had an agent make some enquiries. He has a cousin in Milan who is physician to certain well-placed gentlemen. I can resolve this matter for you, should you wish it done.

—Resolve?

—Should you wish it so.

—My son...is dead.

—Yes.

—You know?

—Yes.

—You can prove it? You can prove that he died?

—Yes. And I can deliver to you his remains, with proof that they are his, for proper burial. And I can give you the man who killed him.

—And for this you want me to sacrifice my family honour, my family name?

—No. For this I ask that you make peace. There is a great deal of profit to be made between you and Seluda. Divided, you are easy prey to the machinations of Faliere and Contarini: they know that while you war together you cannot war against anyone else. Peace will bring great opportunities, and more. More, that only peace can bring.

And for a moment, it seems as if he is considering.

Chapter 23

At night, as she returns, she knows she is watched.

This time she stops in the middle of a square and turns and looks, and does not see the watcher but a glimpse of coat, a sliver of boot as her follower turns into the shadow. She stands straight to show them that she is not afraid. Her mask is bright in the moonlight, and for a while there she stays, waiting, until at last the cold settles on her and she turns and returns home, and is followed no more.

Chapter 24

Belligno sends word.

Bring me the body of my child, he says,—and bring me the man who wrought his death, and I am yours.

The man who wrought his death is in Milan, but she has planned for this too, and knows just the card to play.

Galliard Viole, the Fool. He is a Frenchman who, having discovered himself unremarkable in France, travelled to Italy where the novelty of his being French might be at the very least somewhat more entertaining to the mighty. A short man, he is neither excessively witty nor particularly droll, but has mastered some of the essential arts of being a courtier as heaping liberal praise on the mighty and heavy scorn on those whom he predicts will shortly fall. Indeed, it is this latter characteristic—the ability to lose friends wisely—which has doubtless kept him alive as he journeys, ever hopeful, through life.

She meets him by the pier to Forli, hands him one thousand ducats, a sword and a pistol.

—Ah, Milan! he exclaims joyously.—A beautiful city, if somewhat humourlessly run! I have missed its women.

—You do not strike me as particularly foolish, she confesses as he pulls his cloak tighter about his shoulders.

—Do I not? he asks brightly.—That is very strange. I played in the Gameshouse when I was young, and cheated in order to win. The very same night, the umpires found me, and took me before the Gamesmaster, who said that I had broken the laws of civilised men and would pay the highest forfeit and become a servant to the house for a term of one hundred years, until my lesson was learned and my debt was paid. I laughed in her face and told her that she was a ridiculous, over-puffed old lady in a stupid dress, and the next day my wife died, and the day after that my only child, and on the third day my father fell ill, and on the fourth I knelt at her feet and kissed her white pointed shoe and begged her to stop, told her I was hers for ever, and she asked if I knew now what it meant to be a fool. That was seventy-three years ago. In twenty-seven years, I think she will let me die.

Thene stares astonished at this man, and for a moment does not know where she stands, or what she does, or even who she is to have come to this pass, to be standing now hearing this tale. Is she not Thene, the Jew's daughter? Is this earth not the earth, is the sky not the sky, are those centres of her world no more than the afterburn of the setting sun, a reflected illusion on the horizon?

Then the Fool breaks out into a great guffaw of laughter, slaps her on the back and says,—You are delightful, dear lady, simply delightful—thank heaven for Milanese girls!

And like that, he is gone.

Chapter 25

We remember this man, do we not?

Too easy, too easy for a player, lost in their own cleverness, to forget the moves of other clever men!

A great face of hair, two tiny eyes and a little nose, the rest lost beneath black beard and swagger. He is a proud man, this Knave of Swords, for who would not swagger who had seen death as many times as he has and lived to tell the tale? There is no monarch in this world, no pope or prince that can command him, for he—why, he has seen the fall of men and heard the growling at hellish gates and defied them all.

He was sent to the house of Contarini, that most elusive of all the pieces, a man whose fear is almost greater than his sense—or perhaps rather, as time may show, perfectly matched to that scale of disaster that yet hangs over him. We have watched him on and off these last few days as he spoke to captains and sergeants, made enquiries about doors, noted quietly to himself each motion of every messenger, each movement of every spy, each coin that falls upon the ground at Contarini's boot. Contarini, Contarini, you are being most cleverly played by that unseen man who stands behind the shuttered window. Tiapolo is lost, Seluda has yet to make its move but you, Contarini, you have united Church and state in the name of making money. Few things are as likely to win an election as this!

A message comes to our Knave of Swords, word of a relic hidden somewhere about Contarini's belongings. Destroy the relic, you destroy the excuse the bishops have to make their towers of gold, you destroy the profits that strangers will have in building these palaces to theological expense.

So the command comes down—find the relic. Destroy it. Let us stop Contarini's greatest play before he makes it.

So our knave searches, making most discreet enquiries and abasing himself before the might of others. It doesn't bother him, a proud man, to grovel before men he knows are lesser than he. His cleverness exceeds theirs, is clearly shown to exceed theirs with every lie he tells and quiver he makes—how clever indeed that a man so proud should slobber so extemporarily!

When the end comes, it is without warning. He did not see it coming, did not dream that it was coming, but a stranger whose face is hidden by a mask held a card in his hand, the Sun, whose light shines into every corner and beneath whose gaze all things are revealed—why yes, even our ally, our friend, our rogue sent into another's den.

He stands upon the bridge, feels a hand upon his arm, hears the words,—May we speak?

He turns, and the club that strikes his skull breaks both his jaw and two of his teeth in a single bounce. It is a crude weapon, perhaps fashioned from a cabinet-making project that failed, or chipped from the branch of a rotting tree. Can its owner not afford anything better?

(Yes, he can, but he waited too long to acquire his wealth and invested too much pride in poverty, so now that he flaunts his tatty clothes, his thin shoes and in his proud humility, it is perhaps fitting that he now serves as our sergeant's nemesis.)

They beat him, our Knave of Swords. They beat him so no one can tell between what is swollen and what is broken, whether his features were ever really human. All red, red, the water runs red beneath him, his clothes are saturated with it, so that red seeps from velvet, and now they take him without word, without ceremony, to the house of Angelo Seluda, and three men hold him up while a man in a mask looks towards the high windows of this place, and waits.

He waits until she appears—Thene, her mask as empty as

his—and sure now that he has her attention, turns to one of the men who has helped carry our wounded knight to this place. This man pulls a small axe from his belt, of the kind that might be used to cut away heavy ropes from a ship under sail. Down the axe falls once, and twice, and away they go, leaving the Knave of Swords on the cobbles before Seluda's door.

They carry him inside, and she herself descends with a hessian sack. She picks up his right hand by the tip of the little finger, not looking at her work, then picks up his left, pinching it tight, thumb on the soft palm, finger on the still hairy top. The blood drips through the sack as she walks, and she tells herself that it is but flesh, is but meat, that bounces at her side.

Earth, sea or fire? For a moment she cannot decide, before at last throwing the bag into the ocean, weighted with a stone. It is blissful how fast the waters claw these fingers down, and how little blood is on her hands as she washes them in the fountain before the church.

When she returns, the Knave of Swords is dead.

The blood loss was too great, the shock, the pain—or perhaps with his last glimmer of awareness, as the mercenary saw his hands struck from his body, he resolved that life itself was not worth the living, and let go of it with the same force of will which, until that time, he had lived it.

Seluda says,—Who was he?

—A piece, she replies.—He was a piece.

—Why did they do this?

—I sent him to the house of Contarini to find an object. The player who runs that piece has sent him back.

—I thought players didn't hurt other players.

—You are correct. Nowhere in the rules does it say what may happen to our pieces.

Angelo Seluda is silent at this. We do not think he is a foolish man, and if he did not know before what it is to be played, perhaps he does now.

She retires to her room; does not look back.

Chapter 26

The coin turns, the coin turns.
  She rolls it between her fingers.
  The coin turns, and she does not understand.

Chapter 27

She returns to the Gameshouse.

Faliere's player does not come there any more, nor does Contarini's. The game is too advanced for them to dally with lesser matters.

She does not spare much thought to Tiapolo.

—You play? he asks.

We know this man too, do we not? Silver in the sleeves, a face that is too tired to be young, too soft to be old. It is as if the age has been rubbed away from him, leaving a featureless surface behind which smiles from habit, not from humour. We called him Silver before, the man who challenged her to play, and now he sits opposite her once more but does not move towards the pieces or the dice, but rather asks again:

—You play? Here, still? I thought you were engaged in higher matters.

—I find that the games played here helps focus my mind.

—You should be careful. Others will watch you, learn your style, your techniques. Even in a simple game of dice, your character can become visible, and certain deductions will be made.

She smiles at this and says nothing, and he is surprised.

—You . . . *want* to be seen?

Admiration, incredulity, disbelief, wonder, delight—why, all these things we may hear in his voice, strange to the sound.— You want players to observe you playing?

—Would you like a game? she asks.

—What would you propose?

—Cards. For every hand you win, you may ask a question. And for every hand that I win...

—I understand.

—Then let's play.

She divides the deck.

Deals the cards.

At first, she is rusty, slow to find the pattern of it, and he asks five, six, seven questions in a row.

—Are you winning your game?

—No.

—Can you win?

—Perhaps.

—Do you like your piece, the king you must get a crown for?

—No.

—What do you want, if you win?

—Freedom. The freedom that only victory can afford.

We would imagine, would we not, that after losing nine hands in a row, she would be disheartened, she would fold, but on the tenth hand the game turns, fast now, and with a brisk efficiency she starts reclaiming the cards, taking hand after hand as quickly as the questions come. So now she asks:

—Are you a player in the higher league?

—Yes.

—How long have you played?

—I think... centuries.

—Are you lying to me?

—No.

—Have you been sent to influence, help or hinder me?

—That sounds like three questions.

—I think, if you listen, it is only one, but should it be a concern for you I can break it into three separate parts, win three separate hands and get the answer either way.

—Did you let me win? he asks.—Did you play me?

—You will have to win another hand before I answer that. Now—my questions, please.

—No, no one sent me to interfere with you in any way. I saw you alone and wondered if you would like to play, and here we are, playing still.

—Does the Gameshouse exist outside Venice?

—Yes, but I think you need to find a better way of asking the question that you wish to ask.

The next hand she plays too quickly and loses, and is barely able to hide the intake of breath, irritation at herself, that slips through her lips as he takes the hand.

—Did you let me win our first few hands? he asks.

—Yes.

—Why?

—The questions you ask are indicative of who you are, and the information you hold. It allows me to formulate my own questions more successfully.

At this he laughs, throwing his cards onto the table and leaning back. For a moment he sits there, shaking his head, arms folded, legs crossed, until at last he says,—Lady, I do not know precisely what the situation is with the game you play outside these walls, but let me say that if you are playing it as well as you play me now, you cannot help but win.

——I have more questions, she says, indicating the cards between them.

—I do not think we should play this game any more.

—Why?

—A game should be balanced, and there should be joy in it. I see neither any more. But you are eager, I think, for more answers, and it would be churlish of me not to give them. So I propose an accord, a deal struck between us alone.

—What deal?

—Not here, he replies.—I will visit soon, somewhere else, and we will discuss fairer terms.

—Do I have your word on that?

—You have seen me play. Would you value my word if I gave it?

She does not answer, and when we look again, both she and he are gone.

Chapter 28

A man in Milan.

He is no longer young, but has applied every trick he can to appear so. He wears a wig to thicken out his thinning hair, his stockings are tight, his shoes are curled, the colour of the cloth that tugs against his hips is vibrant orange, a garish, tasteless thing that no Venetian would approve of. He has a cap upon his head from which silver feathers sprout, and he wears no fewer than eleven rings upon his fingers, though secretly he knows only three are gold all the way through.

His name is not important, for he is less than a piece in this game, but we must take a moment now to sympathise with his coming predicament, for he is a man who had a sister, and that sister loved a boy of Venice, and he on learning of this slaughtered the boy and threw him into the river. For two years perhaps, he believed he was free from this crime—though he would not call it such, not crime, no, *justice*, justice for his sister, for his family, for his honour, *justice*—but now retribution comes.

It comes, it comes, and it wears the face of Galliard Viole, our foolish Frenchman, who approaches this stranger in the street and says,—Friend! Friend, my old friend, my brother, it has been so long! Let me buy you a drink!

He buys a drink, and another, and another, and soon both Fool and friend are mightily drunk, holding onto each other, kissing each other's cheeks, roaring with merriment when their staggering tips one or both over to the ground, for how funny it is to be in good company! How noble it is to be loved, how great is the bounty of man, how little matter material things when there is the joy of humanity, of fellowship, of the communion of souls!

Thus proclaim Fool and friend both, and keep on proclaiming it, right to the moment when our unfortunate fellow realises that he is far from home, in a street where no torches burn, and turning to the Fool mumbles:

—I think we should have turned left...

...before he is soundly beaten about the head, bound, gagged and thrown into the back of a midden cart.

Chapter 29

Alvisa Muna exclaims:

—How did you do it? How did you persuade Belligno to switch his support? And to *Seluda*?!

—I had a piece find the remains of his child, slaughtered by a vengeful brother in Milan. I offered a great deal of money. I promised peace. But I do not think it will be enough to win.

—Contarini still holds the support of the bishops.

—And Faliere?

—A ship came into harbour last night carrying his colours, and a stranger from Constantinople.

—Did the ship ride high or low in the water?

—High. The stranger was its only cargo. Zanzano has declared for Faliere too, and he brings with him the cloth merchants and most of San Marco. But Belligno gives you the docks, the fishermen, the fish market. Seluda will be noticed now: it was an extraordinary move!

—Perhaps an unwise one. If he is noticed, he is more liable to be attacked.

—You are ready though?

—I do not know what cards my enemies might play.

—But you know your enemies, yes?

She considers this question a moment, then nods.—Yes, she replies.—Now I do.

That same day, a whisper goes through the town.

Faliere has negotiated with the Grand Vizier of the Ottoman

86

Sultan himself; Faliere has struck terms. Faliere has been granted such concessions to trade with the infidel that if he were to declare now that the Turk had turned Christian, it would be believable, so impressive is this coup!

That night, Faliere and Contarini attend church together, and sit on opposite sides of the aisle. They do not shake hands when the ceremony is done, nor do their wives smile and embrace, but stiff and separate they go their own ways, and people bow uneasily as they pass, trying to direct their homage to neither man specifically but both in equal measure. Tiapolo sits far at the back, his three daughters around him. They say, the whisper goes, that the eldest is to be sent to a nunnery. None of the suitors that Tiapolo has found for her are interested any more.

Thene watches these daughters, their eyes down, pieces that were played upon, and for a moment remembers what it felt like to weep.

Chapter 30

She finds him at the Gameshouse.

—You are Tiapolo's player, she says, sitting beside him.

He looks up from the card table, two fingers of his right hand pressed against his closed lips as if to trap the breath within them. He doesn't wear his mask now, and his eyes are red in the rims, black around the lids from too much work, not enough sleep.

—And you're Seluda's Jew, he replies sharply.—What do you want?

—You've lost the game, she answers.—You played too fast, too soon, too strong; you had nothing left for the end.

—You're here to laugh? he exclaims.—Is that what you want?

—No. You still have cards to play, a piece at your command. Tiapolo cannot be Tribune, and you cannot enter the Higher League, but we may still do a good turn for each other.

—You suggest... an *alliance*?

—There is nothing in the rules to prevent it.

—You've just said I've lost.

—And you have. The question is whether you lose everything.

A shadow follows her through the city.

This time she does not run, does not stop, does not wait, does not fear.

She remembers now how good it is to refuse to be afraid.

She stops on the Rialto. Even at this hour, merchants and hawkers are bartering their wares, and crowds jostle for space across the waterway. Architects and detractors predicted that the bridge would not stand for more than ten years, so absurd was its design of arches and white stone, but here it is two decades later, as implausible and defiant as Venice herself.

She waits, and Silver comes, no smile on his face.

—Shall we walk? she asks before he can speak.

They walk.

Chapter 31

—First Belligno, now Tiapolo throws in their lot with you? he asks as they move through the night-time fires of the city.—You have an unorthodox approach to victory, turning your enemies to friends.

—My approach to victory is that I intend to win. The rest is merely tactics. You mentioned some sort of arrangement? Answers to questions?

—You have more questions than I do, I think.

—And yet you are still interested in me, she replies.—Though I think you are fascinated by my mind rather than any other parts.

—To speak truth, my lady, I think you are going to win.

—Am I? Faliere still controls trade with the east; Contarini still commands the power of the bishops and the builders of the city. I have gained ground, but not enough to guarantee the win.

—But you still have pieces left to play, do you not? A coin, for example—do I guess correctly? I do! When I looked at the board and saw that Seluda had been dealt as a king rather than Belligno, I did wonder what cards might have been given to his player.

—You will have to explain that to me.

—I will, but we must make a deal.

—What manner of deal? I will not compromise the game.

—Nor shall I ask you to.

—Then speak. What manner of deal?

—One day, perhaps in a week, or a month, or a year, or ten years, or more years besides, I will need a favour. I will be in a certain situation, a peculiar difficulty, and at that time I will ask you to lie to someone of whom you are afraid. Do this, and I will answer any questions you have, to the best of my ability.

—The deal you propose is skewed. I have an idea of what I gain from it now, but no conception of the scale of what I might lose later.

—Nevertheless, these are the only terms I will accept.

We walk a while in silence. The city closes in about us; we go further and further from the Grand Canal, from the busy paths of the city, into the dark places, the narrow places, the alleys and the caverns formed by overhanging houses, across waterways too tight for the gondola, too wide to be called a gutter, past shrines to weeping saints and martyred heroes, braziers where the beggars huddle and the cold ladies of the night warm their whitened fingers. We walk, we walk through streets never changing, where blood is as old as stone, ancient blood of ancient families whose grandparents were fed on the water of the lagoon that shall one day be sprinkled on the brow of the newborn infant that shall carry on the name, in the house, in the street, in this frozen city of Venice. We walk, and no one knows our significance or our strength, no one but the knowing, who we greet as familiar strangers, unsung friends. We walk.

Until at last

—All right, she says, and stops herself, and thinks a moment longer. And then,—All right. We have a deal.

—Then ask.

—Is the game I am playing fairly balanced?

—No.

—How do you know?

—If it was a game of equals, Belligno should have been assigned a player, not Seluda. His position was stronger, equivalent to Tiapolo, Faliere and Contarini. Seluda was a weaker piece. Equally, the man who played Tiapolo was not yet ready for the higher league. His tactics were poor, his intentions unclear. The choice of pieces inherently biased it in favour of Faliere and Contarini.

—Why?

—The Gameshouse is...old. It is not bound to any place, but rather has doors throughout the world. This game in Venice is one of hundreds, maybe thousands, being played in places you cannot dream of, and only an entry-level game at that, a little skirmish on the field. The house deals in empires and kings, in armies and Churches, and its players are some of the oldest and...perhaps not wisest, but shall we say most determined... people I have met. With such a purpose, and spread so wide, it should not be hard to consider that a body of this sort could influence events. A piece like Tiapolo is given a player who cannot win; a potential Tribune such as Belligno is not, and through this disadvantage is denied an opportunity to secure his place. We tell ourselves that the Gameshouse has no objectives beyond the playing of the game, but I have lived long enough and played enough games to question this. The nature of the game changes the world, and though I cannot swear to it, I would suggest that the distribution of cards, which should be random, is also skewed to produce an outcome that is more fitted to the Gameshouse's will rather than the player's abilities.

—To what purpose?

—That...I cannot say. It is not a question players—even the oldest—like to ask. Perhaps only the Gamesmaster knows.

—I have been dealt a coin.

—Yes. I thought you might be.

—What is it? It is out of place in the deck, a mundane thing, not a piece that I understand.

—May I tell you a story?

—Is it true?

—It is often repeated—will that serve?

—Tell me.

Chapter 32

It is said, (so Silver began) that there have been only three Gamesmasters in all the years in which the Gameshouse has existed. I know nothing about the first, but the second was a woman, dressed all in white, her face hidden as was her purpose. The Gamesmaster is the head and source of all the games that are played. Her rules are absolute; her judgement is final. She does not play herself, but rather devises and controls the games that others play—except very, very occasionally. When Rome fell, it is said that the Gamesmaster was challenged to play such a game that empires shook with it. When Luther pinned his articles to the church door, it is suggested that the Gamesmaster watched, and that these things which to us seem no more than the turning of the world are—to the ones who wear white—moves upon a board bigger than any of us can see. Whatever the truth of that, what is generally accepted is that the Gamesmaster has been on a few occasions challenged for her crown by players such as you or I. No one knows the game that they play, the master and the rival, and only one such match has there been in all the years that I can remember. It was a game played between a woman of Normandy and the Gamesmaster, and it lasted nearly seven years. During this time, the operation of the house ceased and all things were turned to this single conflict. Wars raged across Europe and throughout Asia. Temples fell in Africa and the New World; peoples rose against the lords of India; plague spread and the wild horsemen rode freely through burning lands—but were these events connected? Were these the signs of a battle fought for the Gamemaster's throne? I don't know, and wish I did.

Whatever the course of the game, after seven years the challenger vanished. Disappeared. And within a day of her disappearance, the Gameshouse opened its doors again as if nothing had happened. A great many assumed that she was dead; others suggested that she was claimed by the Gameshouse in defeat: her body, her mind, her very soul, sucked into the endless corridors of the place to be bound for ever in service to the house. One or two—a very few at that—suggested that no, she had not lost at all, but won, and in victory she had become the Gamesmaster, as bound to the house as surely as if she had lost and been enslaved, for the Gamesmaster may only die when defeated, only leave their office by the same rules that they enforce on the board.

But you are wondering what all of this has to do with your coin, yes?

The woman had a husband. The fashions of the time would have it said that the husband had a wife, a lesser creature to complement his greatness, but in truth he was compared to her, an amateur at the game, as I think your husband is now. He was a besotted fool with just enough wisdom to know to trust in the more vasty intelligence of his wife. For seven years he let her play the game, never fully understanding its scale or import, until that fateful day when she vanished, whether to death or slavery or victory he did not know. All he knew was that the Gameshouse had taken her and, incensed and suddenly awake to that which had been obvious, he hammered on the silver door which leads to the halls of the higher league, begging and threatening for answers as to the fate of his wife. No answers were given, for he was an average player in the lower league, and the rules of the game would not permit him access to those who might know. For years he struggled to find answers to his questions and achieved nothing, for no matter how good he grew at the game, the house would not welcome him to the higher league. At last, desperate, now ill and his wealth lost, rumours came to him of a place in a far-off land where an ancient magician might be able to help him.

Selling the last of what little he had, he journeyed east to a land of high plateaus and long grass, where trees barely deign to grow on the grey mountainside and there are a great, warlike people dressed in furs and armed with spears, who their neighbours call barbarian and who laugh to hear themselves so called, knowing that "barbarian" is their strength, is their fierceness and their rage, and rejoicing that others have wisdom enough to perceive it.

There, his beard grown long and his shoes turned to tatters, at the end of his strength he followed a little stream down to a hidden valley, where great bonfires blazed and people danced in honour of thunder and rain. The people who found him had no word for law—no, not even its concept. Strength and life were the only notions they understood, the only justice that they comprehended, and to enforce anything else by these means was to waste strength itself. They laughed at this stranger then, this ragged creature come to their home, robbed him of what he had left and cut him to see if his blood was red like theirs (and it was) and took him before the strongest and mightiest of their kind in case he had some opinion on the matter and so as not to offend him by making a decision for themselves.

This strong man, this mighty man—how can I best describe him? His beard was black, his hair was straight, his eyes were ocean-green, his skin the colour of walnut but burnt too, reddened by the wind and the sun to a sort of sanded roughness. He was not particularly tall, but had that splayed manner about him, an easiness of leg and arm that sprawled in every direction, confident of himself and his little kingdom, and when the bloody stranger was pushed before him, he looked on this man with no more interest than a soothsayer might look upon an inauspicious sacrifice.

At last he spoke, and the man was astonished to hear his own language pronounced clearly, so far from home.

—Why are you here? asked the king of the valley.

—I've come looking for help, replied the man.

—Help? Help yourself. Why ask me?

95

—I'm told you know something of the Gameshouse.

—Do I look as if I do? Do I look as if I care?

At these words, the man drew himself up a little more before this king, and said,—No, I cannot see any sign of it in your face, but you did not stop to question what the Gameshouse is, but derided it at once, and I think you are therefore the man known sometimes as Bird, and an enemy of the house and the one who rules it. Am I right?

—You bore me, replied the man called Bird.—Your words bore me.

At this he turned away and his subjects leapt on the man and seemed as if they would tear him to pieces, eat him even, until he cried out:

—The Gameshouse stole my wife!

Hearing this, the king of that place turned back a little, though he showed no sign of sympathy, and all his subjects slunk away a little, disappointed to be denied their sport.

—So? he asked.—What is that to me?

—I am ill and poor, replied the man.—I will die, I know it, before I can find the truth. The only way I know to find my wife is to become a great player; the only way I can play is if I have more time; the only way I can win time is by being a great player! So I am trapped, and so I shall die and never know the truth of it. Help me. I had some money but your people took it . . .

At this he held out the only coin he had left, ancient and small, a little Roman thing shaking in his palm.

—Money? replied Bird, his voice rolling with laughter and rage all at once.—Do you think I care for money? Do you think I care for the things of men, for coin and law and truth and kings and husband and wife? These are the false things, the made-up things, the not-of-the-wildlings things that mankind cages itself with. Do I look caged to you? Do I look like a prisoner?!

Incensed, he grabbed the man by the throat so that in his choking half-state he could not speak, could not stammer out some denial, some defence, but rather then thought he would die.

A moment there he hung, this poor would-be player, his life

in someone else's grasp as whose life is not? As whose fate is not suspended in that place between a stranger's whim and the universe's contempt?

Then suddenly Bird let him go, and his humour brightened as he paced a little, smiling at some new thought. The more he thought it, the more it entertained, until suddenly he stopped and laughed out loud, as great and rich a sound as the man could have eaten it. Then he bent down, picked up the discarded coin and, pressing it into the man's shaking fist said,—A game. Very well, little man, a game.

—What game?

—Something near your level, something that would displease the Gamesmaster, but still a game with rules and consequences. Toss the coin. Call a side. Get it right, you'll live, and long enough to play your game, or rather to play her game, the game of the Gameshouse. Choose wrong, you die. A pretty sport, is it not?

—It's chance, not a game.

—All things are chance. Nature is chance. Life is chance. It is a human madness to try and find rules where there are none, to invent constraints where none exist. The only thing that matters is the choice. So choose. Choose.

And the man did.

Chapter 33

—Who is Bird? asks Thene as we walk together through the night-time of Venice.

—Hard to say, Silver replies.—He is neither a player nor a piece; nor does he exist within the Gameshouse. I heard a man from the east once posit a theory—a sweeping, spectacular theory!—that as the Gameshouse exists, so there must exist Bird. There must be an answer to the rules, a house of misrule and chance to balance against the precision and order of the game. However the argument waxed of the philosophical to my ear, so I didn't pay much attention to it.

—You are saying that it's Bird's coin that I hold?

—I am saying that a story tells of a coin which, when thrown, may hold death on one side and life on the other. In a sense such things are anathema to the Gameshouse, for there is no skill, no intelligence or craft in such a judgement, merely the outcome. Then again, it might be argued that such a thing is the purest game there is, unsullied by complexity and true to life, where chance will not change her colour for the wise man or the fool.

—As a player, should you be telling me this? Should you instruct another in the value of their pieces?

—Does it say in the rules that I cannot?

—No.

—Then I can. Players rarely help each other, as I am sure you will learn. Every player who lives too long becomes a rival who must be challenged or displaced. But as you yourself so aptly demonstrate, there is great power to be gained from turning an enemy to a friend.

—Am I an enemy?

—You are a player, as I am.

—But you are playing another game, are you not? He does not answer. She tuts, a little shaking of her head.— Come now, come, she says.—You said you would answer my questions; I am still asking them.

—Yes. I am playing another game.

—And am I to be a piece?

—Perhaps.

—One of my pieces died the other day.

—I saw.

—I had not thought... it had not occurred to me that... silly, now that I think about it. As you say, there is no reason in the rules why a piece may not die, why another may not kill. I simply had not considered it. I had not... but it is done. The game goes on.

—Thene.

He has stopped, and so do we, and as we stop so it seems does all of Venice, the night running cold, the walls bending to listen, listen, conspiracy is afoot.

—My lady, he corrects himself, trying to find the words again.—Do not think that people do not die in this game. Do not flinch now.

—I won't, she replies.—I understand, and have understood from the very first, why a king may want a player to play upon him, why Seluda, Faliere, Tiapolo and Contarini have agreed to be pieces in our hands. Their ambitions are coloured by feeling, desires and commitments; they hear the cries of loved ones, see pain in their friends. A man dies and they must grieve, repent, question their intents and its consequence. Victory for them is a means to ever-changing ends, to fortune and honour, comfort and prestige, and the tools they deploy are daughters, sons, companions and things of value which were hard to earn and once

99

used, cannot be won again. This tangle of things clouds simple intent, and intent should be only this—victory. Victory and the prize. We are players. They are the pieces. Winning is all.

So saying, she turns away and we are...

...what are we?

Are we perhaps a little sad? Have we, who know the turning of the times and have heard whispers of a future not yet named, developed some semblance of sentimentality that clouds us to the truth of things? Do we wish to be victorious *and* humane? How foolish we have become in our old age. How unwise. We must purge this sentiment from our souls and remember again and again: it is the victory—it is the win. The rest is only a cage.

The coin turns.

The coin turns.

And she is gone.

Chapter 34

Five days to go.

Where did the time go?

They are balanced now, she thinks. Faliere in bringing the promise of trade with the east has won a great many men from Contarini's cause, and not even the voice of the abbot on one side, or Zanzano on the other seems to settle the debate. There are some who are pledged and will not turn, but many, many more votes now ready to be captured, and she has Tiapolo and Belligno at her command, their power turned to Seluda's cause.

Not quite enough—not yet. She cannot quite win yet. But she can see how victory might fall out.

Only two cards left—the Three of Coins and the Tower.

The Three of Coins is a beggar, small and overlooked, who lives on the charity of the Church. He seems like nothing, but he too has his part to play.

Not on this, though. Not when the Tower is ready to be deployed.

Thene meets with him and the Priestess both. They sit upon a barge in the middle of the bay, eating fruits and drinking water as Thene says:

—Even if we find this "elbow of St. Simon" or whatever non-sense it is that Contarini is peddling to the bishops, we have the problem that the Senate *wants* Contarini to be right. They want to have a sacred relic come to Venice, and they want to have an expansive and expensive building project that will line their pockets to house it. Stealing or destroying the object is not enough: we must impress upon the bishops and their supporters how such an enterprise may leave them inconvenienced, not aided.

The Priestess is silent a while, agreeing but offering no more, for what can she do to rectify this? What is there to be done?

So our eyes turn to the Tower, who is known as Foscari and at six foot three stands so high and has shoulders so broad that it is a miracle any gondolier would take him on his barge, fretful that the slightest sneeze of this great frame could upset his boat and tip them all into the sewage-chased water. A sometime military engineer, he lost his left arm in an unnamed war, one of the endless skirmishes of the city states, an incident which was denied by both sides as soon as it had been fought, for no one in Italy likes to go to *war* with each other; rather their battles are merely misunderstandings over piddling matters of territory, honour and pride, and the men who died were adventurers on the road, not soldiers, not men of any military sort of the kind commanded by princes, for who knows if yesterday's sworn enemy will not tomorrow be your son-in-law? Such is the necessity of turbulent times.

—I believe it is in our interest to create a need for alternative works, Thene continues.—Ones in which Contarini does not hold the greatest power or interest.

—What do you suggest?

—The Patriarch has a very nice house, she replied.

Silence.

Foscari the Tower seems uninterested, his gaze turning outwards to a pair of flies that are skimming across the water, tangled in each other yet still somehow staying in the air, wings beating with furious vigour as they rise from the water. The Priestess sits and despite herself, despite her decorum and training, her mouth hangs a little ajar and she blurts out at last:

—You wish to *burn* the house of the Patriarch?

The Tower smiles at nothing much; his gaze still elsewhere,

like a child who has heard the parents argue and knows if he can just keep his peace, their argument will end well for him.

—Only a piece of it, Thene replies.

The Priestess sits back, shaking her head, hands flickering up then down from her lap, like a butterfly unsure of its flight.

—The Patriarch is very rich, Thene continues softly,—and a man who is chosen by the Senate more than by God.

—You can't know that, retorts the Priestess, sharper than perhaps she intended.—God is in the hand of the men who vote, and the tongues of men who speak, even those who speak ill, for all will come at the last to serve his holy spirit.

—Even us? asks Thene.—Even this?

Silence again.

Then the Tower turns his great, bearded head and looks up at the sky, seeing in its running clouds perhaps some infant fancy— the back of a dragon, the legs of a horse, the spirit of a dolphin that is blown away—and he says,

—Do you want anyone to die?

—No.

—How big do you want the fire?

—Not so big that the house is considered irreparable, nor in such a place that it may spread too far.

Perhaps this is disappointment we see in the Tower's face, and if it is then here we begin to know that, for all his childish simplicity, his innocent airs, this is a man who has had his fingers round the throats of his enemies and enjoyed it. What was it, we wonder, that bought him to the Gameshouse's service?

(And here it is, the secret hidden, for Foscari once looked upon a town that would not be taken, a place high in the hills, of sloping yellow streets and cracked red roofs, whose very steepness seemed to stretch it out like a map on the landscape that the attackers might see every road, every corner, every home, and mark with the tip of their little fingers which one now was set for destruction. In this place, at this time, with victory assured, Foscari reached out to the cannon which were his lovers, his

103

friends, his power, his all, and as he set to light the flame, a woman dressed all in white stepped to his side, caught his wrist and said,—Don't.

—Don't, she said. The powder is too heavy, the metal too old. This cannon will burst when you fire it, and kill you for sure.

This warning given, she departed, and he, being a proud but superstitious man, ordered his lieutenant to light the fuse, and stood well back, and he was finding dried drops of blood from the man's shattered body in the folds of his doublet for months after, and when the white lady came again to his door he knelt at her feet and said he was hers, and she said,—I know.

Such is the story of the Tower.)

—I do not see how this will help you, says the Priestess, her voice bringing us back to this time, this place, this moment by the sea.—The Patriarch will spend money on renovating his palace and this will only increase Contarini's profit.

—Contarini's entire strategy depends on his relic, Thene replies.—It is the excuse that the bishops have been looking for to build more and richer shrines to themselves, from which construction they may take a profit in money skimmed and gold trim, for Rome will surely send them money for the housing of a sacred relic. Contarini provides stone at great expense, the bishops take the money of Rome, the Senate takes money from the bishops and traders, and everyone profits. But! If the Patriarch finds himself in a dilemma—to invest in building a church for a relic of doubtful providence, or to repair his palace—where will that judgement fall? Certainly Rome will not pay for both, and there is far less profit to be made by the Senate in repairs to a palace rather than in a new reliquary where every piece of gold leaf may be the offspring of five pieces that vanished.

—And the relic? asks the Priestess.—What of that?

—I have one card left to play, she replies.—I must simply choose the time.

Chapter 35

The Three of Coins is a boy, barely fifteen or sixteen years old, all long, hanging limbs and tiny, oval face. Nothing seems in proportion about him, for he is surely too skinny for lungs to breathe, too tall for legs to balance, eyes too small to see, ears too big to hear. Yet here he stands, alive and, for all intents and purposes, well. A sometime thief, a sometime beggar, he is of that sort who is nothing for very long, but rather drifts from easy idea to easy idea, riding the wave of life until he either drowns or is washed up on some alien shore.

He is not the ideal piece for this purpose, but he is the only one she has left.

—Steal a relic? he muses.—I can try, could be interesting, could be boring, don't know.

—I sent a man to find it, and he was murdered.

The Three of Coins shrugs; he doesn't seem surprised by this.—My life ended when the Gameshouse took my card, he explains.—It was made clear that I weren't my own man no more.

A question she wants to ask. She looks, and does not ask it. Does not need to. This boy, this strange, distant boy stares at nothing much. It is the same vacancy she saw in the eyes of the Tower, the same focus in the gaze of the Priestess. It is the thing that hides behind the laughter of the Queen of Cups, the swagger of the Knave of Swords, the slouch of the Seven of Staves. Each piece in each way lived their life by their own definition, but beneath it all, there is a thing she dares not name.

Is this slavery?

A quick dismissal of the idea: slaves are taken by force, held against their will and yet...

...and yet:

Alvise Muna, Seven of Staves: *I had debts.*

Pisana, Queen of Cups: *I bet the life of my child.*

The Knave of Swords: *My sword broke.*

The Priestess: *There are some who made arrangements which they might regret.*

Every piece has come into her hand through the Gameshouse, but what pushed them through the Gameshouse's door?

The Queen of Cups knew she was coming: *I was a player once.*

And what of herself, what of Thene?

She has not thought of her husband once.

There is no shame in that; she has had better things to keep her occupied.

And even if questions could be asked, what is she to do?

Walk away?

Back to Jacamo, back to the life that went before?

A player must play in order to win. A king who conquers the kingdom must slay many soldiers in his path; four men wish to be captain, and only one may rise to that rank. What of the others? What of those who are left behind when victory is won?

History will not remember them.

And so on, Thene, on.

On to the end.

Chapter 36

She had asked a question of the Knave of Swords—a question he died answering. *Where is Contarini's relic?*

Now she realises what a foolish question it was. Contarini, Contarini, frightened, wandering Contarini! You played a card to catch spies in your house, you change the bed you sleep in every night, and certainly you smile and you laugh and you shake hands with prelates and princes, and say how wonderful it shall all be when you are Tribune, but Contarini...the word that has not yet been invented for you, but it comes; the word is *paranoid*.

What cards were dealt, what deals were made to give Contarini his ridiculous relic she doesn't know, nor does it much matter. The relic is not the point of this exercise, merely the excuse—an excuse to build, an excuse to embezzle, to proclaim triumph where there is almost none. But as it is a symbol still, it holds value, and where does Contarini keep a thing of great value?

About himself. Always—but always—about his own person.

Terrible trust!

If only you had trusted in others, Contarini; if only you knew how to smile and mean it, you could perhaps have won this game, but no—no. You never understood the value of such things.

She must tempt Contarini out of hiding.

How better to do it, she thinks, than through the pieces of her enemy?

*

She speaks to Seluda.

—You were friends with Zanzano, you say, before he betrayed you?

—I thought I knew what friendship was, he replies,—and by that clearly mistaken understanding of what was between us, yes, I was his friend.

—Do you have any letters he sent? A note or two? Something written in his hand?

—I may; why?

—Do you want to know? she asks.—Seeing as you still cling to some part of friendship, that is?

Seluda considers, and then quickly absolves himself.—No, he says.—I don't want to know.

A letter is sent.

A reply is given.

The reply—alas, the reply!—is given to a messenger boy who is lazy and easily bribed, and Thene reads it closely as the Three of Coins stands idly by, scraping the dirt out from beneath his nails and flicking it away in little black spots towards the water of the canals.

Thene reads, considers, then pens another letter, seals it again and sends it on its way.

An invitation, written in the name of Zanzano, suggesting that though he has spoken most firmly for Faliere these last few weeks, yet now he has some small doubts, and would Contarini be willing to discuss a couple of matters of mutual concern?

Why, it would appear that Contarini is most willing.

Most willing indeed.

Night in Venice.

Few cities are more beautiful and more ugly in the dark than Venice.

The city is a jewel of contradictions. We stand by the waters of the lagoon, you and I, and watch the moonlight ripple beneath a star-pricked sky. We hear the creaking of the ships, smell fish

108

sizzling in the pan, hear the distant laughter and feel the warmth through an open door, and know that this is surely paradise, the beautiful city, and marvel at how great are the deeds that man has wrought.

Yet turn away, and what is there now in this place that is not a threat? The alleys too dark, the walls too close, the water lapping at your feet hungry, hungry for blood. How many bones were sucked bare by the wide-eyed fish which twist away from the worm and the rod to gorge on sweeter pastures? How many of the crows that nest in the highest towers have, of a frozen night in winter, not swept down to pluck an eye from the still-staring corpse of he who shall by tomorrow have no name to put on his tombstone? Beauty and blood: does the blood give the beauty its edge? Is skin fairer when washed in red? Or is it the blood itself which is beautiful, for surely men will blaze the brighter when they know that tomorrow they may be drowned?

Or maybe here is the most terrible truth of all: that in a city as tide-turned as Venice is, perhaps it is simply too hard to find love, loyalty and truth, and so in other virtues people invest their hearts—passion, beauty, poetry and song—fancying perhaps that these shadows of the former are as great as love itself.

Contarini receives Zanzano's note and, as a good piece must, shows it to his player.

Does his player smell a trap?

Perhaps he does, but then the battle is too close between Faliere and Contarini, the net too tightly drawn to refuse this offer, and if a little something is lost, what a great deal could be gained! The letter is compared to others known to be in Zanzano's hand, the seal is checked, and indeed it seems to be his voice, his style, his composition, and so in the deepest hour of the night when even the drunk boys and merry girls who dance on the tables of the inns have at last lulled themselves into stupored sleep, a gondola sets forth from Contarini's home.

There are four people within it, and a gondolier who says nothing and of whom nothing is asked. Torches burn at either end to guide the way, but the moon is shrouded behind the high walls of the city, and only a little light pushes through the mosquito-humming dark. The waterways at this hour are a place for insects, some crawling along the surface, visible only by the pushing ripples of their darting motion; others zip high, bumping along walls like blind bats feeling their way through the air, indignant to find their journey so disrupted.

Through this, Contarini moves in silence.

Let us consider the others who accompany him.

One man we may immediately assess, name and discard: a guard carrying a short spear that he probably can't use and a chipped sword which perhaps he can. He is a problem, but not an insurmountable one.

Another we have not seen before, his face half shrouded by a velvet hood, but if we were to consider his role, his strength, his abilities, we could give at least a representation of a name to him, and say perhaps that he is that card known as the Sun, whose real name will turn out to be something Germanic, and who used to pass letters for Sir Francis Walsingham and who betrayed the Spanish king and is now what he most excels at being—a spy, a traveller and a watcher of men. He had some aspiration, once upon a time, of playing in the same Gameshouse where his masters sometimes dallied, but for reasons we cannot know, the Gamesmaster never invited him to challenge for the higher league, though his skill was entirely apt to it.

Contarini does not trust the Sun, suspecting what he once was; but for all that he is a fearful man, he is an economically minded one too, for to him a man whose card is held is a man who is now owned. His gaze turns in satisfaction to the final occupant of the boat, a man in a bone-white mask, and Contarini smiles upon him, though if he smiles back we cannot see. How easily has this old, plump man, cheerful Contarini, come to congratulate himself on owning a piece as powerful as the Sun, and somehow managed yet to forget that he is a piece himself. The easiest intellectual option, the path of least resistance, and there you have the man.

110

A guard, a spy, a piece and a player.

Their route to Zanzano's house takes them under four bridges. Two are high enough that the gondolier needs only to bend a little to push them through it; of the other two, one requires him to squat, and one is so low indeed that it is miraculous that the pilot of this little vessel does not lie down flat to propel them beneath its stones. As they approach it, Contarini mutters his usual exclamations against *new money* and the vulgar, unpleasant things it builds, forgetting—choosing to forget—how yesterday he shook the hand of the very man whose construction this bridge is, congratulating him on his superb judgement in supporting Contarini's claim, and hoping to see him very soon for some private chat.

Coming towards this little bridge, it seems that a shadow stirs around it, and at the sound of footfalls, the Sun raises his head.

A sound that might be the scraping of a barrel.

A creaking that could be the drawing of a bow.

The Sun rises to his feet, steady in the still-moving boat, and seeing him rise, the white-masked player asks,—Something?

—Perhaps, replies the man, and then,—I heard...

What he heard we shall not know, for what he next *experienced* was a cracking of timbers and an explosion of sticky blackness across his face as, from windows high above, barrels of honey, mud and egg were thrown, all mixed together by an angry cook of Seluda's, the dark sticky stuff splattering across every soul in the boat which, rocked by this assault and then by the confusion of all within, sloshed first from side to side and then, with a final slow flop, capsized, hurling all into the water.

At this all light ceased, and for a moment five men flapped and splashed, flailed and gasped in the murky dark. How terrible to drown; how much worse to drown in the dark when there is no sense of where safety lies, only water without bottom, darkness without end, clothes swelling up and dragging down, bubbles of air popping from nose and mouth, eyes pushing against their sockets with the pressure of liquid building in your gasping, choking face. Terror, terror to drown, and now the soldier's sword is an anchor and the fine fur lining of your cloak and

111

golden chain about your neck is death that threatens to pull you down, the rich men drowning faster than the poor.

Yet! A light above, voices in the dark, and here are ten or fifteen boys, the forgotten, unloved, undrawn poor of the city. They crowd round the water's edge, torches burning and hands outstretched, and some three or four dive in to help the flapping, spluttering passengers, hauling them, some by the arm, some by the neck, one even by the hair, gasping onto the safety of the bridge.

—Money, money, please sir, money! cries the boldest of these unlooked-for saviours, or:

—I'm strong, you see how strong I am, I am very strong indeed you could use me, yes, as a servant, I work very hard because I am very strong!

Or maybe even the simpler, softly whispered words that are not a threat; no, never that, never threatening...

—I saved your life. I could have not done that, sir, and heaven looked no less kindly on my soul.

Contarini is a man of pride, always one to refuse gifts when offered lest they become debts, and even less willing to hand out his own money unless he is sure of what he shall take in return. Yet now he sits, this great man of Venice, dirty, wet and stinking, as dozens of little hands in a show of straightening his sopping gown pat him down for coins, rings, silver and gold, until the Sun, recovering some semblance of his wits roars,—Get away! and charges at the pack which disperses, laughing like hyenas, withdrawing some little way but not yet giving up the prize, the scent of blood in their noses, their victims stranded in the dark. All except one, who runs into the dark and does not look back.

Then the player is pulled from the water, his white mask lost, and he is an old man, grey hair, grey beard, pale eyes and a mole situated perfectly in the centre of his left temple that seems to be pinkish at the base and then deep, deep brown in the middle, as if a second mole has attempted to grow from the first. He gasps for air, sees the boys, sees his pieces, the gondolier lamenting his battered craft, broken barrels floating in the water, and at once now his mind turns to the most important question—

—The box!

At once Contarini feels within his sopping garments, pushing leaden fabric away from his skin in great, sagging waves, and though he almost immediately feels nothing, still he keeps looking, for it is unacceptable, impossible, that he does not find that which he seeks.

—Who took it? roars the player.—Where is it?!

Now he staggers to his feet, and without care for his own safety or person, squelches towards the gaggle of boys, who laugh tremendously to see this drowned ox come for them and scatter before him, chattering at how funny it is to see old men move, and how much funnier it will be to see old men cry.

This pattern of pursuit and scatter, pursue and scatter leads the player a little distance away from the canal, until with a sudden burst like spring petals on the wind, the boys break away, running barefoot over stones away into the swallowing dark.

We look now at this player, clothes streaming, hair stuck to his head, gasping for breath, burdened by time and water. He turns his head side to side, his feet rooted as if crushed by his own weight, and sees now a figure, cloaked in grey, a white mask upon her face, a lantern at her side.

We can name this woman too, can we not? But he sees only what she is, not who she is, and cannot even bring himself to name her.

—*Whore*, he breathes, having no better wit for the moment.

She steps a little towards him and he tries to draw himself up to his full height, though dignity when you are leaking canal waters from the seat of your trousers is a difficult attribute to obtain.

—Seluda's little whore, he adds.—Your piece will die for this.

—I do not think so, she replies.—Stealing the relic from you was only part of tonight's work.

—It will not be enough: you will lose.

—I do not know if I will win, or if Faliere will beat me to the final reckoning. What I am sure of is that Contarini's claim will not survive past tonight, and you will never see the higher

113

league of the Gameshouse. It is a trait I dislike in players to gloat over their defeated enemies, but in your case I have come not to gloat, but to witness. It has been suggested to me, strongly suggested, that the Gameshouse does not deal all hands evenly. My player is weak, and though I cannot compare my cards to others, not knowing their draw, I am... uncertain... if they were as touched by chance as perhaps I would think. Therefore I wanted to see you, to witness this moment, and ask myself this question: why you? Or perhaps: why Contarini? Or perhaps both. Why would the Gameshouse seek to see a creature as patently vile as you clearly are in the higher league? What is their purpose? Why are we playing this game? I am sure you have no answer. You are a piece, and perhaps so I am. But in observing you, one day maybe I will be closer to the answer that I seek.

She finishes speaking and he steps towards her suddenly, fast, one hand rising as if he would grab her by the throat, breathless, and what is he thinking now? Can he imagine himself killing her—is he that man? We think that perhaps the truth of the matter is that he cannot think at all, and this is just the animal, the stray dog within his soul, that now twists his fingers towards her neck.

Yet she does not flinch, and at the stillness in her features he hesitates, breath meeting hers, his fast, hers soft, so softly waiting. Two rules there were laid out for the players, and he remembers them now.

—Will you? she asks, as he is frozen to the spot.—Do you dare?

It seems that he does not.

His fingers withdraw; he forces them shaking to his side.

—You are no player, she breathes at last.—A player would never fall so low. That's good. That's what I wanted to know. That means the Gameshouse intended Faliere to win.

—This is nothing, he says.—The bishops will still stand with us.

—No, she replies.—I do not think they will.

So saying, she turns away, and he watches her out of sight.

Chapter 37

The sky glows red tonight.

A fire in any city is a disaster, but in Venice! So many buildings so tight together, so much timber waiting to ignite.

Yet this fire is contained, for the building where it begins is kept apart by its status from many others, and there is nothing if not an abundance of water to hand.

A Patriarch should not have so fine a palace, the Priestess tells herself as she watches the flames from across the water. How much we have forgotten. How Christ would weep to see us now.

Chapter 38

And in the morning, the Patriarch of Venice pens a letter to his good friend, Abbot Padova, who we may say perhaps sold his soul to a woman in white and became that card known as the Hierophant, and for what? For a promise of secrets and blessings, whose value we will one day see does not outweigh the sacrifice that must be made.

Be that so, to him the Patriarch writes, telling of the fire which has all but gutted his glorious palace, and the priceless treasures that were lost! Gold melted in the heat, paints blistered on canvas, the faces of the saints destroyed, ancient Byzantine symbols turned to ash, the rosewater boiled in its bowls as glass cracked and turned to sand, a tragedy, a tragedy and an abomination and worse—oh, but far worse! Can the churches of Venice really afford to build both a reliquary for this "elbow of St. Simon" if it is even verified...

(What new question is this, wonders the abbot, since when was verification a concern?!)

...and rebuild the Patriarch's home?

Panic in the priesthood, panic in the Senate. The situation may still be salvaged, the election may still be saved, but here now come Angelo Seluda and Orio Faliere, and though they are enemies, bitter rivals for the crown, yet both of them smell blood and it seems—for just a morning and an afternoon—that they wordlessly combine efforts.

The profits from building a reliquary have been hugely exaggerated, whispers Seluda.—Contarini was playing you all, using

116

you, offering rewards he could never have given, the priests all secretly doubted themselves—do you really want a man as unreliable as Contarini on the Supreme Tribunal?

And Faliere, frozen, icy Faliere, stalks through the halls of the Doge's palace and murmurs with a voice that seems to never rise and yet cuts through every shadow, where is this relic anyway? What is this elbow bone for which Contarini would have the bishops go bankrupt?

Through it all, Contarini struggles, and his player too, begging, imploring, coaxing, wheedling, we can still bring great profit to this city, the Patriarch can have his reliquary *and* his palace too, trust us, trust in what we can achieve, there has been foul play...

...but all for nothing.

And when, at supper, they produce the blessed relic itself, a priest who has buried many bodies in the crowded cemeteries of Venice exclaims,—That is not the bone that you showed us before, and is far newer than any relic should be! and at once chaos erupts as Faliere whispers:

—I would not wish to do my good brother Contarini down, but it does seem that this relic should be questioned...

And Seluda murmurs,—Poor Contarini—it seems he has been the innocent victim of some terrible, terrible hoax, and I wonder that he did not see it sooner himself!

So that, when the sun finally sets over the city, Contarini is done.

We watch him return to his palace, walking this time— shameful walking!—perhaps haunted by his soaking memories of the humiliating night before.

Of the man that was his player, we see nothing more.

And so in the halls of the Doge, when all have departed and the last sunset light burns in sideways and hot through the high windows, all things at last are still. We watch Thene, and do not know her mind. She gazes upon the images of great men, the faces of noble Doges, and the obliterated place where a

Doge's face once was. She walks through images of the history of Venice, the glories of Lepanto, the sacking of Constantinople, memories of crusader princes who others called pirates and rogues. She sees the painted depiction of raging seas upon which the brave Venetians still set forth in brigs, caravels and galleys, mighty men with great shoulders rowing against the crashing waves, ancient Poseidon stirring the oceans below, blessed Jesus calming the skies above. For a moment she thinks she sees the face of Zeus in the bearded depiction of the Almighty as he bestows his blessing on the holy islands of the lagoon. A flicker in her eyes, a question of perspective, for did the people of this land not once worship the all-father Jove, and were they not, in their time, right?

She crosses herself quickly at this thought, and we are surprised.

It is the last time we shall see her make this sign for as long as we shall know her.

And then, quiet as night, he is there.

The man who would make Faliere king.

The two players, Thene and he, face each other down the empty hall. Both are masked, neither speak. Is it coincidence that has brought them here?

Fool you, for asking the question. Shame on you if you thought any of this was not wrought by another's hand, and long before we came to look on it.

At last the man says,—My apologies, my lady. For how I addressed you the night when we played chess. You are a better player than I gave you credit.

—You played with your words, and with me, when you spoke so, and I respect the game, if not the move, she replies with a little nod of her head.—And for my part, and I think it must also be so for you, I have...enjoyed...our game.

—Very much so, he replies,—and I regret that I will not play you again when this matter is done, since one of us must be exiled from the Gameshouse altogether at its conclusion.

She hesitates, then,—I nearly asked you your name.

118

—I would not give it.

—Nor I. It seems...unfitting...to the spirit of the thing. Yet I am curious to know who you are, that the Gameshouse would have you win.

—You think I have some advantage?

—Yes. I do.

—Come, come, he tuts.—That is bad grace from a good player.

—I have looked at this board and see no reason why Seluda should have been played, nor why Belligno was not, save an intention bigger than either of our parts. Contarini's man, though strong, proved to be merely...human...

She pauses on this word, considering it, and finds to her surprise that it is right. For what is a human if not flawed by humanity, tempered by feeling, doubt and hope? And is not a player more? Does not the player strive to rise above all of this and see only the moves themselves?

—...and so I must conclude that you are the strongest of us, given the greatest chance, and I wonder who you are, that the Gameshouse would see you victorious.

—You do yourself down, my lady. You have fought a good fight. Perhaps even stood some chance of victory. Does the Gameshouse not wish you even success?

She opens her mouth to say a name, to explain all, but hesitates, blessed sense, hesitates before she speaks of the man with silver sleeves, of a Roman coin, of a bargain struck, and our heart may beat slow again, breathe, breathe, for we are not ready, we are not ready to play the game that must be done, do not betray us yet, Thene, do not show the strength of our hand to one who serves our enemy!

Her lips seal, thin and tight, behind her mask, and if the other player has seen any alteration in her eyes, any drawing in, we cannot tell, and it may not matter.

—You speak of my victory as if it is still impossible, she says at last.—Yet the election seems even.

He does not reply.

Oh, fluent silence!

Her eyes narrow behind the mask and she gazes now into his blank, white face. Does she see? Does she see?

She cannot know but at once she guesses, for is there not a small Roman coin in her pouch that she has not yet played, and are there not cards in the field, pieces still to be moved, and could all not yet be thrown into doubt?

A recollection hits her now, her own wisdom, wisely given: one day the balance must break.

Faliere and Seluda stand almost perfectly balanced in this fight, the last pieces standing on the board.

What was the beginning of her advice that preceded this thought?

Assassination is a crude move. Let other players expend cards on battling each other, the strong tearing each other down, until they are weak enough that I may strike.

She looks at Faliere's player, and it seems to her that he smiles.

She turns and runs.

Chapter 39

The Gamesmaster always had a sense of humour.

We loved her for that, once upon a time.

She found her inspiration for this game in a pack of tarot cards, matching the meaning to the piece, the human to the name. The Priestess—intuition, knowledge, secrets, that is her meaning. Yet sometimes she is also Isis, the mother of magic, and how disdainful would our Priestess be to hear herself painted with such a pagan brush, whatever the truth may be.

The Fool, full of hope in his journey. Galliard Viole, do you find hope as you wander through the courts of Europe? We do not think so. Sorrow haunts you, behind your smile, and yours is always the loneliness of the road.

The Sun. You burn more than you heal. Your light is fire, not fertility.

The Queen of Cups. They will burn you at the stake someday, not because you are a prostitute, but because you dared to write of heaven as a place where male and female have no name, and souls are equal, and love may be expressed in touch and silence, and without reserve.

The Gamesmaster chose you all, named you all, played you all, as she plays even now, and she was most apt when she named this final card and called him Death, and put him in the hand of Faliere.

Chapter 40

Thene runs.

She runs through the streets of Venice, a madwoman in a mask, and people stare and scatter before her.

She runs, and is not a woman used to running but still she runs, distance irrelevant, time of no import, for she looked into the eyes of the man who plays Faliere, and she saw death there, and knew that the game was not yet done, and so she runs, and runs, and runs! It is a blessing that she knows this city, for in Venice the sun can be hard to find, the streets twist and tangle in on themselves, the canals bend in and out, forming slow sweeps that deceive any innocent traveller. Too many bridges are private, too many guarded by hungry men; you think you have found a landmark, but no, the alleys curl inwards, and when you emerge again you have lost all sense of place, all bearings, and you look for the sun and cannot see it between the high rooftops but do not panic.

Do not panic.

These are you streets, Thene, they are *yours*, you made them yours, you took them because no one was willing to give, you grabbed at a future and made it yours, you have the courage, you have the strength, do not fear, do not fear, and *run!*

The house of Seluda.

Suddenly, dozens of dignitaries are interested in him, men in dark robes and little caps flock to explain that, really, they were always on his side, always supported him in his bid, of course they did—of course! His role as Tribune would be so good for the city and for just a little consideration his support is theirs, just a quick shaking of the hand and a bargain...

She pushes through the crowd, which mutters at her rudeness: a woman, and a stinking, breathless one at that, what does she think she's doing?

Boys with letters, men with money, they have all come now, too many, too many, smiling, laughing, embracing, the best of friends—we in Venice are all the best of friends, and why would we not be, we are Venetian!—and at last comes to Seluda's side.

—You have to go! she hisses.

—Go?

He is smiling now, enjoying the attention, the accolades; it is easy for him to forget that not five days ago he was unregarded, unimportant, the people of Venice expected little of him and so paid him even less attention.

—I believe your life is in danger!

—I am with my friends! he replies expansively, gesturing through the crowd of faces.

She nearly shrieks with rage, at the vanity of the man.—This is why men need to be played, she wants to scream,—for I do not possess such a great ego as you do; I have not invested my heart and my self-esteem in the flattery of other men, only in victory, in *victory* which now you threaten to squander!

These words are not for now, not for Seluda, so firmly she grips his arm and whispers,—I think Faliere may send a killer!

—Let him come! My men can deal with it!

—Can they? Will you bet your life?

Now Seluda turns, and she sees the man beneath the jollity, the mind beneath the pride.—In Venice, he breathes,—death will always find you, wherever you hide. You cannot live your life waiting for it, for then you will not live.

—Nor will you *win*, she hisses.

He shrugs.—Victory is not life.

So saying, he turns away, spreading his arms wide to another man, a cry of—Paolo! My dear friend!

A moment she stands, bewildered and alone.

123

Her breathing has slowed, though her shoulders are high, her back bent, her feet burning from her run.

The crowd surges and pulls around Seluda. One of them hides a blade, or poison, or a pistol, or a rope. She watches the faces, and they all smile, smile and smile, and for a moment she despises them, despises the city, Seluda, and maybe even herself.

Her hand has slipped into her pouch, and though she cannot say when the habit was formed, she feels the little coin between her fingers, familiar and warm from where she has been touching it, pressing it into her skin like a lucky talisman.

And in that moment she thinks she sees the man called Silver, watching through a crack in a door, and knows that she imagines this, for there is not enough space to see him there.

Then she thinks perhaps she sees a woman all in white, moving behind the crowd, but she ducks down low between two traders in Egyptian wheat, and though Thene cranes her neck, she sees the woman no more.

The coin rolls between her fingers, warm and old.

For an instant, her eyes roll through the gaze of a man, whose eyes were ocean-green, whose hair is straight, skin the colour of walnut, but reddish too about the cheeks and forehead, as if burned by too much sun and sea. He is a mighty figure, dressed in strange barbaric robes, fur about his neck, rings of bone about his fingers, but blink, and he is only another supplicant come to pay tribute to the honour of Seluda, civilised men in a civilised time, who smile and smile, and look always for the kill.

And in that second, we, who have so long stood and watched, feel a shudder as her gaze sweeps the room, and know that she sees us too. She sees us, impossible though it is, and she *knows*. She knows who we are, and what we desire, and in that moment when we fear that she will destroy us all, instead it seems to us that she smiles.

Then her gaze lights upon a man, and she knows his face, and can name him both for himself and for what he is, for he is Death as surely as he was once Jacamo, her husband. He is looking straight at her, his mouth a little ajar, but that will not deflect him from his purpose. One hand hangs by his side, the other is buried within his cloak and we can feel now almost as if it was our skin itself on the handle that it is a pistol he hides there.

How did this happen?

How did Jacamo de Orcelo become the card that is Death? How did this fate befall?

(He lost too much gambling at the Gameshouse, too many creditors were howling at his door. The debt, was indeed so much more than his wife had ever understood for the shame, the shame of the gambler who has lost his home, it eats you up, has eaten Jacamo whole. He considered suicide for a while, and with the pistol against his jaw ready to end his days, a woman in white came before him and said:

—I can wipe your debts.

—I know you, he replied.—I have seen you in the Gameshouse.

—You have seen my umpires, she answered.—You have seen my ladies in white. I am their mistress. I control the board.

—What are you doing here?

—A game is about to be played for the control of this city. I am looking for pieces to fill the board. You are about to lose it all; I will give it back to you for a bargain.

—What bargain?

—You will kill a man, at a player's command.

—I, a killer?

—You would kill yourself. I assure you, killing another is easier.

—Why would you do this?

—I enjoy the game. Games are made to be enjoyed.

—How is murder a game?

—Life is lived through things which are not true. We pretend ourselves foolish in order to show our wisdom. We find things funny, which are sad. We smile at those who we would destroy, make alliances with those we do not respect, admire ourselves for our intellect and always look for the ultimate prize. We would be great, every one of us, and to achieve greatness do not bother to look at those we have destroyed in our path. A game is all of this and more, and nobler, for those who play at last transcend themselves, and see both the consequences of their choices, and the board as a whole. I do not think there is a nobler calling than the game, and I would have you a part of it.)

Jacamo de Orcelo.

His gaze meets his wife's.

She wears a mask, but he knows her as surely as she knows him.

He does not smile.

Perhaps even he looks sad, a man she can pity, though she has never pitied him before.

They have their parts to play.

He pulls out his pistol. He is almost at point-blank range to Seluda; he cannot fail but to hit, to kill, and she too far away.

Her fingers close around the coin; she pulls it from her pouch.

His finger tightens about the trigger.

She closes her eyes and throws the coin.

Chapter 41

The coin turns, the coin turns.

I loved the Gamesmaster once, but she loved the game more than she loved me, and the coin turns, and she is gone.

A pistol fires.

Chapter 42

It is the last night.

The night before the election.

The last night before the end.

Orio Faliere paces in his study as he has paced so much, for so long, the floor worn down by his striding.

His player sits behind, mask still covering his face, legs crossed, arms folded.

Thene stands before them.

Silence, save for the stomping of Faliere across the floor.

We wait.

At last Thene says:

—You will withdraw your candidacy for Tribune.

Faliere's player laughs; Faliere does not, but paces—still paces.

—A man attempted to kill Angelo Seluda, she continues,—but his pistol misfired. He lost three fingers on his right hand, and was taken into custody. In custody he died.

Walking, walking, Faliere is walking. Angelo Seluda lives and Jacamo de Orcelo dies, and no one knows who gave him the poison that ended his days.

—You will withdraw your candidacy, Thene repeats.—You will end this race.

The player laughs again, but it is a sound cut short by the silence of his piece, Orio Faliere, pacing still. They wait for the old man, who makes another cross, and another, and finally stops directly before Thene, some seven inches taller than she, and says,—Why?

—Because I know about your wife, Thene replies.

Silence.

The other player leans in, legs unfolding, hands clasped in front of him.

Silence.

—You can prove nothing, Faliere says at last.

—What is this? asks his player, low and earnest.—What is this about your wife?

—I have the sworn testimony of the gondolier who carries her to her assignations. I have the witness of three ladies of the town who have observed her activities. I have the testimony of the servants who clean the beds, the men who bring the food and most importantly, I have the testimony of her lover.

Faliere's player is on his feet now, but Faliere is still, so still.

—My wife's activities mean nothing, he says at last.—I have always known her a whore. The city will forget.

—The city will forget that she sleeps with prostitutes, it is true, though the scandal will always haunt you. Whether it will forgive her lying with other men's wives, I am less certain. Even if it does, that is not the reason why you will withdraw your candidacy.

—He is not withdrawing—we are *not* withdrawing! blurts the player, but Faliere is ignoring him now, watching Thene still.

—You will withdraw, Thene continues,—because you love your wife.

At this, Faliere smiles.—I am told that I love no one.

—You put it about that you love no one. But the truth is you love her. You knew what she was when you married her, and you married for wealth. She does not love you, and you did not love her, but sir, I have had her watched these long weeks and I have concluded that it is not apathy which keeps you away from the touch of other flesh, it is love. You love her. You know about her activities and you seek to protect her. This distance, this coldness—it is not for you, but for her. You love her and you know that this proof which I have will not only destroy your campaign, but it will end her life.

129

—No, wait, this is…begins the player, but Faliere silences him with a gesture.

His eyes are fixed on Thene's.

Silence.

—Sir, the player tries again.—Sir, this is a trick, a lie; she is nothing, she is…

Again Faliere silences him, and the player steps back, reaches out to the wall for support, as if uncertain of his own weight. How hot his belly feels, how strongly pulses the veins in his neck; we watch him and we think—yes, we are certain of it!—we think it is good that he is so afraid. This player was destined to win, and there is great satisfaction when the strong are shattered by the weak.

What would you do to win?

Anything, he might reply, gasping for air. Please! Anything!

But now this player is destroyed by his own piece, for he makes some sounds, some little begging noises, but Faliere is not listening. The piece is human after all! Faliere is more than a symbol on a board.

—May I have time to think? he asks.

—You have until dawn, Thene replies.—You know where to find me when you wish to answer.

Chapter 43

Thene walks through the city at night.

These are her streets.

She does not fear a soul.

The sound of fabric nearby.

A sense of eyes on her face.

Dawn will come soon and she is ready for it, though she knows already what Faliere's reply will be.

She is not even certain if she needs to destroy him for victory, having defeated so much to come to this point, but it is false, she concludes, to say that victory is the sweeter when it is snatched from the jaws of defeat. She will win a great many battles in times to come—let her first be triumphant.

Footsteps on the cobbles of Venice.

Water laps against old, smooth stones.

A woman's voice.

—May I join you?

We look, though it hurts so much to see her now. Dressed in white, her face hidden by the veil, even in these grubby paths she is so clean, so bright, so perfect, her voice soft and thunderous, her step gentle and long, we loved you once, we loved you, and you left us.

The Gamesmaster steps up to Thene at the other's gentle nod, and walks beside her.

A while they walk in silence, as dawn begins to reflect off the skies above Venice.

Then:

—This is a game which has been played before and will be played again, says the Gamesmaster.

—I thought as much.

—You have played it beautifully, my lady.

—Thank you. It has been an honour to participate.

—I have watched your progress and enjoyed the manner of your moves. You will be a fine addition to the Gameshouse.

—Addition?

—A fine player.

—Thank you.

They keep on walking. Then:

—A man spoke to you, did he not?

—You shall have to be more precise, my lady.

—A man known to some as Silver.

—I partially know the name. We played chess a couple of time, and cards. Is that wrong?

—Not at all. The Gameshouse welcomes all games, even the lesser ones. There are no rules against this. Tell me: did this man make you an offer?

—What manner of offer?

—That you must tell me.

They walk a while, silent still, as Thene considers her answer. Dawn spreads, the grey light flecking with colour in the thin shutter of sky overhead. The Gamesmaster walks in silence, a ghost in the shadows, an anonymity all in white.

—Before I answer, she says,—may I ask a question?

—Certainly; outside the house we are but two women discussing mutual friends.

—Then tell me this: was the game evenly weighed?

—Of course! she replies, high and indignant.—Of course it was!

Then,—No, Thene says at last.—The man you are referring to made me no offers.

—Very well, the Gamesmaster replies.—That is all I wished to know.

And like the passing of the night, she is gone.

132

Chapter 44

Later—centuries later—a stranger asked Thene what the first game was she ever played.

He meant it in the Gameshouse manner. Not a question of backgammon, checkers or chess, but the game that won her admittance to the higher league, where the currency is life, time and the soul, and the game is played in worlds and kings.

She was silent a long time, and I think the stranger realised then how much bigger the question was than he had thought when he asked it.

At length she answered so:

"The game I played which won me admittance to the higher league was one of kings. My king was Angelo Seluda—no one remembers him now—who wanted to be a Tribune of Venice. These days, we forget what the Tribunes were, but at the time, the matter seemed very important to him. Four other kings were ranged against him—Tiapolo, Contarini, Faliere and Belligno, but of those, Belligno and Tiapolo were destined to lose. Contarini was badly played, and Faliere...in the end, Faliere outplayed his own player, I think. He chose to be a husband before he was a piece, and for that I can admire him. I have played hundreds of games since then, and thought very little on that first but still...I remember not so much the victory, as the pieces. The Priestess, alone on her island. The Seven of Staves, scuttling for ever in busy obscurity. The Knave of Swords, dead by a violent man's axe. The Fool, empty-eyed and distant; the Tower, who loved to set fires and stare at flies. Death, who gambled too much and paid too high a price. They, I think, stayed with me more than the victory, which was itself no great thing. Somehow still, I remember the pieces."

At this, the other players laughed, saying, "Pieces? Pieces come and pieces go, and only the game continues!"

"No—but there is more," she replied. "You asked me what the first game was I ever played, and I told you of the game of kings. But there is another question, more important, which is what is the first game that I was ever played *in*. That game began, I think, long before I ever competed for the higher league, and though I have not yet seen its shape, its battle is still ongoing."

At this, the other players fell silent, uncomfortable, perhaps, at an idea that many had felt but few dared express.

Then Thene smiled, and gestured to the table before them and said, "Will you make your move?"

Dice roll.
    Cards fall.
    Kingdoms topple.
    Emperors burn.
    The young are born and the old pass away.
    And always the Gameshouse, the Gameshouse, it lives, it turns, the Gameshouse waits.
    And my love too.

The coin turns.
    The coin turns.

And we are gone.

THE THIEF

Chapter 1

The great game is coming.

Not yet, not yet, the board is not quite prepared, the pieces not in place, but it is coming so soon now. Why has she not destroyed us? Beautiful one, graceful in all things, why has she not crushed us when we were so much easier to crush?

Perhaps because in all things, the greatest game is the one you most enjoy.

Chapter 2

Remy Burke was drunk when he took the bet, but that does not excuse him. He had been a player for some fifty years, though he looked not a day over forty, and should have known better. We watched him turn down the first drink that was presented, politely once, then firmly again, and respected his wisdom in doing so. Yet when Abhik Lee sat down opposite him and in a single gulp drained his whisky down, Remy Burke's pride was raised, for here was an opponent of some seven years playing, a whippersnapper by the standards of the Gameshouse, daring him with his grey-green eyes to be the coward.

"Are you not drinking?" asked Lee, and at those words, Remy was drinking, he was gulping it down, for he knew perfectly well that he could hold his drink and doubted nothing that this was a game he would win against the half-breed player before him.

Six whiskys in, he growled, "What are we playing for?"

"Nothing at all," replied Lee, draining his glass. "Sometimes the game has no meaning."

Oh, reckless Remy!

Foolish Remy, buoyed up on drugs and pride!

Every game has its meaning.

Every single one.

You should have asked us; we would have whispered in your ear, told you of the day Lee played a New Jersey arms dealer at a game of battleships in 1933. Two cruisers and a frigate went to the bottom of the sea that day, and when Lee was declared the winner he won not only the other man's fleet, but his sea legs and iron stomach, and the beaten player had chronic diarrhoea to the end of his days. We thought perhaps, on the eighth or ninth glass to have stepped forward, to have warned you—but the umpires were there in their white robes, and they caught our eye, and we knew that you were playing now, even though you did not know it yourself.

Oh Remy, you should not have underestimated your opponent, for he would not have dared you to drink if he did not know he could win.

Yet the drink was not the game; at least, not the game that Abhik Lee wanted to play.

It was merely the opening of the trap.

Chapter 3

The Gameshouse.

There have always been houses where games were played, but this is no common parlour, no place for dice and the snap of a card upon the table. Surely if that is the distraction you desire, you may play in the lower league with the lesser men, who bet only money and pride. But if you are good enough—if you have the will to win—then step through these silver doors and come into the higher place where we ancient souls and scheming players lay our bets down in life and blood, in sight and souls. I could tell you of the games I have played—of the castles I have captured and held, seven thousand men at my command to protect a flag from my opponent! Of the kings I have enthroned and overturned, the monuments I have built, the risks I have made upon the stock exchange, racing my player to a monopoly of oil, of timber, of iron, of men. Of the murderers I have pursued and the times I have been hunted; of the races I have undertaken across the world, a crew of twenty and a single caravel at my command, and the strange pieces and men I have played to achieve my victory.

But not yet—not yet. It is not yet my time.

Therefore let us, you and I, look again at poor Remy Burke, who is a good, if unflashy player, and who woke one hot morning on the floor of his hotel room in Bangkok in the high summer of 1938, the taste of bile in his mouth and a hangover popping out through his eyes, and in a moment of stark terror, *remembered*.

Very little of the drinking he remembered, it is true, nor is he entirely sure how he came to be in this place, at this time. But as he raised his head from the floor and beheld the cotton trousers and linen suit of the man who sat before him, recollection returned and kicked against his skull almost harder than the hammer of the liquor within his belly.

He made it to the window in time to puke violently, wretchedly into the street below.

Remy's father was English; his mother was French.

This was a most unfashionable union.

His people were something in India; hers were something in Laos, but that was long ago and far away, all dead, all gone. The Gameshouse gives life to those who play it well, but they are few, and they must learn to leave lesser things behind. Yet for all that Remy won many a hand and lived for many a decade, perhaps something of his family haunted him, for always he returned to the lands of his birth, wandering through the islands of Malaysia, the hills of Laos, the great rivers of Vietnam, until at last, like a moth to the flame, he comes again to Bangkok.

The French and British empires glowered at each other through South-East Asia, grabbing a peninsula here, an ancient people there, until at last only one country remained, Thailand, blessed Thailand, ready to be crushed like the butterfly beneath the leopard's paw. The king looked at the British and saw that only the French could save him; looked at the French and saw that only the British would keep them at bay and in this state, and implausibly somehow, through gunships and concessions, Thailand remained free, a worm of neutral territory between the jaws of colonial sharks. Yet how free can any country be when all around great empires prepare for war?

So, like Remy, to Bangkok we are drawn, and now we sit, unseen observers, to see what new fate will befall our player as he wipes the last of the night's excess from his lips and slips down to the floor by the window-sill.

"What did I agree to?" he asked at last.

141

The man in the linen suit didn't answer immediately, but half turned in his wicker chair to look out of the hotel window. In the street below, the city was all change. Imported black cars idled irritably behind pony traps laden with straw and rice; three-wheeled rickshaws bounced round bicycles and grumbling trucks. Bangkok was a city where worlds collided; the smart suits of Western men and Eastern men who aspired to be more West than the West; the dusty sarongs of the running children; the torn trousers of the street-seller hawking his wares; the robe of the Buddhist monk pawing at passers-by, clinging on until they paid.

"Tell me it isn't blind man's buff," groaned Remy at his companion's quiet. "The last game took seven months and I was on a walking stick for five."

"It's not blind man's buff."

"Good, then . . ." This sentence was interrupted as Remy once again crawled, with surprising speed for a man so chemically damaged, up onto the window's edge, supporting himself by his elbows and, half gagging, half spitting, stuck his head out into the street and failed to vomit. If the sight of an over-six-foot Anglo-Frenchman with grey-flecked beard and deep brown hair attempting to puke into the street below aroused any interest, no one remarked on it. This was Bangkok; the city had seen worse.

Nausea came, nausea went, and down once again he sat on the floor, gasping for breath.

The man in the suit lent back in the chair, one leg folded over the other, hands steepled together, the tips of his fingers bouncing rhythmically against the end of his nose. His face was young—an unnatural young: too smooth, too soft, as if all the time had been sanded away—but his hair was silver-white, paler than the suit he wore. At last he said, "What I don't understand, Remy, is how you could possibly have let yourself get so drunk. And with a man like Abhik Lee! We all know that he's as malicious a little wart as ever set foot in the higher league."

"It wasn't part of a deadly plan, if that's what you mean."

"Abhik takes things personally."

"He's young; he'll burn out. Ten years—twenty at most—he'll

play a stupid hand for a stupid stake. You feel so strongly about it, Silver, why don't you pull him down?"

The man addressed as Silver shook his head softly. "Abhik won't play me. He hunts around the fringes, looking for smaller fish to fry. One day he might have the guts to take me on—but not yet."

"Thank you very much," croaked Remy. "Care to tell me which pan I'm sizzling in today?"

"You still keep cash under the mattress?"

"Got about fifty baht."

"You'll need it."

"Silver," growled Remy, shifting his still-uneasy weight on the floor, "what's the game?"

"On your eleventh shot, I believe you agreed to a game of hide-and-seek."

Silence.

Remy closed his eyes, head rolling back. "Right," he said. Then thought. Then, "Right."

Silence again.

"What's the board?" he asked at last.

"Thailand."

"What—all of it?"

"All of it."

"And the cards?"

"I can't say what the seeker's been dealt, but I imagine the resources are substantial. Assume he has some high cards in police, government and the temples. He's probably also drawn a few mercenaries, ex-spies, ex-cons, maybe a banker or two."

"How long have I got to beat?"

"You're asking me Abhik's form?"

"Yes—you watch everything—yes, I'm asking you his goddamn form."

"Last time Abhik Lee played hide-and-seek, the board was Palestine. He remained hidden for fifteen months, and when the sides were swapped he found his opponent in eleven days. You don't have to hide for long if you know you can seek fast."

"That's great, because in this country I probably can't hide more than a week."

"Abhik Lee is a proficient player of this game; I'd urge you to try and hide for a little longer than that."

"What were the stakes?" Again, silence from the man called Silver. "Don't give me that face: what were the goddamn stakes?!"

"Abhik bet twenty years of his life."

"That's not so much."

"It is for Abhik; a huge wager for one so young, in fact, fascinating in its boldness."

"I can afford to pay if I lose."

"You bet your memory."

Silence.

Silence.

When Remy spoke again, his voice was soft, and very sober. "All of it?"

"All of it."

Silence.

"How long do I have?"

"The game begins at noon; you have twenty minutes. I imagine that Abhik is already preparing the assault against this hotel; I'd urge you to be ready to run when the clock strikes."

For a moment, Remy was still. Then, with a half-nod of his head, he wiped his mouth with the back of his sleeve and crawled on hands and knees towards the bed, hefting the mattress to one side to reveal a paper envelope beneath. Travel documents, a little money—less than he would have liked—when had Remy got sloppy, we wonder? Doubtless as he looked through his meagre haul, he wondered the same.

As he crawled to his feet, bile again rose in Remy's throat and he leaned against the wall a moment, waiting for the feeling to pass.

"Any rules I need to know about?" he asked through heavy breathing.

144

"No deployment of resources beyond those on the board."

"Meaning?"

"Don't write for help to your banker in India or the hunter you won in Rangoon."

"You know about the hunter?"

"As you said: I watch people's form."

"All right. Only resources in Thailand. What else?"

"They can hurt you."

"Really?"

"The seeker has to verify the win in person, has to touch you to make the tag. Killing a player is against the rules, but if Abhik's men catch you before Abhik arrives on-scene, they are permitted to hold you even if you resist until he arrives."

"Can I hurt Abhik?" he asked, with teeth-grinding relish.

"You can kill his pieces, and I suppose you could try to injure him—however it might be unwise while you're hiding."

"Anything else?"

"Not as much a rule, as a bit of advice—Abhik wanted to play this game. He got you drunk and you went for it and then he challenged you. He chose the board; he made the rules. He'll have done his prep, checked up on your resources. He'll be watching your known contacts, waiting for you to run to them for help."

"I guessed as much already."

"Sobering up?"

"What time is it?"

"Quarter to twelve."

"Where do I start?"

"Here."

"And Abhik?"

"The Gameshouse."

"That's only twenty minutes away."

"Twenty minutes on foot," corrected Silver. "Five by car."

"Five minutes head start isn't much."

"Bangkok is big, and you were drunk." Then a question, fast, pushing its way through Silver's lips, the thing he had wanted to ask and had fought, and now which demanded to be known. "Why does Abhik want to play you, Remy?" he asked. "This game smacks of the personal. What did you do to him?"

"Honestly, old thing," replied Remy, pulling a bag down from the top of the wardrobe, "I have no idea."

Chapter 4

We watch.

We watch Silver slip away round the back of the hotel at five minutes to noon. The game has not yet commenced—that comes with the ringing of the bell—but it is bad form, bad manners, for one player to be seen helping another too particularly. It might raise questions in the house about what that other player really intends.

We see Abhik Lee pacing up and down before the silver doors of the Gameshouse. How did this house come to be here? We have seen these doors in Venice and London, Paris and New York, Tokyo and Beijing, always the same doors with the lion's head roaring from the metalwork, and yet wherever it is, wherever it appears, the Gameshouse seems old, a fixture, slotting into the architecture of this place as if it always was, and vanishing again without a scar.

We ask ourselves, you and I, who controls this motion through the world? Who is it who proclaims that here, now, in 1938, a door to the house shall open in Bangkok?

Then we ask ourselves another, far harder question: why?

Abhik Lee asks no such matter. He is a higher-league player of the Gameshouse. He has only one objective, the same as commands every man and woman who has ever set foot in those hallowed halls: he is determined to win. Every other thought is merely a distraction.

Observe Abhik Lee for a minute. His heritage is all mixed up. Persian, Bengali and Nepalese met a few generations ago with a

Scottish sergeant from the East India Company, who fell in love with India, shaved his beard and swore never to eat meat again, and whose grandchildren were more beautiful than any in the village, black-haired and green-eyed, and who were shunned for being strange. Abhik was shunned too, but he stumbled through the doors of the Gameshouse where the white-robed umpires were waiting for him, and there he discovered that a skill at cards could bring more than passing glories.

Smart grey suit and smart black shoes, cut in London, perhaps, or Paris—he must be hot in all that wool, we muse, but he is never out of it, never seen with a crease in his shirt or a smudge on his trousers, for now that Abhik has these things that other men desire, he will not be seen without. Abhik Lee will change for dinner in the Sahara, wear sock suspenders in the Taklamakan, because he can and because you cannot. He has seen the election posters in Bangkok and heard the winds of change, whispers of Japanese troops eyeing nearby Singapore, of army generals who no longer care what the once sacred king believed—and he doesn't care. These are merely the unfolding events of history around his life, and history will pass while he endures.

His watch has a silver case, and never loses time.

It strikes noon, and the hunt begins.

Chapter 5

Bangkok was built when a capital city was destroyed. Ayutthaya, cultivated city of noble kings, burned to the ground, the royal family butchered or taken as slaves. When that city died, a tradition began of generals taking power where no better alternative arose, and the offspring of those generals now sat, uncomfortable and quiet in the great palace of Bangkok, while new generals gave new orders, bowing to the kings who had to remember not to bow in return.

At some time, a palace was built on a swamp, its houses, shops and warehouses little better than floating wharves, rafts that bobbed against that uneven muddy shore where water and land could not decide which was the mightier. But though a young city, she had grown fast, and now sprawled away from the Chao Phraya river inland, criss-crossed by brown canals where the mosquitoes swarmed. The streets of Bangkok were as strange a medley of societies as ever grew on any corner of the earth. Shacks of tottering wood; longboats rotting at the seams; great embassies and European mansions of shining stone topped with tiny ramparts as if the inhabitants feared an assault by toy men, or feared so little the men of Thailand that even in defending against them, they made them dwarves. Temples—the great stone wats—none more than a century and a half old, yet within ancient carvings and stern lessons had been dragged from across the country to give an age to all things which the erosive action of damp and sun had not quite yet achieved. But even within these newly raised Buddhist shrines could be found the cackling green of long-tongued Kali dancing on the skulls of her ene-mies; the smiling hand of Krishna, the many arms of Vishnu; and scholars of theology debated furiously in Hindi, Thai, Malay and Mandarin which the most righteous path to heaven might be, while from their embassies and wharves the Christian men and women of the West looked on in wonder and marvelled that anything so beautiful could be so wrong.

Into this city as the clocks struck noon tumbles Remy Burke, hungover, bewildered, a bag upon his back containing one pair of pants, two pairs of socks, a box of matches, a stub of can-dle, two hundred baht in various pieces, a pencil and a knife. In any city in the world, such a man might cause some remark, and now such remarks were death or as near to death as ever he could imagine.

Had he bet his *memories*?

Such bets were not unheard of in the Gameshouse, and he had no reason to doubt Silver's word. Should the umpires have not intervened? Should someone not have stopped him? (Games are not always fair.)

Too late to wonder now.

He runs.

Chapter 6

Only three ways out of Bangkok. Train, boat or road. Each has their disadvantage.

Alternative?

Stay in Bangkok.

Hide out in an embassy with foreigners like himself?

But no. Too obvious: the embassy would become a trap, a prison; he'd be found, he had no doubt, Abhik catching him within a few days, a week at most. He needed to get into the country, find a forest or a mountain, keep moving.

No time to stop and think it through. Dammit! No time.

Train, boat or road?

He was less than a mile from the central station, and from there to anywhere, the growing tendrils of Siam's railways spreading out before him, but it was obvious, easy, the trains infrequent and unreliable. There existed no real timetable, only a blackboard with departures scrawled up by a grinning man in a crooked cap, a promise of good intentions rather than a guarantee of escape.

Or perhaps he'd get lucky. Perhaps there'd be a train.

Road?

Cars are still rare, the property of the very rich; better to steal a bicycle.

A six-foot-two Frenchman on a bicycle peddling through the fields of Thailand might still excite some remark; but that's a problem he'll have wherever he goes, whatever he does.

Oh, he has been played, has Remy Burke! He has been played long before this game began.

He makes a decision, the middle way, and runs for the river.

Hey hey! Let us stand a moment together you and I on the banks of the Chao Phraya and listen to the calls, hey hey! You want something, sir, you want to buy? Here, I have gold, silver, gems, totems of sacred power; I have herbs, spices, rice wrapped in banana leaves, locusts deep-fried, very good, very tasty, sparrows on a skewer you can eat whole, prawns bigger than your fist, hey hey! Slow down, sir, slow down, it's very good, you're foreign, yes, you're rich, yes, you've come to the East to taste something wonderful: try this, buy this, buy her, buy him; come sir, come! The floating market is always here, a hundred little rafts and boats, a dozen great steamers, a handful of clippers that wormed their way up from the bay to the south: we are here, all of us, waiting for you, as you have waited for us, gold flowing along the Chao Phraya river.

Remy does not buy.

He has fifty baht in his bag and the clothes he wears. Every satang now counts; every grubby coin and haggled bargain. He runs, breathless and sweaty, the air a humid cloak that smothers the skin, faces turning in amazement at this gasping stranger, for who runs in Thailand? *Keep a cool heart*, tut the old men in the doorways. *Be happy and keep your heart cool.*

In other times he loved this country for its immersion in relaxation. The sun is too hot, the people seem to say, the ground too wet, the mountains too high, the rice too green for stress, so be calm, wind down, the train will leave when the train feels like it, the tide will turn when the river is ready so why do you pant and stamp your foot?

He stamps his foot because he will die, his mind will die, if you do not get out of his way!

The waterside. The river has not yet been fully tamed; it still carries memories of those good old days when the city floated on top of it, and only the Grand Palace stood in its way. In

Ratanakosin, the kings of this land built stone walls to protect their homes, their vaults, their stolen emerald Buddhas, but away from those fine places of gilt and gold, wooden wharves, sticking out into the water like dead leopard tongues, are man's greatest incursion against waves. The sea is to the south, but there is too much danger of hitting international waters, of breaking the rules, and if Remy fears one thing more than defeat, he fears the umpires, white-robed and unrelenting, who find their prey in any place. Now the gnats buzz over the edge of the water, the flies cling to the empty sockets of the dead fish laid out for sale, the easy-time girls coo at the foreign buyers and sellers come to port, at the neat Japanese who sniff and tut and head to a more important meeting with more important men; at the wandering Chinese, thrown by war and politics from their own country to seek new meaning in new places; at the Malay labourers looking for a taste of freedom; and the Anglo-Indian scholars who have lived long enough to wonder what "freedom" even means. They come, they all come, to the market, and so does Remy, praying that in this crowd even he, ridiculous-looking he, will not stand out.

"Nakhon Sawan! I am going towards Nakhon Sawan!" He addresses the boatsmen in Thai, but they laugh at his flushed face, panting breath.

"Take the train, Frenchman!" advises one, casually throwing barrels of silver fish over the side. "You'll like the train!"

"I want to go by boat."

"Why? It'll take much longer, you look in a hurry."

"I like the river."

"Take the train, French! It's much better for you!"

So rejected, he looked at his watch.

Twenty past twelve.

What would he do if he was Abhik Lee?

He would raid the hotel, hoping to catch Remy with his pants down, certainly. But he'd also send pieces to the station, set watchers on the roads, set a cordon round Ratanakosin, and of course—but of course—he'd send pieces to the waterfront.

153

Not as many, perhaps, as he'd put on the trains, but still enough that he could be spotted. How long would it take? If he was lucky, Abhik would have sent too few people to apprehend him immediately; or perhaps not? Perhaps Abhik's hand is that good, every piece he plays a master of muay boran, every one a killer.

He looked along the shore and saw no one obvious, no one staring at him too hard, too long, but then again on this water-side, this teaming waterside of barrels and crates, of bartering and discord, *he* is the most obvious thing about it. Poor Remy Burke, the most obvious man in Thailand.

(He looks, and does not see, but that does not mean that his enemies are not already there for lo! we spot the woman that his eyes skim over, her hair blue-black, her eyes laughing, seemingly at the antics of a group of children who prod a still-crawling crab with sticks along the quay, but who sold her soul to the Gameshouse when she was just fourteen years old, barter-ing away her freedom to save her baby's life, and who now is a piece in someone else's hand.

She smiles to see the children play, and turns from the water-front to send a skinny boy on a bicycle to the train station to summon up more men.)

A boatman unloads barrels of still-living snakes. He har-vested them from the swamps to the east, great tangled masses of red, black, brown and green that snap at each other as they are hooked on the end of a pole. His four-year-old daughter sits in the front of his barge playing with a tiny one that has taken a particular fancy to the twist of her wrist, before her brother, ten and all grown up, pulls it by its gaping jaw and tosses it with the rest of its kin, condemned to a culinary destination or a medical fate.

On the pier, the wife haggles. Her arms are lightly pocked with a dozen snake bites which she brushes off now as easy as a fly. Her clothes are not so much worn as wrapped all about her, great twists and barrels of cloth in faded blue and brown, spun around her chest, her waist, her head, her feet, and we can feel perhaps a moment of sympathy for the man who is on the receiving end of her tongue, as forked as her cargo, sympathetic as a fang.

"No!" she proclaims. "No, no! You pay the price we agreed or we go elsewhere!"

"Where will you go?" demands the buyer. "Where will you go? This is an inferior cargo!"

"It is not inferior: it is exactly what we agreed; you pay what we agreed..."

As they row, Remy eyes the boat. He kneels down by its prow, smiles at the boy, who glares like a man. "You came down Chao Phraya?" he asks softly.

The boy nods, shoulders back, chest puffed; a little warrior.

"You know Nakhon Sawan?"

"Hey! You want to buy snakes?" The father steps forward, boat bouncing unevenly. "I can sell you snakes, good for you to eat them, good for the heart, good for being a man! My wife handles all the money things."

"Are you going north?" asks Remy. "Towards Nakhon?"

"Yes, north—but not all the way. The people aren't so good there."

"But out of the city?"

"Yes—you want to come?"

"I do."

The husband runs his tongue around the inside of his lips, looking Remy over. "I'll talk to my wife," he says.

"Could we leave immediately?"

"Once we've unloaded snakes!"

The wife is there quickly, a tiny woman cowing all before her, glaring up into Remy's face. "Where do you want to go?" she demands in rata-tat-tat Thai straight from the front lines.

"North. Out of the city."

"Why?"

"Honestly, ma'am—I made a bet and now I need to get away."

She sucks in her breath, long and slow, clicks her tongue, looks at her children, her husband, her barrel full of snakes. "Five baht!"

155

A fortune—a veritable fortune! He can pay it a hundred times over in the normal way of things, but this is not the normal way of things. "Three baht."

"Five!"

"Three, ma'am. There are many boats which would take me further for three."

Her eyes wander across the wharves, assessing her potential rivals, hungry for profit. "We aren't going to Nakhon."

"But you are leaving the city?"

"Three baht...you are a villain, but three!"

He smiles.

"Let me help you unload."

Chapter 7

We watch the boat slip away from the land.

We are not the only ones.

Four minutes after it has reached the centre of the stream, knocking against the sneaking currents of the river, three cars arrive. Three are two more than are usually seen in Bangkok, save when the king or the generals go about their business, but there they are, black, American-made, carried over the Pacific by a great white-painted steamer, decks scrubbed and windows clean, which will be sunk in four years' time by a German U-Boat prowling the shipping lanes for arms and men. We are impressed that Abhik Lee has such good cars ready to do his work, but then we remember—he has been planning this for a long time, hasn't he? Nothing is chance in the Gameshouse.

Abhik Lee steps onto the quay, shields his eyes against the glare of the high-noon sun, squints against the river. Thinks, perhaps, that he sees the shape of Remy Burke, huddling low but still clear, against the side of the little rocking boat. Seeing is not enough—he must tag his target.

"Get on the water," he barks to the men from one car, and then to the other, "Get ahead along the river. Don't lose sight of the boat."

How close he is! He can win this in a day, perhaps. What a glorious victory that would be.

*

Two hours later, a police boat pulls alongside the little barge of empty barrels and shed snake skins. The officers scream at the family to obey, to stop, where is the foreigner?

The husband clings to his oar; the little boy cries.

The wife stands in the middle of the boat, arms flapping, tongue lashing like rigging in a storm, proclaiming you pigs, you dogs, you come here, you speak to us like this, how dare you, how dare you, look at what you people have become!

Abhik Lee leans forward on the railing of the police boat.

"Ma'am." His voice is quiet, courteous, unstoppable. "Where is the foreigner?"

The foreigner paid three baht to be taken north, but handed over only two and they hadn't travelled more than a mile before, without explanation, he demanded to be rowed to the easterly bank of the river, and hopped overboard.

"How long ago was this?" sighs Abhik Lee.

"About an hour! He didn't even say thank you!"

Abhik Lee's face contorts briefly in a scowl, which vanishes as quickly as it blooms. He at least is courteous, always so very courteous. Lose courtesy, and you lose control; lose control and you lose yourself.

Shall we peek?

Oh, go on then.

Let's look at the cards in Abhik's hand.

We ease open his jacket pocket, slip our fingers down towards the silver cigarette case where he so discreetly stashed them, slide it out while he is otherwise occupied and flick through the papers.

My—my, oh my! What a hand was here dealt!

Police inspectors, spies domestic and foreign, a communist saboteur, chiefs of little villages where surely the Gameshouse should not have reached (and yet how far it goes), two abbots and a nun, an anarchist rumoured to have planted a Malaysian bomb or two, a criminal overlord and his son, two majors, three industrialists, one colonel and a general! With cards like these, you could stage a coup, topple a king, start a war! These are extraordinary cards you have been dealt, Abhik Lee, and for what?

To hunt a single man, alone and hungover, through the rivers of Thailand?

We slip the cards back into Abhik's pocket, our presence unknown, our thoughts unexpressed. We are the watchers that take no part, the umpires that judge all but can never be judged. We play the players.

Run, Remy Burke. Run.

Chapter 8

For seven hours, they hunt high, they hunt low. Abhik Lee plays three cards fast. A policeman stops all trains leaving the central station, saying a murderer is here, searches every compartment of every truck. The passengers sit around on their suitcases and bundles, chins in their hands, waiting until at last, five hours after the first train to the north should have gone, Abhik says, "Enough," and the policemen lets them go, pumping great black clouds from the stacks of the engine and creaking slow over the too-quickly rusted tracks as they head away from the city.

A colonel sets up roadblocks on the main roads from the city. There was a threat against the king, he explains, a foreigner with a gun, and now everyone must be stopped and checked. The French ambassador and his mistress were heading out into the countryside for a few days of light hand-holding and poetry-making (as some might put it) and, since they are foreign and heading away, they are stopped and held at gunpoint while the colonel examines their papers, their faces, their lives. The French ambassador threatens gunboats and retribution, not so much in indignation at his condition, but in terror of his wife finding out, when word trickles back to the embassy, of just who he was with when so slandered.

The colonel examines the ambassador and says, "No—it's not him," and lets him go.

On the river, the police boat chugs up and down. Its highest speed is eight knots, but on the Chao Phraya that is something almost extraordinary, and the boatmen tut and shake their heads

160

as the police churn by, exclaiming, "In such a hurry! These busy people and their crimes, so stressful, so much stress!"

By the time the sun is down and the mosquitoes are out, Abhik Lee is very quiet and very calm.

"It's fine," he says. "A quick capture would have been ideal, but we are prepared for the long game. Let him run; let him hide. We'll have him within the week."

This said, he goes directly to the telegraph office and begins to raise his forces through the rest of the country.

Chapter 9

Darkness settles.

We settle with it.

So still, so quiet. We—you and I—we are so used to the bright lights of the city, to the sky flecked with the reflection of our business, but here, in this time and in this place, all is darkness, all is quiet. The roads of Siam are peopled by day with trudging barefoot men and baby-swaddled mothers; with skipping children, ear-flicking donkeys, ponies and their traps and even, if you head far enough from the city, the occasional slow-marching elephant and his rider, hauling great logs of timber or pallets of clay to their destinations. There are cars, surely, and trucks too, but they are few and far between, and we may stand now, you and I, and turn our faces towards the stars and see an infinity of light that shines in the heavens, but not, we think, upon the earth. Dao Look Kai, the seven little chickens that threw themselves into the fire where their mother burnt, a tiny cluster of starlight that we might call the Pleiades. The crocodile, Dao Ja Ra Kae, look on him and remember always to do good deeds so you will be rewarded. Dao Jone, the brightest star of all. Children born under his light will become robbers, and the dogs that would have guarded the house all fall asleep under his silver gaze.

Stop.

Listen.

A van approaches! Most rare sight, a Russian-built thing, perhaps? No—not Russian. A British van come up from India, a tarpaulin upon its back, crates bouncing with the light rattle of green celadon pottery, delicate cups and narrow-lipped vases which are gently going out of fashion as the spread of the West to the East begins to overwhelm the once fashionable spread of the East to the West.

This van stutters along a nowhere road in a nowhere place, the driver sucking a fat cheroot which he has savoured for nearly thirty miles, leafy ash dripping onto his trousers when—bang! An axel cracks, a tyre bursts, something shifts in the back of the vehicle which should not, but he only rolls his eyes and slows to a halt, for this has happened before to him and will happen again for the coming fifteen years in which he will continue to drive this van until that fateful day when the engine bursts past all repair and too far from replacements.

Cursing all the way, the man steps from his driver's seat and, feeling his way in the star-black darkness to the back of the van, throws back the tarpaulin.

The light is faint, the moon a thin crescent behind skudding clouds, but it is enough: as he pulls back the covers from his crates, he sees a man, and the man sees him.

The driver jumps back, a faint cry coming from his throat, not sure whether to run or fight.

The man hidden at the back of his truck raises his hands imploringly, calls out, "Please, no—I'm not going to hurt you!"

"You're right you're not going to hurt me!" retorts the driver. "This is my van—what are you doing?!"

"I needed a lift."

"Haven't you heard of asking? Why are you hiding at the back of my van?!"

"I thought there might be roadblocks."

"Roadblocks? Are you a criminal? If you are a criminal then you should know that I will die to defend my property!"

This statement, coming as it did from a potter's son whose nearest equivalent to martial prowess was the time he was beaten up by Sunan for looking funny at Sunan's sister, is perhaps louder and more indignantly rendered than it needs to be.

Remy untangled himself from the tarpaulin, slipping uneasily to the ground, hands still raised in a placating way, fingers open, palms turned towards the driver. "I just needed a lift," he murmured, eyes running across the empty land, flat fields, flat mud, low trees, darkness. "Where are we?"

"Where are we? *Where are we?!* You hide in my van, you scare me half to death and then you ask, 'Where are we?' We are in hell, foreigner! I have driven you straight to hell and there is no escape from it!"

Remy turned his attention fully to this bouncing, indignant doomsayer, and straightening up a little, said, "In that case, I'll leave you to it."

Slinging his bag across his shoulder, he looked back the way they'd come, then on towards the dark, and with a little shaking of his head and a shifting of his weight, turned and began to walk.

The road was packed mud; the night hummed with insects.

His trousers were muddy from jumping too quickly from the snake-seller's barge. What had he seen that had frightened him?

(He had seen three cars pull up to the riverbank as they sailed away and known that three was three too many. You may be hungover, Remy, but you did not enter the higher league for nothing.)

He had hidden in the pottery man's truck because it was going the right way at the right time. They'd taken a back road out of the city so that the potter could say goodbye to his second-favourite aunt, the one who always gave him something sweet mashed with coconut, and in this familial manner had dodged the roadblocks.

Remy hadn't eaten all day, or had anything to drink.

His stomach contracted in tight physical pain at the recollection, but he shook his head: he cannot stop; a stranger in a familiar land, he must not stop.

Behind, the driver of the van flaps and curses and, when the darkness has swallowed Remy whole, stands still and shakes, chewing his bottom lip though he cannot say why.

*

Five miles later, the fixed truck chugged by Remy on the road, the headlights dimly illuminating him. They swept past a few hundred yards, then stopped. Remy sighed and kept walking. The passenger door opened, the driver stuck his head out.

"Hey!"

"What do you want?"

"You want a lift?"

Remy stopped, turned on the muddy road to look up into the dimly-lit face within. "What?"

"A lift! You want a lift?"

Hunger bites, thirst sucks.

"Yes," he said, climbing inside. "That would be very kind."

Chapter 10

The driver's name was Looknam.

Rather, his name was Kalayanaphan Angthongkul Somboon, but as a child his mother found him a mewling, difficult boy and so named him for the larvae of the maggot, and called him Looknam, and for reasons of speed as much as anything else, Looknam he remained. For four years as a child he barely made a sound except for crying, but aged six some switch was flipped in Looknam's soul and from a creature of few words he became near impossible to silence, speaking both volumes and—worse—tactless, honest volumes of words where none would have been preferable. By the age of twenty he'd achieved the remarkable accolade of having lost four jobs in fewer years, and at twenty-one he was finally given to his uncle by his despairing mother in the hope that the wealthier potter could find some use for his garrulous nephew.

Rather unkindly, that use was driving the truck.

"I think my mother thought that it might make me quieter, a better man, you know, having no one to talk to? I drive thousands of miles every week; I go to Rangoon to sell to the British or Vientiane to sell to the French; and I pick up the clay on my way back south and my uncle says that one day I might be allowed to do something else, like sell things instead of deliver them, but I don't mind: I like driving; it's relaxing, and my friend Gop says that everyone's hoping I'll drive off a cliff or get stuck in a river or something somewhere, because the truck wasn't really built to do all this hauling over such distances and it would make more sense to put the pottery on a boat and sell directly to India but I say that we've got family in Rangoon and they buy at a really good price because you know the people who come to that city to trade, well, they're really stupid, much more stupid than in Bangkok so it's good that we can sell there and if I'm the only one driving the truck then it's not so expensive and in Bangkok people know what good pottery really is so we can't sell this stuff—I mean, it's not bad, but it's not great; actually it's not very good at all, but the Chinese used to make better stuff but that market dried up, my sister says, so maybe it's okay really, but anyway, like I said, I don't mind driving: I enjoy the quiet."

Silence, for a few seconds.

"Also I like picking up people; there are people going places in this country; this is a moving country ever since the generals stepped in and I know that people talk about how it's not a good thing, and that the king is in danger and we have to protect the king but I say how's the king in danger? These are his generals doing the best for his country and I know there was some . . . but it's all settled down now and we're all going to be fine really, as long as the Japanese don't invade which they won't because why would they? They're not interested in us, just the British, really, just Singapore and India and that's fine, really, although the Japanese are almost as bad as the Europeans but if they don't bother us who cares?"

Who did care?

Not Remy, it seemed.

"But one day I'll stop driving and meet a woman and we'll get married and have five children—three girls and two boys, but the boys will be the oldest and protect their little sisters and the youngest girl will be my favourite, not that I'll have favourites but I will really because, well, we do, don't we, and she'll be very shy until one day when she starts singing and then everyone will say how brilliant she is at singing and she'll become the most famous of them all—not the richest: the boys will be rich, and they'll look after me and my wife in our old age—but my

167

daughters will all be famous and all take it in turns to come and feed us when they're not travelling the world performing."

Silence.

"What do you think?"

Silence.

Remy sucked in the side of his cheek, feeling the soft tissue with the tip of his tongue, exploring the interior of his mouth carefully as if seeking out unwise sentiments that might have lodged between his teeth. "I think it sounds very pleasant."

Silence.

Then, "Do you want a cheroot? I pick them up in Rangoon, much better—*much* better!—than what you get here, cheaper too, everything cheaper."

A cigar, wrapped in grey-green leaves, fatter almost than his wrist, was offered. "Thank you, no."

"Mind if I . . . ?"

"Not at all. As you say, it's your truck."

"My truck, yes! Can't believe you hid in it; I would have given you a lift if you'd asked; what is it—law trouble? Don't worry about it, everyone's had trouble with the law before, it happens; you know a lot of criminals go into the monasteries now? I mean, I'm in favour, whatever the monks do I'm sure it's good, but I don't know, some take the robes and I'm sure they get better but some, some are just—well! You know what some are like, don't you? But I'd never say anything, I'm sure, because it's not my business, just make merit and pray for good karma, that's what you do, isn't it? Do you pray?"

"No."

"You should pray, you should pray, it's very important, even if you don't pray to the right things you must pray, you must make offerings otherwise you'll never have any hope; it's the law, the law of the universe—are you sure you don't want a smoke?"

"Thank you—no."

Looknam shrugged. "More for me!" he exclaimed merrily, and chatted on as they drove through the dark.

168

Chapter 11

The village lay on the water.

Those words could be spoken about most places in lowland Siam, and therefore as geographical descriptors went, they meant nothing at all.

Remy slept in the back of the truck while Loknoom snored in the front. Dawn came in reflective grey streaks, bouncing off the still water of the lake. Remy woke with the cawing of the crows, knelt in the mud and washed his face, drank a handful of water down, felt hunger in his belly, fear at his back, looked around at a four-house town, Loknoom's truck the only vehicle in sight; knew he could not stay.

"I'll take you to Rangoon! I've got a cousin there, his wife—you should see his wife..."

"I can't leave this country."

"Why not? You're foreign—you can go wherever you want!"

"Not today I can't. Thank you for the lift."

"Where will you go? There's nothing round here!"

Remy shrugged, and walked away.

Impressions of a man on the run.

He has forty-eight baht in his bag. What was that worth? A month's rent for a small room in the city—if he didn't eat. A couple of journeys by train. One night of drinking at the French club in Bangkok. A gun and a few bullets. A few weeks' food and drink, carefully measured. Not enough—not nearly enough.

Dawn rises to the day. The day is hot. In February, the locals

169

call it mild and luxuriate in the sun; which turns Remy's skin lobster-pink as he boils. In May, even the oil-skinned men who hunt snakes on the water confess it too hot to work after 9 a.m., and sit and wait for the rains. It is April. It is the worst of times to get sunburnt.

He steals fruit from the trees and eats in an explosion of juices and sugars. He tries to steal a chicken, but it's too fast for him and he lands on his face.

He walks for five hours without seeing a car, a bicycle, a truck or another village.

The only people he sees are two farmers, their trousers rolled above their ankles, wide hats upon their heads, leading three heavy-limbed buffalo to a field. They stare at him, openly amazed, perhaps the first foreigner they have ever set eyes on, but he puts his hands together in a greeting and is careful to bow lower than they do, for this is their land, their fields, and he is a stranger trespassing on their roads.

He stops shortly after midday, sweating, still hungry despite his stolen fruit, thirsty enough to risk climbing through flooded fields, drinking from water that he has no doubt contains its fair share of leeches and snakes. He must survive off this land, he knows, since he hasn't the resources to live by any other means, and to do so first he must stop fearing it.

After an hour, he carries on walking, his head now pounding, not from alcohol—though that ill-fated start to the journey did not help—but heat and hunger. He cannot say after a while if it's the sun that moves about the earth, or he who moves about the sun; cannot swear that he isn't walking in circles, chasing sunset. It isn't until the sky is turning orange and pink on the horizon and the glare has gone from his gummy eyes that he comes to another village, a cluster of houses roofed with dried leaves spread across a wooden frame, whose adults stare at him as if he were a walking ghost, and whose children, knowing no better, flock around him in fascination, too shy to ask questions, too curious to run away.

An old man approaches. He is almost as thin and fibrous as the

170

stick on which he leans, skin like bark, hair like cobweb. He is the village elder but unlike his father, who was the elder before him, he has retained his wits and knows better than to glare with suspicion on the unknown.

"Who are you?" he asks. "Are you lost?"

"A traveller," Remy replies. "Not lost; just wandering."

Ah! Revelation dawns in the elder's face, for he knows, though he has never met anyone like this before, that foreigners go very easily mad in hot climates, and here clearly is a deluded poor fool struck down by too much sun.

"Come inside, come into the shade," he commands. "Eat with us, eat!"

Remy obeys.

Chapter 12

Remy ate rice in the shade.

Took off his boots.

Rubbed the blisters, put his boots back on before he could scratch them until they burst.

Found a leech feeding busily against his calf.

Knocked it carefully off. Do not pinch it at the back, or squeeze too hard. Do not scald it with fire or salt. These remedies, though traditional, make the leech regurgitate its meal, filling a wound with its stomach. Ease it off gently—so gently— or let it gorge until it flops to the ground, the anaesthetic of its saliva numbing the bite.

The villages watched him silently, asking nothing until, when her father's back was turned, the daughter of the house lent forward and said:

"Is it nice in the city? Is there a lot to do?"

Remy opened his mouth to reply, and found that only banalities or shallow half-truths were willing to manifest. A longer, more honest reply would have required more energy than he had.

"It's all right," he said, "as these things go."

When he tried to sleep, the elder's wife came over to him, offering a bag of what seemed to be powdered white chalk. He didn't understand, and she demonstrated, rubbing it into her face, her arms, her legs, her hands, until every exposed part of her seemed to become a ghost, an eager, grinning ghost, offering her gift to him. He cautiously rubbed some on his face, and found it cooling. She nodded and smiled, encouraging him as you might encourage a frightened child.

He lay down on the wooden floor of the elder's house, and slept without being invited, and without being disturbed.

He slept for five hours.

The sound of engines woke him.

A terror in the night, a dread of discovery. He sat straight awake, saw the sweep of headlights across the roof of the hut, crawled on hands and knees to the window, peeped out.

Already the people of the village were gathering, curious, if not particularly surprised, for first a foreigner had come, and now this car: these things were most certainly connected, and most certainly unremarkable in being so.

A man steps from the car; then another; then a third.

They are smartly dressed. One is Thai, another Japanese, the third is of that wondrous medley of bloods that has no real place to call its own, but is of everywhere in the world. Abhik Lee, you could have been beautiful if you were not such a player.

The elder of that place greets them, points them towards his house.

They run inside, but Remy Burke had slept with his boots on and is not to be seen.

Chapter 13

A miserable sunrise.

He crawls in the night through mud and field, and at day-break looks back to see the clear path of destruction his journey has sown through that tranquil land. Torn stalks, broken flowers, fallen purple petals and uprooted wild celery mark the path he has taken, and the village is still visible behind him, his way clouded by darkness. His feet are sodden, threatening to rot inside his boots; he shivers though the air is growing hot.

He cannot use the roads—not now, not with Abhik so close. The hunter moved fast, so fast! He saw that his prey had escaped Bangkok and must have followed the roads, sending out tendrils to ask where a stranger had been seen. Remy needs to change his face, and soon, but there has been no time, so fast the chase follows.

He staggers, back bent and lungs gasping, through the rising day.

A car swerves by on a nearby road. He hadn't even seen the road; it was a thing lost behind the bushes, just a path of mud carved through more mud still. He hides, belly-down among the thin green shoots of the field, until it has passed. A pair of water buffalo eye him suspiciously, not sure what this walking puddle is doing in their kingdom. His appearance will be a problem, he knows. If there is anything more distinctive than a six-foot-tall Anglo-Frenchman walking alone through the lowlands of Siam, it is a six-foot-tall Anglo-Frenchman who is covered in mud. Such an appearance is not the colonial way, and Bulldog Britain or La Belle France would be most displeased to know that one of their native sons was so dishonouring their noble ways as to appear...dishevelled. Uncouth. Inferior. There is no mud, the ambassador might proclaim, in noble England. Even the beggars are hungry for better things.

He knows that he cannot keep running like this for long. What would he do if he were the seeker?

He'd set up a cordon, the radius of a running man's reach, let nothing in and nothing out. Setting up such a cordon around Bangkok was a challenge, the city too big; out here in the countryside, with two roads in and one road out, it is not so hard to do.

At noon he hid in the shade of the matum tree. Grey fruits, not yet ripe, swayed in the branches overhead. A bird with a shaven head and extravagant tail feathers stared down at him, and cacked its displeasure at his presence for a while before losing interest and returning to the task of preening.

He set his eyes on a range of low hills in the distance. The sun had burnt all the clouds away, and they seemed bare and harsh in this hot noontime light. As he neared, he could see the beginning of forest and scrub clinging to the low rise, green-grey leaves, spiny and broad, as if the palm trees of the south and the hardy evergreens of the north had met in this country and fused together in ultimate genetic victory.

The path became harder as he neared the hills. The pain in his feet had reduced to steady throbbing; the throbbing was not good news. The aching in his head whispered of heatstroke yet to come, but he couldn't waste time on puking, not now, not when Abhik was so close behind.

At some hour of the early afternoon, he heard the sound of an engine, louder and clearer than even the cars that had sometime rattled across this mud-shaped land. He ran until he reached scrubby bushes which rose to his waist, threw himself down in their embrace, twigs snapping at his skin, a startled rodent racing from its lair. There he stayed as the engine noise circled once, then twice, then a third time overhead. His clothes were the colour of grey mud, his hair, his skin, all things caked in dirt, and that was probably what saved him.

The plane turned and turned again, then flew on by, its spotters having seen nothing to report.

He reached the edge of the low forest by dusk. The last few miles had been the longest, paths running out, fields growing to tumbled-over towers of tortured foliage. He fell beneath the shade of an acacia tree, heard the shrill night callings of the beautiful creatures that paraded through the day, their feathers vibrant golds and greens, their voices like the battle-cry of a barbarian granny, and for a few blissful minutes, Remy slept.

The night was all about compensating for the day.

He puked what meagre contents were in his stomach, then puked thin, white bile.

He lay curled up in a ball, head pounding, arms shaking, his blanket a bundle of freshly fallen leaves, his skin twitching from the landings and departing of myriad flies. In the dark he thought he heard something large, panting, stir in the woods, and wondered whether tigers ever came this close to humanity, or if wild dogs slumbered. It would be simple to light a fire—but not yet. Not tonight. Not with Abhik's men so close by.

Shortly after midnight, by the rising of the moon, he heard voices in the distant forest. Sound travelled strangely in this place, carried on the leaf-rustling wind. He pulled his bed of leaves higher above his head until barely his eyes showed between their damp edges, and watched distant flashes of torchlight play in the woods before fading away with the sounds of men.

Abhik Lee had a tracker; of course he did.

It would have been foolish to expect anything else.

Chapter 14

He rose with the sun, having no alternative.

A wild boar, furious and panting, sprang away from his den as he shook himself free, startled to discover that it had spent a part of the night near a creature bigger than itself. He wondered if anyone else would hear the commotion of that passing beast.

As the sun climbed higher, so did he. Beneath a fallen tree trunk, he found a nest of nameless scuttling insects and collected a handful in a scoop of leaf to serve as breakfast. Hunger made them taste better; perhaps even good. The ones with long antennae about their head and little spots of brown across their carapace reminded him a little of prawns.

A dip in the land hinted at water but the stream he found at its centre was barely an arm wide, a running trickle of nothing. He buried himself in it, turning his head against the flow to let the water run across his face, his eyes, into his mouth. He didn't dare take his boots off for fear that his swollen feet would never get back inside.

He wondered if he should stay here by this little stream, eating little insects, but looking back the way he had come, he could see too easily the muddy imprints where he had walked, the broken twigs he had snapped, the undergrowth disturbed, and so he kept climbing.

The shadow of the forest made moving easier, sheltered from the heat of the sun, but made navigating harder. He climbed, trusting only to motion, until he came to a ridge of spindly grey stones which rose above the top of the highest trees, and there, feeling his way along in search of an easy route, he found a path, narrower than a child's waist but still distinctly a thing carved out with knives and boots, which snaked over the ridge of the hill and ran down the other side.

He followed it a while until he came to a tiny fork, a bare disturbance in the way, and seeing it had already been disturbed by other feet before his, followed that.

It curled a little down the way he had come, and he was almost ready to leave it when, pushing through an insect-crawling shrub, he came to a small clearing. Here, from a nondescript pile of grey rocks, the little stream rose where he'd earlier drunk, and there, carved in the same stone and decked with yellow and green lichens, were the faces of a dozen gods.

Tallest among them, though a little shorter than Remy, was the smiling, beatific Gautama, his hair held high and his ears hanging long, hands together in a *wai* of greetings. Either side, smaller but no less worn or carefully carved, he glimpsed Vishnu and Krishna, Ganesh the elephant god and Kuanyin, goddess of mercy, standing together like a happy family, and in one corner, an arm sadly chipped off at the elbow, another saint with Indian features and a Buddhist robe, who wore about his neck the sign of the cross and smiled as contentedly as any on this hill.

A woman sat before these icons. She squatted on her haunches, picking at a ravaged piece of fruit, her eyes wandering over the statues with no particular focus on any one divinity. Her head was wrapped in bright fabrics that swept back to a point; her neck was circled with metal bands that pushed her chin up high above her shoulders. Her teeth were stained black and red with betel juice, her wrists were skinny and old, her ankles narrow enough he could have wrapped his thumb and little finger around them and still had room to clench. At his approach her head turned up, revealing her stained smile, film-coated eyes. She squinted through the pinprick vision of her cataracts, saw a stranger, a shape without distinction, and grunted a sound which might have been greeting, might have been contempt. She couldn't have been a day under seventy, yet somehow

178

she'd made her way up here to eat fruit and rock back and forth before these ancient stones.

Remy bowed, palms pressed together, asked her, "Excuse me, revered lady, do you know if there is somewhere I can trade for food around here?"

She took so long to answer, he began to speak again, but she cut him off with a shaking of her head and a shifting of her weight from one foot to the other.

"Trade, trade, nothing to trade," she tutted.

"I'm hungry; I need help."

"Help? Hungry? Nothing to trade—no, nothing to trade."

"Is there a village near by?"

"Village? No, no village."

"Any people?"

"Down the hill, down the hill perhaps. You should ask my son."

"Where is your son?"

"There, there, over there." She flicked one wrist back up the path, fingers flashing out like the tail of a horse swatting at flies.

"Is it far?"

"No, not so far, not so far."

"Do you...are you all right here?"

"I've got fruit. You want fruit?"

He looked at the half-eaten remains and his stomach churned. "That's very kind, but I'll find my way."

He left her, praying alone to deity unknown.

Chapter 15

There was a downward path on the other side of the ridge, which turned into a scratch in the ground which dissolved into nothing.

At the place where it dissolved, Remy stopped, looking for someone, something, a sign of human life. Birds shrieked in the trees, leaves flapping like sails. The wind was cold, the sun so hot that where it peeped through the foliage it burnt little marks on skin and earth. He listened.

Something creaked between the trees.

Someone cursed, their words lost to the breeze, but then they curse again: "Idiot, idiot, I told you to tie..."

The wind carried the voices away.

Remy turned, and kept turning, listening, looking.

On his third rotation, he saw the elephant. It stood barely fifty yards away, where it had been standing all along. How, he wondered, could a creature so large, so ponderous, hide so well? It looked at him; he looked at it, its ears brushing thoughtfully against the insects that clung to its wrinkled side, its trunk twisting as if trying to chew the air.

For a moment neither moved, paralysed, it seemed by their own mutual surprise at being so encountered. Then a man, tiny and lithe, burst round the side of the elephant's flank, a sack on his back and a stick in his hand, saw Remy and stopped. His head was shaven, his clothes were an explosion of colour, his trousers torn at the knees and crotch, badly re-patched and the patches torn again, but he didn't seem to care.

"Hey!" he said at last, when the silence grew too long. "Hey! Have you seen my mother?"

The elephant driver's name was Songnoom. He was his mother's second son, king of the forests, master of his tribe. Where, Remy wondered, was the first son?

(He ran away to be a monk; what a disappointment. It's all very well seeking spiritual enlightenment, his brother would say, but how's that going to feed anyone?! We shall never speak of this again.)

Songnoom had a rifle. It was an ancient, rusted thing, a remnant of some war. Perhaps it had been cutting edge when first it fired in the Crimea, but each shot needed to be loaded, rammed home, the pan primed, and it was only good for shooting rabbits at very short range, and scaring strangers far from home.

Now Songnoom waved it towards Remy—not the barrel, just the weapon as a whole, as if he himself was uncertain if he was intimidating an enemy or welcoming a friend on a lonely path. Like his mother, his teeth were stained red and black, but unlike his mother he had lost two as a young man and so chewed almost entirely on one side of his mouth, creating a pattern of streaks which faded to pink away from the mashed-up betel nut.

At his command were seven other men, of whom two were brothers, four cousins and one they'd picked up as a child and brought along, and who suffered terribly for his lack of genetic bondage. He also had three elephants under his authority, which regarded the great turbulence of the humans about them with the patience of wily priests who have seen rebellion and heard the changing of the psalms, yet looked up and known the heavens never altered for man's delight.

Any impression that these men might be foresters or locals vanished at the sight of their antiquated arms, and the suspicion dawned—and how right you are—that these might well be traders of a less salubrious sort.

(We peek into their packages and yes, oh yes! Sweet intoxicant poppy, the sap dried out into great beige bricks in the sun, wrapped in linen and sent on its way. This is not China—you will not be beheaded here for your practices—but still, still a risky business, the times being what they are! We cannot blame you for avoiding the road more travelled.)

Questions: who are you? What are you doing here?

Answers: I'm a traveller; I'm lost.

And then, sensing perhaps their illicit goods, seeing their uncomfortable attitude: the British accused me of something I did not do. They hunted me all the way to Bangkok. I'm trying to get to the north, towards Vientiane.

On foot?

I don't have any other choice.

Silence in the forest.

We have arrived at a tricky moment. These are not bad people, these smugglers, are they? How would we define "bad"? Songnoom loves his mother, and for that love would surely do anything to protect her, and if protecting her extended to killing strangers in cold blood, well then, surely that is not a "bad" act, in and of itself, merely the logical conclusion of our line of thought?

We consider our options, balance the pros and cons.

It is the game we play now, and the dice, when they fall, will not fall without some weight. "Chance" is a concept for children.

Perhaps Remy too can hear the rattling of bones inside the case—a player of the game should always have an ear for such things—but what's he to do? He calculates every move he might make, and they are few, and they achieve…nothing. His fate sits in the hands of a second son, his lips stained like ancient blood. Throw the dice, toss a coin, wait for it to land.

Songnoom's fingers drum against the butt of his rifle.

Remy looks at the gun and realises he played the moment wrong. He appeals to the brotherhood of bandits, but in confessing that he is hunted, he also admits to being a prize.

A voice calls out, "I dropped my spoon."

Our eyes turn, as does the whole forest it seems, to see the smuggler's mother, moving well for a woman whose neck sticks out almost horizontally from her back, waddling down the forest path. Her lips still glisten with the remnant of consumed fruit, her fingers are sticky nectar to gathering flies, but her voice is clear and her feet are steady, for these are her hills, her forests, and though the young boys laugh at her and call her granny, she has known stories that they will never understand.

A little gesture from her son, and those of his boys who were hiding knives in their hands and in their eyes, turn away.

"I dropped my spoon!" she exclaims again, wandering towards the elephants. "I dropped it."

Remy moves a little away, ready to run as son and mother reunite. Songnoom flaps over his parent, Remy temporarily forgotten; helps her mount an elephant where she sits, tiny on its great back, as comfortable as a queen on her throne. Remy is heading away, slipping between the trees, but perhaps some tendril of filial piety, of honour or gentler thinking has been kindled in this smuggler, because as Remy turns to make good his escape, Songnoom calls out after him.

"Eh!" he cries. "You want something to eat?"

Chapter 16

A picnic with smugglers and their mother in a forest.

They laugh at how eager he is to eat until they see that it isn't an act, a passing fancy, but the devouring of a man who might otherwise have starved to death.

His clothes are ruined but still curious enough that the youngest of the clan, a boy of some fifteen years, trades them for an old shirt and baggy trousers that he was taking to sell. They are too small for Remy, but big enough that they merely look strange, not uncomfortable. They were too large for the boy anyway; where did he get them, we wonder?

(Won in a race with his elder brother; which brother is not with the clan now, because he is slow at running and likes to gamble, and neither vice is acceptable in a streamlined business operation. The older boy will die in 1943 in Kuala Lumpa with a card sharp's knife through his throat; the younger in 1945 when the Japanese retreat and chaos ensues. When he dies, he'll be wearing a shirt patched with pieces cut from Remy's clothes. So much for chance; so much for fate.)

Remy offers to pay, a few coins, a bare handful for his meal, but the smuggler's mother is sleeping now and something in the peaceful manner of it, the easy way she lies against the warmth of her elephant, which could crush her spindly form with a flick of its trunk, a bump of its side, and yet now waits as she peacefully slumbers—why, perhaps this sight stirs Songnoom to charity which he might not otherwise demonstrate, and so with a merry, "Good luck, foreigner!" he waves Remy freely on his way, to whatever fate might await him.

So much for a picnic in the forest.

Chapter 17

Food, drink, a little sleep in the shelter of the trees. He takes off his boots at last, and his feet are swollen, raging red. He makes a nest between some rocks, starts a very small fire, tiny scraps of kindling, lies down to think.

Where is Abhik Lee?

(Five miles outside Nakhon Sawan, waiting for you to come to him, Remy, waiting for you to walk into his trap.)

Where are Abhik's men?

(Three still scour the hill looking for you, less than four miles away, a tracker and his friends. They are the nearest and most immediate threat, but they have been diverted by the smuggler's paths, tricked into thinking that perhaps you too have followed these routes. Another fifty men and women are circling this area, some on boats, some by bicycle, some not even aware that they are playing the game, but rather pieces played by pieces, given your description and told to find you out with no idea of why. Make no mistake, Remy, you are still in the hive, and the hornets are buzzing.)

What will Remy do now?

He lies back to think, while the sky fills up with stars.

Chapter 18

We look down from the sky above, and between the swaying leaves of the forest, whispering with the sound of a shingle sea, we do not see Remy.

The tracker finds the place where he slept in the morning, but the fire died long ago and he left at sunrise, climbing bare rocks which leave no trace where a man might tell that his foot has fallen.

For a while they follow, guessing at the fugitive's most likely course, but to no avail.

Remy Burke slips away, like breath.

Three days without sighting.

How far may a man on foot go in three days?

Three miles an hour, fifteen hours a day at the very maximum, three days—one hundred and thirty-five miles.

Not possible—no *chance*—that Remy has gone so far!

On the fourth day, Abhik Lee sits down with a map, draws a circle with a hundred-mile radius of the village where last Remy was seen, and ponders. A hundred-mile radius contains within it a vast area of land, but it is easy to eliminate certain points. His men have been on the rivers, in the towns, at the railway stations, and a foreigner attempting to pass these points would have been noticed. No stranger has been seen in any of the major towns nearby, and though his cards are limited, the resources they can deploy are many. Policemen, soldiers and spies roam the countryside looking for Remy Burke, pieces played by a man who is himself being played, all by Abhik Lee.

Oh, Abhik, do you really think the game stops with you? Do you, as you move your pieces across this map, as hypothetical a board as any chess or backgammon set, do you really think that you are the master of all that unfolds?

We forget, sometimes, how young you are.

Rumours proliferate, of course. A stranger seen in Ratchaphon turned out to be a British journalist, a slave to gin and malaria in roughly equal parts, who was taking a few months out from his posting in Singapore to reconsider his life, and muse whether the time had not come to join the communist party. Another man, glimpsed in Nong Klang was a German archaeologist and his wife. Rumour whispered that the German was, in fact, a Jew, and knew as much archaeology as a killer whale does the tea ceremony but, being a man disowned, invented whatever name it seemed most suited him and thus increased the odds of his survival. A Dutchman twelve miles to the south was searching for precious gems, a crew of thirty quiet locals at his back who neither smiled nor frowned as he paced up and down shouting, "Come, come!" and "Go, go!" at everyone and everything who came near him, these perhaps being the only native words he knew. He was convinced he was going to strike diamond and make it rich, but when the Japanese came he was interned as an enemy alien, and when he was freed in 1945, his voice was broken, though his back was still straight.

All these rumours, Abhik pursues, sending out his pieces to explore every one and knowing, as he does, that none of them are Remy.

The very absence of Remy makes it easier to narrow options.

Somewhere in the wild; somewhere in the wilderness. Sooner or later, he'll have to show his face, and Abhik knows, without a doubt, that within the circle drawn on his map, he'll find his prey.

Chapter 19

Day four.

Day five.

Day six.

No sighting.

And what of Remy Burke?

Where are you now?

Why, he sits by the side of a river—no, not even a river—a tributary, a worm of water wriggling through the land that has no name save colloquialisms given by the locals—and fishes.

He was not here yesterday; he will not be here tomorrow. He stole the line and tied it to a bit of wood, skewers his catch on sharpened sticks and cooks it over low ashes. He is tired, muddy, picked over his entire body by insect bites and gently seeping cuts, but his feet are no longer swollen and his belly is occasionally full. One morning he woke to find a snake sizing him up, stretched out to its full length beside him as it assessed whether it could swallow him whole. (It could not, and at his stirring it lost interest.) Another, he woke to find two children—a boy and a girl—staring at him fascinated, enthralled by this leaf-and-bone man hiding in their forest. They ran away when he sat up, and he left his hiding place that very hour, knowing that they could not resist but tell their parents, and their parents would tell a friend, and the friend might tell the police and so, in as little as a few hours or as much as a few days, he would be exposed.

(They told their parents; their parents told their friends. A friend's cousin, whose wife's brother was something in the local police, told his brother-in-law, who had received word six days since from his boss in Nakhon Sawan of a man on the run, a half-breed Anglo-Frenchman with dark brown hair, and at once he alerted the authorities and they all rushed to the place where Remy had last been seen to find only the guts of a fish eaten for breakfast and a few grains of stolen rice gobbled in a banana leaf to indicate his passing.)

Remy wanders, and isn't as frightened as he was before. After the initial shock of his predicament, he has some semblance now of equilibrium. He walks, he walks, his feet passing through agony until at last, hardened like the black scaldings on thick rattan wood, they settle into their shape within his battered boots, and still he walks. One day he steals a bicycle, abandoning it twenty miles up the road in dense undergrowth and following the course of the river instead. The next day he finds a stout stick which is straight enough to be used for walking, and sleeps in the porch of a high-walled temple which he thought was abandoned, until a monk emerges in the middle of the night to give him some water and a little rice, laying cup and bowl beside him without a word, and an older, more portly monk emerges at dawn with a broom to chase and berate him away.

He will move, and he will hide, and he will avoid people as much as he can, until circumstance conspires against him. And if he must meet people?

He will assume the worst and keep running.

Chapter 20

On the seventeenth day, the woman surprised him. The path ran between rice paddies, laid out with wooden boards. He walked it alone beneath a grey sky threatening rain in the early-morning glow before colour invades the land, and when he looked round, she was there, a bicycle propped against a tree, a chicken in the basket, its feet tied together with string, still alive, head sticking out, watching all things uneasily.

She stared at him hard as he approached, and he smiled and bowed a little, and kept on walking.

Her stare was on his back as he walked away.

Two hours later, on a different path up a nearby hill, he heard the rattling of pedals, the bouncing of hard wheels on rough mud. The chicken was gone from her basket, but this time the woman slowed, pulled up a few paces ahead, lent her bicycle to one side and said in heavily accented French:

"Are you all right, sir?"

He replied in her language and saw the surprise on her face. "I'm very well, thank you."

"Do you know where you're going?"

"North. I'm on a pilgrimage."

"Are you . . . a holy man?"

"No. Just walking."

This little exchange was enough to carry him by, but she dismounted and caught up with him, matching her pace with his to walk alongside. "How can you be on a pilgrimage if you're not a holy man?"

191

"I think pilgrimages are meant to make people holy."

"Or wipe away sin from evil—that is the other meaning, is it not?"

"In some cultures."

"You look like a man of some cultures."

Now he looked at her more closely, taking in her man's clothes, her broad-rimmed hat, her skin roughened by the sun. With a little work she could have passed for a boy, but she made no effort either way and the effect was oddly attractive. He looked away. They walked together a while in silence.

"Have you been on this pilgrimage long?"

"Not so long, no."

"Why did you go?"

"I had a gambling problem."

"Ah—that is a terrible thing!"

"I made a bet that I shouldn't have made. It may cost me dear. I think—at least, my friend says—that I was tricked into making it, that something more than the drink was behind this mistake. But it was still me, still my voice that agreed, still my game." He spoke quickly, low, surprised to hear his voice. How long had it been since he'd had human company? The days stretched in the wild when you hid from human sight.

"So you are running away from your debts?"

"No. I am walking to win the game."

"But you said you were on a pilgrimage."

"Can it not be both?"

"I do not think a pilgrimage is a proper pilgrimage if you are also using it as an excuse to visit your favourite aunt, or buy silk cheaply to re-sell," she murmured sombrely. "That's just business dressed up in orange robes."

"Yet here I am, walking alone, and though my intentions may be one thing, could we not suggest that the road also changes me?"

"Very well: in the best case scenario, you *are* on a pilgrimage, but you could be on a far more effective one if you were also not walking to win."

"I can...accept that premise."

They walked again a while in silence.

"Why are you talking to me?" he asked. "I don't have money."

"That's a pity—I don't either."

"Most people avoid me."

"Of course they do—you are strange."

"Does that make you strange for talking to a stranger?"

"I am a widow. If I talk to a man, people whisper about me. So I talk to you."

"Because...I am not a man?"

"You have chosen the loneliest hour and the emptiest road to walk down. And you are foreign—that makes you something other than a man, and in speaking to you I am something other than a widow. I lived with my husband on the shores of the lake. He used to sell fish to a Frenchman there, a priest come to convert us. The priest wasn't very persuasive, but he liked the climate and the food, and said that if God had given so few people into his hands, then surely this was a sign that he should stay where he was for longer, rather than move on in search of easier pastures. He made this thing a joke. Then my husband had a pain in his ear, and he died."

"I'm...sorry to hear that."

"After, I was going to be a nun in the temple."

"Why didn't you?"

"Women cannot pray with the men. They cannot be blessed—it is unclean for the abbot's hands to touch a woman's head, even a baby's."

"What about nuns?"

"Nuns can touch the children, but nuns sweep and run errands and do not engage in the discourse."

"You...wanted to be a nun to engage in discourse?"

"Of course I did. The generals rule the country; the king is confined to his palace; the communists fight the nationalists who fight the Japanese in China and in India Ghandi walks to the sea to harvest salt. Of course I want to debate and meditate and pray."

193

"That seems...good."

They kept on walking. Finally she said, "Are you heading to Sok Prah?"

"I don't know. Where's that?"

"It's the village on the other side of this hill."

"Then I suppose I am."

"That's where I live."

"I see."

"I don't think you should go there."

"Why not?"

"The monks there are narrow-minded."

"That's a terrible condemnation for a monk."

"It's an easy trap to fall into. You pray, you think, you pray, and in time you forget that the world is bigger than your thoughts. It's noble for men of business to spend time at temple. I think it is also noble for men of the temple to sometimes spend a week down a mine or delivering babies, yes?"

Despite himself, Remy smiled. "You might be on to something there."

They walked.

"Also," she said, "two days ago, two men came into the village: soldiers. They had a picture of a white man, a foreigner, which they stuck to the wall of our elder's home. He's a stranger, on the run, a reward of five hundred baht for anyone who helps find him. Five hundred baht is a lot of money in these parts."

They walked.

"Thank you," he said at last. Then, as an afterthought, "If they said I committed any crimes, did anything violent, they are lying."

"Are they?"

"I...play a game sometimes. That is all."

"What kind of game?"

"Hide-and-seek."

"Like the children play?"

"Exactly like the children play. I am hiding; someone else is

194

seeking. When he catches me, we'll swap sides and I'll seek him. The winner is the one who stays hidden the longest."

"You are playing a very odd game."

"I was drunk when I said yes."

"And this game you also call a pilgrimage?"

"A good game does more than make you smile. Is there a road that doesn't take me through your village?"

"No. But there's a path that will take you to a temple, and from there you can climb down to the river."

"This temple...full of cantankerous monks?"

"They might not sell you out for five hundred baht. Although," she smiled, "it only takes one, doesn't it?"

They walked.

"I live outside the village," she said eventually. "They say that widows bring bad luck. I am poor."

"And the men who came to your village are rich," he conceded.

"Are you playing for money? This pilgrimage game of yours, these debts you are afraid of—is it money?"

"No. If I win, I gain life. If I lose, I lose my mind."

"Those seem like very high stakes."

"As I said: drunk."

"Does your game let you kill people?" she asked, sudden and bright, not slackening her pace as she walked beside him. "Is that something you do?"

"There's no rule against it, but I would still have to make that choice."

"Would you kill me to keep me quiet? I've seen you on this road—I could cycle ahead, go to the village, to the town, to the railway station; they have a man there who speaks Morse code—I could be rewarded. For five hundred baht, people will forget that I'm a widow. If you bet your life, are you willing to take my life to keep your secret safe?"

"I don't think so."

"Why?"

"Your body would be found; people would search."

"Not me; they don't care."

"Perhaps they wouldn't search for your murderer because of any fondness for you. Perhaps they'd only look for fear for their own daughters, wives."

"Ah—that is a good point! So you wouldn't kill me because it doesn't gain you anything?"

"I also like to think I have a code."

"But the code is not within the game?"

"No."

"Does it help you win?"

"It...Possibly not. Yet I still have it. But as I said, the situation hasn't arisen."

"And so you haven't been tested? Perhaps you're right," she mused. "Perhaps you are also on a pilgrimage."

"You want something," he said, stopping, turning to look into her face. "Tell me."

"I wanted discourse," she replied. "You are the first person to talk to me for five months."

With that, all words die on his tongue.

What do we see here, in this moment? This woman, stick-thin beneath her baggy clothes, standing stiff and straight before a stranger. The people of her village avoid her gaze, turn away; she brings bad luck; she is twice cursed—once for being a widow, and a second time for having no children to support her in her state. Husbands die, but wives who do not produce an heir—they walk in the devil's shadow! Good people, good monks, good friends, they do not wish her ill—they just wish her elsewhere. Life is too hard for complexity; let questions of the "right" of things be asked when there is more rice in the bowl, more fish in their bellies. Let someone else shake society to its roots; let those who have more time for it wonder at the lot of widows.

She speaks, and it is the first time in five months that she has spoken so many words altogether. For a while, in her isolation, she spoke to the stars, to the dawn, to the birds in the trees, to the Buddha and all his aspects, and to herself. But her words became repetitive and banal, and so she fell silent until now.

Remy Burke has not spoken for four days, and thought he might go insane from it.

"I have a little money," he said. "May I buy some food from you?"

Chapter 21

Her name was Fon. She was born on the day that the monsoon began, and the winds had blown so violently that the roof of the hut was shaken with it, and water poured in across her face, a blessing, her mother always said, not a sign of nature's rage.

Her hut lay outside the village, up a stairway of mud cut into the side of a small hill, obscured by low-drooping palms and scarred boulders. The hut was a single room raised up by poles a foot or so above the earth, with a roof of leaves. There had once been a door of tough, dry leaves threaded through a frame, but the frame had cracked and the door now rested on the ground, waiting for repair, the room open to the night. She cooked outside in a pit of charcoal and rounded stones. They ate as the sun went down, listening to the change in the pitch of the forest noises. From the top of the low hill, they could look down into the village, a little circle of candles and cooking fires picked out against the darkness. She said that the hut had belonged to her mother, who had died there four years since, and whose spirit— so the people said—still haunted this lonely hill.

He slept on the floor at her feet, as the wind tumbled shreds of nightmare dreams around them.

In the morning, she said, "I wanted to make the door better, but it's hard to do alone."

She already had the tools she needed—wedges cut from fallen branches, a few nails carefully salvaged from her trips to the town, a hammer and a rusting saw. She commanded him with perfect precision and he obeyed, and by noon, the thing was done. In the afternoon she sat down to mend a fishing net, and he watched, until without a word, he joined her, and she said, "I've been doing it a little at a time."

"I'm not going to be much use—it's not something I do often."

"You'll be of use," she corrected firmly. "It's good to have company."

When the sun fell, she looked down towards the light of the village and tutted and said, "I shall have to go down there tomorrow."

"What do you trade with them?"

"Herbs I collect from the hills. Fish, if I'm lucky. Squirrels and birds I catch in snares. But they know I live alone, so it's easy to rob me. They aren't bad people—just hungry ones. Their children are hungry. If you could get something more to feed your child, wouldn't you?"

"Probably."

"If it was within your code?"

"As I said before—it hasn't been tested."

On the third day, she cycled into the village, and he collected wood to burn and checked snares, and when she returned she laid her bicycle against the wall of the hut and said, patting the handlebars, "Without this, I think I would have died a long time ago."

At the end of the first week, they sat side by side in silence, watching the stars come out between the trees, until at last he said, "I have some money you can have."

"You help me with my work; I don't need money."

"Nevertheless, I have some; you could use it. Please don't be...please accept it."

"No," she replied softly, pushing his open hand away from hers. "If I started spending baht, people would suspect. They'd wonder where I got it, and you'd be in danger."

"There are ways around that, surely?"

"You play your games—tell me, are there any ways that aren't a risk?"

"No. Probably not."

"There you are."

On the ninth day, she touched him lightly on the arm, an unconscious thing, a brush asking for attention.

He looked up, smiled, and she pulled immediately away, holding her fingers in the palm of her other hand, like a woman stung. Said a few empty words—we aren't interested in what—and walked quickly away.

She could not remember the last time she had touched another person, but we can. Nine months and twenty-four days ago, a woman helped you pick up your bag when you dropped it, but you did not enshrine the feel of her fingers against yours in your memory, not knowing that it would be the last time a person would touch you for so many long, cold nights.

On the morning of the twelfth day they walked through the forest, setting snares and collecting roots, until at last she asked:

"Why is the game so important?"

"I told you—if I lose, I lose everything."

"But why do you play? Why does it matter so much to you to be a player?"

"It's... I like the victory. The... challenge. My days are not mundane. I do not sit and solve logistical problems; I do not try to get the trains to run between Mandalay and Rangoon; I am not tasked with moving crates in the harbours of Hong Kong or digging pits in Xian. It is not... daily dullnesses that oppose me, but rather brilliant minds. I fight brilliant minds, and when I win, when I know that I was better... but even in defeat, sometimes, there is joy. In witnessing the beauty, the brilliance of another player, of feeling your heart race, your face burn with the excitement of it, with the excitement of your plans, their plans; chance doesn't enter as a factor: it's not luck; it's not nature; it's just... *me*. My mind, the pieces and the game. It is... incredible. Perfect. I... would find it hard to give that up."

They walked together a while longer, until she said, "But you were drunk."

"What?"

"When you agreed to this game, the game you play now— you were drunk."

"I...was. Yes. Abhik...played me well in that regard."

"Did no one try to stop you?"

"I don't know. I have a friend—I say 'friend'. He's a player, one of the oldest, possibly the very oldest still alive, friendship is always part of something else, enjoyable, perhaps, as all games are, but still...things within the house are never quite what they seem."

"I don't think that is what I'm asking."

"Then what?"

"I think...I am asking if you are sure that this thing you are experiencing is happiness. Or, if it *is* happiness, if it is worthy."

"It is only a game."

"Does it do no harm?"

"It...I have a code," he replied. "The game is what it is, but I have a code."

"I think you have answered the question, therefore, for yourself."

On the fifteenth day he put his hands on her shoulders, a silent greeting, a wordless comfort as she watched the forest. Her body turned, as if one part wanted to run, the other sink. Then she swallowed, lifted her chin, stood up and moved away.

That evening he said, "I cannot stay in one place too long."

"Do you think your enemies will find you here?"

"I am sure they are still searching. Perhaps they assume I have slipped the net and have given up on this area. But I doubt it. Abhik will have cards he can play across the whole country— I'm sure he'll be holding some pieces here. And I...there are things I must do."

"What things?"

"Victory comes to the man who stays hidden the longest. I am a stranger in this country; even here, even with you, I cannot stay hidden for ever. I have questions that need answering. I do not understand why Abhik wanted to play this game. I do not understand why the Gameshouse permitted it to happen."

"You said you were drunk?"

"The game isn't balanced. Abhik has a natural, immediate advantage. He can hide in this country; his face is not remarked. My skin makes it harder for me to hide. He has resources he can access; had time to put his pieces in place—pieces more than those dealt in his hand. I did not. A game isn't fun if it's merely the inevitable destruction of an opponent. The Gameshouse might have intervened, balanced the bet before it was made, but it didn't. That is...curious."

She nodded quietly, eyes turned away from him into the forest. "If it is important to you, you must do it."

In the night, they lay together on opposite sides of the hut. She turned her back to him as he undressed, and pulled her thin blanket high about her chin as she settled to sleep.

They lay, faces turned away, eyes open, pretending to sleep.

Chapter 22

The following morning he woke, and she said, "I'm going to get supplies."

He watched her cycle down in the grey morning light while the forest whispered and the flies gathered with the rising day. He paced the edge of the hut for a while, and as light burnt the moisture away and the heat began to beat down even into the shade, driving it back, he paced the edges of the forest.

The sun rose higher and he walked and sat, and walked a little more, and drew dirt patterns with a stick on the floor, and stared into the sky, and walked, and waited.

Shortly after noon he heard the clattering of a bicycle on the path. He stood, breathless, though he didn't know why, until she appeared, a bag on her back, basket full of fruit and uncooked rice tied in leaves. He opened his mouth to say—what?

A moment of could-have-been. We take in breath as he does, find ourselves ready to say sorry, farewell, hello, goodbye, adieu, let me stay, forgive me, be with me—why, all these dance on our tongue at that moment of inhalation, but for Remy...

...he said nothing at all, for she spoke first, slinging herself awkwardly off the bicycle which dropped where she left it, scampering towards him, her hands pressing against his arms in an instant, holding tight.

"You've got to go!" she hissed. "You have to go now!"

"I don't..."

"I went to the village and they all stared at me, then looked away. The children stared, the old women stared, the mothers

203

stared, the fathers stared, and when I went to go, the farmer's son turned to his mother and said, 'Will they take her too?' The richest farmer in the town has a cart he rides to market—the cart wasn't there and neither was he, but the market isn't for three days. They must have seen you—you have to go."

"This isn't proof," he replied, pulse pounding in the soft flesh beneath his tongue, throat tight, air thin. "This doesn't mean..."

She pushed a bundle of rice wrapped in leaves into his hand. "You have to go," she repeated. "They know."

He gathered his meagre belongings in a daze, didn't complain when she pushed a cup into his bag as well, and a wooden spoon. Then he stood before the fixed door of her hut, she in it, and said like one in a daze, "What about you?"

"I am not in danger of my life."

"Aren't you?"

"This game—will you win it?"

"I...Maybe. I don't know."

"Go," she repeated with a little shake of her head. "Just go."

He didn't move.

"If you lose you are useless to me," she said. "Go."

He did.

Chapter 23

Anger is not a helpful emotion for a player.

He walks the rural paths again, away from the road, away from people, away from anything but the beating of the sun and the turning of the wind, and reminds himself that he is not angry. Angry at himself, angry at Fon, angry at Abhik Lee, angry at the Gameshouse, angry at...

Nothing of significance, he tells himself, and feels immediately guilty for feeling any thoughts except gratitude towards his sometime host.

He is not angry.

Angry is not helpful.

He reminds himself of this many times as he walks through the forest.

Chapter 24

At night, he settled down to sleep beneath the sheltering leaves of a drooping palm tree, and thought himself safe until he woke with a start and saw the torchlight flashing through the forest, heard the voices murmuring to each other in the dark, the crack of feet. How had they come so close, five hundred yards, maybe fewer, maybe four? He pulled his bag onto his back and ran, blind through the dark.

At the commotion, the others, the wanderers in the night, turned their light towards him, and someone gave a cry, and they ran also, charging after him through the busy, buzzing dark.

He ran until he came to a stream, and then he ran along that, gasping for breath, face streaming with sweat and tears, legs shaking, lungs breaking, and still they came behind him, one ahead of the others, barefoot and nimble, dressed in a long shirt and shorts held up with rope, his hair braided to his head—a tracker, no doubt *the* tracker, a piece played from Abhik Lee's hand, more potent and dangerous than any hired help.

Remy ran, until he tripped and got straight back up, and knew the hot nothing he felt in his ankle would be a price he would pay later, and kept on running until his legs gave way, and his lungs failed, and belly burning, face popping, he dropped onto his hands and knees in the soil, rolled onto his back, shuddered and shook.

The running of his pursuer slowed a little behind him. Blinking back tears, he stared into torchlight, half glimpsing the reflection of the man who stood behind it, lean as a chestnut tree, a void in his expression that was all professionalism, a man about the job. He edged closer to Remy, and from his rope belt pulled a machete, and from around his belly undid more rope and, edging closer one step at a time, hovered over the fallen player, resting the tip of the blade just above Remy's chest.

"You won't kill me," gasped the player in Thai. "It would be against the rules." The man didn't respond, showed no understanding in his face. "Abhik wins only when he tags me himself, only if I'm alive," he said again in French. "You won't kill me."

French seemed to be more comprehensible, for the man's blade immediately turned, the sharpened curve resting just below Remy's right eye.

Alive, said the blade in silent steel, doesn't necessarily mean unharmed.

Slow—so slow—the tracker squatted down by Remy's side, the blade not moving from its point. Behind him, struggling to keep up in the dark, were the sounds of the other pursuers, less fleet of foot and sure of their way than this man. In a moment, the hunter would call out to them, summon them to the kill, and that would be that: game over.

Remy closed his eyes, drew in breath, and the hunter, perhaps sensing something of what this pertained, closed his lips tight. Then Remy rolled, knocking the blade to one side with the back of his arm while kicking up as hard as he could towards the hunter's face. The hunter rolled too, pulling the machete free, but Remy threw himself bodily on top of the other man, ignoring the blade, ignoring the fingers that clawed at his face, trying to get purchase on his eyes, digging for the sockets. A moment in which all was leg and arm, too many limbs for anything to do any good, no order to the fight, merely elbows in guts, knees in groins, fists in faces, then Remy wiggled his elbow free from the medley and dropped down, point first, his entire body weight into the man's throat.

The hunter's eyes popped wide in his skull. He wheezed, staring up at nothing, and hands which had clawed and scratched now fell dully to the earth. Remy rolled free from his stricken attacker and, hearing still the sounds of the others in the wood behind him, turned and ran.

Chapter 25

Bitter wakings on a clouded morning.

Abhik Lee wakes to see the face of one of his players—a hunter, a good piece which he played well—standing before him.

The face is swollen, the neck bound up with cloth as if that might alleviate the puffed-up redness some. The hunter, when he speaks, does so in French, which he does not speak well, and his voice is hoarse.

"He got away."

Abhik Lee leans the tips of his fingers against the spot between his eyebrows where, some have said, an invisible third eye resides, or where perhaps he simply felt the most irritation.

"He was on foot?"

"Yes. Going north. We are still looking; he won't be far. He was injured."

"How injured?"

"We fought. I hit him several times. He was limping too when he ran away."

"You couldn't catch a limping man?"

"He was more violent than you gave me to think. You said he would surrender easily; he was soft, fearful. You led us to believe that he could not survive in the wild for more than a few days."

"That was the impression I had of him, certainly."

"Your impression, monsieur, was wrong."

The corner of Abhik's nether lip contracts just a little, and again he taps his paired fingers against the centre of his forehead, once, twice, three times, steadying thoughts. He is not used to hearing that he is mistaken; it is an uncomfortable development for one of his inclination, and being uncomfortable, he now makes the greatest mistake of all, and ignores it.

"He will not survive long," he repeats. "He doesn't have it in him."

And what of Remy?

We look, and here we find him at last, barely spotting him where he has fallen. He is nestled in between three stones that have no name, by the side of a rushing waterfall. He wakes slowly, in that he has barely slept and that grey land between sleeping and waking is all the expanse he now wanders. When at last he is fully alert, he simply lies there, looking up at the sky. He has lost the time and the direction of the sun; all he sees is cloud. His ankle is vastly swollen, and were the notion not so unproductively absurd, he might now lie in self-pity and weep.

Now he dreams of returning to Fon, and laments all the foolish things he both said and did not have the wisdom to say.

The sun rises and so must he.

We sit together, you and I, on a high rock above the waterfall, watching the foam surge in the depths below, and from this vantage point, we watch Remy limp away.

Chapter 26

A risk, but he has no choice.

At twilight, before a small monastery of aged monks and scuttling boys, he collapses.

The door is opened by an old man, who tuts and sighs at what he sees and leaves Remy there while he goes to fetch younger boys.

Two children, ten and twelve years old apiece, help him limp to a room which smells faintly of mould.

The very oldest of the monks, a man who walks with the aid of a round-headed stick, sits down to examine Remy's leg, mutters and proclaims that yes indeed, it *is* beyond the monks' medical skill! Bed rest, if you please—bed rest.

"Are you a criminal?" asked the young man, seventeen, orphaned and left to the care of the priests at two years old, as he sat by Remy's side.

"No," he replied.

"How did you get this injury?"

"I fell."

"Are you sure you aren't a criminal? We welcome everyone here, regardless of their past."

"I'm not a criminal."

"Ah—but you are on the run, aren't you?"

"Not from the law."

"Are you sure?"

"I swear it."

*

In the morning, the oldest monk came back to inspect Remy again and grumbled and proclaimed, "Yes, yes, bed rest, just like I said!"

In the afternoon, the abbot, younger than the oldest monk but vastly more political, came to greet their unexpected guest.

"Novelty upon novelty!" he exclaimed brightly. "A foreigner, injured, who speaks our language! Do you know anything about the path to enlightenment?"

"I hear rumours," grunted Remy from his pallet on the floor, "that by good deeds and the making of merit for yourself in this life, you may advance through the wheel of the universe."

"I think it is a wonderful thing that you have come to our monastery," chuckled the abbot merrily. "For you, for us—for everyone!"

So saying, the abbot returned to his room and wrote a letter to his senior in the larger temple in the town informing him that the man wanted by the police had come to his temple and was there still a sizeable reward posted for his capture, and sent a boy to make sure it was posted and waited happily for the reply.

Chapter 27

On the second day of his stay in the monastery, the rainy season began.

Remy sat within the shelter of a dripping porch, listening to water on the slates above, watching the ground turn to a shimmering black mirror.

The youngest monk, the orphan, sat next to him and said, "First I am the breath. Then when I am the breath, I am the air. I am the wind that moves through the sky. I am the leaves bending in the trees. I am the earth turning, the soil splitting, the dust that blows away. I am here and above and in all the corners of the earth. I am in the first gasp of the newborn child; I am in the last sigh of the dying mother. I am the sobs of the abandoned lover. I am the laughter of the delighted child. I am breath, I am wind, I am life, and when I am all of these things, *I*, the *I* that was simply me, that sat by you now, was nothing at all."

At dinner, the abbot asked if any post had come and was told that the rains had made the roads difficult and muddy, and he smiled and said it was to be expected and that he was not worried at all, and Remy watched him from the corners of his eyes and the edges of his smile, and said nothing.

When the bell rang at three in the morning for the monastery to wake and pray beneath the moonlight, the oldest monk came to wake Remy, tutting all the way.

"Good for you," he said. "Come, come, good for you, try it!"

And when the bell rang again for breakfast, the youngest

monk came to him quietly, pulling him into a room away from the others, where he saw his bag, a dry sarong and hat, a stick to lean on, sandals and rice wrapped in leaves. The monk said:

"Two weeks ago we were all told to look out for a foreign criminal on the run. The abbot said it was of great merit to hand him to the police or the soldiers, and so has decided we shall."

"Why would you tell me this?"

"It is interesting, isn't it?" asked the monk with a smile. "The others tell me I am not wise in my speech."

So saying, he turned away, and Remy picked up these meagre goods and slunk away without a word.

Chapter 28

A strange sight!

A man, with an overgrown brown beard, brown hair, pale skin burnt by the sun, dressed in a medley of clothes that are halfway between a smuggler's shirt and a monk's robes, a rucksack on his back, limps towards Lampang.

The land in the north is more mountainous, wild and beautiful. The water that sweeps down from the mountains carves great valleys, as if the rotation of the earth itself has turned all things into gentle curves: curving plateaus and curving streams; curving roads and curving trees. It is a land of pineapples, teak trees and white pottery fashioned with delicate kaolin clay. At dawn the low cloud caresses the tops of the mountains, burning away as the sun rises. By sunset the shadows have turned, a great twist of grey sweeping across the land, and the wind whispers through the forests and over the rivers with the smell of rotting leaves and fragrant flowers which open when the rains cease.

Alone again, and injured, Remy Burke heads north to Lampang.

Twice in two days he was nearly caught.

The first—an army truck that came out of nowhere on a deserted, muddy road. The bridge had gone down on the main causeway, swept away by a flood, so the truck took this less travelled path, and Remy, hearing it approach, runs for the undergrowth, throws himself into its cover, cowers there as the soldiers drive by, heads down, tarpaulin flowing with the rains.

The second—a police roadblock near the flat blue waters of Mae Wa. Someone must have seen him and spread the word—who? we wonder (a poacher and his son, who told a friend, who told a cousin, who knew the chief of police, who had received his orders in this regard not five nights since, and a warning that the suspect was most likely headed in his direction)—for there they were, three indolent policemen, their trousers splattered with the mud of the road, chewing betel nut and spitting red juice into the puddles at their feet, miserable in the rain, waiting for him to come.

He watched them from a ridge some quarter of a mile above the curve of the road that they defended, lying on his belly as he assessed them and his path. He'd walked twenty miles to find the junction they guarded, and did not want to go back, not with his shoes rotting from the rains, his legs black with mud, his belly empty, his ankle sore. He hid instead in a little clump of dripping trees, eating his last banana and its flowers, shivering from the rain. Cold and damp now were settling in his throat and mind, making one ache, the other cloudy. How much longer could he keep this up?

Not long.

As long as it took.

Shortly after sunset, the policemen on the road abandoned their mission, pedalling back to town. He slapped wet-footed past their cordon, saw the lights of a village ahead, did not dare approach. He slept badly that night and woke with a fever, fished on the lake in the morning and caught very little, and felt sick after eating, but at least managed to keep his food down.

Fever trapped him where he was. For three days he lay on the edge of the lake, drinking and stealing fruit from the trees, shaking and whispering comforts to himself. Sometimes he spoke French, sometimes English. Sometimes he remembered a story his father would tell as they walked together by the ghats of Varanasi, back in the days when empire was great and the rituals of the Hindus washing themselves in prayer was a thing to be indulged, a childlike game which the British would point and snigger at, and the polite ladies would turn away from, flushing hot to see so much flesh so easily displayed in the brown waters of the Ganges. Then his mind wandered to his mother, who took him one day to see the temples of lost Cambodia, whispering in his ear that he shouldn't tell his grandfather she had brought him there, for it wasn't considered right that a dignified lady take an interest in the barbaric traditions of the locals. Then she knelt by him and showed ancient carved texts, images of gods and kings, the graffiti of long-dead children scratched with a blade's point across holy icons, the fallen stones of a place where once people went into the jungle to pray for rain to feed their crops, sunshine to harvest in. He'd run up and down the carved stones of the broken temples and laughed and asked if he could play hide-and-seek, while around them the jungle shrieked and the lithe monkeys blinked suspiciously over their trove of stolen mangos.

That had been before the games he played became . . . something else.

On the fourth day, the fever broke, and he lay naked in the water of the lake, eyes closed, head back, and listened to the rumbling in his ears. He caught one last fish and cooked it on hot charcoal, and watched a little boat sailing across the water, a parasol protecting its sole inhabitant, three lines suspended off its prow, until the owner of the boat saw him and, waving slowly, paddled closer.

The man was a fisherman, sixty if he was a day, missing three teeth, two on the bottom of his jaw, one on the top.

"Are you lost?" he asked.

"No, not lost—looking for a way across the lake."

"Get in, then, get in!"

He got in.

Across the waters, the fisherman talked brightly, of his wife (dead), his sons (noble), his daughters-in-law (not good enough though at least they tried) and his grandchildren and great-grandchildren (beautiful, all of them, so very beautiful). His seven sons had themselves married and produced between them some thirty-eight grandchildren for him to call his own, and of these thirty-eight, twenty-nine were already churning out offspring—each of which he could name and character—bringing the total number of direct blood relatives within a twenty-mile radius of this lake to seventy-three.

"It would have been seventy-four," he sighed, "but one of them moved away."

Which was, in its way, a kind of death.

On the other side of the lake, Remy stood unevenly on firmer shores and said, "How far is it to Lampang?"

"If you follow the road, about two days' walk—but the road is on the other side of the water."

"And how far if I stay away from the road?"

"Four, five days of hard walking. But you don't want to do that—you're injured, you've been sick. Stay at mine a while; my daughter-in-law will look after you."

"I cannot. When you go home, you will find that people ask after me. A foreigner, a tall man with fair skin. They will tell you I'm a criminal."

"You're not a criminal!" chuckled the old man. "I've got seventy-three children—do you think I don't know a criminal when I see one? You're a pilgrim, sure as these eyes can see by sunlight!"

"Then you understand why I take the harder road."

The fisherman shrugged. "The Gautama tried starving and suffering on his path to enlightenment, but it was only with a full belly that he truly achieved Nirvana—at least, that's what I think."

And as they turned to part ways, Remy hesitated, then turned back. "May I . . . ?" he began, then stopped, stumbling, not on the words, but the very notion of what he was about to speak. Trust had grown thin, so thin, and now it stuck in his throat, but he took a long, slow breath and tried anyway. "When you tell people about me—and feel free to do so—will you tell them . . . ? . . . tell them I asked the way to Phrae. Tell them that my ankle was very bad, and you did not take me across the water. But if you would be very kind, do not tell them for a day. Or two? I have nothing to offer but my gratitude, and my word that you do no harm to any man and a great deal of good in doing so."

The fisherman sucked in his lips as far the tip of his nose slanted downwards, seemed to quiver on the verge of being swallowed whole, a face collapsing into a face. Then he smiled, waved his hands joyfully in the air and said, "Well, no one listens to me anyway!"

Remy bowed low and walked away.

Chapter 29

Four days later, hobbling out of the forest and the hills, he came to Lampang.

Once the pride of the Lanna kingdom, the city still maintained its walls, its gold-plated temples, its fondness for spiced banana and its pride, seeming in its mountain-shadowed way to proclaim that it was still a state unto itself, needing little of the outside world to bother it. Go to Chiang Mai or Bangkok, or cross the border to Myanmar if you felt the need to run to work, to argue in the streets, to buy exotic things or banter in loud voices through the dead of night. Lampang was a quiet place for quiet people, and heaven forefend that it change.

Remy stood a while on the side of the hill, watching this little place, houses on stilts on the rolling Wang River, which, like so many waterways in this land, flowed eventually back to the Chao Phraya and south to the sea. He listened to the sound of the horse-drawn traps bouncing through the streets, the cry of the elephant drivers hauling their goods into town, the rattle of harnesses and the slosh of oars, all noises travelling gently upwards, amplified by the distant rising of the mountains on either side.

To enter Lampang was a risk, for there would be authorities there that would be watching, however well he had lost his pursuers in the mountains, and no matter if they believed the fisherman's tale of his turning east towards Phrae, not west to the river. (Good fortune: the fisherman lied, feeling jubilant as he did so, and the word reached Abhik Lee, who diverted a general

220

and all his troops to Phrae at once, and sent his hunters back into the hills and found no trace of Remy as he did.)

Yet whatever his fortune, he would be noticed, and his position given away by his entering the town. All of Abhik's resources would turn, they would come seeking him, and he would have to run again, where before now he had merely wandered.

A great risk: a terrible danger.

One that now, with a half-nod of his head, he took.

Chapter 30

Oh Remy, oh Remy, what are you doing?

You are buying two tickets at the railway station in Lampang—one to Chiang Mai, the other to Bangkok.

We watch the bewildered expression on the vendor's face as you make your purchase, precious baht which you have nursed so carefully coming from your bag.

We watch you head onto the platform, a tattered man in tattered clothes, an every-which-way ragdoll—the police will come for you soon, they will come, but first comes the Chiang Mai–Bangkok train, a great new roaring thing with a diesel engine, black and proud, clattering like a laughing dinosaur's jaw, easing into the station with a scream of steel. You board, heading north, bold as anything, smiling your most serene smile, sit in a compartment with two other travellers—a woman who holds a sleeping baby, and a man in a business suit, Japanese, who smiles courteously at you over his newspaper and then looks away and never looks back.

Remy studies the landscape as it grumbles by. There is much he needs to note.

(Who are these travellers? Why, she goes to visit her mother who is dying for the twelfth time and will die three more times again, each time complaining vociferously to the assembled, summoned relatives that she has been abandoned by her family, before finally she passes away in 1947 from a fall in the street which knocks her head, and from which she doesn't wake. And he? Why, he knows about railways, has studied railways and studies now the railways that connect China to India, and will one day very soon, from an office, orchestrate on maps and with carefully marked little notes, the construction of railway lines by captured slave labour, and say when the war ends that Japan only meant to bring freedom to the people of the East, only an end to tyranny. So we see them, these fellow travellers on this train, and they being known, we turn away.)

At Chiang Mai, you get off this train, then board the train heading in the opposite direction, south to Bangkok, and as it begins to move from the platform, you jump off again, hopping from the open balcony at the back of a carriage onto the gravel, rolling as you land, then pick yourself up and dust yourself off, and run from the track.

We watch Remy—now we watch him, squatting by a little well outside the square line of the city's moat, pumping water into a cup, shaving with his nearly blunted knife the great growth of beard that smothers his jaw and chin, dragging it back to reveal the pale skin beneath, shockingly untouched by the sunlight compared to the browned rims of his eyes. He sits now and scrapes the hair from his head, blood flecking water as he scratches it to near-baldness, before popping a wide straw hat on top of the exposed flesh and wrapping his skinny, burnt body in a dusty robe.

What does he look like now? A wandering monk, perhaps, if you do not look too closely. A beggar. A madman. A holy man. A parched prophet from the desert.

Whatever he is, he does not look much like Remy Burke.

He sleeps rough on the streets of Chiang Mai that night, while the wild dogs circle each other and wonder if he is prey. It is one of the most peaceful nights of sleep he has had for a very long time.

When the sun rises, he steals a bicycle and pedals some twenty miles out of town, arriving in a stinking sweat a few hours before midday. He reaches a bridge across a low stream, a single-track thing of already rusting iron, which no train dare cross at more than a snail's pace, and as the flies gather around

223

him and the forests ripple, he sits down cross-legged on the side of the track to wait.

He breathes, and it seems to him that his breath is wind, that wind is air, that air spins across the world, through the lungs of Abhik Lee, pacing the platform of Lampang waiting for the train, through the flamed nostrils of the players and the pieces of the Gameshouse, across the waters of the Chao Phraya, and out to sea. It seems to him for a moment that he is nothing, and he is not afraid.

Then comes the singing in the tracks, the pumping of the engines, the growling of the train. He rolls down on his belly, waiting for the train to arrive, hidden in the undergrowth. The Chiang Mai–Bangkok express, heading south, kills its speed as it approaches the bridge as it did yesterday when he rode it north, the engine barely chugging, and at a meagre four or five miles an hour, it begins its cautious crossing of the ways.

Remy waits until the first few carriages are over, then without a sound rises up from the undergrowth, jogs until he is running, running until he is keeping pace, and with a great heave and flap of robe, pulls himself aboard the rear of the last carriage of the train, and up into safety.

Chapter 31

Stops on a line.

Lamphun, Phitsanulok, Lopburi, Ayutthaya, Don Muang.

Remy sits and watches the countryside and cannot remember the last time he felt so relaxed.

The compartment is empty until Ayutthaya, when a British man in a linen suit and his wife get on. The man smells profoundly through the layers of his sweat-stained jacket, but this doesn't stop his wife wrinkling her nose at the sight of Remy and whispering in prickling English, "He smells *terrible*."

"He's just a monk, darling," whispers the man.

"Can't we go to another compartment?"

"Darling, you're making a fuss—we can't always avoid the natives."

With a grunt, the wife settles down in the seat as far away from Remy as she can, while her husband positions himself between them as a form of shield. He looks at Remy and smiles, proclaiming in extraordinarily accented Thai, "Good morning."

"Good morning," Remy replies in the same language, pressing his palms together, and turning away to look out of the window before they can see his own smile.

A world outside. Motion without movement. Workers resting beneath the shade of a banana tree. Mangos rotting on the earth. Nets thrown into a river by stick-skinny girls. The banging of the gong from temple. Many stops, waiting for another train to clear the narrowest point in the track ahead. Sometimes the rain falls; sometimes the skies clear, brilliant blue flecked with white that turns black again as quickly as the clouds parted, and turns the distant hills and fields to dusty grey.

The British man says:

"Can't trust these people, these Siamese, to do anything. Can't trust them to get a job done. 'Tomorrow,' they say, and then the next day: 'Tomorrow.' You ask what the hold-up is and they say, 'I'll do it tomorrow,' and when you insist they say, 'I need to order a part.' Why didn't they order it yesterday? 'I'll do it tomorrow,' they reply, and that is the end of the argument! No, better off with a Chink. Hard worker, your average Chink, but wily too, will rob you if you blink but if you show him who's master, make it clear you're not having any funny business, they'll do all right by you. Your Malay is the laziest of the lot, but responds well to the rod, but your Jap! Gotta admire a Jap, you have. Damn me if the blighters aren't almost like us!"

Remy listens, his face turned away, and says nothing at all.

He is still as the train moves.

He is motion.

He is a fixed point on the earth.

He is the earth as it turns.

He is here.

He is everywhere.

He is nothing at all.

As they pull into Bangkok, the rain is falling from black skies, the drops so fat and hard they bounce off the skin, exploding off the heads of people running for shelter. Remy leans out of the compartment window and sees a queue stretching away from the platform's edge.

Soldiers, two dozen or more, stopping every man and woman who try to pass them by. Remy looks up the other end of the platform, but there are more men, armed, watched over by the great benevolent portrait of the king which hangs high above; all eyes turn to the train from Chiang Mai.

With a little intake of breath, he pulls himself back into

the compartment, while the Englishman and his wife mutter together.

"He looks funny..." whispers the wife.

"Darling, you can't say that."

"But he does..."

...as they climb off the train.

Terror now in Remy's breast. He has walked across half of Thailand only to return to Bangkok but his movements, it seems, have been predicted, his presence marked. How did Abhik know? How did Abhik come to monitor this station?

He sits breathless in the compartment of the slowly emptying train and realises he doesn't know what to do. Stay on the train a while longer, see if it will carry him north again? Run and hide? Make a break for it? If he makes a break for it and is seen, his plan will be ruined, the whole purpose of this dangerous exercise destroyed. Getting on the trains was an operation in opportunities, an expansion of options, no longer *this* section of wilderness or *that* area of farmland could he be in, but wherever the trains roamed, Padang to Nong Khai. Yet here were soldiers, waiting in Bangkok, and it can only be that his ruse has not worked!

The conductor came along the carriage, checking each compartment, calling for the last stop. At his approach, Remy pretended to doze, an instinctive move, and the conductor called him briskly awake, telling him to get off the train. He nodded and smiled and made to gather his things as the conductor walked by, shuffling into the corridor with no idea where to go.

Blend into the crowd? Hope that the soldiers guarding the platform were working to an old description: a bearded foreigner, a man in tattered clothes, a wounded stranger?

A great danger, but what alternative did he have? He pulled his hat down lower upon his head, put his hand upon the door, took a deep breath and heard a voice call his name.

"I say, Remy," it said, "you do look extraordinary."

Chapter 32

A moment to pity—shall we pity—Abhik Lee?

Poor old Abhik, you thought victory would be so easy! Remy Burke, an indulged, pampered player, who drinks too much and talks too easily. You had him chalked up as an armchair general, a great player of games of risk and the stock exchange, a wily gambler who knows how to deploy his troops and diplomats by telegram and hastily scrawled letter, but not a *runner*. Not a man who could run, who could hide, who could stay hidden. You misread your opponent, Abhik Lee, and we are glad.

What a merry runaround you have been given! You scoured Nakhon Sawan, tore through the forests to the north, sent scouts into farms and villages, boats onto lakes, soldiers onto trains. You pestered the police chief of Phrae so much the man started crying at you down the telephone, only for word to come from Lampang—Lampang of all places!—that a man matching your quarry's description was seen buying train tickets to both Bangkok and Chiang Mai!

Then you had to reposition in a terrible hurry, soldiers to one end of the line, policemen to the others, spies in all the trains in between. You raced across the country to Lampang, but by the time you were there, your quarry was in Chiang Mai, and by the time you reached Chiang Mai, your target was gone. Yet close: so close! So close you have come, you can feel it, you know you have been almost close enough to touch (at your best moment since he fled Bangkok, you have only been three miles away) yet somehow still Remy, indolent, indulged Remy, has slipped through your net.

Where is he now?

Over three hundred miles between Chiang Mai and Bangkok, who knows where he jumped from the train?

But you are persistent, Abhik Lee; you have a plan.

That must be why you left the troops in place at either end of the line.

Chapter 33

"Won't you come in?"

Remy turned to see the source of the voice which called his name, speaking confident French, from the open door of the compartment next to his.

The owner of the voice was neither young nor old, neither remarkable nor plain, but rather of that middling sort that is nothing at all, of no country, no time, no place. We have seen him before, you and I, right when the game began, and can give him a name, and call him Silver.

"The conductor won't bother us for a little while," he added with a smile as Remy hesitated in the corridor. "He's not as interested in his job as he pretends."

Slowly, head still half turned towards the teeming platform, Remy slipped into the compartment, and Silver pulled the door shut behind him, settling down in a seat away from the window.

For a while, the two men regarded each other, and said not a word.

"There's a price I'm going to ask," said Silver at last.

"A price?"

"Yes."

"What kind of price, and for what service?"

"I would have thought the service was obvious," replied Silver, hands resting across his folded legs. "I will get you out of this station, and in Wiang Sa district in three days' time, a man will see a foreigner who matches your description walking through the woods. That should buy you a little time to do those things that you have come here to do."

"And what things have I come here to do?" he asked.

Silver shrugged. "None of my business, old thing."

"How did you find me?"

"I have some resources."

"Why would you help me?"

"I am not interested in seeing you lose."

"That is...unusual for a player. The Gameshouse promotes the victory of the strongest: that is its very purpose. The weak fall and new challengers arise; the games grow more complicated, the stakes evolving with time. If it is my time..."

"It is not," replied Silver quickly. "That is...I do not consider this game you are playing to be balanced. Hide-and-seek is an ancient game with a fine tradition, but the context of this match is not fairly suited. The lesser player is going to defeat the stronger one because the board was skewed to this effect."

"I took the bet, Silver; no one forced me."

"Indeed, that was reckless of you, and only you can carry the responsibility of that particular indiscretion. But the very wager you made is telling. If you win, you get some snippets of life; not as much in the grand scheme of what I know you have already won. If Abhik wins, he takes your memories, and such memories they are, Remy! With his ambition and your experience, Abhik Lee could be a phenomenal player, stronger than almost any other in the higher league. And the game—hide-and-seek in a country where everything about you, your present fashionable attire apart, makes it nearly impossible for you to hide? You are a good player, Remy, no one would deny it, but I have some sense of the cards Abhik Lee has been dealt, and I would wager that when you receive *your* cards, they are of a lesser sort. That is not in keeping with the spirit of the Gameshouse, and things which are not in keeping interest me. Do you know why Abhik is so interested in beating you?"

"I cannot imagine."

"Have you played him before?"

"Not at a higher league game, no."

"But at a lower one?"

"We played poker once."

"Who won? You?"

"I had a lucky hand."

Silver's smile briefly withered into a scowl. "'Luck' is a dangerous concept in the Gameshouse."

"Nevertheless. I needed a straight and got one against the laws of probability."

"I cannot imagine the game swung on this one moment."

"It did not but it was a big bet towards the latter parts of the game and the hand which, I think, broke Abhik's will to victory."

"What did he lose?"

"Money, nothing more."

"No life, no sense, no memory, no emotion, no...?"

"It was a lower league game, Silver," Remy barked harder than he'd meant, eyes flickering again to the rapidly emptying platform outside. "We didn't play for anything that mattered."

Silence in the carriage. Outside, the rain hammered on the roof of the station and the last of the train's passengers were shuffled through the cordon of men. A captain, looking to have a bright idea, gestured a few of his men onto the train, starting at the engine, moving down the carriages, checking each door, every nook, just to be secure.

Remy shifted uneasily in his chair. "You mentioned a price," he murmured.

"Yes, so I did."

"You can get me through the station undetected?"

"I can, and spread a little of a false trail for you—not much, not so much that anyone could say it was cheating."

"And in return?"

"I will need you to show mercy to someone, when the day comes."

"That doesn't sound so hard—what's the catch?"

232

"You'll be very afraid when you have to do it."

Silence. A leak in the roof of the station let a thin trickle of water fall, like a rattling string, into a growing puddle. A seller of bananas was hustled on by a soldier who hadn't received a bribe. A child cried, frightened of the engine. Silver waited; Remy stared at nothing until at last a little smile spreads across his face.

"You're afraid of Abhik Lee," he murmured.

Silver raised his eyebrows and said nothing.

"You already admitted it. His ambition, my memories—he would indeed be a deadly player. Perhaps good enough to challenge you."

"He would lose if he challenged me," replied the other, a sharpness breaking through the good-humour in his voice. "But as a piece in someone else's hand, he could present...an inconvenience...in larger games."

"To prevent him, you help the lesser player?"

"You are not the lesser player, Remy."

"Am I not? As I said: I chose this game. That already makes me weak."

"Weak in Abhik's mind, perhaps," he replied. "Abhik thinks that a game can only be won with ruthlessness and calculation. Were this chess, he would be right, but you, Remy, you have the greatest gift of a higher league player—you remember that your pieces are human. At a superficial level, some might say that makes you kind, but I would suggest it makes you beautiful. To play people is a vastly more elegant skill than mere number-counting."

Silence. Remy lent back in his chair, fingers folded together, lips pursed. Outside, a soldier called to another, "On me—come, come, let's look."

Silver spoke a little faster, eyes flickering to the compartment door. "There are...anomalies...in the Gameshouse. We tell ourselves that the games we play are fun, sport, selfish, merriment. But we play with countries. We command armies. We toy with economic goods, with ideas and men. We have crowned

233

kings, toppled tyrants, guided generals to a victory that would not otherwise have been their own. We have, through our merriment, shaped human history, altered it, changed the fate of men. The structure of our activities as a game, a sport, gives us great advantages. We have a ruthlessness, an intellectual vigour, which might be denied from a queen who was fearful for the welfare of her son, or a captain who had grown to love his men. To us, these things are merely pieces, resources to be moved to the greatest effect, and from this brutal mathematics, we pluck victory where there might otherwise have been defeat. All for the game. And where does that game come from? Who puts the pieces in our hands, shows the board, umpires the event? Why, *she* does. The Gamesmaster. She controls us because she controls the board, and though the Gameshouse claims that all its games are even, sometimes you can find a flaw. A competition to crown a king where the players are not evenly matched, or the pieces are handicapped without this disadvantage being declared. A player who is dealt a general where you only received a major. She drew Russia; you only found Belgium in your hand. A challenge which should not have been accepted—terms struck which should not have been agreed to, and sometimes the Gameshouse intervenes and sometimes it does not, and for a house that lives by rules, I have yet to see reasons given as to why. Why did the house let you bet your mind, Remy? It is not an even wager. Why did it let you take a bet in a country where your very face was a handicap of almost insurmountable difficulties? Umpires have intervened to prevent lesser imbalances; why not now?"

A sound at the end of the carriage—soldiers voices, boots, the opening of compartment doors.

Remy said, his eyes not leaving Silver's face, "I chose this. This was my mistake."

"Perhaps it was. Perhaps I am wrong. Or perhaps we are merely pieces in the Gamesmaster's hand, and she has decided to discard you for someone new."

Voices in the carriage, nearer. Remy didn't move, hands

234

together, breath soft. "So you are going to challenge her. You are going to play the great game."

A moment in which Silver didn't answer, his eyes darting upwards in search of thought. Then he looked back at Remy and smiled, and said simply, "Yes. Do we have an accord?"

The door to the compartment opened. Two soldiers stood framed in it. "Who are you? Why you are here?" they barked. "What are you doing?"

And then, seeing Silver's pale face and Remy's too:

"You are the foreigners! Put your hands up now! Get up! Get off the train!"

The two of them moved slowly off the train, hands on their heads, the soldiers poking them from behind. They stood on the platform and waited while one man fetched the captain, and then two men returned.

The captain looked into Remy's face and nodded in understanding. Then his gaze turned and he looked into Silver's eyes, and his expression froze.

"Well?" asked Silver, his eyes not leaving the soldier's face. "A bargain?"

Remy smiled and found that as he smiled, he began to laugh. He lowered his hands from his head, pressed them against his sides and laughed. "Yes!" he exclaimed. "To hell with it, yes; I'll play your game."

The soldiers watched, wordless, silent. What terror was in the captain's eyes as he looked on Silver's face? (The terror of a man who played to enter the higher league and lost, lost his wife, his home, his child, until a stranger with silver hair came in the night and offered to give them back in exchange for a favour not yet disclosed. He who giveth, so they say, can taketh away.)

"This is not the man you are looking for," Silver explained to the captain, indicating Remy. "Please inform your men of this fact."

The captain nodded again, then turned to his soldiers, wrenching his eyes from Silver's face as if from the leering gaze of a corpse, and barked, "Wrong! Wrong—didn't you pay attention? These are not the men—wrong! Go back to your posts!"

The soldiers obeyed.

*

Silver walked Remy out of the doors of the station and together they stood for a moment in the porch, looking at the pouring rain. Silver's eyes wandered upwards as if trying to read the motion of every drop that fell. Remy watched him a while, then held out his hand and said, "A bargain, then."

Silver's eyes drifted down from the grey sky overhead. He smiled, shook Remy by the hand. "A bargain," he agreed; then, as an afterthought, "Good luck."

He turned to walk away.

Remy called after him. "Silver!" he said.

The other man stopped, look back, questioning.

"No one ever wins against the Gameshouse. You know that, don't you?"

Silver smiled and walked away.

Chapter 34

Eight days in Bangkok.

With what money he had left, he bought a suit, trousers, a new hat, dressed himself in every way as the smart European gentleman. It was easier here, and easier still now that Abhik Lee was stretched so thin. He had fled Bangkok when Bangkok was being torn apart looking for him; but now! Now no one knew where Remy was, and so Remy returned here to blend with the expats and thrill-seekers, the spies and the refugees.

He rented a room in a cheap hotel away from the water, slept beneath a net, took a bath, inspected every cut and bruise, scrape and swelling, scrubbed at his feet, his face, his hands, his nails, until every part was pink and tingled.

He slept until four in the morning, then dressed again in his ragged robes and headed towards the embassies and the clubs where embassy men go. The man he mugged that night was a British sub-consul, drowsy on opium, high on the scent of adultery, his wife waiting for him patiently in Aldershot, the smell of sex still clinging to him like the anaesthetic jaws of the leech. Remy didn't have to hit him more than twice to cow him into submission, and he stole forty-seven baht from the bewildered man who, rising slowly from his opium lull, had the good sense not to report the crime to any of his seniors.

From a Singhalese man with a drooping lower lip, he bought the papers of a dead Frenchman whose corpse had been washed onshore four days earlier and whose name would never be reported to the police. In a whitewashed clubhouse built in the

Washington style, with fans overhead that never turned and a bartender who sold, at a quarter of the price than that on the advertised menu, home-brewed gin and deadly rice wine he made himself, Remy found Winston Blake, sometime journalist for the London *Times* (when he could be bothered to file a story), occasional spy, affable drunk, goodtime man waiting for the divorce, fingers in every pie, sometime player at the Gameshouse until he lost a game that he could not play and was cast out into the night with another man's asthma as his prize.

"Remy," he muttered, as the other slipped onto the stool beside him. "Not dead, yet?"

"Not yet, Winston," he replied, gesturing at the bartender for a drink. "Can I top you up?"

"Don't see why not, sport, don't see why not."

They talked.

"The Japs don't want to invade Siam, you see," he grumbled. "This place is a little fish, something that can be scooped up easily enough once they've got the prize."

"And what's the prize?"

"Singapore! Malaysia! Take out the British first, take out the big resistance, get your guns ready to do India and once you've got all of South-East Asia in the bag, nibble up Siam as an afterthought."

"And what are the British doing about this?"

"Bugger all, lad, bugger all!" he wheezed, panting for breath in the settling evening heat. "What can they bloody do about it? Hard enough time keeping the natives in line, let alone dealing with some imperialist samurai whatsit. You see that man over there...?" He pointed with a purple-tinted finger, subtle as a torpedo, delicate as a hurricane. "He's one of the Jap lot. Lovely man, really. Genuinely believes—this is the part I love— genuinely believes that he's going to free Asia from the colonial oppressor. That Japan will come as liberators, not conquerors, and that by going to war against the Brits and the Frogs and that lot, he's *defending* his country from the inevitable European scourge! At least the Europeans have the good grace to have given up on any pretence of dignity or generous feeling. Bless him—" he waved cheerfully at the victim of this analysis, who tilted his drink in reply—"he's a good sport, and a not half-bad spy, but he's terribly mistaken."

"In what way?"

"His bosses! His bosses talk the whole 'liberation from the colonial' stuff, but they're ideologues and bullies, the lot of them. No good having a decent middle management if the word from the top is cleanse the ethnics and that, is there?"

"And what about you?"

"What about me?"

"Where will you be when all this happens?"

"Oh, India, I think. Or Ceylon. Far from here as I can get, really!"

"Another drink?"

"You're a sport, Remy, always have been, always a sport."

And later:

"Do you remember Abhik Lee?"

"God, yes! Unpleasant sort, but good at the game, if I recall. Played an extraordinary hand of monopoly once against a Yank who was something big in rubber. Won half the plantations of Malaysia, a U.S. senator and the love of the Yank's wife, all because the other's tanker got caught by pirates in the Strait of Malacca. Personally I thought the wife business was a bit much since he clearly didn't love her, but he was always a vindictive little sod, was Abhik, winning things he didn't need simply to prove that he could."

"I'm playing a game with him."

"Good God, are you? Which one?"

"Hide-and-seek."

"You're seeking?"

"Hiding, as a matter of fact."

"Bloody hell, sport, you'll do better than to come round here. Half the people in this godforsaken place are trying to get into the Gameshouse, you know how quickly they'll rat you out?"

"I've put up a smokescreen."

"Won't last—chap like you stands out."

"That's why I'm doing a little legwork now. I was wondering if, in your easy way of things, you knew where Abhik lived?"

"Don't get me involved in your stuff, Remy; I'm out of the Gameshouse and have the failing lungs to prove it. Bet my sclerosis against his asthma and look where I am now!"

"Perhaps I could help with that?"

"Only if you win, sport, only if you win."

"Well then—help me win."

And the night after that...

He caught her as she was getting on a ferry heading south towards the sea. She wore grey; he wore a large hat pulled low against the torchlight; she saw him in the corner of her eye and smiled anyway, recognised him for what he was.

As the ferry chugged slowly through the waters, he worked his way round to her until, like two strangers meeting upon a lonely voyage, he stood by her side, hands folded on the railing, and said,

"Thene."

"Remy."

"How are you?"

The woman called Thene considered, her lips thinning and stretching as she toyed with an answer. "Well," she said at last. "Still here." Beautiful Thene, we remember you from another time, another game, do we not? And you are still here, your dark hair shorter now, your smile older, your features as beautiful and unchanging as the moon. You wore a mask once, and played to crown a king in Venice. That mask is gone, and yet perhaps all it did was sink into your flesh, become your flesh, a thing invisible that you wear still.

"I hear you're in the middle of a game," she murmured.

"Indeed."

"Silver mentioned something."

"Ah—I wondered if he would."

"How's it going?"

"Abhik's going to win."

"I'm sorry to hear that. I assume you haven't come to me for help?"

"There's nothing in the rules which says I can't."

"But to ask another player for assistance would be... *extraordinarily* dangerous," she mused, turning her weight on the rail to regard him better. "Think of the concessions I could get from Abhik if I were to tell him about this conversation now."

"You could," he conceded, "probably get more from Abhik than I can offer you, and in doing so you could guarantee that he wins, whereas by helping me you merely shift the balance of probability against my losing."

"The matter is settled then—I must help Abhik."

"However..." he interjected, laying his hand gently on her cold arm, "...if you did help me win, you would have in your debt a player far older, and far less temperamental in his loyalties than Abhik is now."

"A player who got drunk and took a foolish bet," she retorted, pulling her skin gently free from his touch, "is not a player whose services I can rely on."

"Then help me for your code," he said, moving round quickly to block her view as she turned away.

"My code? I am a player," she replied. "I have no code except victory and the game."

"I think we both know that isn't true, Thene. I have played you in both lower and higher league games, and you have beaten me every time save once. The one time you did not win, you would not sacrifice the life of the woman you had embedded in my minister's palace. You knew what he would do to her when her treachery was found out and though exposing her would have won you the game, you played a different piece and were mistaken, and it was the only game you lost."

"Sometimes I make mistakes."

"You lost two oil wells, a railway company, a seat in the Politburo and your appreciation of the taste of strawberries from that game. I have never seen you make mistakes of that kind since."

"I won back the taste of strawberries over a game of snap," she answered easily. "Where, if memory serves—and it always does—you lost your perception of the richness of the colour purple."

"Which only proves my point—that you have always beaten me, except that once."

She sighed and turned back to face the water, her eyes elsewhere, but her body still here, still waiting. We watched and waited with her as Remy waited too, holding tight to the edge of the railing as Thene studied the waves parting before the ship.

"What do you want, Remy?"

"I need to learn something of Abhik Lee's past. Where he came from, games he's won, his form, his style."

"You have pieces; why use mine to gather this?"

"My pieces are outside this country. If I accessed them, I would be in violation of the rules of the game."

"My," she murmured, "Abhik really did nail you on this one, didn't he? Why did you come here, Remy? You were drunk and you agreed to play a game in a country where you have no resources. You should have stayed in India where you have enough pieces to have an advantage in any game."

"Where would be the challenge in that?"

They watched the water a while, the two of them in silence. Then he said, "Silver's going to play the great game."

"I know. He's been preparing for a very long time. Don't look so surprised. As you say, I am a very old player. I have observed my enemy's form. Silver has been gathering pieces into his hand for centuries now, building up a reserve to rival the Gamesmaster for when he eventually makes his challenge."

"And when do you think that will be?"

"Soon, perhaps—soon."

"And do you think he can win?"

242

"I don't know. Both he and the Gameshouse hide their resources and their intentions. You would be unwise to trust either."

"Do you think the Gameshouse has an agenda?" She didn't answer. "Thene. Your silence speaks volumes."

"You interpret as you will," she replied, eyes not rising from the river. "My silence will not sway you from your course."

"Will you help me?"

"I will need something in return, some day."

"Name it."

"I don't yet know. A favour. Information. A piece. Something of that ilk—in proportion, of course, to the risk—in proportion. We must always be balanced in these things, must we not?"

"It's yours."

"Then I shall see what I can learn."

"Thank you."

"It is merely an exchange," she replied, turning away from the water and drawing herself up straighter. "This too is part of the game, though perhaps we flatter ourselves in thinking that we are the ones who play it."

So saying, she walked away.

Chapter 35

The next morning, a report reached the ears of Abhik Lee that Remy Burke—or at least a man conforming to his appearance—had been seen in Khon Kaen. So certain was the news that Abhik Lee at once boarded the first train heading north, leaving behind him three other entirely separate yet plausible sightings of Remy in Bangkok.

We wave goodbye to Abhik at the railway station, and he does not return the courtesy.

That night, information came to Remy Burke and two hours later, he lets himself into Abhik Lee's private rooms in Ratanakosin.

Thrilling intrusion! We drift through Abhik's life, seeing spread in all the things he possesses the story of this man. We feel god-like, naughty, wonderfully intelligent as we pick through his belongings, knowing him to be far away. Who would live a normal life when they could live like thieves and umpires as we do now? He has lived in this place a good long while, not three streets from the Grand Palace. The fans swirl slowly in the ceiling overhead, the flies press against the mesh across the windows, the shutters closed behind them. A mosquito net hangs across a dishevelled double bed—dishevelled because he had not time to make it when news came to send him north, dishevelled because Abhik Lee will trust no man with his privacy, his possessions.

He has taken all information regarding his pieces, those generals and colonels, diplomats and ministers who he has been playing from his hand—but there is still plenty to examine. Shelves of books: *Das Capital* to *Mein Kampf*, Dostoevsky to Hemmingway, Ishwar Gupta and Kavi Kant, Sunthorn Phu and Sei Shonagon. When did Abhik learn to read medieval Japanese? (A game of detectives in an Iranian country palace. A minor princeling was found dead and Abhik caught the killer before his rival could do the same. Abhik had bet his knowledge of Hindi versus the rival's study of Japanese—a good bet fairly played.) A kitchen stocked with rice and vegetables, nothing too sugary, no meat at all. No alcohol, but water three-times filtered, boiled and cooled. So eager was Abhik to leave Bangkok that a bowl of rice stands cold and glutinous by the sink, the dirty spoon hanging off it, flies coming to feast. Seven different kinds of tea, including a jar consisting of several different kinds stirred together in perfect proportion. A map of Bangkok—abandoned—and when he dials the telephone exchange, the last number they connect him with is the personal number of the Minister of the Interior.

A small table set with incense. A small pillow on the floor before it, curved with the shape of Abhik's knees. It might have been an altar, so carefully is each part arranged, but no deity stands watching, no symbol is invoked. A gramophone player. The music is the Indian sitar. He rifles through records underneath as the music plays. Wagner, Elgar, Mozart, Duke Ellington and Billie Holiday.

The bathroom is small and bare. Cracked tiles on one wall in blue and white, a gently rotting bathmat flung across the side of the tub, a basin stained faintly yellow around the plug. He opens the cupboard and finds it bare of essentials—Abhik took his toothbrush at least to Khon Kaen. He rummages through the small wicker bin below and pulls out a brown glass jar with a dipper in it. A label on the front has Abhik's name, a date and a trademark—Oculimol. The bottle is empty, the date within the last three weeks. Remy had lost track of time until his return to the city.

He slips the bottle into his pocket and lets himself out the way he came in.

Chapter 36

On his fifth day in Bangkok, a letter was posted under his door.

How the letter came to his door—how Thene found him—he will never know, and we, respecting the privacy of a player, will not tell.

Within it was listed every game Abhik had played, the stakes wagered, the prizes won, the prizes lost.

In seven years, he had been busy, winning a small fortune in territorial concessions, willing governors, questionable executives, busy generals. In the last nine months he had gone to some extraordinary lengths to win prizes in Siam, including, Remy couldn't help but see, a great many of the military men who had so recently seized power—always, but always!—in the name of the king. In this country most things, we know, are in the name of a king. Only once did Remy see his own name—that night he played poker with Abhik, a lower league game, nothing of significance, surprised, impressed even, that it cropped up on Thene's list.

He read the list once, and then read it again, and only on the second view did he find the game he was looking for.

On the sixth day, Abhik Lee returned to Bangkok and that same night, Remy thought he saw two men watching his hotel. He moved that very hour, fleeing through the dark, but he was fearful now, his deal with Silver done, an end coming to the chase.

He has run for nearly three months. No one could have believed that Remy Burke would stay hidden for so long.

*

On the seventh day, as he walked towards the river, he heard the sound of a motorcycle behind him, and looking back, saw two men approaching, one riding behind the other, arms about his waist. He did not recognise their faces, but he knew their intentions, and ran. They followed, swinging round and past him, the man on the back of the bike throwing himself into Remy's path, the driver coming back to cut off Remy's escape. Too soon, too soon, they had found him too soon!

Remy runs straight at the nearest man, tackling him with a bear-hug around the waist. They both tumble; someone strikes someone else, someone falls, someone kicks, someone snarls, someone—Remy!—bites the other's man face! He bites him like a dog, gnaws and gouges, a wild animal; where did this come from?! (It came from the forest, from the mud, from the heatstroke and the hunger, the thirst and the fear.) And for a moment—for an implausible, incredible moment—Remy is winning. Pounding a stranger to death in a dirty street in Bangkok, while the wives look on from their open windows and the passers-by know better than to get involved, involved with a *European* at that, a man who'll complain to his embassy who'll use it as an excuse to commit...some implausible excess not yet fantasised in the ambassador's mind...the people look on until, coming up behind him, the driver of the motorbike starts pummelling Remy as hard as he can with a tin helmet.

Remy falters.

Stumbles.

Falls.

Blood runs down his face, his neck.

The skin is shredded from his knuckles.

His arms are red and will soon be purple, brown, black.

This is it, Remy Burke, we whisper to him. This is the last game you will ever play, the death of your mind, the destruction of everything you are. Abhik could have been kind, challenged you to play to the death, but no! He wanted you to live, ignorant and forgetful, wanted to steal your senses, your memories of the prayers of the holy men as they crawled towards Varanasi, the smell of the fires besides the Ganges, the shrieking of the jungles that encroached on the holy places of Laos and Cambodia. He wants the memories of your mother's song, your father's stories, the touch of your fingers on bare flesh, the excitement of a tongue in your mouth, the smell of moonlight, the thrill of victory, the line of Fon's back as she turned away, he wants your *soul*. And when he has it, he'll watch you wander, bewildered and afraid through the world, and laugh at you in silence, and turn away without another thought. This is what Abhik Lee will do to you when he's won, so get up! Get up and *fight!*

Remy kicks out, blind, blood in his eyes, and catches someone's leg. He kicks again, and the man who stumbled is now collapsing, a foot buried in his stomach, winded but whole. The breath buys him a moment; he takes it. Remy rolls to one side, chest burning, face streaming, heart rushing, crawls on his hands and knees to the edge of the road, strangers parting about him, crawls to his feet and, half blind, he staggers up and runs.

He gets nearly half a mile before he collapses in the doorway of a house.

A woman opens it and starts screaming.

He manages another quarter of a mile before he falls down again. Three men and two women walk by before a woman with a child stops to ask if he is all right, if he needs to get to a hospital.

No hospital. Abhik Lee knows now he's in Bangkok, and will know too that he's injured. He'll be watching the hospitals.

Water, he begs, and the woman brings him water from a pump.

How do I look? he asks.

Terrible, she replies. You need help.

No help. You're very kind. No help.

Remy crawls on, towards the gathering night.

Chapter 37

Here we are.

You and I, here we are again, standing before the doors of the Gameshouse.

It is night over Bangkok. A bone-rattling, engine-snorting, ting-a-linging, come-all-ye-unto-the-roaring night. We knock on the silver doors of the Gameshouse and they let us in, shutting out the city. Here, the sound of the sueng, plucked by an old man with a red hat upon his head, ears grown long, gold around his throat. A pair of girls in blue and pearl duet on the many-stringed khim, while a singer pushes her voice as high as the eagle's flight to tell the story of sad kings, broken hearts, lost empires, forgotten lives. Here the players of the lower league—so many players, so many mighty men and women looking to be something more!—challenge each other for gold and time, favours and secrets, as if they matter. As if this board is the one we have come to love. How many of these would-be great players will end up pieces? (Twenty-two of the fifty-eight here assembled. Twenty-two of the gathered players will bet a little too much, lose a little too heavily and when they are in the pit of their despair, a woman in white will come to them and say, "Can I interest you in something different?" A high number indeed; a significant percentage of those congregated here, as though, we muse, as though there are those called to the Gameshouse to play only so that they might be played upon, and in their falling increase the sum resources of the Gamesmaster, of she who sits on high. Yet these are thoughts for another time, another roll of the dice, and so we move on.)

Through another pair of silver doors, lions roaring from the panelling, up a corridor too long for this building, to the place where the higher league plays. Oh now here, *here* we see the true players, the men and women who know that the world is a board, and only toss a coin when they are sure which way it will land.

We are looking for one player in particular, and tonight we find him.

Godert van Zuylen. He was sent, so the rumours say, to a tiny island in the middle of nowhere after he got his boss's daughter pregnant and would not agree to the marriage. The population of that place was seventy-three, but no! Seventy-three, it transpired, was the number of those people that the Dutch authorities had actually managed to count, and being as they were uninterested in the interior, they had not found the two thousand that lived on the side of a volcano and worshipped the fire and the sea. Van Zuylen found them, and even here, even they, it seemed, had heard of the game, for one day a door was opened at the back of a cave, and within he found the sound of cards, dice and the beating of the ritual drum.

Now he owns the father and the daughter both who had him sent away. He won them in a game of codebreaker's scrabble in 1917, by use of a one-time pad dropped behind Austrian lines. Two thousand men died that day, and he was victorious by the rules of the game and he never looked back.

We approach, but wait!

Another approaches first. Remy Burke, fancy seeing you here!

His appearance causes some commotion. Blood still clings to the collar of his shirt, laces the ends of his hair. His trousers are torn, knees scuffed, fingers dirty, knuckles swollen, jaw red, eyes black. He makes directly for van Zuylen, and others part before him, though many stare.

He sits down opposite van Zuylen and says to the white-clad waiter who cautiously approaches, "Water please."

Water is bought in a cup chilled with ice, a slice of lemon in the side, a sprig of mint at the bottom. Where does the Gameshouse find all these things? A low priority on the list of questions we must ask.

At last van Zuylen says in careful French, "You look terrible, Remy."

"You look well."

"I had good fortune in a game I played."

"Ah—that explains your youthful glow! How much did you win?"

"Only five years. It was a brief skirmish, that was all. My planes had the better engines."

"Of course they did—you are a professional."

"Indeed. May I help you?"

"You played a game against Abhik Lee here some seven months ago."

"Ah, the delightful Mr. Lee. Yes, I played him, though I do not think it is good form to discuss the matter, do you?"

"It's not a discussion that interests me: it's the wager."

"I do not think it's good form to discuss that either—unless, that is, you propose to offer something in return?"

Remy is silent for a moment, staring down at the table. At last he says, "I am in the middle of a game. I cannot access my resources until the game is done."

"Then I fear we cannot..."

"How about cards?"

Van Zuylen hesitates. "You are already occupied, are you not?"

"A lower league game, a skirmish, nothing more."

"And what could you wager for this game?"

"What would you like?"

The Dutchman purses his lips, turns his head thoughtfully to the ceiling of the room. "How about... the affections of the last person who loved you?"

"That's a big wager for a small game."

"You seem... desperate."

251

"I'm not sure the umpires would appreciate you taking advantage of my condition."

"It is a lower league game, that is all. Backgammon, perhaps, or chess? I'll let you decide."

"I had always thought you were more sporting than that, Godert."

He shrugs. "The word is you agreed to a game with Abhik Lee while drunk. Most likely you will lose. What is the good for me in playing a man who is already beaten, unless I get to pick at some of the bones?"

Remy smiles thinly. "Chess then," he says, and his voice is dry. "You can be white, if you like."

Chapter 38

A game of chess.

We watch.

So does half the Gameshouse.

These people have seen a lot, but a blood-soaked player, in the middle of a match of hide-and-seek, staggering into their halls? Why, that—that is still a sight to see. We are drawn, we are drawn, by the smell of blood in the water.

Who was the last person who loved Remy?

He is not sure he can say for certain, but we can, and so can you too, Remy, if you try. She waits for you in a broken hut in the forest, the moon above and the waters of the lake below, your widow in the woods. We do not think you shall return to her, and neither does she, but such a predicament does not diminish the force of her affection. Van Zuylen will have her, if he wins, like a trophy on the wall.

You should not gamble a thing that is not yours, Remy.

You should not bet a thing you cannot afford to lose.

It is not in keeping with your code.

We watch, waiting for Remy to lose.

He plays black; van Zuylen is white.

He opens aggressively, swaps a bishop for a knight, a knight for a bishop, opens up the centre of the board, pawn takes pawn takes pawn takes pawn. The pieces fall, the centre is exposed. King's castle, racing to opposite sides of the board, taking cover. The queens square off, Remy eyes an exchange, van Zuylen...

...flinches.

It is not yet time, the Dutchman seems to say, to take the most powerful piece from the board.

Remy studies his face now, as the queen moves away.

It is not an error per se to retreat from the exchange, but it is...indicative.

Does van Zuylen see something in the bloodied features of his opponent?

(He does. He sees the chief of the tribe on the unnamed island where, as a philanderer who'd philandered too far, he has been sent. He sees the ancient man dancing with the bones of slaughtered sharks around his neck, hears the beating of the drum, feels blood in his face, his neck, his fingertips, rises up spontaneously to dance himself, spins round and round with the chief and the chieftain's daughter and the chieftain's wife until he realises that the flesh he was eating is raw, and the drums are now silent, the whole village watching him gorge, and him alone. There is a darkness in their silence, a violence waiting to spill, but they do not move, do not speak as he crawls away back to the trading post in the bay, and the drums do not beat, and he does not dance again. Now van Zuylen looks again into the sun-soaked, blood-soaked face of Remy Burke and sees violence in it, and power, and tastes raw flesh in his mouth, and hears the beating of the drum, and is mightily afraid.)

A piece falls; only a pawn, and at some tactical risk.

Van Zuylen reclaims the next pawn four moves later, then another, his pulse rising as he sniffs victory.

He is wrong—not a victory, a trap. He was lured in by the taste of easy pickings and now his rook is trapped, pinned by a combination of king and knight. He tries to run, has nowhere to go and with a sigh throws away his rook for one last pawn, and knows that the game is nearly over, though he is not sure where death will come.

Death comes three moves after the inevitable queen exchange.

He resigns when it becomes definite, and the watchers, save for us, drift away.

Remy says, "You owe me some information."

"What would you like to know?" the Dutchman asks, and finds that he is exhausted.

"Seven months ago you played Abhik Lee at a game, and Abhik lost. Here's my question—what was his forfeit?"

Van Zuylen smiles, though his hands are shaking.

"Oh," he says. "Now I understand."

Chapter 39

It is the small hours of the morning, the glow before dawn, when Remy leaves the Gameshouse.

The streets of Bangkok are at last silent, save for the distant ringing of a ship's bell, the thump of a door slamming in an alley, the shriek of a stray cat.

The men are waiting outside: three soldiers and a colonel. We know who tipped them off, and we understand—Abhik Lee is a good player to have on your side.

This time they leave nothing to chance. Two men have grabbed Remy by the arms, a third snapping the handcuffs on, and before he can tut and say, "So it goes," they bundle him into a car and rush him through the empty, grubby streets. They take him to a house above a canal, bundle him up three flights of stairs, push the door open to reveal a room where the slowly rising light of dawn now creeps across the floor in perfectly defined squares, showing a desk, a chair, a bed, an oil lamp burning down. They sit him in the chair, and from the room next door the sound of water in a bowl rises, sloshes, ceases.

They wait.

Abhik Lee dries his face, his hands, the side and back of his neck with a towel, and steps at last into the room. He wears a waistcoat and long shirt sleeves, a watch hooked in his pocket, the chain slung across his tight belly. Perhaps he slept like that? How, Remy wonders, did he avoid crinkles?

"You did well, Remy," he says, reaching forward to touch the side of Remy's bruised face. "Better than I thought you would."

"Thank you."

Abhik hesitates, his fingers hovering above Remy's skin. Then he lets his hand drop, brushing his enemy's sleeve, his arm, squeezing tight a moment against the bruises along the bone, hard enough to make Remy flinch, before gently letting go. He turns away from his prisoner, straightening his tie, and as he examines himself in the mirror breathes softly, "Tag. You're it."

Chapter 40

They gave Remy three days' grace.

Time to heal, they said.

On the third day, he was given his deck of hands.

Majors, the wives of ministers, a handful of priests, some nuns, a couple of traders, a medley of spies, a hunter from South Africa, a tracker from Nepal, a good hand, no doubt, a decent collection of pieces to play, but not nearly good enough.

He wondered then what Silver would say.

(He would smile and say nothing at all. Remy has not seen Abhik's hand but he has sensed its power, and senses now perhaps that the cards he holds, the randomly shuffled, randomly dealt cards, are bad. If they were random at all.)

He smiled at the umpire who delivered them to him and said, "Thank you very much."

The umpire's face was invisible, hidden behind her veil as she walked away.

On the fourth day, he summoned two of his pieces—a Bengali soldier, famed for having first killed then fallen in love with the great mountain tigers—and a Bangkok gangster, who boasted that his cousin owned all of Hong Kong and had dealt opium to Queen Victoria herself! The thief had a car; the soldier had a gun. Together, they went to the Gameshouse.

The umpire stood outside to wait with them until the allotted time. They lounged on the bonnet of the car, chewing tendrils of squid until twelve p.m. struck, at which point Remy put his watch away, slipped into the passenger seat and said, "I'm thinking about a show."

They went to the cinema. When the national anthem played, the entire audience rose in solemnity and stood again when newsreel footage showed the king inspecting some general's latest triumph.

> *We, servants of his great majesty,*
> *Prostrate our hearts and heads,*
> *To pay respect to the ruler, whose merits are boundless,*
> *Outstanding in the great Chakri dynasty,*
> *The greatest of Siam.*
> *. . . May it be that whatever you will be done,*
> *According to the hopes of your great heart,*
> *As we wish you victory, hurrah!*

When the film was done, Remy looked at his watch again and, tutting, said, "How about temple?"

They went to Pathum Wanaram, assured by the thief that it was out of the way enough to be quiet, but royal enough to be majestic. The soldier stayed outside, refusing to enter the grounds of a place so ornate and contrary to his faith. The thief galloped in, bounded up the steps two at a time, bought a great handful of incense and prostrated himself before every monk and icon he saw. Remy watched a crowd saluting the ashes of a long-dead king, sat a while by the roaring mouth of a kylin, a half-dragon, half-lion which guarded this royal place, heard the beating of the gong and watched the shadows stretch and said at last, "Wasn't that nice? Let's have some supper."

They ate prawns and fried fish, octopus legs and crinkled green cabbage purchased from a vendor by the river, who swore that his father was the greatest fisherman of the bay, and had once caught a shark bigger than his boat which took three days to die even after it was hooked and harpooned and dragged to land.

"It didn't die even on land?" asked Remy politely.

"No! It only died when my mother cut its heart out, still beating, and threw it back into the sea! True story!"

All the truest stories, we knew, ended with these sacred words.

When the sun was down, and they'd washed the oil and grease of their fishy meal from their hands, the thief said, enthused by the adventure that the day had begun:

"Where next, sir?"

The soldier sighed, and at Remy's expression shrugged and said, "I was brought here to hunt."

"How many hours has it been since the hunt began?"

"Nine, ten?"

"That should be long enough," he replied, and turning to the thief, "Take me to the Gameshouse."

Chapter 41

Again, the silver doors; again, the sound of music.

Again, the rolling of the dice; again, the laughter of strangers who will never really be friends, not truly, not while they play the game.

Heads turn as Remy enters, his soldier in tow, the thief left with the car.

"He can't come in here," says the umpire guarding the gateway to the halls of the higher league.

"He is a piece, and I am a player," replies Remy firmly. "We are playing a game."

The umpire hesitates, then nods, and the two of them go in.

Through the halls, heads turn, people stare; we move past the lives that are being made, the dreams that are being broken, the wonders won, the lives lost, the battle of mind against mind, brute intelligence and skill; governments fall, empires turn; this is the Gameshouse, where humanity is a symbol, the world an object—come and play if you dare; come into the Gameshouse.

A smaller wooden door at the back, a darkened stair heading up. Usually it is guarded but as Remy approaches, the umpire stands back because the umpires—why, they enforce the rules of the game, and Remy is a player, the game goes on, on, yay even up this dark flight of stairs where usually only the umpires go, up and up too many floors, we think, for this house, too many doors leading to either side but Remy keeps going, knows in his belly where to go, up towards the place where the Gamesmaster, so beautiful though she is lost in white, so beautiful, until she became what she is, up even there to where the Gamesmaster resides, ruler of the house, lady of the game.

The umpire pushes back the door without Remy needing to knock, and he enters a room hung with silks, all whites and silvers, obscuring furniture, obscuring shape or size, but not obscuring *him*.

Abhik Lee, sitting by a writing desk of red lacquer. He turns as the door opens, mouth opening, perhaps to give some command, ask some favour, but as he turns, he sees, and his mouth widens, pen and paper fall from his fingers to the floor.

Abhik Lee.

"Tag," says Remy, catching him by the arm. "You're it."

Chapter 42

The soldier stood outside.

Remy stood within.

Abhik sat, frozen by the moment, still in his chair, papers at his feet, a crystal beaker of water half consumed by his elbow.

Neither man spoke.

Then Remy said, "Your side of the wager was twenty years. When you pay the forfeit, you will be an old man. Your mind will wither as well as your body. It will be a difficult loss for you to come back from. I once lost fifteen years in a match in Poland, and I nearly died while trying to claw them back. I will release you from this forfeit, spare you this death—and, I think, given how this game has gone, it will be death—if you answer some simple questions."

Silence.

Then, "How are you here?" breathed Abhik Lee, and we have the impression that he asks this not so much of Remy but of himself, or some unseen other, who stands silently by. "How are you here?"

"I followed your eyedrops," he replied, pulling the little glass bottle from his pocket, Oculimol on the side. "You played a game against van Zuylen seven months ago; when you lost you acquired the corneal scarring that has bothered him ever since a nasty eye infection. The scarring, while irritating, isn't blinding, but has to be continually soothed with eye drops. You use Oculimol; it is difficult to find outside Bangkok. Finding it made it seem more likely that you would not risk leaving the city, even in a game of hide-and-seek."

"I removed all trace," he whispered, voice rattling over dry tongue. "There was nothing in my room."

"There is nothing in your room now. But I came back to Bangkok over a week ago in order to investigate you, *before* you became the hunted. There is no rule against it—merely risk. By coming to Bangkok and showing myself, I permitted you to catch me, but the danger was worth the prize. When I found the Oculimol in your rooms, I went to every pharmacy I could find. Only two receive shipments of this concoction, and only one had been asked to send a large supply to the present address of the Gameshouse. As I said: there is no rule against my hunting you when I am the hunted. Nor is there any rule forbidding you from hiding in the Gameshouse. Players stay here for weeks, months at a time. I would not think to look here since the idea is so absurd, and if you were willing to stay put in this gilded cage, avoiding contact with anyone who might be sympathetic to my cause, your preparations all in place, for a few hours longer than the time I spent running—than the hard, lonely time I spent running—then you would win without even experiencing the discomfort of an itchy eye. You did not break the rules, Abhik Lee, nor did I. Nor can it really be said that you violated the spirit of the game, or any code of honour. Your code is victory and the prize. Nothing more. Such a situation as this could bring out the vindictive streak in me; yet as I said, I will forgo my prize for a little information."

Abhik swallowed. "What kind of information?"

"Why did you challenge me?"

"You were weak."

"I am an old player—you'll have to do better than that."

"You were weak—a weak old man in a country not your own. I could win—I knew I could win."

"Did the Gameshouse ask you to challenge me?"

He didn't answer.

"Did the Gamesmaster offer to help you?"

No answer.

"What were the cards you were dealt when you hunted me?"

No answer.

Remy smiled, head on one side. "It has been a long road to this point, Abhik Lee. I travelled far and wide before I realised how I could beat you. You had me frightened and afraid, focused only on hiding, on being your prey. It took me too long to remember that I would soon become the hunter and, Abhik, I am a good hunter. I have played too long to be anything less; do not dare underestimate me. Why did you challenge me to this game?"

"I knew I could win."

"Why challenge me?"

"You cheated!" The cry, sudden, sharp and shrill, rose as Abhik did, clawing his way up from his chair, his body shaking with rage. "You cheated—the umpires should have your soul, your body—you cheated!"

"No. I am within the rules of the game."

"Not now, not *now*," he snarled. "Not this game, not *now*. Before!"

"Before?"

"When we played cards, you cheated!"

We struggle with Remy to place this accusation, find the heart of this raging voice. Was this...cards? Is this a game of poker, a flash of cards on the table that has Abhik raging like the lion? We think it is, and we are amazed.

"It was poker," breathed Remy. Then, more pertinent to the point, "I did not cheat."

"The game was mine; I had you; it was mine—you cheated." A growl, a paring back of teeth, a pulling in of breath, Abhik was ready to burst with it and held it in under great pressure.

"I didn't cheat."

"You cheated."

"I got lucky! It was lucky, a lucky hand, that's all!"

"There is no luck!" Now Abhik let his voice burst through; now he swiped the beaker from the table, glass shattered on the floor, water speckled the white silks hung all about. He kicked at his ancient lacquered chair, beat his fists against his chest, roared and roared again, *"There is no luck!"*

Remy waited.

We waited.

Silence settled.

A silence of slowing, forced breath, of bulging eyes, of bursting veins.

We waited.

Silence.

Remy said, "What did the Gameshouse offer you?"

Silence.

"What did they promise? Better pieces? A twist in the balance of things? A prod towards weaker prey? What do they gain by my defeat?"

Silence, and the slow panting of Abhik's breath.

"I will give you back your life," Remy murmured. "I swear it, I will forfeit the prize, but first you tell me."

Abhik's breath slowed more. He reached out for his chair, found it broken and overturned. Sunk down against the edge of the desk, couldn't seem to quite grasp it, slipped, fell to the floor. There he sat, legs splayed, eyes staring at nothing, breathing fast and shallow, not the deep gasp it had been before.

Remy squatted down in front of him.

"Tell me. Let me help you."

Slowly, Abhik looked up. He seemed to see, as if for the first time, not his enemy, not his defeat staring back at him, not even another player, but rather he looked, taking in all the shapes of Remy's face, the scars and the wounds, the marks of great hardship etched by the sun onto his skin, the freshly clotting blood, the freshly sinking bruises, the tired eyes that had squinted too long against the bright, hot day and closed only fearfully in the long, howling night. All this he saw, and for the first time seemed to see a man, and for a moment his lips parted as if he would speak, but something then moved in the curtains behind Remy where his back was turned, and Abhik's lips sealed once more.

What was it?

We turn to look, though Remy does not, and imagine we see a figure, drifting away, vanishing into silk, from where she came. We pursue but whiteness blinds us, and we cannot find her in this place. Not yet—not yet.

Then Abhik says, "No." He speaks again, and is more confident in the sound. "No."

Remy straightened, shaking his head. "I give you this chance," he said.

"No."

"I will have your life if you do not answer me."

"I . . . will not answer."

"Do you fear the Gamesmaster so much?"

Abhik was silent a moment, head turned to one side. Then, very quietly, "*No*," but as he said the word, his head nodded and his eyes were fixed on Remy's own, digging into Remy's own, but then his lips sealed, and he said no more.

Chapter 43

Is this victory?

Remy stands by the Chao Phraya river, waiting for the sun to rise over the bustling waters.

Is this victory?

He closes his eyes and breathes, and it seems to him that his breath is . . .

. . . only breath.

He walks along a muddy road, a road carved in his memories, but the shapes that were so vivid before, the stories that were so bright seem now a thousand miles away.

Is this what he played for?

Is this success?

The sun peeps over the eastern-most edge of the city, a nail-thin sliver of light that grows so fast, fast as the turning of the earth, spreading upwards into the great, waiting sky.

He feels . . .

. . . very tired.

Though if we were to look, we would perhaps suggest that there was a youthful quality about his skin, a freshness to his eye, a brightness to his hair, a softness to his hand that is not . . . that cannot be . . . of his usual seeming.

(And if we were to look, we might see a man walking away from the Gameshouse. He walks tall at first, though without direction, but shortly finds that his back aches and his legs are frail, so he stops and pulls a branch from a tree, and walks with it supporting him. His spine curves gently down, and when he rubs at his now-throbbing head, strands of hair come away from his fingers, their deep blackness turning grey in his hand. He looks up, and the street seems distant now, softly out of focus, and as Abhik Lee walks away, he starts to cry, the tears rolling down the ancient wrinkles and rivulets of his old, cracked face.)

Is this victory?

And then, she is there.

The Gamesmaster, all in white.

She stands beside Remy, watching the sun rise higher above the buildings, filling the sky with golden pink. The breeze off the river ripples the veil that covers her face, but though the heat is rising, she still wears gloves, trousers, robes, every part of her hidden except her voice, which now speaks clear and quiet.

"You were drunk when you took the bet," the Gamesmaster explains. "You were drunk when you took the last five."

"I won the last five games I played," he retorts, not turning his eyes from the rising sun. "I *won*."

"You played for low stakes, skirmishes barely worth the gamble. You are an old player, Remy Burke, and a good one. We were very sorry to see you losing...interest."

"Losing interest?" he breathes, barely holding back the anger in his voice. "Is that what you saw in me? A player 'losing interest'? Is that why you told Abhik to challenge me?"

"The Gameshouse does not control the game, nor the luck of the draw, nor the things that its players do."

"But you didn't stop him either," he growls. "You let him come at me; you let an uneven game be played..."

"Was it uneven?" she replies quickly, cutting him off. "Was it unfair? You have wandered hundreds of miles, Remy Burke, and found, I think, a little bit of something which had in recent years grown occluded to you. You found, we think, a reason to play, and you won. Whatever advantages it may have appeared that Abhik had, clearly they were not overwhelming."

"The game was uneven..."

"You won," she repeats, cutting him off. "You won."

Silence. Then:

"Silver is gathering pieces to himself," she says. "Have you not told lies to win a hand? And would you not discard a piece if a better one presented itself? Do not mistake his easy words for truth."

"Silver gathers pieces," he replies. "And so, I think, do you. It did not violate the rules, but only by your consent could he have hidden in the Gameshouse; only by your consent could such an uneven match have been played, for such a harsh wager. If Abhik had won, if he had taken my memories, he would have been a devastating player; if he won because of an accord between himself and you, he would have been an even more devastating piece."

"Yet he lost," she replies. "The stronger mind defeated the lesser, and we are honoured to have you play in the Gameshouse, particularly now we know the full extent of your...qualities. Who would have imagined you had so much to give; incredible what men will do when tested. Now it is known, we look forward to seeing how you play in future matches. You see, Remy, the Gameshouse wins whoever is victorious; we are enriched by your successes."

He has no answer.

Only breath and air.

The sun rises, the earth turns and he is...

...something. Something solid, something burning, something strong, something old, something new, something that has a name which now returns through the crumple of his frown, through the clenching of his jaw, through the tightness in his fist and here it is, the thing that washes away the road, stills the circling of the universe, pins the stars in their place and makes the moon wax and wane, only for him.

He is a player.

He straightens up a little more, turns his face away from the sun.

Then she says, still watching the rising light, "A great game is coming, Remy. It has been centuries in the making, but the time is soon at hand. When the game begins, be careful where the pieces fall."

"I am a player," he says. "I know how to read the board."

The Gamesmaster smiles behind her veil, and turns away.

He watches her go, and when he turns away we watch a little while longer, until she is out of sight.

THE MASTER

Chapter 1

We have come—at last—we have come to the end. You and I, we have played this game so long, and never once made a move.

Come now, come.

The board is ready; the cards are prepared.

The coin which was spun must fall at last.

Chapter 2

There is a story which is not a story told about a place which is not a place.

It is the story of the Gameshouse, where the great and the ancient go to play. Come, generals and kings, priests and emperors, you great factory men and you ladies of letters, come to the Gameshouse. Come and play for the mastery of a city, the conquest of a country, the wealth of a civilisation, the history of a palace, the secrets of spies and the treasures of thieves. Here our chess-boards are a grid which we lay across the earth; dice roll and strangers die; the cards fall and the coin turns, it turns, it turns, and when we are done, armies will be shattered, oceans will rise, and we will win and live, or lose and die. For it is not petty things that we play for in the Gameshouse, but life, time and the soul.

The curtain is parted, the music ceases and the player takes the stage.

Chapter 3

They call me Silver.

My real name was lost centuries ago, gambled against a barbarian king. I cannot remember my name now, but he who won it was a sometime lord of horses and lost his life in battle, never knowing that he was a piece on that field, played by another hand. When he died, the death of my name was sealed, and it is no comfort to know that he too is not remembered. Only she knows it now—she, the Gamesmaster, the woman all in white who guards the halls wherein we play—but she is above all things, and will not tell.

And so, having nothing more, I am simply Silver.

Of the players in the Gameshouse, only one is older than I, and she has no interest in these things.

("I have seen the world change," she murmurs, spiking thread through needle, needle through cloth. "But the game does not. I am a player, interested in the game, not the world, so what is your adventure to me?"

"What if I said I played for love?" I ask one night when I have had too much to drink.

She laughs, raising her head briefly from her work to look at me with chiding eyes. "Silver, you love only the game, and she is a cold mistress.")

I have played many games for many prizes, but the greatest game must now begin.

Chapter 4

New York in summer. A city of two climates. Indoors, aircon-ditioning lowers the temperatures to an Arctic chill; outside, the extraction fans add to the already shimmering heat until the air seems to melt in sweat-soaked, skin-slithering despair. I remember when New York was a colony on an island of mud, not deserving of even a few rolls of a lower league dice let alone a door to the Gameshouse. Yet there it stands, silver doors in a street where they do not belong. Lions' faces, teeth bared, snarl-ing at all who dare knock. Red brick above, a fire escape pushed awkwardly to one side as if the Gameshouse has transplanted itself into the architecture of this place, shuffling pre-established buildings a little to the left, a little to the right, to the confusion of the mortar around. Which, of course, it has.

The corridor inside hung with silk, feels old, smells old, and the closing door cuts off all the sounds of the city as if time had frozen upon a single second when no birds sang, no engines roared, no delivery boy shouted at the taxi that cut across his path, no siren soared, no door slammed in the city. Three weeks ago, this old place did not exist, and soon it will not exist again, and no one will remark on it, save those few players new enough to care.

The Gameshouse often comes to New York. It likes to be where the power is.

Come; follow me.

We move through corridors hung with white silk, smell the incense, hear the music, descend a flight of stairs to the club room where the newest players play, UV lights and champagne, cocktails with olives in, a fountain of ice, chess sets, backgammon and baduk, cards and counters, the usual paraphernalia of the lower league. New games too: *Cluedo, Settlers of Catan, Age of Empires, Mario Kart, Mortal Kombat Whatever* fought between a shrieking bishop and a deputy mayor. A judge, a police commissioner, a gangster, a congressman, a chief of staff, a general, a consulting doctor, a research fellow, a professor, a hit-man, a pharmaceutical king, an oil magnate, a seller of used cars and cheap cocaine—all the men and women who think they are someone, could be something more—they all come here as they have come through the centuries, across the world. They dream of passing through the doors which now open for me, and how many, I mused, will be played, rather than players? Most—perhaps all. That is one of the truths of the Gameshouse.

So much for the lower league; I do not slow my step for it. Next, the higher league: another hall, larger, where the ancient and the learned, the oldest players of the game, now gathered over TV screens and digital maps, plotting their next game. Why, there, one who wagered her good health on the price of gold and won—after some market manipulation—the excellent eyesight of the now-blind man who limps away. There, another who played battleships against an air force and lost his carrier in the first wave, now growing old and shrivelled as his life is forfeit. Why, she won a court case, he won a city; she won a state, he lost an oil rig and on, on the game winds, the game that covers the world, the game we tell ourselves we have played all these years for joy, all these centuries for joy, and which has, by our playing, changed the world in the Gamesmaster's form for she . . .

She.

She is waiting for me.

I climb the stairs at the back of the hall, and no one bars my way. Usually two umpires—all in white, their faces veiled, their fingers gloved—stop trespassers, but not tonight, not me. She is waiting upstairs, as she has been waiting for so long.

She sits, her face covered, her arms in white, on a curved

cream sofa beneath a shroud of silk. I have not seen her eat or drink or smile since she took the white, but she is still her, still after all this time.

She says, "Is it that time already?"

I find I do not speak.

She offers me water.

I find I cannot drink.

She says, "You look tired, Silver. You look old."

"Not as old as I feel."

"It doesn't have to be this way," she murmurs. "As long as the house endures, so can you."

"Thank you; I have had my share of eternity."

The gloved fingers of her left hand ripple along her thigh, just once, a pianist warming up with a scale. "So," she says, "shall we?"

"Yes." My voice is not my own; I speak again, louder, claiming the sound. "Yes."

"You do not have to. Once you make this move, there is no going back, and I know you are not ignorant of what will come when you fail."

"I will not fail."

"Will you not? You have spent centuries preparing for this, but the house is mine, the players are mine and of the two of us, I was always the stronger."

"I will not fail."

"The house will have you if you lose. It will have your soul. I would be...saddened...to see that become your fate."

"The house has me already, ma'am," I reply. "I have been the house's slave for almost as long as you."

I imagine a smile behind her veil, and that imagination perhaps leads me to hear it in her voice. "Very well," she says. "Then make your move."

I draw in breath.

I speak the words.

"My lady of the veil," I say, "my lady Gamesmaster, mistress of this house—I challenge you."

Chapter 5

What is this?

Are these...

...tears?

I walk away from the Gameshouse and there is a hotness in my eyes.

What *is* this?

I taste the moisture on my lips and it is salty.

It cannot be sorrow, nor is it a useful response to fear. For so many centuries I have waited for this day, and grief faded with time.

Or did it? Perhaps grief never leaves us but is merely drowned out by a flood of life overwhelming it. Perhaps the wound that bled once is bleeding still, and I did not notice it until now.

I find the thought unhelpful, and walk away a little faster.

There have been only three challenges that I know of against the Gamesmaster.

The first was before my time and exists only in allegory and myth. I will not bother with its telling.

The most recent was in 1774, and none of us expected the challenger to win. Nevertheless, for nearly forty years the Gameshouse closed its doors, and the Gamesmaster and her rival fought the Great Game, setting assassins, spies, kings, diplomats, armies and faiths against each other until finally, in 1817, the challenger was defeated, his princes dead, his armies smashed, and he vanished into the white. Who he is now, no one knows.

Death is simple and the Gameshouse does not grant it easily—rather, it eats its victims whole, and somewhere beneath the white veils that are worn by the servants of the house, I do not doubt that he lives still, slave to the bricks and stones of that endless place.

And the other?

Why, the greatest challenge was made before, in 1208, and the woman who challenged the Gamesmaster was...

...a player greater than any I have ever known.

For twenty years they fought each other, the Gamesmaster and the player, and by the end of it no one could say for certain who had lost and who had won. All that was known was that the player vanished, some said into the service of the house, lost to the white, others said no, no, not at all! She vanished into *victory*, she conquered the Gameshouse, but who can really conquer that place? She is not the player any more, they said, but rather the Gamesmaster. In victory she became her enemy, and perhaps in this manner, her success was her ultimate defeat, for she is no longer herself but only the Gamesmaster again.

Did she see it so? Could she see anything greater than the game? Could she see me?

The coin turns, the coin turns.

Let the game begin.

Chapter 6

We agreed terms long before I issued the formal challenge.

She said, "*Assassins?* No—too crude. Hide-and-seek? Too juvenile, perhaps. Risk—it's been a while since I played Risk."

I replied, "Risk lost its appeal with the onset of the nuclear age."

The Gamesmaster sighed. "Very well: chess it is."

Four weeks later, a player by the name of Remy Burke, a man who owed me a favour, sat down next to me in a bar in Taipei, put his elbow on the table, his chin in his hand and said, "Tell me you didn't agree to play chess with the Gamesmaster."

"I can tell you a hard truth, or a comforting lie," I replied.

Remy let out a long, low puff of breath. "Silver," he breathed, "the Great Game is one thing, but letting her play *chess* under Great Game rules is a death sentence."

"It's still only chess," I replied. "We eliminate each other's pieces and position our own until we are in a position to capture the king; there is nothing remarkable in this."

"Except that you *are* the king."

"And so is she."

"And your pieces are going to be the fucking World Bank!" he hissed. "For bishop, read pope or ayatollah, summoning the faithful to crusade or jihad. For knight, read Mossad; for pawn, read the government of Pakistan, Silver! It's not your death that troubles me here, though I am certain that you will die—it's the death of every pawn, rook and queen the pair of you throw at each other as part of your game. Great Game rules mean you bring your own pieces to the table, and how long do you think it will be until she breaks out the big guns? Are you going to let countries fall, people die, economies crumble just to move a little closer to finding and capturing her for this game?"

I thought about the question a while, rolling the cold stem of the glass between my fingers. "Yes," I said at last. "To win the Great Game: yes."

He rolled back in his chair as if pushed in the heart, and for a moment he looked disgusted. I met his eyes and attempted to see my face in their reflection, my condition. Was there shame there? Did I feel a start of doubt at the lives that would be destroyed, the cities shattered, the countries overthrown, all for a game?

He turned his face away and I realised that I did not.

There are no cards dealt in the Great Game save those that you bring with you. There is no mercy either.

I fled through New York.

Fled in that it was my person, my body, which the Gamesmaster must capture if she is to win the Great Game. And not fleeing, not so much, in that already I was putting pieces into play. I called the police captain whose services I won over a game of blackjack; the admiral who swore he would do anything for me, anything at all, if I spared him his forfeit when the last card fell; the arsonist whose burns I helped to heal when, gambling his life against a powerful man's skin, he stumbled on the final move. I called the FBI agents who had assisted me when I played Cluedo in a house in Oregon, and whose lives I had saved before Colonel Mustard could finish his work with the candlestick. I called the senior engineer in the traffic control centre whose husband had bet his fortune on a throw of the coin, and whose life I had rebuilt after the dime had fallen.

All these I called through a single number, for they were pieces which I had gathered in preparation for this moment, an opening move I had already prepared, and by the time I reached JFK airport and the chartered jet—one of nine—that would carry me to my next location, traffic in Manhattan was at a standstill, protests blocked the bridges, fires were blazing in Brooklyn and FBI agents were conducting drug busts on East 39th Street, where the Gameshouse stood.

Or rather, where the Gameshouse had stood.

For within minutes of my leaving it, it was gone.

Chapter 7

Preparations made on a plane out of New York City.

In a lower league game of chess, you can see your king, the piece you must secure. In the Great Game, the board is the planet, the pawns are legion and finding your target can be as challenging as checkmate.

The pilot on this chartered plane, on which I am the only passenger, is Ghanaian. He lost his licence when the father of his fiancée discovered their liaison and called the ministry and screamed that his would-be son was a Muslim and a terrorist and a villain and had dared to sleep with his beautiful girl. I gave him his licence back, and a plane, and his wife lived in Paris, and his children were seven and nine and knew they were going to be astronauts or dinosaur hunters and had never asked why granddaddy didn't visit.

"Where to?"

I sunk into the co-pilot's seat, handed him a slip of paper. "There are coordinates for an island in the Atlantic."

"What's it called?"

"I'm not sure it ever had a name."

"Father-in-law trouble?" he asked with a smile, a pain that he had made a joke.

"More like fiancée."

"Oh man, you should never run away from love. If it has to end, it has to end, but don't just leave things unsaid!"

"It's not like that."

"If you say so; it's your life."

*

We flew for three hours.

One thousand and eighty-nine kilometres off the coast of America, a senior officer in GCHQ ("sometimes the cards just don't fall the way you want") alerted me to a satellite re-tasking over my rough location.

I alerted a cybercommunity called "Big Brother Lives". Their leader ("I can beat anyone at this game; you just watch me") responded within twenty seconds to my message, and launched the DDoS attack against the responsible servers.

Forty minutes later we landed on an island with no name, little more than a basalt blip in the ocean, where I boarded the French coastguard vessel that was waiting for me and headed into the night.

The captain said, his face lit from below by the lights of his control panels, "I didn't even know this place existed. What is it—a villain's lair?"

"No—no hollow volcano, you see."

"Then why is there a landing strip and no people?"

"It's a long way from radar."

"That sounds villainous to me."

I smiled at the man, whose mighty beard and grubby cap declared that here was a man who served the oceans first and *la belle France* second. Poseidon was his god, the water was his lover, and Liberté, Egalité and Fraternité would be welcome on board only if they were willing to row. He didn't know why he was here, and that was fine. The orders had come from higher up, from a man who had said, "Please don't take my mind," and whose mind I spared in exchange for favours yet to come.

"It has some lovely and rather unusual diving birds on it," I said at last by way of comfort. "I don't know how they got there since they are better at swimming than flying—yet there they are—nature's hiccup."

"Nature doesn't have hiccups," he replied seriously. "When she farts an island out of the bathwater, she does so deliberately."

*

My cabin was below decks, a hammock in a space made for pipes, no air save hot blasts from the engines, noise without cessation, rocking that would throw you from your bed if you fought it, soothe you to sleep if you permitted yourself to sink into its embrace.

I had used some thirty per cent of my New York resources to escape the city, and deployed a GCHQ mole and an anarchist cyber group in my defence. She—my enemy, my lady of the veil—had tasked an NSA satellite to find me. Pawns played in an opening move, feeling out the shape of the board.

This was acceptable—I could be patient in the early days. The Gameshouse had shut its doors and now somewhere she walked the earth, and being as she was, so very mighty and so very skilled, I didn't need to make any great efforts to find her yet; not until I was secure in my own position.

The more moves she made, the more pieces would be revealed, and the easier she would be to find.

I closed my eyes to sleep.

Chapter 8

Moves made from Ville de Valverde.

I set the FBI onto the NSA, attempting to trace the satellite that had tracked me down.

The NSA wasn't having any of it, and within forty-eight hours my agents were reassigned to desk jobs in Dallas, torn away from their friends, their families, their careers and their utility as pieces. Pawn takes pawn.

I tried an alternative tack, pushing from GCHQ for intelligence, but the Americans simply ignored my requests. The Gamesmaster had her pieces well positioned in the NSA, and they deflected my assaults without a thought. Tactical stalemate.

This being so, I settled back for a little while to consider. Villa de Valverde is a capital city, population 1,691, little white houses on a little green hill. Walking round it took approximately twenty-five minutes before returning to the tiny room above a taverna which served as my headquarters, resolved to try another tactic. The more pieces I threw at the NSA, the more pieces I risked compromising, revealing my hand to the Gamesmaster.

Instead, I deployed a mercenary and his handler in Sri Lanka, flying them to the U.S. to attempt to kidnap a likely NSA employee who might be in the Gamesmaster's employ. This they succeeded in doing, and held him for all of twenty-two minutes before a SWAT team broke in and took them down.

Three hours later, the mercenary, pushed full of what chemicals I knew not, confessed to having received his orders from a man in Colombo who matched my description—which indeed he had—and I waited with baited breath for what doom might come.

Very little doom came indeed. Colombo remained distressingly uninteresting for nearly four days until finally a journalist for Al Jazeera knocked on the door of my double, asked if he could have an interview and, told no, simply shrugged and walked away. A pawn, sent to test whether there was indeed a king hiding in the city. The Gamesmaster was not willing to risk bigger pieces on unlikely outcomes yet. She was moving carefully, feeling out the board; a slow opening game.

On my ninth day in Villa de Valverde, my landlady asked me if I wanted to join her and her husband for dinner. She was seventy-three and had the energy of a twenty-year-old; he was eighty-one and relied on the twice-monthly medical drop from Santa Cruz to supply the drugs and oxygen that he needed to stay alive. She cared for him constantly with unflagging cheerfulness, and it seemed as I sat at their uneven wooden table in their tiny kitchen smelling of fish, that her great energy had been drawn, vampire-like, from him so that as one waned the other waxed, though her waxing was all, all of it, in love for him as she grew to fill the void that his decline created.

She cooked with divine inspiration, fish and beans and wine, prawns bigger than my fist, sauce to lick from the cracked blue plates on which it was served, and as she cooked she talked constantly, a merry litany of stories and adventures from the tiny island in the middle of the sea.

Many tourists, she said, many indeed but not so much, not so many as Tenerife and people said that was a bad thing, a tragedy, a shame, but she preferred it, it made it better, and what tourists you did get were a better class, not the kind to just sit on the beach but the kind who cared where they went, what they saw, yes, better, so much better. And you, Mr. Vagar, what about you, you come here but you never seem to leave your room—is it not the sun, the climate, the people, the sea...?

Writing a book, I explained.

A book; how marvellous; what on?

Mathematics.

Mathematics! That sounds...very nice. What kind mathematics?

Decision theory. I used to study zero-sum problems, where the outcome of a decision by one agent led to an equal and direct loss of material in another. Now the times have changed—we look at asymetrical models of decision-making, stochastic outcomes, differential games and so on.

I see, she lied. And tell me, Mr. Vagar...what's it good for?

No malice in her question, nothing but genuine concern and interest. I opened my mouth to explain, to talk about outcomes and opportunities, models of human behaviour, and found my words had run dry.

The next evening after the table was cleared, she nudged her husband, subtle as an orca, and winked at me and said, "Do you play cards?"

I did.

She dealt three hands, an old game, a game of pairs and additions, and her husband took his cards in shaking hands and played each one slowly as if the little squares were almost too heavy to hold, as if frightened he would drop them, and he won—resoundingly, he won—though his breath wheezed in his throat and his eyes drooped as his wife wheeled him up to bed—and at the moment of victory I thought I saw a thing in his eyes that I had seen a thousand times before.

Not merely joy. Not merely satisfaction at a victory.

I saw in him, in his face like dried seaweed, *power.*

Power over the game.

Power over the world that was within the game.

Power over the players that he had defeated.

Power over this moment, this second of triumph.

Power over himself.

Our eyes met as he was turned away, and for the first time that evening, he smiled.

*

Two days later, lying on my belly on the single bed in my little room, a small, spotted, brown lizard edging ever closer to my right elbow, its curiosity aroused by my stillness, its tongue licking pinkly at the sizzling air, I saw my own face on an Interpol wanted list.

It had been a while coming—a big move, an obvious move, but more importantly, a move that demonstrated again the extent of her power.

I hired a boat and sailed south across a still, grey sea.

Chapter 9

Resources launched against Interpol; not an all-out assault, merely a little prodding around the edges.

Through an officer of the Bundespolizei, I requested more information. What was the crime of this unnamed criminal who had my features?

Theft, came the answer. Terrorism. Arson. (Did it matter?)

And what were the leads?

The criminal was probably in Europe. Links to cyber-terrorists. Links to paramilitary groups. Assumed dangerous.

And where had the request come from for his arrest?

Bulgaria, came the reply.

He's wanted primarily in Bulgaria.

That was unwelcome news. Did the Gamesmaster own a piece of the Bulgarian mafia as well as a shard of Interpol? That applied pressure from both the legal and illegal ends of the spectrum of professional body-hunters.

I rifled through my memories, lists of contacts, names, gathered down the centuries in expectation of this moment. My resources in Bulgaria were thin but I eventually settled on a senior civil servant who had bet his all—his life, body, soul—with the wild overconfidence of a man who was never going to win and who, when the umpires came to collect, had kissed my shoes and cried out for mercy, and who had received back from me his life and his body—but not his soul.

"I can't do it!" he hissed down the satellite phone. "I can't ask those sorts of questions!"

"You can," I replied calmly, feet dangling over the side of my boat, sun hot on my skin, salt in my mouth and on my tongue. "You will."

Three days later, I docked in the village of Palmarin on the Senegalese coast. The water was the colour of oceans on maps, a perfect pale blue where the eye skimmed over it, fading to clear as you looked down to the sandy bottom below. On the beach, three boys in baggy shorts watched me approach, prodding the sand with long sticks, huddled beneath the shade of a palm tree, and when at last their patience broke they ran all at once, like a river through a dam, to dance around me and holler, "Money? American? Money?" and hop and pull nervously at my sleeves until their mother, swaddled all in blue, tushed and tutted and chased them away and called them vile creatures and said their father, God rest him, would be ashamed.

They laughed at that and ran back to the shade of their tree to watch for the next stranger with the stern intensity of a lighthouse.

"You'll like it here!" exclaimed the woman who led me to the best supply store in town, owned, though she did say so herself, by her cousin who was the only honest trader I'd find in these parts. "We have sun, we have the sea, we have fresh fish and good drink—not like other places, not like Dakar or Mbour—there they only have noise and bad people."

Her cousin, for all that he wore mismatching flip-flops and grinned as if tetanus had locked the muscles in place, was an honest trader who sold everything at a price barely above what it was worth, and threw in four bottles of clean water when I was done with a cry of, "Take, take; you'll need it!"

At sunset I sat on a wicker chair by the sea, and drank palm wine and read a fourth-hand thriller which had sat on the counter of the store between the tins of dried fish and the stack of bicycle tyres, every size, and which quite possibly hadn't been for sale were it not that the enterprising owner would have sold everything he could, even his mismatched flip flops, if there was some profit in it.

Goddammit, exclaimed the text in my lap, *you tell those goddamn CIA punks to get their house in order!*

I laid my book aside and watched the sea. The stars began to grow in the sky. I tried staring into the darkest part of the darkness, but the more I looked, the more stars I could see there. The wind turned cold off the water, and I enjoyed its touch.

My phone rang and I found myself briefly annoyed by the sound.

I let it ring nine times, then answered.

A voice, speaking fast in Bulgarian: my civil servant.

"Damn you," he rasped. "Damn you, now they're after me, damn you to hell!"

"What have you learned?"

"That you don't fuck with the fucking mafia! That you don't fuck with the fucking mafia-run police! That you don't fuck with the minister of the interior or senior judges; that you don't fuck with this fucking stuff!"

"Tell me what you've learned."

"That you don't fuck with the SSLP! They've put a fucking hit out on you, straight from the top this comes, ten million euros to the first fucker to pick you off and you know, when I started asking...I think they put a hit on me too. I'm leaving. I'm fucking getting out of here before they get my wife and kids, fuck you, Silver, fuck you!"

He hung up on me before I could say anything more.

Twenty-two hours later, he was dead.

Chapter 10

An inspector in the Istanbul police ("win some, lose some") filled me in on SSLP.

"Security Solutions and Life Protection," he explained cheerfully down the phone. "Shit name for a bad insurance company. They're mafia through and through. Joined the market few years back: money laundering, protection rackets, drugs—the usual. Recruited a lot of its muscle from old rivals, but also did a neat number with the kids. Opened wrestling and boxing clubs across the country, survival courses, community meetings, that sort of shit. Tea and cake for the mums, one-oh-one on how to fuck people over. Nice, traditional Hitler Youth stuff—get them young and they stay loyal till they're old. That's the theory at least—first generation are hitting their thirties about now so I guess we'll see how good 'loyalty' is in a psycho!"

I pictured him, my hard-won piece, sitting with his feet up on his desk, a tulip glass of cool Turkish tea in his hand, rocking gently back in his chair, and in my fantasy he rocked now a little too hard and fell backwards, spilling both his tea and his casual attitude towards the people who'd put a ten-million-euro hit on my head, across the floor of his too-tidy office.

"Who runs it?"

"Georgi Daskalov, but he's untouchable."

"Where is he?"

"Not Bulgaria—shit, you think a guy like that would stick around in his own country?! Italy somewhere. Up by a big lake, you know the kind of thing. Hell, I'd like to live by a lake in Italy, but I guess some of us have to suffer for our sins."

A secretary in the *Servizio per le Informazioni e la Sicurezza Militare* ("whatever debts my husband owes, you forgive them; my skills are more useful to you than his") confirmed Daskalov's location.

"We all know who and what he is," she sighed. "But even if we could prove it, what good would it do? Bulgaria would request his deportation and he'd be free within a week, or he'd just bribe or shoot his way through judges until someone stupid enough came along to let him go. You don't get to touch men like Daskalov—the best you can hope for is damage limitation."

"What would happen if I did take him down?"

"Maybe the whole thing would collapse. Maybe things would get better. Maybe someone else would take his place, and it'd just carry on regardless."

"He's a powerful piece in my enemy's hand. Removing him might open up the board a little bit."

"He's a murderer, a human trafficker, a dealer in vice and drugs," she corrected. "All the rest is talk."

I set sail the following morning, heading north towards the Mediterranean.

Chapter 11

On my third day at sea, an email arrived in capital letters, marked "urgent." It came from the Swiss cyberwarfare experts I'd acquired over a game of Diplomacy (seventeen months of hard play and at the end, as it always seems to, the game came down to an artillery exchange over Grozny and an ignominious retreat for my opponent into Siberia, surrender finally agreed six hundred miles from the Pacific Ocean after I'd sent in tanks).

It read:

> At 22.33 GMT, your laptop was compromised.
> Destroy and evade.

The time was 23.08 GMT.

I threw my laptop overboard, made one phone call before throwing that into the water too, ripped out the transponder from my boat, shut down the radio, killed all running lights and made a sharp turn east towards land. From beneath a bench I pulled out three lifejackets and a box of emergency supplies, lashing them together with rope and throwing them, still tied to the ship, over the side into the water.

At 00.12 the first plane flew over, slow and low, its engine groaning like an overweight bee exhausted from the toils of life. It circled me once, twice, its lights popping in and out of thin cloud as it nailed my position, before it drifted upwards, out of earshot. At 00.32 two fighter planes took its place. I jumped overboard when I heard the jet engines, cutting the rope that connected my floating bundle of boxes and lifejackets to the ship with a knife and, clinging to this makeshift raft, kicked away from the boat. It seemed to take the fighters an inordinate amount of time to circle round for the kill. When the missiles struck, I was nearly two hundred yards away, but that was near enough for the heat to singe the back of my neck, for the force to slap me under, for the shockwave beneath the ocean—moving slower than the air—to then pick me up and spin me round, my tightly shut eyes burning against the half-glimpsed sight of burning fuel on the water, my mouth full of sea, my nose full of sea, my head full of foam. I clung to my raft and kept kicking away, and when the fighters circled back once, twice, three times, strafing what little remained of my boat, I pushed myself under my raft and held my breath until my eyes were going to burst from their sockets and my lungs were two shrivelled vacuums in my chest, and then I surfaced, and coughed and gasped and dived again, the busy world under the ocean illuminated by cobwebs of fiery light which drifted into the sea from the remnants of my boat until at last, their job done, the fighters turned away and the night was silent again.

I was in the water for eleven hours.

I didn't move, but let the ocean do what it would with me, carrying me with the broken remains of my boat. A little bubble of warm formed around my submerged legs and waist; my arms shivered and shook where they clung to my raft of lifejackets. Above, the ocean stars turned, beautiful, a sight just for me, just for my weary eyes, a universe that no one else could perceive. In a little while, I felt burning across my back and shoulders, and for a moment the salt water where it seeped into my wounds was agony, and I screamed into the silence, until the antiseptic touch of the water against my skin was in fact a blessing, and the cold was a blessing, and the heat was a blessing, and all things at once seemed to me a blessing, and I closed my eyes and thought how nice it was to be blessed and dozed a little, and woke dreaming of drowning and found my nose slipping beneath the water, and

I thrashed and gasped for breath, and wondered if I was going to die in this place, and if she would miss me when I was gone.

Probably not, I said, and then:

That's not what you're playing for, I replied.

What are you playing for? I asked.

Vengeance? Pride? Justice? Love?

I laughed at that.

You're so funny, I said. You're so funny I could die.

The sun rose quickly over the ocean, and there was no land beneath it as it climbed into the sky. How fast it went from a blessed relief to a torment, too bright, too pervasive, no shelter from its glare. Hell was an ocean, I realised. Hell was an endless sea. I wondered if there were sharks in this water and having wondered, imagined teeth tearing at my feet, my legs, my blood calling to them, no game yet invented which could tame Mother Nature.

"This is a check," I said. "You are a king and she has put you into check, nothing more."

"Nothing but the sea and the sharks," I replied.

"Where's your wisdom now?" I asked. "Where's your wit?"

"Keenness and quickness of perception," I intoned through broken lips. "Ingenuity. Humour, finding humour in the relationship between incongruous things. Wit: a person of exceptional intelligence."

"Tell it to the sharks," I replied. "Tell it to the seas."

When the boat came, I thought it was a product of my laughing, bewildered mind until they called my name from the prow and I remembered that I had summoned it, the last thing I'd done before throwing my treacherous mobile phone and laptop over the side.

They sent a diver into the water to help me onto the palette which they lowered over the side. Once on deck, they carried me, still in the orange litter, to their infirmary where an officer all in white, accent as tight as the little black hat on her head, asked me my name (which I could not remember), what day it was, if I knew what had happened.

Eventually, I remembered the name by which I had summoned this boat, and how I had won it (a game of Monopoly—I bought the utility companies; she bought the high-end hotels, and utility companies, it turned out, were the better investment as tourism fluctuated in southern Florida) and drank the water that I was given, and lay on my belly while the medic dressed the burns across my neck, shoulders and back, and asked how I had received them.

"Two fighter jets blew up my boat," I replied. "I think it must have happened then."

She tutted and sighed and said, drink more water, and gave me something else to drink besides which made the world— for a little while—seem more peaceful than it had been in the morning.

Chapter 12

The boat was a cutter with the British Royal Navy and it deposited me in Gibraltar some ten hours after it had picked me up in the sea. I had no passport to be checked at customs, nor no contacts or proof of identity.

I asked permission to phone my lawyer to see if he could get the relevant documents faxed over, and when they said yes, I dialled the piece in the admiralty who had so obligingly secured my rescue, and told him to get me freed, and that for this all debts were paid and his game was done.

He nearly sobbed with relief when I said as much, and thanked me, thanked me, thanked me, and got it done.

Alone, empty-handed, bandages on my back, I walked along the seafront of Gibraltar, a place that was neither one thing nor the other. The streetlights were pure English seaside, wrought black metal. British flags flew in the shops which sell obligatory sand buckets and bags of dried starfish; the Lord Nelson pub smelt of beer and chips, yet the Anglican cathedral had something of the Moorish about its curved arches and white walls, and the hotels that lined the seafront and chic marinas were pure Mediterranean slabs of functional tourism, square and turned into the sun. I walked until I found a tourist office; they stared at me, scalded skin, cracked lips, salt-washed hair, but politely directed me to the banks and buses.

Only one bank in Gibraltar carried any resources that I could use, and those were limited, planted some twenty years ago when I was passing through in expectation of this day. My signature on the account got me access to the bank manager; my fingerprint permitted me into the vault. My safe deposit box hadn't been updated for seven years—sloppy on my part, but I hadn't pictured myself shipwrecked in this part of the world, let alone so early in the game. The passports within were all out of date, save for a Swedish one which was two months from expiry. The five thousand U.S. dollars and five thousand euros within were still in currency, and the gun, I was relieved to find, hadn't rusted inside its padded box.

I bought myself a new laptop and three new phones, and took the ferry to Tanger-Med that evening.

Tanger-Med is a half-excuse for a port in a half-excuse for a place. Billboards and helpful public information posters declare that soon—very soon—this place will be the greatest cargo hub on the Mediterranean. Tired men in grubby uniforms sit around on empty public benches smoking thin cigarettes, the ash flicked onto the empty marble floors of the empty passenger terminal. By the great wharves where the cargo ships dock, cranes crawl back and forth, yellow lights flashing, and lorries wait to be loaded by the fluorescent-clad labourers, but the cruise ships do not like to stop here, and the men and women who crawl off the passenger ferry in the small hours of the night have the looks about them of lost tourists, or itinerant workers who know that this is merely a place that is a stop on the way to somewhere better.

I hired a car and drove through the dark tree-clad mountains and agro-giant fields to Tétouan, windows down, the cold night wind keeping me awake while the radio played boy-band pop and the raised voices of pundits who could not keep silent in the face of the other's foolishness.

I arrived in Tétouan just after dawn and slept in the back of my car until a policeman knocked on my window to see if I was dead. When it transpired that I wasn't, he shouted at me, telling me to get a hotel, to move on, move on already, and so I did

303

and found myself at last in a shady room at the back of an old, cracked building where the flies stayed on the ceiling and the old woman in a black veil who ruled over it all muttered through her nicotine-stained teeth, "Good, good, good…bad, bad, bad…good, good, good…" as her gaze inspected and judged all about her.

I slept.

I had planned on sleeping only a few hours, and woke thinking I had done precisely that until the old woman told me I had slept an entire day, dawn to dawn, and it was bad, bad, bad, good, good, good that I had done so.

"Sleep sleep wastes life!" she chided. "Doctor tells me I have slept for twenty-five years already, bad, bad, very bad. I love sleep. No one says stupid things; no one makes me cry when I'm sleeping, good, good!"

Head craned awkwardly to see the green-flecked bathroom mirror, I peeled the dressing off my back to survey the damage. Light burns still scar, and even if they do not, they still hurt. I smelt no infection, saw no pus, applied ointment and, contorting myself like a praying mantis, wrapped myself in fresh dressings and skipped the painkillers.

At last now—at last—I turned my laptop on.

Chapter 13

All things through the darknet, and carefully, so very careful. An email from a dummy account to another dummy account, which forwarded it to a lawyer in Dhaka who forwarded it to a company in Belarus who finally, at last, forwarded it to my cyber-experts in Switzerland.

They were, to my surprise, still standing.

We met on a message board where heroin dealers and credit card fraudsters conducted their trade.

For sale—x 5000 credit card details with full names, addresses and DOBs, proclaimed the ads that popped up around us. *Carefully collected over three years of hard work. No time wasters, please.*

How was I found? I asked my experts when they came online.

NSA, they replied, then: *it may not be safe for us to deal with your case any more. The NSA have been looking at our systems too.*

Advice? I asked.

Don't use the same computer twice, they said. And then, having thought about it a little while longer, they added, *And never contact us again.*

At that, they disconnected, and that was fine. They were not running away from the game—their utility was done, a pawn which had been passed by another stronger piece, and which fell now from the board.

Chapter 14

The NSA was a problem.

Twice the Gamesmaster had tasked it against me, and both times it had done sterling work. I had set a DDoS attack against it which had slowed it down, but to truly undermine its ability to get in my way, I needed to do something a little more distracting.

I wandered through my mental lists of pieces at my disposal and settled on a big gun.

I called a number in Washington DC and, when the phone was eventually answered, I asked to speak to the senator.

Moves on the board.

A U.S. senator comes into information that the NSA has illegally been spying on U.S. citizens on domestic soil, violating the privacy of good, ordinary Americans.

The NSA denies.

Civil rights groups stand up and say it's an outrage, a horror.

The NSA denies.

Newspapers ask for evidence of the claims. (Al Jazeera, I note with a sigh, runs a largely accurate article slamming the senator, and I add it to the list of assets under enemy control.)

The senator calls for an enquiry.

The White House says such an enquiry would be counter to the security interests of the nation. (Is the White House also compromised, I muse, or is this just politics?)

The senator begins to waver under this pressure.

But this is the U.S., where fact is second to volume, and just as I think that this line of attack is going to fail, the fringes of the Republican right, God bless them, God keep them, rise up to a ferocious man and woman and proclaim, how dare the NSA violate our civil liberties? What happened to the constitution? What happened to freedom? How dare big government intrude into our private lives, how dare they? We've read thrillers; we know what these people are like; we know because we are the only people left in this country with sense!

I watch all this from afar on NBS broadcasts and Fox News, and at the indignation of the right, the pundits rise again, righteousness in their voices, hunger in their eyes, and though my senator is shuffled to the back room and chided for having dared unleash such a shitstorm, your career over, your future over, never again, my son, the work is done.

I don't have the resources to destroy the NSA—or rather, I will not spare those resources yet—but I can make it much, much harder for them to catch me.

Finally. A blow against the Gamesmaster. The board opens, just a little, a tiny peek, a sense of the flow of the game.

Chapter 15

The Moroccan-Algerian border was closed, and had been for nearly twenty years. I rode a cargo ship from Nador to Almeria, and as my senatorial crisis in the U.S. unfolded, drove through southern Spain.

Fried eggs in Sorbas. A child saw my white hair, my young face, kept young by many games won, many lives destroyed. Her face crinkled in suspicion and doubt, and finally she walked up to me, folded her arms and said, "Are you a monster?"

"No," I replied.

Her face tightened to a crinkle around her nose as she considered this, before finally concluding, "I think you're a monster!" and, laughing, she ran away before I could eat her up.

Roadworks on the motorway between Puerto Lumbreras and Lorca. When a lorry's engine burst in the heat in a one-lane corridor of diverted vehicles, the traffic stopped and we all got out of our cars to fan ourselves in the smiting summer heat, children running from car to car asking if anyone had water and playing hide-and-seek behind the ticking hot bonnets.

"It's always like this," sighed the driver of the car behind mine. "People don't dare say it, but I will—corruption. Corruption, corruption, corruption. In India, they protest against it; they have rallies, political prisoners against it; but here? Here we blind ourselves, we say, 'No, it can't possibly happen here, not to us, not in the EU!' but I say, 'Hey, wake up, wake up already—can't you see that's exactly why we do have it, why it's everywhere, because we're so smug and so self-satisfied that we don't even bother to open our eyes to see it!' Money rules this country, not democracy, not the people. We're just little pieces moved around by big men, statistics and numbers ruled by capitalism and consumerism. You think you're free? You're just a wallet that spends, earns and dies— that's the sum of your life. It's disgusting, is what it is."

"Sometimes roads break," I pointed out.

"Sometimes roads are broken," he retorted. "Sometimes people break things. Sometimes countries are broken. Sometimes societies are broken. Sometimes people are broken so badly, they don't even notice that's what they are."

At Tarragona I stayed in a hotel next to a church, and woke with a start at 4 a.m. thinking the world was over, the game was over and I was done, only to open the shutters of my window and look down to see three monks, all in black, unlocking the gates of the church to go in and pray. I went back to bed, and did not sleep, and left at 7 a.m., a spread of cold meats and hard-boiled egg on my dashboard, the taste of oranges in my mouth.

The customs booths were gone at Le Perthus, torn down by order of the EU, but the French flag still flew and policemen still glowered from stations by the roadway. I wound through the Pyrenees behind a slow but steady line of crawling traffic, turning off before Le Boulou to stretch my legs, eat some food, watch the mountains. Two vultures turned slowly overhead, riding the thermals higher into the sky. Thin white clouds formed and dissolved on the mountain tops, caught as if by a needle in the wind before being blown away into the empty blue sky. Sheer cliffs dropped down into river gorges, grey stone, black buzzards, dark trees clinging to every angle and edge.

I sat and ate my lunch on an outcrop above a ruined monastery, where once hermits had fled from the world, and I was alone and could have stayed here, I thought, for ever.

But the sun grew hot, and the wind was cold, and my meal was done, so I drove on.

Chapter 16

Preparations made as I crawled through southern France.

I abandoned my car in Perpignan, and on the train to Montpellier I sat, laptop on my lap, phone tucked to my ear, and organised a military assault against Georgi Daskalov, head of a criminal gang which had put a ten-million-euro hit on my head, a piece that had been played by the Gamesmaster.

I had no pieces in the Italian military, but a few in the Carabiniere.

"I can seal the roads for you, keep eyes away," said my most powerful, "but no way, no fucking way, not a chance can I take down Daskalov for you."

"That's fine," I replied. "You're the wrong piece for the job anyway."

In the end, I settled on an ex-special forces team run out of Tampa, which touched down in Milan three hours before my train arrived.

As we drove north towards Lake Como and the jagged Alps, I turned on my laptop to discover that 178 million dollars had been wiped from my assets. The move had also taken 2 per cent off the value of the New York Stock Exchange, and looked to be a general attack against over thirty companies that I *could* have been affiliated with, and which in fact had crippled only seven that were mine.

How had she found them? I had played plenty of pieces which

might require paying, but hadn't even begun to dent my carefully cultivated funds.

Perhaps she hadn't found them at all—perhaps it was guesswork. But no—the Gamesmaster didn't strike out without purpose, she knew that somewhere within the companies she was now assaulting lay my assets. To defend or not to defend?

I considered the state of my finances and let it go. In chess, you must learn to read which attacks matter and which are merely flourishes before the main event. 178 million wasn't so much in the grand scheme of things and, if nothing else, I could now mark up the U.S. Federal Reserve and Treasury Department as potential lines of investigation, should it come to it.

We drove on, into the mountains.

Chapter 17

Two kinds of rich lived in Lake Como. Old rich that had fallen in love with the water and the mountains, with the long paths by sandy shores, the yachts beneath clear blue skies, the flowers that bloomed in every garden outside every mansion—a rich that had forgotten that it *was* rich, as long as it had owned and enjoyed the smell of magnolia, the sound of water by its gate.

The second rich lived behind closed gates and high walls, on balconies above the eyeline of the gawping tourists. Like a poor man freed at last from a prison sentence, great leaps of imagination had been dedicated to the spending of money, and even greater feats of self-justification to explain that no, the water really did taste better when it emerged from gold-plated taps and yes, the quality of conversation was improved by at least one party holding a phone clad in diamonds while they spoke.

Or perhaps not. Perhaps sometimes—as in the case of Georgi Daskalov—the only reason needed for why every one of the seven cars he owned in the garage beneath his three-storey palace was upholstered in tiger, leopard, lion and bear skin was because he could. Because others wanted it, and he had it, and there an end.

We broke in shortly after 3 a.m. The security system he'd installed was valued at six million dollars, but the men who manned it had fallen victim to the twin Swarovski Alize vodka bottles they'd received in exchange for favours unnamed, each bottle clad in pink diamonds fit for a fairy princess, each cup thrown back with the gusto of champion wrestlers newly returned from throttling giants with their thumbs.

The security alarm went off as we slipped in across the upstairs patio, a silent alert at police headquarters (who did not respond) as well as the security office (which responded groggily) but by the time the first sober man had pulled his Uzi from the wall, three of his colleagues were dead, and Daskalov was sat in his underpants on the end of his eighty-thousand-dollar bed, hand-cuffed and sulky. I let my men deal with the rest of the house as I sat next to him, balaclava over my face, pistol in hand, silk shifting beneath me, the smell of drink heavy in the room.

His underpants, being the only thing he now wore, were Lycra. I looked into his face and briefly wondered if we hadn't caught a body double, a not-quite-Daskalov, or perhaps he merely liked the feel of synthetic fabrics against his nether regions and lamented to his friends that all this silk and gold, all this cotton and organic food, it wasn't to his taste at all—but one did have to keep up appearances, didn't one?

Then he said, not lifting his eyes from his study of the floor, "You're fucking dead."

"Mr. Duskalov," I replied in his language, "you recently put a hit out on a man to the sum of ten million euros. Last I heard, going price for such assassinations was fifty thousand. What's so special about this target?"

"You hear me?" he asked louder. "You're dead. Your wife is dead. Your kids are dead. Maybe you're lucky—maybe you die first so you don't watch, but I swear to you, they die, all of them, all dead."

"I have no wife. I have no children, no family, no friends and no name. Do you know who I am, Mr. Duskalov?"

For the first time he looked at me, and he did.

"You will lose," he whispered. "You will lose."

I radioed the commander of my little troop. "Tear the place apart," I said, and it was done.

Chapter 18

Data salvaged from a mobster's home.

Contacts, emails, photos, the names of friends, family, loved ones. Duskalov thought he was clever, thought he kept his business secure, but everyone makes mistakes, and he had made plenty.

We were in and out of his home in less than fifteen minutes. Twenty minutes after we departed, I watched the place where the mansion stood turn to a pyre of smoke and flame, hit by who-knew-what ordinance fired by who-knew-whom. If the Gamesmaster had hoped I was dead before, now she knew I was not, and her blowing up the place where I might be seemed more like a fit of pique than a sound tactical move.

Or perhaps not. Perhaps she was sending a message.

I have all the missiles in the world, she said, her words whispered in the remnants of velvet slippers and ancient masterpieces fluttering to the ground. How long do you think you can keep this up?

A series of quick moves.

Numbers traced, bank accounts accessed, payments followed. I deployed a firm of German forensic bank accountants and two police forces, and we found her accounts, the accounts through which she'd paid Duskalov the upfront to put out a contract for my head, five minutes and twenty seconds after she drained them completely.

We salvaged fifty-two of her most recent transactions—not

a one of them for less than a million dollars—before the virus she'd implanted in the system wiped out all trace of it, and the servers of half the banks in Switzerland.

The next morning, I drank hot coffee and ate cold bread, and watched the Swiss Head of the Federal Department of Finance gabble to the journalists that it was just a blip, nothing more, normal business would resume within a few hours, do not be alarmed.

By the end of the day, we had traced forty-eight of the fifty-two transactions on the Gamesmaster's account, and I turned two investment banks and three financial authorities loose on them, capturing eleven of the companies that the Gamesmaster had routed her finance through, and shutting down a further twelve.

At midnight, the Swiss banks announced they would need another day to get their systems up and running, and the finance minister resigns the following morning, though in practice she has done nothing wrong. By the time the dust settled, the Swiss economy had lost 1.3 billion francs and I had seized a mere seventy-three million dollars' worth of the Gamesmaster's assets. In the days that followed, I rounded it up to a neat ninety million, pushed a mayor out of office in São Paulo, destroyed two companies in Japan and pulled the plug on a computer laboratory in Mumbai, but it was merely a scratch against the surface, a gentle clawing at the Gamesmaster's skin, and ultimately insignificant. Have I spent too many pieces in doing it?

Perhaps not. Neither she nor I were pulling out the big pieces yet, but we probed at each other's defences to see what might give way.

Chapter 19

Places and moves.

In Istanbul, I drank salty ayran and heard the call to prayers and rode the ferry to the Black Sea, watched the translucent jellyfish pulse and wriggle in the grubby waters beneath the prow. Not so long ago the waters had been clear, the fish fat and juicy; pollution had changed the ecology of this place. Once I'd played backgammon with a sultan on the Golden Horn, and when he'd lost he slapped me on the shoulder and said, "Sometimes the dice just don't fall the way you want them to, eh?" and we'd had fresh fish by the sea and he'd told me that his dream was to capture Vienna, but even if the Roman Empire fell, there'd still be enemies, unless the world was in his hand and all people were one.

That had been in the early days, only a few centuries after my loss. Then I had played with the fire of a man scorned and cursed, and sweated and raged over every game, and lost a fair few to my own enthusiasm until habit and the cold turning of the years had diminished all feeling, all fury, all hope into no more and no less than the motion of pieces across the board.

As I settled into the cargo hold of a ship carrying tin towards Batumi, a car bomb detonated in Cheltenham, killing three GCHQ staff and seven strangers. Of the three, only one had been my piece, but I imagined the killers hadn't been able to narrow it down so precisely and thus settled on eliminating the most likely suspects. My pieces were falling, and I was no closer to bringing the Gamesmaster down.

*

In a park in Vologorad, where stood a monument to the children who had died in war and who now played for ever in mutual delight, I launched a tentative assault against the sometime colonel, now general of the PLA who had replaced a deposed piece of mine in Beijing. A few careful enquiries revealed that yes, he had sometimes been seen to enjoy a game and yes, his fortunes had seemed to decline and then soar again, indicative, perhaps, of an outside party helping him through a difficult time. I circled round him slowly, slowly, a little poke at his finances here, a gentle exploration of his family life there, before finally setting a careful but thorough agent (yet not so thorough that he had not lost when we played mah-jong) in the Ministry of State Security against the general and his affairs.

Contacts unfolded, information blooming like a flower. I let it all come to me as I slipped through southern Russia, riding an ancient rusted bus and clattering, wheezing train along the banks of the Volga until my agent whispered that the newly formed general suspected something, and if I was going to strike, the time was now.

Go forth, I replied. Take him down.

In the operation that followed, the general, two colonels, a major, three senior politicians and their aides and, to my delight, a high-ranking delegate of the Communist Party who had been tipped for senior office, all tumbled, all fell, and were sent away either to prison or vanished into the unknown realms of re-education. How many had been in the Gamesmaster's hand, I couldn't say, but China certainly seemed a more hospitable place at their fall.

In a wooden shack that served as a garage, in the middle of a forest of dark pine and lazy flies—fat things that sat like fluff in your hair and bumbled through the air like wind-blown feathers—I played dominos with Leonid and Oleg. A wood-stove burned in the corner of the room, and you could buy for a small consideration tins of salty fish, tins of beans, rice cakes, black bread, tins of fermented vegetables and, from a rack proudly displayed behind the counter, a shotgun, a fireman's axe and a genuine—if you believed their oaths—Cossack's sword which had been wielded in the greatest battles of the Crimea.

"Russians are getting soft," complained Oleg as pieces spread across the table, a mathematical sprawl of battles won and skirmishes lost. "They've been blinded by foreign ideas. Everyone says, 'liberty', 'freedom', 'tolerance' but it is not 'freedom' if you're being oppressed by people you don't agree with, by capitalists and Jews. And 'tolerance'. You want me to tolerate homosexuals? Why? They don't respect me, they don't respect my values, and my values say that all homosexuals are fucking child-molesting pigs, that they're offensive in the eyes of God, and actively—yes, *actively*—want to destroy this blessed society I live in. You want me to tolerate them? They don't tolerate me! They call me 'backward' and 'redneck' and other things and I say yes, yes! If 'backward' means I honour the traditions of my fathers, if 'redneck' means I love the earth and this land and would shed my blood for it, then I am all of this, and your 'freedom' is just a prison to put men like me in, but worse— worse! You, with your words and your talking, you want me to imprison myself. The only advantage we have is that they, those Jews and those faggots, they are too cowardly to take up arms. We aren't. We believe in something more than they do. That's why we'll always win."

I listened to his words, and watched him lay a bad piece on the table, and saw a way to win the game, and considered my hand and, very slowly, and very carefully, lost.

In the evening, Oleg slapped me on the back and said, "You're all right, for a stranger," and invited me to join him in the hot cabin in the woods, where burning rocks were carefully lowered into sizzling steam, and the air seared our lungs, and we lay naked on wooden planks and beat each other with birch branches, skin gleaming, oil and moisture and sweat, and where Oleg slapped his naked thighs and proclaimed, "This is what men do!"

When I left the next morning, hitching a ride on the back of

318

a truck busy with squawking chickens, Leonid took me to one side.

"Oleg's a good man," he whispered, "but he's never left this place. On this road, in this forest, he is a king. He's frightened of what he'll be if he goes somewhere else."

"What about you?" I asked. "Aren't you afraid?"

He shrugged. "I went as far as Kazan once, and stayed in the house of a Jew. He seemed all right. He liked to watch the TV too loud, but always turned it down when his wife came home. One day, I think, the world will be full of people; that is all."

I thanked him for his hospitality, climbed up between a pallet of chickens and waved goodbye as the truck drove on. Oleg and Leonid stood side by side, waving back until we were out of sight.

Chapter 20

Beneath the white arches and faux-chandeliers of Novosibirsk Trans-Siberian Railway station, I drank terrible coffee from a cardboard cup, knees cramped in a chair too low to sit in, and listened to the talk of two women waiting for their train.

He said that?

He said that.

Barbarian.

He thought it was funny.

Does he think it's funny?

He thinks it's funny.

It's not funny.

No.

Guys like that think you're a prude when you say no. You've led them on by looking like a woman, by being who you are, by being there, by being at all, they blame the women, because women are strong and men are weak and so if you say no...

...it's your fault.

It's your fault.

Or you're saying "no" to be a tease.

Because you want to...

...though you don't...

...in their minds...

...in their minds everyone wants to...

With them.

Because all of this, all of it, it's always about them, isn't it? You have no freedom.

Because you're a woman. Hard-wired to look at a man and want him, hard-wired to be happy when they...so that's it. That's all we are. That's where the logic leads. And me, I've looked at men and I've thought...but I've heard their voices, I've seen them laugh and smile, I've assumed they will say no because they can, because they will, because that's life, but he...

Exactly. He doesn't see you, just himself reflected.

It's not funny.

No. It never was.

The trains in the station ran on Moscow time, three hours behind the local zone. A woman behind the ticket counter, her face collapsed like a muddy cliff, fossilised features revealed beneath the falling loam of her skin, grudgingly sold me a ticket to Krasnoyarsk. "Twelve hours," she snarled. "No food on train."

"That's fine."

Her lips curled downwards at this, as if to say that whatever my naïve assumptions now about my ability to endure twelve hours on the train, time would prove them wrong.

In the station toilet, a woman handed out grey toilet paper one sheet at a time, studying intently the faces of those who purchased this proffered good, wondering perhaps what manner of waste product we might produce and whether, as the consequence of a bad meal perhaps, or a hard night of drinking, we might come back for more paper in a moment, desperate and vulnerable, and if a tip would be on offer should she oblige.

I sat alone on the Eastbound 002M from Moscow and willed my eyes to shut.

They closed, they opened again. A sound, a terror, an unnamed fear.

Sleep, I said, for God's sake, sleep.

You sleep, I replied. You leave yourself vulnerable and exposed, alone in the night with strangers. You sleep, if you're so tired.

I laughed at that, and wondered when my own company had become so unpleasant to me.

A long time ago, I whispered. I started to hate you the day you started playing for the sake of the game, rather than the cause.

It's not true, I replied. It's not true.

It's not true.

The train rattled on through the Siberian night.

Chapter 21

At Ulan-Ude, I sat on my bag in the car park outside the station and waited for my Mongolian visa to clear. An official in a dark uniform with shiny cufflinks inspected my passport, examined my face, examined my passport again, turning it this way and that as if some embedded secret might be found in reading the writing right to left, bottom to top as well as through more conventional means, before laying it aside and saying, "How did you get to Russia?"

"Through Georgia."

"I didn't think that was possible at the moment."

"It is if you're not Russian or Georgian."

"What is the purpose of your trip?"

"I'm a teacher."

"What do you teach?"

"History."

"Why are you coming to Mongolia?"

"For the history."

"What history?"

"All of it."

"What bit of history are you interested in?"

I sighed, and considered any number of smart answers that would have slowed my journey before saying the two words that he needed to be said. "Genghis Khan," I sighed. "I'm interested in Genghis Khan."

The customs man perked up considerably at this. "You must visit Ulan Bator!" he exclaimed. "And take the bus to Tsonjin

Boldog. They have a statue of the Khan there that is a hundred metres tall!"

I thanked him courteously as he returned my documents, and did indeed visit Tsonjin Boldog. The statue, a monstrosity all in metal, wasn't a hundred metres, but was at the top of a hill in the middle of nowhere, which may have helped create an impression. The stern face of the Khan glared out from the back of his rugged, long-tailed pony, a golden whip encased in his fat-fingered hand, the whole edifice erected on a strangely European-looking visitor centre which proclaimed proudly that Mongolia was finally ridding itself of the shackles of oppression to become proud in its own identity, and the history of its Khans.

I caught the onward train that evening, heading south across open grasslands beneath an endless sky towards Beijing.

Two hours before we were scheduled to cross the Sino-Mongolian border, my phone rang.

The caller was a member of the Australian Secret Intelligence Service whose fealty I'd won in a game of Old Maid, and who, as the last pathogenic vector was eliminated from the field between us, threw her hand in with a shrug and a merry cry of, "Shucks, I guess this is a game-changer, yeah?"

"I'm a good player," I replied. "I never sacrifice a piece unless I have to."

Now she was on the phone and there was a satellite delay between us, but she kept to the point. "You in Mongolia?"

"What makes you think I am?" I asked carefully.

"Got a hit on you crossing the Russian-Mongolian border. Some bright spark thought you looked a little suspect, did some digging, now half the intelligence services of the world have got their guys descending on you, not to mention a whole bunch of folks I've never even heard of. Might not be you, might be a hiccup, but I figured if it was you, you should know that you're probably fucked."

"Thanks for the warning—I'll call back."

I hung up, threw my phones and my laptop out of the window

of the still-moving train, gathered my bag and walked for three carriages before bumping into a Chinese tourist and his wife heading the other way, whereupon I stole his phone.

Eight minutes later, the train slowed for a long curve towards an ancient bridge, and as it dropped to near running speed, I creaked open a door between two interconnecting carriages, threw my bag onto the tracks and jumped out after it, rolling, knees to chest, as I fell.

Chapter 22

Mongolia is one of the most sparsely populated countries on Earth. Her beauty changes with the eye of the beholder. To a man freshly flung from a still-moving train, it is flat, vast, terrifying, a desert of grass where you might roam for ever, still bleeding, still stinging, and see barely another soul. To a tired wanderer, it is a blessed place, rolling hills and dry shrub where you might start a fire, a warning of mountains in the distance, but an infinite space between you and them. To a thirsty man, it is a damned place, bare and infertile, until you find a little stream running down from a stony hill, when Mongolia becomes again the most beautiful place on the surface of the earth, a hallowed sanctuary from the intrusion of brutal men, an uninhabited wilderness built only for pilgrims and the sky.

I saw in Mongolia all these things, but mostly I saw danger. The irritating customs official on the Mongolian border had known someone, or said something to someone, which now put me in danger, and so I walked from the railway line only far enough to find a little cover, and on my purloined telephone called the only suitable piece I had in play within the Mongolian steppe.

Batukhan, when he answered, bellowed, "Who's this? What do you want?"

"It's Silver. I want you to make a move for me."

He fell very quiet then, and breathed a long while before he said at last, "What do you need?"

"A pickup, and a lift across the Chinese border."

"I'm very busy right now, very busy..."

"Your soul is mine," I replied. "I won it and gave you your freedom where other men would have sucked you dry. Now I claim my debt."

Silence again. Then an overdramatic groan, a flustered sound to cover the terror he would not permit himself to feel. "Tell me where you are."

"I'd say about a hundred miles north of Erenhot."

"That's eleven hours' drive from here!"

"Then I suggest you get going."

He drove; I walked.

I walked with my stolen mobile phone turned off until it would be needed. I had crunched something in my ankle and, while it wasn't unbearable, the discomfort slowed my pace. I could see no trees for miles save for a single scrubby thing of white bark and no leaves which hung in the far distance like a signpost to a hidden cemetery. I walked through a landscape of no roads, no fields, no farms, no people, only sky, until I came at last to a dirt track, no wider than the width of my left foot, near-overgrown save that the odd unnamed animal (my mind leapt to predators and creatures of sharp temperament) had kept it clear. Where there were animal tracks, there was some thin hope of water, so I followed it to a downward curve in the landscape I hadn't observed coming, and then down a little more to a soft gully where a stream flowed and where, set to one side of the water, stood a low grey wall, half tumbled to obscurity, the land risen to meet its stones so now a man could climb over it in an easy step. Within, a few more broken walls, places where once words and names had been scratched into stone, gone, only an echo in the dust. I wandered through it as the sun began to set, until my eye caught a glimmer of metal beneath the earth. Kneeling down, I brushed away a little dirt to see the corner of a bell of bleached brass, ancient characters still visible on it, cradled by what at first seemed to be a mound of clay, but which, when I pushed a little deeper, I found to be a human arm, dry-grass bone shrouded in faded cloth, and following the line of this stick which still embraced the bell, I saw that the mound I had took for soil was in fact a skull, shrouded also in fabric, a second arm pulled across its face as if the unknown stranger in this place had pulled the cloth across his eyes to shield himself and his precious possession from a storm, and died just so, too weary to live longer.

I left the corpse and the bell, and sat by the stream instead, thumbing my mobile phone back on as the sun set so that Batukhan could find me in the dark.

Chapter 23

Batukhan, five foot two, smuggler, gambler, petty crook, dealer in used cars and bad horses, would-be player who lost on his very first game, ("I don't know how I lost—perhaps it wasn't me losing; perhaps it was just you who won?") and whose life I acquired and spared, drove a monster of a truck with the casual ease of a teenager on a bicycle. One hand on the steering wheel, another gesturing in the air, a bad Chinese cigarette hanging out of his mouth, all windows down and the speed gauge hitting sixty miles an hour despite the total lack of roads as we bounced across the midnight steppe, he exclaimed:

"You're in real trouble! Real trouble, Silver, like trouble I haven't seen before, and I've seen trouble!"

"What kind of trouble?"

"The Chinese closed the border crossing three hours ago— no trains, no cars, no planes, no nothing! Then two hours ago, the Russians closed their borders too! The government is panic; everyone says we're about to be invaded, the PLA sent helicopters into Mongolian airspace, denied it of course but we know what we saw—every pony-riding nomad's on Sina Weibo these days anyway, posting pictures of special forces guys, armour, guns, the whole works, getting on the train and threatening to shoot anyone who looked even slightly Western, slightly like you! They stopped *Dae Jang Geum* to show a picture of your face—I nearly died! My mother was on the phone to me: 'They've interrupted *Dae Jang Geum*,' she was screaming, I tell you, screaming, 'They've interrupted it, just when we were going to find out if it was exile or death—what am I supposed to do?' 'Mother,' I said, 'they'll resume broadcasting in a second, just you wait,'—my mother, you see, my mother—but I love her, of course I do—your *face* on TV! You're famous, you are."

"I could do with anonymity."

"Is this a game?" he asked abruptly as we bounced our way across a surge of stones. "Are you playing a game?"

"Yes. It's a game—*the* game, in fact. She's putting me in check again, removing options, forcing me to…" I hesitated. He was too frightened to hear the words left unspoken. What pieces could I sacrifice to protect myself? Was Batukhan more useful to me dead or alive?

"Well, it's a disaster! My mother, my mother screaming—the government's mobilising the army, do you know that? Not to catch you—at least, probably not to catch you—but because the PLA is massing on the south and the Russians are massing in the north and the border's been closed and the mining companies are asking what's going on and no one seems to know but it's all about you, your game ruining my mother's calm. And when she's angry, I'm angry, and I have to take my anger out on someone, so if you've got someone you're angry at, you should call them, right now!"

He slapped the steering wheel for emphasis, then clung on tight as a sudden, unseen lurch in the landscape bounced us in our seats. The motion seemed to knock the fury from his lungs, and for a while we rattled on in silence, our headlights tearing through the gathered dark like gunshots through silence.

"Can you get me across the border?" I asked at last.

"Sure—sure I can. I'm me, this is my country, these are my hills, I can do anything." Then, as a sullen afterthought he added, "I'm a player in these parts, I am. I'm a proper player."

The words, no sooner spoken, fell dull into the night.

We drove on in silence.

His plan for getting me across the border was a travelling family who, as the eldest woman shuffled me into her yurt, proclaimed

330

through her toothless gums that they were of the Baatuds, an ancient and noble people who had been destroyed by other worthless tribes down the centuries until only a few now, only a few, carried their sacred songs and stories, and would I like coffee?

Batukhan babbled at high speed outside with the woman's husband, a dialect I didn't know, and when it seemed that an agreement might never be reached, the old woman rose up and hollered at them both in the same language and they hung their heads, and that seemed to settle the debate.

"They'll get you into China," said Batukhan as the woman padded round me and pushed me onto what I suspected was her finest rug. "Any problem, you don't call me, okay?"

And with that, he was gone.

Impressions of a family travelling through Mongolia.

There were fifteen of them. Grandpa Baatud (nominally in charge), Grandma Baatud (mistress of all she surveyed), two sons and their wives, a daughter and her husband and seven progeny. The eldest of this brood was a boy of fourteen, his face scaled red by the wind, who rode a brown and white pony and glared with a fire that his father lacked, daring anyone to deny his right as eldest, strongest, smartest—a little man in a tiny world. The youngest was a four-year-old who stared at me with astonished eyes and, over the course of the five days I spent with them, only once dared touch me, and having done so clung on, as if unbelieving that I might not dissolve before her. I let her cling; the strength of her arms around my leg reminded me of...something. Something distant which had faded. Something that might have been like trust, but more. Something more, which had vanished with my name.

They rode a mixture of ponies and sour-faced camels. They travelled with two yurts, which could be raised and lowered in a matter of hours, the fine-boned internal structure whisked away and the thick skins that covered it unfurled almost too fast to follow motion; yet the ropes that bound these goods to their animals' flanks were bright blue, nylon-woven, and as she trotted along, one of the middle daughters, an eleven-year-old who looked at no one, finding no one interesting, kept checking text messages on a mobile phone which was recharged from a solar battery the size of a small frying pan. This heavy object seemed indulgent for just one teenager to use for her social needs as we travelled through this empty land, but lo, when we stopped for food on the second day, out it came and her brothers and sisters leapt to charge their devices while Grandma looked on and said it was the school holidays, and the children did miss their friends when away.

I said nothing, swaddled in a loaned jacket, hat pulled low against the glare of the sun, the grumbling camel beneath my folded legs burping toxic gases in sulky criticism of my presence on its hump.

We ate dishes enriched by camel butter, and drank hot cups of camel milk. The husbands and sons sang songs at night, tales of ancient battles and dead witches, whose contents I barely understood, while their children sat around to listen, the youngest agape, the eldest silent in the face of unappreciated repetition.

Once, a military fighter plane flew over, and during the three hours that followed, I heard engines higher in the clouds. One of the sons declared he knew it to be Chinese by the sound, having served in the Mongolian army, whereupon the second son laughed and said his brother couldn't tell the difference between a vulture and an eagle, let alone a Chinese or a Russian jet, and he was to stop boasting about his time in the army, given he'd only served for three months before being dismissed as unfit for duty. Then the eldest son flushed red and said at least he'd served, at least he'd travelled, and an argument broke out between them, silenced at last by Grandma who proclaimed that they were giving her a headache and didn't they know better than to put her into one of her moods?

It seemed they did, and they fell silent.

Grass dried, thinned, failed.

We swathed ourselves in bright fabric dulled by sunlight, wrapping it around our faces, our fingers, our clothes, barrier against the dust and the sun. My eyes burned, skin flaking from the lids. My face, even shielded, began to crunch to the lizard-like redness of my companions. I craved water, but drank only when they did, obeying their rules, knowing their rules had been formed to survive. The daughter stopped texting after a while; the dust took the inclination from her. I wondered what she might have said? *DESERT SUCKS SO BORED ATM. CAN'T WAIT TO GO BACK TO SCHOOL* <m>L</m>

I laughed out loud thinking about it, and the convoy stared at me and I laughed no more.

On the fifth night, as the fire blazed in the centre of the camp, and the men sat round boasting of impossible deeds while camels churned and ponies slumbered, I saw shapes move on the edge of the dark and, fearing the worst, made to run. Then the shapes resolved into the form of the women and their daughters, moving against the edge of the starlight, and creeping further, I saw hands sweeping across the turning skies, and heard soft voices whispering secrets, and strained my ears to catch some few words of the truths being told there.

By this star you may find north, whispered a mother, and by that you may know how far you are from dawn in winter. When you head south, you will see this constellation grow brighter, and may count the hours by the turning of this light as it journeys through the heavens. Remember these lessons, they whispered, for one day you may find yourself lost and alone in this land, far from friends, and only the earth beneath your feet, the water of the rivers and the rains of the skies, the journey of the sun, the shriek of the eagle as it returns to its nest and the turning of the stars will guide you. Believe in these, believe in yourself, and you will always find your way home.

The next morning, without any ado, as we travelled in silence across a plain of yellow dirt, Grandpa Baatud half turned in his saddle to look back at me and said, "This is China."

"Is it?" I looked for sign of life, a change in the land, an appearance of people, but the landscape was as empty as it had been, the sky as wide.

"Oh yes," he replied merrily. "We've been in China for a while now. You can tell by the smell."

I sniffed the air and smelt nothing new.

Two days later, we came to a village in the middle of yellow sand and white rocks whose name translated as something akin to "The Beginning of the Sun Near the Death Tree", and whose inhabitants, all two hundred and twenty-nine of them, had the same sun-blasted, sand-scraped, wind-scrubbed features as my guides. I looked for signs of a police station and saw none. I looked for a military presence and saw none. I wrapped myself in my scarf, buried my face in my hat and asked in Mandarin if there was anywhere I could stay. Eventually, the mayor of the town, a man who had more than a little of the Mongol in him, put me up on his sofa, which was in his bedroom, which was his house, and refused any payment for his kindness.

Alone, in a nowhere place, in a nowhere land.

Grassland had yielded to dust. Desert is not merely a place of dunes but of dryness, of solid packed earth and dust, of stones and rocks and flatness that will not be dug, sky that does not forgive. I asked the mayor why there was a town here.

"There was copper," he said sadly, "but that was a long time ago."

So it had been; yet it was no more. I did not ask further.

The nearest town was four hours' drive away.

I caught a lift on the back of a truck loaded with rubble.

"It's all we sell," explained the driver. "People seem to find a use for it. Why are you here?"

"Just travelling."

"No one travels here," he replied. "Here is death."

"Everyone travels to death sooner or later," I replied with a smile. "In one way or another."

He stared at me in surprise, then turned away and looked for a brief moment like the loneliest, saddest man in the world.

*

The next town had a population of nine hundred and thirty-three, and a market on Thursdays, and the last gasping remnants of a mine nearby. It even had a guest house with four rooms and a visitor balcony. I sat on a wobbly plastic chair on the balcony watching the dust rise from the mine nearby, smelt chemicals on the air, heard the grinding of great machines tearing through the earth.

It had been over a week since the Gamesmaster plastered my face on Mongolian TV. Will she have the power to plaster it on China's networks too?

I watched TV on a tiny black and white set in my little, roach-crawling room, and saw no evidence of this. One computer in the town had an internet connection, and after a great deal of bartering with the man who owned it (something middling in the mining corporation) I secured twenty minutes on it, watching the system crawl into reluctant life.

My face, it turned out, was not on the Chinese evening news, but the Interpol search warrant had somehow evolved into a thing that had both the Russian and Chinese police forces excited at the idea of finding me. The FBI, I was relieved to see, had yet to join in with this mania—clearly my control of that institution still exceeded the Gamesmaster's.

Twenty minutes on a computer was not enough to wreck any real havoc against this exasperating move, so I deleted my internet history, shut down and moved on.

There was a bus to the next nearest town, population fifteen thousand. As we drove through the desolate landscape, I looked out of the window to see machines bigger than swimming pools crunching through solid rock, great axels like tearing teeth rending the earth into shreds, men walking along gantries within these creatures' bellies, dust flying, flying all around, turning the windows of the cramped bus grey.

Ten miles outside town, the bus stopped at a road marking in the middle of nowhere, a place with no name, and a man got on. I looked at him and he looked at me, and I thought I recognised in him a thing that I did not like and looked around at my fellow passengers to see if anyone else had that instinct, and at least three or four had turned away.

On our arrival in the swollen red dusk, at a bus station that smelt of urine and rotting eggs, I got off, and the man who'd boarded ten miles ago got off with me, walked up behind me, drew a gun from the holster underneath his black padded coat and a badge from inside the pockets of his trousers and said, "Stop, please."

I stopped, turned, faced him, clinging to my meagre bag, watching his hands, his face, his body. He held the gun but his features showed no expression.

"Show me your face please."

He had already seen enough to make a decision, but I pulled my hat from my head, my scarf from my mouth. He considered all these, taking his time, a man confident in his skill set and his judgement, before saying, "Please face the wall. Do not turn around until ordered."

"Am I under arrest?" I asked.

"Yes. You are under arrest."

"For what crime?"

"Travel through a military zone."

It was a lie but one he turned out so easily that clearly it had been tried and tested a dozen times before, and not yet been found wanting. I hesitated, still facing him, and at my doubt, he raised the gun a little higher. "Please face the wall."

I obeyed.

"Do you have a passport?"

"Not on me."

"Where is your passport?"

"In my hotel."

"Where is your hotel?"

"Beijing."

"What is your name?"

"David Fields."

"Please come with me."

"Why?"

"You are under arrest."

"Where are we going?"

"The police station."

"May I call my embassy?"

"At the police station. What is your nationality?"

"Canadian."

"You may call your embassy from the station. Please come with me."

I considered my options and, remembering that a king may be put into check by a pawn, obeyed. He took my bag, handcuffed me and led me away, one hand on my arm, a simple man conducting a simple arrest.

Chapter 24

The police station had two cells, one office, and one other constable in it.

On seeing me, he exclaimed, "What the hell is this?"

My eager captor pushed me into a wooden chair that creaked uneasily beneath me and made no answer, stepping round his junior colleague instead to play with the computer, which was possibly even older and even clunkier than the one I'd borrowed in the mine manager's office. I waited, listening to the hum of the fluorescent tubes overhead, the slow *thunk-thunk-thunk* of a broken extractor fan, smelling the bleach on the tiles in the tiny bathroom, the old cigarettes stubbed out in an aluminium ashtray. Finally the policeman found the picture he was looking for, and conferred with his colleague and at last straightened up, walked round the desk, pulled me by the arm to face the screen and said, "Do you deny that this is you?"

I looked and saw my own face, beautifully rendered mugshot style—though I had no memory of posing for the photo—and a list of crimes that range from the banal to the impressively imaginative.

"It's not me," I replied. "I don't know who that is."

"Do you deny that this is your picture?"

"I do. I do deny it. I would like to call my embassy. My name is David Fields. My embassy will confirm it."

Another debate ensued at this. Finally I was pushed back into my chair, and a phone was passed to me, the number already dialled. "You have two minutes to speak to your embassy."

I waited for the phone to be answered.

"Hi," I said in French to the attaché who eventually came on the line. "This is David Fields. I'm in a bit of bother."

The two policemen glanced at each other uneasily—French was clearly a language beyond their comprehension.

"David...Fields, was it?"

"That's right."

"I can see your file right here, Mr. Fields, sir."

"Could you get onto the relevant parties, please? I'm in... where am I?"

"Huanshi Lu," grumbled my captor, when asked in Mandarin.

"You got that?" I asked the embassy.

"Huanshi Lu—yes, sir. Are you injured in any way, Mr. Fields?"

"No. But you probably have less than three hours to get to me before I sustain terminal injury."

"I'll be right on it."

"Pull out all the stops on this one—I'm in serious trouble."

"Absolutely, sir. We'll have something with you imminently."

"There's a danger they'll try to move me."

"Procedures are already being activated, sir. We'll have you out before you know it."

"Thanks."

"A pleasure, Mr. Fields sir—a pleasure."

He hung up and the policemen reluctantly put the phone back on the receiver.

"Your embassy didn't want to talk to us?" demanded the senior officer.

"No," I sighed. "You're only pieces in this game, I'm afraid. My friends are going to look rather higher."

They threw me in the cells.

I could hear the sound of voices on telephones for an hour after they locked me up, and praised inefficient bureaucracy for getting in the policemen's way.

After an hour the telephones stopped, and silence fell.

I waited.

After two hours and two minutes, the phone rang, just once.

I couldn't hear the conversation that followed, but when it ended, silence again.

Then voices, raised in argument. Junior arguing with the senior. That took nearly twenty minutes. When they were done, the two policemen came into the cellblock. They now wore bulletproof vests, riot helmets, and carried guns.

"Up!" barked Senior, and I got up.

They handcuffed me, rougher than they had been, and pulled me from the station, turning the lights off behind them. They put me in the back of their one, unmarked, battered beige car, Junior keeping his gun trailed on me all the way, and in the dead of night, headlights rippling against dust, began to drive.

"Where are we going?" I asked, and, "Shut up!" was the only reply I received.

I sat in silence as the town receded behind us, and at last said, "Do you have orders to kill me?"

"Shut up, shut up!"

I looked sadly from one man to the next and saw terror, gut-clenching, soul-biting terror in them.

"It's okay," I said. "It's okay. It's only a game."

Five miles outside the town, they pulled off the one, arrow-straight road onto a dust track that led nowhere at all. Two miles further on from that, they stopped, and Junior pulled me out of the back and pushed me into the glare of the headlights, and then pushed me further and a little further still, until I hovered on that dead place where light loses shape and spills into shadow. Then he forced me to my knees and levelled his gun against the back of my head, and shook and shuddered, and did nothing.

Then Senior said, "Do it!"

and Junior said, "No. I won't," and turned away.

An argument ensued. Senior was, I realised, even more afraid than Junior, raging first about orders, instructions, their careers, before switching to wheedling, begging, cajoling, explaining

340

that he had a family, that they had to do this for the family, that Junior didn't know what it was like, what it would be like if he lost this job, everything, everything would go too.

To which Junior said, "I won't kill a man."

"He's a terrorist!"

"No man deserves to die without trial. I have never killed a man in cold blood, and I will not start now."

"He has to die; you heard the orders!"

"I refuse them. They are not my orders; they are not orders I recognise within the boundaries of the law."

"Do it!"

"You do it."

"I can't."

"Why not?"

"I . . . he's just . . . not while he's just *there*."

At this, Senior fell briefly silent, and for a while the three of us remained there, a locked tableau of mutual terror.

Then Senior said, "Give me the gun," and took the weapon, and marched up behind me and pressed the barrel against my skull, hand shaking, breath ragged in his throat.

He was concentrating so hard on the act of murdering me that he didn't see the laser sight as it flashed across the sand finding its target. Junior did, however, because he cried out a warning a fraction of a second before twin sniper bullets blew out his and his partner's brains.

Chapter 25

They were special forces of some flavour or another. They had the black body armour, the black balaclavas, the silenced weapons, the exotic range of expensive tools and above all, they had the quiet demeanour of men who'd killed in terror and killed while calm and realised that, either way, there was a dead man on the floor and that was all the job required.

They freed my hands, and as they secured the area I knelt by the body of Junior, who'd refused to put a bullet in my brain, and thought for a moment I might cry. Why? He had been a piece in another player's hand, and his face, any semblance of humanity, had been obliterated when the bullet ripped through his skull. I was tired, I told myself. I was so very tired.

"Sir?" said one of my rescuers. "We need to go."

I nodded, and didn't move from the blood-splattered sand.

"Sir?"

Still I didn't move. Someone caught me by the arm, muttered, "*The shock...*" in Cantonese under his breath and helped me to a truck. By white torchlight they gave me a brisk once-over, checking for injuries which I might have been too numb to declare. Finding none, they gave me a blanket, water, a couple of sweet biscuits to chew on, and their leader, his face hidden behind nylon and wool, patted me on the knee and called out over the roar of the engine in cheerful Mandarin, "Good evening, Mr. Fields. The ambassador and the general send their regards and say to tell you that they can't make moves like this all the time."

"I nearly thought they weren't going to make it at all," I replied.

"They said you might say that, and to tell you that you were a fool to come to China. In the last ten days, the army has been purging senior officers by the dozen, the party's in chaos, the police have been put on high alert and for twenty-four hours, the government genuinely thought that the air force was mutinying!"

"You seem...happy about this."

He shrugged. "I'm just a man doing a job. I get a call middle of the night, get to some shithole in the middle of nowhere to rescue some man called David Fields—that's my job—I do it, I get paid, I go home. The machinations of big men in high places are nothing to me—not while I've got my health, my apartment and my kids."

"That seems reasonable."

"Gotta know what you're fighting for," he replied brightly. "Gotta keep your eye on the important things in life."

The trucks drove for five hours, and when they stopped they were at an airfield in the middle of a yellow field above a brown river. A man in white shirt and flapping brown shorts ran towards us, owl sunglasses bouncing on his head, the sun rising behind his bald spot.

"Unacceptable!" he snapped. "Impossible!" he added as the captain of our little band took him to one side. More cries of this ilk—ridiculous! Disgraceful!—resounded around the field as the men and I sat on the dusty ground or lounged against the side of the truck, waiting for his ire to pass. I said nothing. Sometimes a king has to hide behind more powerful pieces than himself.

Cash changed hands, his fury abated and as the sun crawled towards midday and the fat river flies settled on our shoulders and backs, nuzzled in hair and wriggled towards the soft warmth of our flared noses, I heard the hum of an engine. A two-seater plane, white and wobbly as it bounced in off a westerly wind, no sooner landed than it had stopped, no sooner stopped than I was bundled into it."Bye-bye!" sang out my rescuer cheerfully. "Have a nice trip!"

They waved at me as we departed, a line of ex-special forces mercenaries, assassins and killers, sending me on my way, smiles on their faces, rifles on their backs.

The pilot was a woman with hair cut tight to the back of her neck and a conversational flare that started with "good morning" and finished with "please don't touch anything, thank you". The sun moved around us as we headed south, and through the changing cloud cover I saw land the colour of pus, factories pumping thin spreads of grey into the sky, roads of locked red lights, rivers that barely seemed to flow. I half closed my eyes against the glare of the sun, and when I opened them again the land had grown green and mountains rose like fins from a puffer fish. In the heat and dry air of the cabin, sleep came easily, and when I looked again, the sun was red to my right, vanishing into a grey haze before it could reach the horizon, and below the lights of towns and cities glowed like yellow living tumours, fibrous tendrils of road and river reaching out between each nodule to connect the whole.

We landed on a little airstrip halfway up a mountain, the air clear and cold, a single shack by a single road guarded by a single truck. An old woman shuffled into the half-gloom of falling night as our engine stopped; she smiled and bobbed at me, gave the pilot a hug, a babbling tenderness in her greeting that my stony companion seemed to little deserve, and shuffled us inside. She fed us soup of cabbage and noodles, plied me with tea, chatted to the pilot about the weather, the news, the TV, the radio, the rude woman she bought eggs from at the bottom of the hill, and when our bowls were empty said, "You'll be wanting something for the road, yes?" and pushed rice cakes and a hot flask into my hands, and like that, we were pushed back out into the night, and my pilot hauled me back into the passenger seat and the refuelled plane back into the air.

*

344

We flew on, low, into the night. I wondered if radar would detect us as we swung slowly around the peaks of mountains, hugged the sides of river valleys, dipped in and out of low, threatening cloud. I wondered if anyone cared. I had played my hand well when I called the Canadian Embassy as David Fields. My eyes closed of their own accord as we flew on towards the sea.

Chapter 26

My pilot woke me as the sun was rising over the airstrip, and I jumped.

The engine was silent; the tarmac was empty. A flock of birds, heads turning upwards with the coming dawn, fled for the skies as I roused myself in my cramped corner.

"Taipei," she explained simply. "Twenty miles that way."

"Thank you."

"I just did my job."

"No—you did more. Thank you."

She shrugged. "Don't tell me where you're going," she said as I slipped, weak-kneed and stiff-backed, to the ground. "I don't like knowing that sort of stuff."

Twenty minutes later, she was in the sky again, and I watched her go as the sun rose.

A taxi took me to Taipei, no one bothering to check my passport.

A bank accepted my signature, details and fingerprints, and handed over fifteen thousand U.S. dollars, no questions asked, in various notes.

I converted one thousand then and there and bought myself a night in the nearest five-star hotel I could find. From my room, I had a view across the city, all light, noise, glass, concrete, traffic, the blare of horns, the rush of people, the mountains blue in the distance, Taipei 101 obscenely huge against the diminished enormity of its neighbours, spiking the sky.

I had a bath, a large meal and, as was my wont, stepped outside to buy the best laptop and satellite phone I could find.

China was in turmoil.

At the UN, the Mongolian government screamed violation of its airspace, its ground-space, violation of treaties, of rights, of dignity, of—of most things, not that the UN particularly cared, China being what she was.

More interesting, in Beijing the government rocked, shaken to its very core. Senior generals, admirals, air marshals, spies, civil servants, ministry men, policemen, media magnates, news stations, governors, mayors—how many, how many of the great and good had suddenly proven to be unsound? Troops mobilised without orders, borders shut down, strangers searched, all seemingly with a purpose yet no direction. Terror—now terror had set in—for how much of her own government, wondered those few apparatchiks of Beijing who weren't obviously compromised, but how much had been suborned to this...whatever-this-was. To this purpose unknown.

Purges followed.

Arrests, exiles, even a couple of executions, for if there is one thing a military will not tolerate, it's a breakdown in command structure. Human rights movements cried foul, financiers shifted uneasily in their boardrooms, governors fell and elections were cancelled. The U.S. State Department issued a communiqué to the effect that, while it wasn't interested in China's domestic affairs, it hoped—for the sake of regional security—that a solution would be found to this problem sooner rather than later. The Russian ambassador was recalled to Moscow for urgent talks. Two army units threatened mutiny. A prime minister fell.

All this I watched, first from my room in Taipei, then a room in Singapore, then an internet café in Manila, then on my laptop in Hawaii and finally, as the few strong men left standing crawled their way to the top of the broken podiums of power, and men who'd been too weak to be of much note now eyed up newly vacated positions, I watched it all with distant curiosity from my apartment in San Francisco.

The Gamesmaster had ripped China apart in search of me, and I didn't need to do anything now but watch the pieces fall. The system would self-correct, and in doing so a great handful of the Gamesmaster's assets would be wiped from play. In expending so many resources on my capture, she had lost control of Beijing, and the field was open now for my pieces to take control, assuming I had enough pieces in play; assuming the investment was worth my while.

I considered the matter for two lazy days in San Francisco, making no moves, playing no pieces, merely pondering the board.

On the third morning, I reached a conclusion and set the pieces in motion.

Chapter 27

The Great Game.

The opening is done. We have made our moves, staked high, lost heavy. Now the board is open and we move slower, careful, wearing our enemy down, looking for the king, looking for the capture.

This is the middle game.

I consolidate my pieces in China; she focuses on the EU and U.S.

Beijing is threatened with a trade embargo, accusations of cyber-terrorism, espionage, foul practice economically, foul practices against humanity.

I activate the Union of South American Nations; she plays two of the big four oil companies. I launch environmental terrorists and an insurance broker in retaliation. She turns the Greek police against the head of the insurance company; I turn the interior ministry against the police. She unleashes a nationalist opposition movement against my minister; I play an orthodox patriarch and evangelical Christian TV station back at her.

For a moment, all things hang in balance. Seven DEA agents are gunned down in Guatemala; an American intelligent network are arrested in Tunisia; the oil companies waver; the CEO of one, and deputy CEO of another stand firm, and I see that they are her pieces, the heart of her play, and one is killed by a cartel, the other in a road accident on a cliff by the sea. She kills the leaders of a terrorist group, shuts down the insurance company and the bank that was linked to it and, in an act of spite, kills my Greek interior minister with a car bomb that also murders his wife and eldest son, and leaves his twelve-year-old daughter without her right leg and suddenly alone in the world. I manage to salvage my patriarch by sending him on hermetic retreat to the Ukraine, but look back in sorrow as my evangelical TV channel is taken off air for "hate crimes".

All this takes five months.

And as I move, I move, and the world turns.

I smell sulphur in the hot springs of Greenland, listen to the erudite arguments of the overweight Icelandic IT men in their suits and furs. I ride the ferry through the great glacial valleys of eastern Canada, watch white beluga surface and dive in her sandy bays. From a balcony in Cape Town which looks south towards Robben Island and the sea, I launch a botnet attack against a series of servers in Oman which have been targeting me. From a grubby little hotel room in Malawi, where the bus never comes and the children have come too late to the library, all the books stolen by their fathers who have now forgotten how to read, I orchestrate the arrest of a man who looks like me, sounds like me, has nothing to do with me, but who is taken down by the Glasgow police as the face behind the irritating Interpol warrant she has served against me. And always, I move, and so does she.

Twice she comes near to capturing me directly, once unleashing the full force of Egypt's military as I flee across the Sinai desert, saved only from capture by a hastily deployed team from the Israeli Defence Force and a mechanic in the driver's seat of my truck who could fix almost anything with duct tape and a hammer. The second time, she nearly gets me with a hit squad in Tehran, who swing through the window of my room and kick the door down in true commando-style, and are thwarted in their execution only by the humming of my refrigerator which has been so erratic in the night that it's driven me to wakefulness. They shoot my bed rather than me, and I jump two floors out of the nearest window, landing in the lovingly tended rhododendron bush of my wealthy next-door neighbour with a crack and a splay of glass, and limp across the Iranian border into Iraq some eight hours later in search of urgent medical aid.

The doctor whom I eventually called on for assistance tutted as she dressed my injuries. She was a higher league player, though only incidentally, finding herself increasingly drawn to the affairs of her own country over the machinations of the Gameshouse and dabbling only when she urgently needed something which she could find by no other means.

"I heard the house has closed its doors," she tutted, slapping ointment onto my face in thick, stinging dollops. "They say you're playing the Great Game, and the Gameshouse will not appear again until the game is done. Is this true?"

"Yes."

"You think you can win?"

"I don't know."

"And what will you do if you do win?" she demanded, swatting at the sole fly which dared hover nervously near the one light in the middle of the bare, blue medical room. "Have you thought about that?"

"Yes."

"Well?"

"I will destroy the Gameshouse."

"Why? It is the thing which sustains you, which gives you life; why would you destroy it?"

I didn't answer for a while. Then, "It destroys lives."

"It changes outcomes; that is all. That battles which are fought are fought between people, and would happen regardless of the house. The players merely change the result."

"No," I replied. "What you're describing is merely politics and death. I have played those games too, in some of the greatest battles that have ever been fought. I handed out rifles in the American War of Independence; I was there when the guillotine fell on the French king's head. I saw Martin Luther King die, played *Assassins* in the halls of the Kremlin. There are ideas behind these events, notions that are sometimes as stupid as nation, race or creed. And sometimes there are ideas too which

351

are as potent as liberty, brotherhood, justice. We will enslave philosophers and kings to our cause, sacrifice good people and bad to achieve victory, even if that victory is for a tyrant. All that matters is the win; the rest is nothing. That is the game; and do you know what I think? I think that the Gameshouse chooses the games we play, chooses the shape of human history, chooses which ideas will flourish and which will fall, and in playing, we serve it in creating an outcome that is not of *humanity's* choice."

"Silver," she replied, "I'm helping you now because of... favours...that are owed, but don't fool yourself. There are thousands of players out there who depend for their very lives, for everything they have, on the Gameshouse existing. If the Gamesmaster tells them that your victory will mean their defeat, don't imagine for a second that they won't jump at a chance to take you down."

"I know. That's why I'm avoiding them."

"You're a good player but you won't be able to hold out for ever. They'll come for you—not just the Gamesmaster, but the whole house. I don't see how you expect to win."

"I'm waiting for a mistake."

"The Gamesmaster doesn't make mistakes," she replied. "Not her. Not ever."

More moves; more chess.

The first time I put her into check, it was in New Delhi—but by the time my SWOT team reached her address, she was gone, and all they found was a bomb which killed four of them, and a CCTV camera which showed the back of her retreating head as she fled for a car two hours earlier. A weak attack on my part, easily evaded by moving the king.

Eight months later, I nearly caught her again, changing planes in Heathrow, and this time I unleashed the Metropolitan Police and UK Customs against her, grounding all flights and locking down British airspace. For two breathless hours, I thought, perhaps, perhaps I had her, but at the last minute she played the

Home Office against me and in the ensuing bout I lost a police commissioner and a deputy head of the British Airport Authority, while she exposed a cabinet minister and a high court judge in her efforts to escape. The minister I removed with a carefully judged sex scandal; the high court judge was only four months from retirement so I let him live. She fled to where I knew not, and the game continued.

For three years, it continued.

Governments fall and economies decline. Banks shatter, computers fail, militaries rebel, borders close, deals collapse, pipelines run dry, satellites burn, men die, the world turns and the game goes on.

Lying alone on a cheap hotel bed in Addis Ababa, a bowl of peanuts and an empty beer by my elbow, I did a mental inventory of the things we had destroyed in the name of this game and found it extensive. Not merely the pieces sent to their death or prison, but the lives broken every time we played a killer, removed a judge, shredded a government, crippled a bank. We—she and I—were the parents of civil unrest and carnage, the consequences of our actions spread now so wide that the pundits had begun to call the time of our game, "autumn years", as the hope of previous "spring" years now gave way to the savagery that preceded winter.

On a cargo ship crossing Lake Victoria, the flies crawling so thick above my mosquito net I could barely see the tiny porthole and its little circle of light beyond, I encountered the first attack against me by another player. Godert van Zuylen, who played a savage game without much finesse, launched a group of some fifty regional separatists against a governor I controlled in southern Turkey, killing the governor, setting the regional assembly on fire and prompting a crackdown far bloodier and greater than any I would have commanded. It was, as assaults against my position went, marginal, and ill-judged. It was, however, a disturbing sign, worrying enough for me to divert from my path and, with a small group of armed policemen, track him down to his apartment in Makassar, breaking into his rooms shortly before three in the morning and cable tying him, naked and gleaming with sweat, to the end of his bed.

He didn't shake or beg or scream as I pulled off my balaclava and squatted before him. If anything, he sighed in disappointment, not at my actions, I concluded, but at himself, having been so easily discovered.

"Silver," he said. "I didn't think you'd waste the effort."

"Godert," I replied. "I was going to say the same about you."

Even naked, exposed and on the edge of death, he had the old player's pride. He had won too many victories, seen too many people fall before the power of his intellect, to believe that the same might happen to him now. "It's not personal," he explained. "My life is the Gameshouse—quite literally. If I cannot play, if I cannot win life, comfort and strength from weaker players, then I will die."

"You've lived a very long time," I replied, "and the Great Game has only been playing for five years. Surely you can wait another five for it to reach its conclusion without wading in against me?"

"You make it sound easy—five years is a long time for a man of my talents to be patient."

"Right there I think is a measure of just how limited your talent is."

He smiled, the smile of a man who, though he may seem weak, defeated, still knows he is strong. To a player of the middling sort, this confidence is a boon, a gift, for it empowers you to make decisions that others might flinch from, pushing pieces against positions that seemed—but are not—impenetrable. Van Zuylen was of the middling sort; his confidence was a lie, and would do him no good now.

I reached into my pocket. Pulled out a coin. It was small, faded and bore the head of a long-dead emperor on one side, an eagle on the other. The writing was almost worn away around the edges, but once proclaimed in ancient Latin the eternity of an empire which had fallen thousands of years ago. I rolled it around my fingers, and the smile faded from van Zuylen's face.

"Do you know what this is?" I asked, as he watched the coin. He nodded, once.

"Would you like to play a game?"

"Not with that," he replied. "Not like this."

"Did the Gamesmaster command you to turn against me, or was it your own idea?"

"Silver..."

"Come, come; I have, as you pointed out, expended a few slight resources in tracking you down. You owe me something in return."

"I owe you nothing."

"Then choose," I said with a shrug, squeezing the coin tight in the palm of my hand. "Heads or tails."

He shook his head, licked his lips, his confidence faltering. Above us, a fan spun slowly in the ceiling; in the room below, the TV was turned up too loud, a series of *aiiii*s and *hi-yaah*s proclaiming that the observer was a fan of martial arts movies, and doubtless minions were being crashed even now beneath a hero's boot. In the street outside, a woman screamed at her faithless boyfriend; a cat shrieked in the dark.

"We turned," he whispered. "She told us to and we did, of course we did: she's the Gamesmaster; we're..." He stopped, voice drying in his throat.

"We're what?" I asked. "We're the players of the Gameshouse? The great and the brilliant, the masters of the higher league? We're great, we're powerful; at our command civilisations fall and gods are made? Is that it, Godert?"

No answer. Confidence of the iron sort that van Zuylen's was, when it breaks, it breaks entirely, a shivering, a shattering of strength.

"We're pieces," I sighed, when he did not speak. "All of us, every player in the house, we are pieces in her hands. You played the higher games, and she played you. And now she's turning you against me, is that right?"

No answer.

The coin rolled between my fingers.

355

Then, "Everyone," he hissed. "Everyone. The whole house. We're all coming for you, Silver. Even the ones you trust. You think you've got friends? We're players; we turn with the dice. I saw her two months ago and you know who was by her side? Remy Burke, the nearest thing you had to a brother. Even he's turned against you; even he wants to live. She's going to make you a slave. She's going to put you in white and shackle you to the house, just like the umpires. Just like your wife."

The coin stopped, poised on an edge between my index finger and thumb, and there it remained.

"Have you ever wondered what the Gameshouse is?" I mused. "Have you ever asked yourself what it is that the Gameshouse wants? We tell ourselves that the kings we have slaughtered, the armies we have defeated, the nations we have crushed—they were set on their path anyway, and we merely played the game, no more. But in 1914, I sat back in amazement as the game of diplomacy that had been so carefully played by such masterful adversaries for fifty years on the European board tumbled into carnage. How could this happen? I wondered, and then I looked again at the board, and I re-read the rules of the game and I saw that the dice were loaded. Millions have died in the course of our games, and we have changed the destiny of the world with our little sports. And for what? For a pattern on the board that only she can see; a future for humanity that only she can shape. We are pieces, Godert. We are nothing more than pieces."

So saying, I straightened up and slipped the coin back into my pocket. "I was inclined to give you a chance," I said. "Fifty-fifty odds. But you are a piece in the hand of my enemy, and I have played pawns to take you out of play."

I turned, and walked away.

He began to beg as my hand touched the handle of the door—no, Silver, please, Silver, I didn't mean, I didn't want, I'll never again...

I closed the door behind me on the way out, and the breeze-block walls somewhat muffled the sound of gunfire.

Chapter 28

A submarine sinks in the Antarctic. A passenger plane is shot down over Georgia. Mexico teeters on the edge of civil war. Extreme nationalists come to power in Spain, and start expelling and imprisoning its enemies. A religious war breaks out in Mali. Russia cuts off gas to the EU. Three suicide bombers kill two hundred and eleven U.S. Marines in Washington State. Two prime ministers are assassinated, and a president dies under suspicious circumstances. The interest rate of the Federal Reserve drops to 0.1 per cent and six banks fold, taking with them two hundred and eighty thousand mortgages, five hundred and seventy-nine thousand pensions and, once all the investors they shatter are counted, nearly eighty thousand jobs.

Would these things—and more, so much more—have happened were it not for the Game?

Perhaps.

But probably not.

How long could I keep this up?

Not as long as her, perhaps. Every day that the game went on was another in which pieces were weakened, the board edging slowly in her favour.

I was tired. I was so very, very tired.

On the three thousandth and eleventh day of the game, more than eight years after it had began, I sat in the bar of the overnight ferry from Portsmouth to Saint-Malo and listened to the one singer on the stage belt out old Motown hits from beneath rhythmless flashing purple lights. At three a.m. the barkeeper disappeared, though the shutter was still up, and at four a.m. the two teenage boys in the arcade gallery next door finally gave up, their electronic guns falling silent, their slain digital enemies screaming no more. Only I remained, staring at nothing. I didn't notice the music stop, barely noticed the singer reaching behind the bar to pour herself a whisky.

You take the ferry a lot? she said.

A bit, I replied. I travel.

Why do you travel?

My job.

What's the job?

Consultant.

She smiled at that, drained her whisky down, her skin flushed from the exertion of so much song to such an unreceptive audience. The engine of the ferry shuddered and whirred, the ship bumped a little as we hit a swell, rocking the bottles on their shelves.

Consultant, she murmured. Hell—that could mean anything at all.

To my surprise, I laughed. Yes! I said. That's exactly right. That's exactly what it is. May I buy you another drink?

I don't drink with passengers.

There aren't any passengers here. There isn't anyone here.

You're a passenger.

No. Not really.

A moment—a silence—in which we waited for each other. She half smiled and turned away, and I put my hand on her arm, gentle, the lightest of touches and said, If not a drink, how about a game?

We played arcade games until the sun came up over Saint-Malo, an ancient town that had been destroyed and rebuilt, a strange mixture of medieval ideas and 1960s building materials. I was beaten at seven road races, died five times and only once managed to knock her out with my kung-fu special attack as we mashed controls and shrieked like children.

I haven't had this much fun since...I don't know when! she said.

Me neither, I replied.

The company—they have this policy. Always smile, always polite, always say "please" and "thank you," nothing more. They're scared that if you laugh, or if you make a joke, someone will take it the wrong way and sue them. Everyone's so scared of being taken the wrong way, these days.

Yeah. I guess so.

Isn't it good just to laugh, though? Isn't it good just to have fun? To be silly, to be happy, to forget about it all for a while? Isn't it good to stop thinking about the world, and the mortgage, and your lover and your worries, and just have fun and be free?

Yes, I replied, unable to look away from her eyes. Yes, it is.

A moment in which 2-D figures in capes and tunics kicked and punched their way across the screens around us, in which music played and high scores flashed, and I wondered if I could just walk away. Step off this ship into the ocean, straight down, sink beneath the Atlantic waves, away from the Gameshouse, away from the Gamesmaster, away from the noise and the numbers and the pieces and the field, away from the game. All things stopped.

When was the last time I had simply been me?

I can't remember.

I can't remember who I'd been before the game.

She says, "You look sad."

I say, "It's nothing."

She says, "You want another game?"

She says, "Why are you crying? Are you okay? Why are you crying?"

"It's nothing," I reply. "You just brought back some memories. Come on—let's play."

We shot alien invaders and undead hoards, and I was resoundingly, joyously thrashed, and laughed a little at that, and kept on playing until the captain came on the Tannoy and said we were nearing harbour, and would drivers proceed to their cars, but not start the engines until asked.

She puts her plastic gun down, kissed me on the cheek, said I was nice, it had been fun, maybe she'd see me another time, on the next ferry out, maybe.

Then she was gone.

Chapter 29

The time had come to castle.

In chess, this is the action of moving the king behind the protection of a rook, and hunting the Gamesmaster, I had the growing suspicion that she had already made this move, was fortified in some permanent base from which she could easily coordinate assaults against my still vulnerable, wandering self. Was castling safety or a trap? Perhaps both.

I had an ongoing project. As the game turned and pieces fell, I fortified one corner of the board, transformed it into a little castle of my own, quietly, quietly, so she wouldn't see it until it was ready to play. I set it up in Kyrgyzstan, near enough to the Chinese border that I could call on PLA air support, if I needed it. Seven years it took me to get it into place, but still one piece was missing.

On the ninth anniversary of the commencement of the Great Game, the Gamesmaster launched an all-out assault on Jammu. In the fifteen hours in which battle raged, she poured the Indian army into the city, hunting me through every alley and down every dirty hole, and I launched mercenaries, separatists, criminals, idealists and extremists at her. The sound of gunfire blasted through the cold night, tracer bullets picking across the sky, and three times I made a break for the edge of the city, desperately seeking escape only to encounter tanks, squads of hard-faced soldiers, blockades, helicopters—the full might of India's military—turned against me. The government said they were pacifying domestic extremism, and army trucks blared out commands to stay inside, co-operate, as men with faces hidden by metal helmets, shotguns in hand, went door to door looking for me.

In the end, my pieces merely held the line; it was the Pakistani military, acting on its own initiative, which saved me. They put fifty thousand troops on the Kashmir border, and enough of the Indian government believe the threat to pull back from Jammu, leaving eight hundred and seventy-one people dead, and a single, plain-clothes hit squad which managed to take out the convoy I was fleeing on as it heads down the Sunderbani Road.

I crawled from the wreckage of my overthrown vehicle to the sound of submachine gunfire, the scream of men, the smell of petrol, the splatter of flames and the dull pulsing of shrapnel embedded in my shoulder, and survived by hiding under the corpse of my driver long enough for the following convoy to arrive and draw the enemy off.

A man and a donkey helped me over the mountains between Sunderbani and Kotla Arab Ali Khan. I remembered very little of the end of the journey, and woke in a dentist's studio to find a man with a surgical mask and the largest pair of tweezers I'd ever seen pulling bits of embedded metal from my torn flesh. He wasn't a piece, wasn't a player.

"I help people," he said with a shrug. "That is my duty; that is what I do."

I struggled to understand his words, and blamed fatigue for my confusion.

For two days I hid in the dentist's basement living room, eating rice cakes and mutton, until at last he found me a mobile phone and I called in a piece in Lahore who owned seventeen hotels, one TV station and, most importantly, a plane, and who smuggled me onto a flight carrying frozen sheep sperm to Ho Chi Minh City.

Five days later, I was in the USA, arm in a sling, the lacerations to my face and neck fading to pink scars, and India is in turmoil. Like China before, I attempted to propel my pieces into the vacuum left by the fall of those pieces the Gamesmaster had expended on my capture—but this time, my every move was blocked, and I lost seven pieces to arrest and assassination before I was forced to conclude that the pieces she'd played in Jammu represented merely a part of her Indian assets, and I simply didn't hold enough pieces to make the assault worthwhile in the sub-continent. The realisation was a bitter one: the Gamesmaster had unsuccessfully invaded Kashmir and still had pieces to play.

I couldn't match that kind of power.

Cold and weary, I rode the Greyhound bus down Route 15, listening to the screaming of the baby, the snoring of the great fat salesman in the seat next to mine, and knew with an absolute certainty that her strength exceeded mine. I could not defeat the Gamesmaster—not on these terms.

I closed my eyes and considered other plans.

Chapter 30

A stop in the desert.

There was no town to the north, no town to the south. Sunlight and dust, as far as the eye could see. A sheriff in an oversized hat and brown shirt boarded the bus, asked folks to stay calm, walked down the aisle inspecting every face, stopped at my seat.

"Can I see your ticket, sir?" he said, his hand on the butt of his gun.

I showed him my ticket.

"Could you get off the bus, please?"

I got off the bus.

"Can I make a phone call?"

"No, sir, sorry."

"What's going on?" I asked, as the sheriff's deputy took away my bag, found my six mobile phones inside, looked askance at me, and one by one pulled their batteries out.

"Nothing to be worried about, sir; we just need to take you in."

"What for?"

"Routine enquiries."

"You just stopped a bus in the desert—that doesn't seem routine."

He smiled, a smile which proclaimed, not unkindly, that I was right and this was wrong, and there was nothing to be done about it save be civil in my obedience. Then the deputy found the gun at the bottom of my bag, and asked if I had a licence, and I said sure—at my destination. Let me call my lawyer, and I'm sure he'd sort it out.

That's when they handcuffed me and put me in the back of the car.

Chapter 31

A dusty road in a dusty nowhere, where somehow, incredibly, people chose to live. We drove for two hours, passing through eight towns on our way, and one drive-through burger joint where the sheriff was greeted by name. He ordered a double with double of everything for himself, a single without the onions for his deputy and a cheeseburger and fries for me. I ate without complaint, hands still locked in front of me and, as we pulled away, asked again why they'd arrested me.

They just chuckled—a paternal amusement at youthful ignorance rather than a thing sinister unto itself—and said it'd all be sorted out in town, just be patient. I leant my head back against my seat and wondered if this was it, if this was how I died, and felt in my pocket for a little Roman coin which they hadn't bothered to take away from me, rolled it between my fingers and wondered if things were desperate enough yet to give it a throw.

Then the road widened and widened again, and there were lights ahead where there should have been none, too bright, too colourful, an explosion of neon and traffic, declaring bigger, brighter, better. Low houses in grubby straight streets grew taller, whiter, burst up in a sudden leap of concrete and glass, and then grew brighter still, a thousand bulbs glistening above hotel doors, gold and brass on every handle, all real vegetation chopped down to be replaced by shimmering metal facsimiles, fountains lit from below and fireworks above, the stench of petrol fumes and the chatter of voices, aeroplanes circling overhead in a queue to land, the prostitutes and the punters jostling each other in the doors of restaurants and bars and of course, in the centre of it all, the casinos, the churning stomach of this city, for this was Las Vegas, impossible place in the desert, where impossible things almost never happened, and fortune and life was lost in the hope that the mathematics lied. It was a city of flesh and drink, of dollars, dollars, dollars, of loud, frantic hopes and smiles that stretched to the tips of every sunburnt ear, of quiet desperation and the little shuffling men that others avoided, lest their bad luck rubbed off and dragged them into the shallow dark places from which there was no escape. On a street corner, a lone voice proclaimed that vice would bring about the end of the world, and the police were already moving him on, young officers in ironed shirts that stuck darkly to their backs and armpits. Cabbies hurled abuse at each other from across the street, and that was fine because this was a city of winners and it didn't matter how you won, what force you deployed or what loses you suffered, as long as you were victorious.

Into the heart of this place we went, riding the freeway to Frank Sinatra Drive, where billboards three storeys high proclaimed wonders of musical performance by last year's pop divas, boxing bouts between had-been giants, celebrity glamour and the kind of life that you had only ever dreamed about—you, you little people, stuck in your little lives reading glossy magazines. This, said the signs, this was where the writers of those magazines came to get their inspiration, this was the heart of hope, the centre of your aspiration, so lay down your cash, roll that dice and be the star.

So said every palatial casino/hotel we passed, but we didn't stop at the front—we drove through smaller streets to the back of one such giant to where a service door designed to admit two lorries at a time stood open, and men in white hairnets and rubber gloves shouted familiar abuse at each other and unloaded crates of fish on beds of ice, bottles of champagne and loaves of bread in their plastic packaging, boxes of oranges and bags of potatoes, flung from arm to arm like flimsy balls, before being sent down a service shaft to the unseen bowels below.

A few of these men glanced at us as the sheriff pulled up, but they'd worked there long enough and seen enough to ask no questions, expect no replies. They pulled me through a concrete maze of service corridors, past catering units banging food onto crystal plates, laundry rooms smelling of starch and soap, staff locker rooms stinking of sweat, maintenance offices with tools hanging from homemade racks on the wall, until at last we came to a lift with a plain metal door and only one option for where it might go—up—and only two floors it could go to. As they pulled me inside, I felt the coin in the palm of my hand, and felt that this was it, the last moment, the final call, and stayed still and quiet between my captors, though my breath came faster than I could contain.

I wondered if I was ready to die, and discovered that I was.

I wondered if I was ready to become a slave of the white, a piece of the Gameshouse, for ever nothing, for ever no one, trapped beneath the veil, and found that the idea paralysed my very thoughts.

The lift rose a long time. When it stopped, we were inside a bookshelf. The bookshelf was pushed back, revealing itself to be no more and no less than a crude, painted thing, ugly in its pretentiousness, crude in its concealment of the lift. Beyond the bookshelf was an office. I counted twenty-three steps between the door and the single desk set in the centre of its pink marble floor. Water ran quietly down the back wall, a crinkled surface of polished copper and brass, flecked with green, draining into a small pool whose bottom was lined with polished pebbles of silver and gold. Down one side of the office ran more painted books; down the other was a window which looked out across the entire city, lit up at night in all its grid form, like a firefly net or a chess-board.

Behind the desk, a chair of white leather was draped with a tiger's skin. Opposite it, two far smaller leather chairs were bedecked with the remnants of slaughtered bear. Into one of these I was pushed, my hands were freed and, without so much as a "so long, sonny" my two captors turned and went back the way they'd come, and I was left alone.

*

367

I waited.

The city went straight ahead or left and right beneath me, a million lives clinging to the roads, red lights one way, white the other. A helicopter landed on the roof of a casino nearby, disgorging wealth in high heels. A police car whizzed by below, silent in the darkness. I waited. The desk in front of me was empty, save for a set of two bright green plastic dice, a single chip valued at five thousand dollars and a spikey-haired troll doll no bigger than my hand, its frock of straight pink hair shaved to no more than stubble against its plastic skull, a smile drawn on its already smiling face in red felt-tip pen.

I waited.

Silence in the office.

Water fell and I waited.

Did not move.

Felt eyes watching me.

Waited.

Want to talk about it? I asked.

No, I replied, squeezing my eyes tight. No. Just . . . No.

Behind the blackness of my eyelids, faces came unbidden. Van Guylen, dead at the end of the bed. A dying man playing cards; a singer on the ferry from Saint-Malo. A doctor who helped out of duty; children laughing on a beach by the sea. Tracer fire over the city of Jammu; a hit squad shooting down at me as I fled through Tehran.

Go away, I sighed. Go away.

Two Chinese policemen gunned down in a nowhere place, in the desert near a town which produces nothing but rubble.

I refuse them. They are not my orders; they are not orders I recognise within the boundaries of the law.

A pair of Russians cheerfully beating each other with birch in the woods, proclaiming hate as they smiled warmly over the dominos set. *We believe in something more than they do. That's why we'll always win.*

Dead pieces played for small gains. *I'm fucking getting out of here before they get my wife and kids, fuck you, Silver, fuck you!*

"Get on with it," I snapped, and was surprised to hear my own voice ring round the room. "For God's sake, just end it!"

I felt something bite into my hand and, looking down, saw the Roman coin I had been clutching all this time pressed so hard into the skin that it was starting to bruise; and then there he was, striding into the room from behind his ridiculous painted bookcases, white cowboy boots pulled up to his knees, pink shirt, white tie and a black suit. The suit was pinstriped, though so subtly as to be almost imperceptible to the naked eye. The thin threads of not-black that ran through the silken material were gold; threaded gold, I realised, as the owner of it perched, one leg across the corner of his own too-large desk, and beamed at me. I added up the value of the thin metal embedded in the silk and concluded it was probably worth more than a small house in downtown LA, and wondered if you could put it in the washing machine. I considered this question long and hard, as in thinking about it, I could avoid looking at the face of the man who wore it—the smiling, grinning face—until at last he said, "Have you gone and got blood on my chair?"

I realised that the wound in my shoulder was very gently bleeding, seeping through the fabric of my shirt.

"It's okay," he said as I made to cover the wound with my hand. "It'll add a certain character."

I closed my eyes tight, turned my head away, then opened my eyes fast and looked into the face I had longed not to see again.

"Hello, Bird," I said.

"Hello, Silver," he replied, then smiled and pressed one hand against his lips. The fingernails were long, brown, ragged, curving to the end like claws, though the rest of him was perfectly pressed and pampered. "Shit," he chuckled. "I nearly called you by your real name."

Chapter 32

There is a story told.

It is only one of many, but isn't that always the case where the Gameshouse is concerned?

It is the story of a brother and a sister a long, long time ago. He was wild, brave, strong, adventurous; she was quiet, learned, studious and wise. They loved each other with the kind of tussling love that siblings have, and one day, as they were walking by the sea, they had an argument.

Said the brother, "People are savage, reckless, governed as the animals are. Instinct and the will to survive, power and the scent of blood—these are what drives people in everything they do. Love is power; kindness is selfish; society is a tool that is used by the strong to grow stronger, a system of ascendency and might, no more. Pierce through the pretty clothes of civilisation, and you will find blood beneath, just as it has always been, as it must always be."

Said the sister, "I do not think so. I believe that humanity betters itself every day. We formulate laws to govern our behaviour, aspire to reach beyond ourselves in imagination and deed. We overcome our animal needs, our base emotions, and become creatures of reason, and in reason we find a definition of that which may be 'good'."

"Poppycock!" exclaimed the brother, though this being many thousands, thousands of years ago, he may have used a different word to convey his meaning.

"Very well," she replied. "I will prove it to you!"

So a conflict ensued, the brother and sister each trying to

prove their point, and in time they both grew old and they both grew great, and when they should have died they would not, for there was still this battle to be won, and as they were now both very powerful, they lived, gathering to themselves the means to victory, until, after a few centuries had gone by, it was almost as if they could not remember the point they had to prove. So it was that the sister withdrew to a perfect place, a house where logic, reason and the rules of law could be deployed by great minds to overcome any problem, and where the power of human thought could be shown to be greater than any petty emotional need. Some naïve philosophers argued that she was an embodiment of some sort of "order" or "law" or even finer notions as a "yin" which opposed a "yang", but in truth, these were markers that spoke more about the men who applied them, than her.

"The house," she once said, "proves that it is reason, intelligence and logical minds which shape the destiny of humankind."

For his part, the brother retreated to a valley in the mountains and gathered to him the wild people, the dancing people, the people who fed on human flesh because they were hungry and drank blood because it was rich, and who learned hunting from wolves and lusted to be masters of the sun and moon, and screamed in the darkness when it could not be so, and raged at the world. Again, philosophers attempted to apply their ideas to him, calling him chaos and barbarism, but he just laughed.

"Take your proofs somewhere else! Can you prove love? Can you prove passion? Can you prove humanity? We are the wild things that need no words, and you shall never imprison us with your language."

Thus it was, when I first met Bird. His people beat me as they dragged me through the valley because they could, and because I could not stop them, and because there were no laws save strength and blood. They threw me at his feet, and as I begged for my life he tutted and said if I was too weak to win it, I was too weak to have it.

He said, "Why do you want to live at all, being such a wretched little thing?"

371

I replied, "My wife. The Gameshouse has taken my wife."

He said, "So?"

I said, "Ask me anything, any service, anything at all, I'll be yours, I swear it; I'll be yours for ever..." but he dismissed this offer as insignificant, unwanted, uninteresting, and his people howled with delight and made to cut out my heart, my tongue, peel off my flesh, until an idea struck him that seemed to entertain, and from a bag full of teeth and little ground bones, he pulled out a small Roman coin.

"You like games, do you?" he asked as I lay begging at his feet. "She who runs the house—she likes games. She finds they impose patterns on the world, make order where there is only chaos. Let's play a game, you and I. I throw this coin, and if it lands on a certain side, you live, and if it doesn't, you die. You can pick which side gives you life—not that choosing makes a difference."

So I chose, and tossed the coin.

The coin turns, the coin turns.

Empires rise, empires fall, and only the turning remains.

Chapter 33

He said, "Would you like something to drink? Have a Ritz side-car. Cointreau, cognac—I usually charge five hundred bucks a glass in the bars downstairs, but for you I'll do it free, for old time's sake."

He didn't wait for me to answer, but produced a handful of bottles from a drawer, a couple of cocktail glasses and, beaming at his own cleverness, a little purple umbrella. I watched him mix the drink, chuckling as the ingredients combined. He downed his in a single gulp. I didn't touch mine; it sat on the table between us.

"Ain't you gonna drink it?" he asked, his accent a thick California drawl, and before I could speak, he grabbed it from in front of me, shrugged, said, "Hell of a waste," and drained my glass down too, wiping his mouth with the back of his sleeve. This done, he slung himself into his office chair, boots up on the desk, legs crossed, arms folded across his belly, and beamed.

"So," he said at last. "How long's it been? You took your sweet time getting round to challenging the bitch."

"I wasn't ready before."

"Looks to me like you ain't ready now!" he replied brightly. "Getting blood all over my shit, that is."

"I...didn't expect to see you here."

"Where else would you expect to see me? In the fucking mountains, freezing my balls off? The wild tamed civilisation, Silver, the wild got into civilisation's veins—this is the place; this is where it's at. You okay to walk? Walk with me."

I walked with him, hobbling behind as he swept across the thick red carpets, the marble halls, past the mirrors of polished bronze, the bell boys and card sharps, executive hosts and VIP managers, gamblers, tourists, drunks and hopefuls of the hotel. Subordinates shuffled out of his way, middlemen tried to smile, then looked away. He beamed at all who passed him by and they faltered, feeling perhaps the thing that lay behind the smile, the power, the joy. We swept through the backstage corridors above a concert hall where a woman with two stars over her breasts, one over her groin and very little else, suspended by a wire seven feet above the stage, spun and spun in the white light of the follow-spots.

He beat me, he mistreat me, but that's okay, he's my guy . . .

Below, three thousand people stared in wonder, their faces sparkling in reflected light while oiled, muscle-bound dancers pounded and thrust their way through a routine, faces contorted into grimaces of pain, feet stamping, skin bulging, sweat mixing with grease down the sides of their thick, tanned necks.

I want it hot hot, she sang. *I want it now now. I want it more more.*

Bird let me watch for a moment, then pulled me on, dragging me by the sleeve like a kitten playing with its prey. In the lift, a man and a woman were tangled in a drunken embrace, fingers clawing at each other, pulling at clothes, skin, hair. I turned away; Bird watched, chuckling to himself, and they didn't care.

Onto the fifth floor, through crystal doors and down corridors of silver and blue, we came to a quieter lounge, a long bar of polished titanium white and black marble floors, where tables were laid out for the greatest and the grandest to play their games. Dice tumbled and cards fell; a hundred thousand dollars were lost and the loser shrugged; stacks of chips dragged into the house's hand as the high rollers sipped champagne, three hundred dollars a glass, and caressed the thighs of paid-for strangers, and rolled fortunes away like children throwing stones at a bucket.

Down again, down to the bright light where everything beeped, buzzed, banged, twiddled and turned, where the tourists wore

374

Hawaiian shirts and high shorts, and the regulars wore sweat patches which had embedded themselves into stiff crumples of yellow, and the hostesses swayed at the hips as they walked, and bent down to whisper in the ears of familiar faces, buttocks out, breasts down, lips wide and eyes innocent, another roll, sir, your luck will turn...

On a balcony above it all, like an emperor inspecting his troops, we stopped, and Bird threw his arms wide in triumph and pride. "Roulette!" he exclaimed, stacks moving across the green surface of the tables. "Slot machines!" Wheels turned, wheels turned, and the house won. "Blackjack." The cards fell; the player lost. "Twenty-one, baccarat, the roll of the dice." The dice rolled, the dice rolled, and the house won. "The turn of the coin and look at them! Just look!"

I looked around a hall plastered with light, a brightness almost too bright to look at, hear the pinging of the machines, the chattering of the tables, the cries of the winners, the sighs of the loser, and as he chuckled again, "Look, look," I strained my eyes to see what it was that his broad grin and wide arms took in.

"They're smiling!" he cried. "They're smiling, they're laughing, look at them! They're going to be fucking broken—I'm going to fucking break them, rinse them dry, take their fucking souls and they're gonna love me for it all the way. Do you see it, Silver? Do you see?"

"Yes," I said. "I see."

"Do you see this victory?" he asked, face burning with joy. "The banks bet big and countries fall; the numbers grow and the numbers shrink but people—the clever, clever people, reasonable, rational people—they don't play the numbers, they don't play the maths, they just play greed. Lust! Lust and blood, that's all there is, all there ever was. Behind every smile there's only sex and need, in every gift there's a debt that will be paid, power that will be reaped, this world, these people, they are the wild things, the savage things, just like I always said, just like I promised—I was right! There is no reason; there is only the fire and the dark!"

"No," I breathed, watching the slots turn and turn again on the floor below. "You're wrong."

He hit me. The slap, open-handed and hard, was so sudden and unexpected that it pushed me off my feet, sent me falling to the floor, and there he was, stood over me, the king of the mountain, the lord of the wild things. "Stop me," he breathed, and as I made to stand up, he kicked me, knocking me down. "Stop me," he repeated louder, and though some people saw, everyone turned away, no help coming, no one who dared to care. I reached up and he stood on my hand, ground his heel into it until I whimpered with pain, then bent down, his face hot next to mine, holding my head up by the hair. "Stop me," he whispered. "They say you're the one of the greatest players who ever lived, one of the smartest men alive. Go on. Use your words; use your wisdom and your wit. Reason until I stop."

I tried to speak, couldn't, only pain and breath left.

"You play for vengeance," he breathed. "And now you pant and beg and bleed, and nothing can save you except chance and blood. You're an animal too."

So saying, he let me go, turned his back and I hauled myself onto my uncertain feet, leaning across the railing of the balcony to gasp down breath.

A while we stood there, he staring at nothing while I watched the slots. Three cherries in a row; two pineapples and a raspberry; bonus, bonus, bonus! The wheels turned, and the house won. The house always wins, and still the players play.

Then Bird looked back, and he was smiling again, a glitzy cowboy in a millionaire's suit. He caught my hand, pushed something into it before I could say no, holding me tight by the wrist. I felt a thing, warmed by flesh, which he closed my fingers around, still smiling, still looking into my eyes.

"You're gonna lose," he breathed. "It's a shame, after all the time you've wasted, but you can't beat her; you ain't got what it takes."

"You don't know that."

"Sure I do. I've watched players for ever—I know when they don't have the heart for it and, Silver, you lost your heart a long time back. I can help you; I can give you what it takes to bring her down."

His hand around my wrist, his fingers pressing over my fingers.

"In exchange for what?" I asked.

"If you win, you get the Gameshouse."

"No: I destroy it."

He tutted. "And what a waste that would be! You take it, you make it what people really want. No more boards, no more brains, just the joy, just the money, just the blood—you get it? You burn the chess sets and you put in fruit machines. You smash the baduk board and build me a roulette table. And in the higher league, for the ones who get that kinda luck, you make sure when they give the chamber a spin that the ammunition is live; and when the cards fall and the forfeit is the guy's soul, you see to it that the whole house is there to take a piece, to eat him raw. You promise me that and I'll help you take the Gameshouse. Or say no and I'll let the bitch chain you to her fucking wall."

He pulled his hand away from mine. I looked down. A dice lay in my hands, small, polished, perfectly square, carved from yellowing bone. Bird's face was open with curiosity, waiting to see what I'd do. I closed my fist tight around it, let my eyes sink shut, feeling its warmth.

I opened my eyes, handed him the dice. "Thank you for your offer," I said. "But the answer is no."

Surprise flickered across his features but he took the dice, slipped it back into his jacket pocket. "Your decision," he said with a shrug. "Stupid for a player." A flash of a grin across his face. "But then, that kinda just proves my point, don't it now?"

I turned away, feeling suddenly tired, in pain. He didn't try to stop me, didn't move, but as I headed for the door, he called after me.

"Silver!"

I stopped, not looking back.

"Luck is sometimes merciful; the game never is. Remember that when you change your mind."

I walked away.

Chapter 34

The day my funds dropped to their last hundred million dollars, I crossed the border between the U.S. and Canada on a tour bus of enthusiastic Argentineans who *oooh*ed and *aaah*hed as we rattled across the Thousand Islands International Bridge, craning their necks to see the waterways wriggling below, the snow-capped forests all around. Our guide, as we entered Canada, stood up and proclaimed:

"Canada is famous for maple syrup and moose!" and everyone applauded.

In Montreal I ate chips with melted cheese, and as the winter snows began to thicken, crunched through knee-high piles to the bus station to catch the coach northeast, following the river to Quebec, then on into timberlands and the north.

The ferry to Tadoussac was delayed by bad weather, but eventually edged its way across the fjord into a town whose already-white houses were now turned whiter by the thick winter. The sun, when it peeped across the bay, was pale and brief, uneasy to be caught rising and fast to set. The main road through the town was silent save for the great lorries, loaded with timber in one direction, petrol in the other, growling past the little houses in the dead of night.

I found her in a little house above the bay, away from the rest of the town in a thicket of pine trees. The light was on in the living room, the stove was hot in the kitchen, but she still wore two woollen jumpers over her dressing-gown and, when she answered the door, she took a moment to recognise me through the hats, scarves, gloves, coats which shrouded my figure.

"Oh," she said, as realisation dawned. "I wondered when you'd turn up."

She made omelettes, cracking each egg in the fingers of one hand, no need for knives. I huddled near the stove, while a curious black and white cat rolled around my legs and, finding that I wasn't hugely interested, jumped into my lap to enforce the need for attention.

"I like it out here," she explained, pushing a plate across the table. "When the Gameshouse closed its doors, I concluded it wouldn't be long until we came under pressure, particularly the older players. Remy's gone over to her side, you know?"

"I know."

"It surprised me: I thought he was one of yours."

"The endgame's coming," I replied. "I'm losing ground."

She nodded, without expression, pouring ketchup into a round puddle on the side of her plate. "I thought you might be; figured you'd call."

I smiled uneasily over my fork, studying her face. Thene, beautiful Thene, she had put on a mask so many centuries ago and, though the mask was gone, its impression remained on her skin, unchanging, unflinching, unreadable. She had survived in the higher league more than most, playing slow, careful games, building her resources, and yet, being so cold in her demeanour, it was as if the rest of the house had lacked the emotional involvement to ever truly challenge her. She provoked no fear, no envy, no dread, no rage, but was merely all that she was—a player. In those words were the be-all and end-all of her existence, and the rest was merely frost on a winter's morning.

"We struck a bargain, a long, long time ago," I said. "Before you knew what the game was. I need to invoke that bargain now."

"I know. I realised a long time ago what our deal would

379

entail. The Gamesmaster plays, plays the players, using us to shape the world, and by our actions we did that—we created kings and destroyed ideas, launched rebellions and pushed society towards change; change of her choosing, that is. But then I looked a little closer and saw another game running behind it all, and you, Silver, were pulling the strings, gathering players into your hand, pieces you were waiting to play. I have only one move I will make for you—our bargain gave you only one move you could play—but I will play the part well and true, otherwise what is the purpose of the game? So." She laid her knife and fork down carefully at the side of her plate, locked her hands together, elbows below, chin above, leant forward. "What is this lie you need me to tell?"

Chapter 35

Endgame.

I was going to lose, and as losing men sometimes do, I staked my defeat on one final gamble.

I set the board up near Jengish Chokusu, in the snow-capped mountains where no road ran, no tourists wandered, no miner dug, no adventurer came. For days a man could walk in this place and find no sign of life, and yet, in this same ridge of nothing, some forty years ago, the Soviets had built bunkers against invasion in a place where no army would reach, paranoia outweighing strategic sense.

To these bunkers I went, walking for days on end to find them, and in this place I set up my tools: the cameras, explosives, data networking, bugs, traps and locked doors. I play a unit from the Kyrgyz military, deploying three hundred men into the bunker and the mountains around it. A training exercise, my piece told them—nothing more. Then I permitted one of the soldiers to catch me in the edge of his photo frame, as he took a selfie on this tedious exercise to send back to his wife.

The photo I intercepted and enhanced and, after two months of preparation, forwarded it to Thene.

"Contact the Gamesmaster," I said. "I know you know how. Tell her you found this—make the lie plausible. That's all."

"The Gamesmaster is a hard woman to lie to."

"I know. That's why I chose you."

Two days later, a message came from Thene.

It's done.

The IP address from which those words were sent disappeared immediately after. She had made her move and I had made mine, and all there was to do now was wait.

Three days later, the invasion began.

She played Russian special forces, sneaking them in via helicopter in the dead of night. They killed seventeen of my men before the alert was issued and the sky lit up with flares, forcing the invaders back.

The next day, she played a larger unit of Russian operatives, backed up by a team of Chinese mercenaries, but my troops were ready, and a small arms battle raged in this nowhere land, snipers on ridges taking potshots at each other as men fell from cliffs and died in valleys.

On the third day, she launched MiGs against my positions, and the commander of the Kyrgyz unit desperately radioed his headquarters, asking what was happening, what was going on— but she'd jammed his kit, the soldiers' phones, and in a frantic meeting in the middle of the mountain, the unit concluded that, alone and isolated, all they could do now was fight.

They dug in, securing positions in and around the bunker, which she could not penetrate.

On the fourth day, she air-dropped in artillery, which took a further eight hours to be manoeuvred into firing positions. They started firing at seven-thirty p.m. I took them down with a unit of Chinese fighters launched out of Xinjiang, slipped under Kyrgyz radar while my pieces looked the other way.

On the fifth day, she dropped in Russian, Uzbeki, Chinese and Tajik special forces, a groundswell of troops for the first time outnumbering my defenders. For two days, my men held out, but by the end of the week, they were down to a hundred and twenty-seven men and supplies were running low.

Now I unleashed the full force of the Chinese military and government which I had been so carefully nurturing since she chased me through Mongolia. I bombed her positions, sabotaged her planes, assassinated those pieces who she'd played to muster such forces against me, airdropped supplies to my men, unleashed viruses against the satellites and telephones she was using to coordinate this strike and in one bloody night of fire and dust, reduced her forces back down to a mere two hundred men.

The next day very little happened.

The next day, very little again.

On the tenth day of battle, the Indian air force succeeded in dropping two hundred and fifty men, supplies, mortars and heavy weapons into the valley below my bunker, while unknown separatists simultaneously blew up my airfields in Xinjiang, assassinated two of my generals and, in a stroke of beauty, launched an all-out assault on the government offices of Ngari near the Indian border, diverting Chinese attention (and my pieces) away from our quiet, undeclared Kyrgyz war.

Within twelve hours, she had pushed my troops back into the bunker itself, yielding all the positions they'd held outside. Four hours after that, the unit was down to fifty men who debated whether to surrender or fight to the death. Thirty surrendered—twenty swore they would die fighting.

Eight hours after that, the twenty who were left alive, were still fighting, pushed deeper and deeper into the bunker. I detonated booby traps as they withdrew, helping them on their way, sealing off corridors and butchering enemy men who came after them, until at last they were in the lowest part of that place, in the darkest corner from which there was no way out, and the enemy stood at the doors and said:

We can kill you all now with a couple of grenades. You have nowhere to run. Be smart—surrender.

They answered with gunfire and died in a flash.

When the smoke cleared, the bunker was taken. Hundreds of men were dead, the mountain shattered from within. In China, rebels raged through the westernmost towns; in Russia, fighters burned on their runways, while in Kyrgyzstan the Gamesmaster's troops opened the very last door to the very deepest part of the bunker and found looking back at them my camera and network server, and six pounds of C-4.

I detonated the explosive from my room in Tokyo, watched the screen go black. I turned to the men and women in the room, the spies, hackers, cyber-terrorists and cyber-experts, the forensic accountants and military advisors, special forces and retired generals whom I had gathered, the greatest assemblage of pieces that I could muster, and said:

"Did we get it?"

They conferred for a little while, their screens still hot with rolling data. Then an accountant from Maine put his hand up and said, "Yes."

Chapter 36

Every battle has an alternative history.

As men screamed and died for a nameless mountain in Kyrgyzstan, I and my assembled team gathered data.

First, we were based in Yushu, but by the third day of the battle, enough of the Gamesmaster's soldiers had been identified, by unit or uniform, to pinpoint the pieces which had deployed them. As the vast majority of pieces she was playing were being deployed from Russia, we had headed north to Changji, only to change our minds and divert south when the spies and satellites I'd placed over the battlefield detected Indian troop movements to the south. By the tenth day, we had identified thirty-two of her pieces—generals, spies, prime ministers—and by the eleventh, had full access to their communications and finances.

On the thirteenth hour of the eleventh day, and for the first time in ten years, I heard her voice.

It was a phone call to a self-styled colonel of a mercenary band heading into the conflict zone. She said:

"Leave none alive."

By the morning of the twelfth day, when the last of my troops fell, we had tracked that call—and a dozen others—back to a single point. The accountants ransacked the transactions leading to the bank of every mercenary and captain she threw against us, every helicopter pilot and every paid-for bullet, and even as our plane touched down in Tokyo, they confirmed what all other sources suggested: the Gamesmaster's orders were coming from Japan.

When the last bomb went off in the last room of the bunker, we had data on every single man who'd died, every piece that had been played, every command issued.

And, as the dust settled over the dead of the mountain, an accountant from Maine turned round, raised his hand and said, "I think I've found the debit card she's been using to pay for her mini bar."

I looked at the screen that he looked at, looked at the last transaction, noted that it was twenty minutes ago and five miles away and said, "Okay. Let's go."

Chapter 37

Racing through Tokyo in a convoy of trucks.

What do I feel?

Bright lights, tall buildings, treeless streets. Glass and steel, the taste of salt in my mouth.

I have orchestrated the deaths of over seven hundred men, and from their deaths an accountant has managed to trace a mini-bar bill that may or may not be the place of residence of the Gamesmaster.

She castled several years ago, fortifying herself at the top of a tower in Tokyo from which all things are coordinated. In attempting to break down my castle in Kyrgyzstan, she has revealed her position. Safety or a trap? Castling can be both if you are careless with your positioning.

Lights in the streets of Tokyo. Katakana, hiragana, imported characters and exported words. Mitsubishi, Nissan, Sony, Honda: once upon a time these were samurai clans which were turned to merchant manufacturing when the old order fell. Then the Americans came after the Second World War and declared death to all zaibatsu, the corporate conglomerates. Now the youth of Japan compete with a mania that borders on disease to get lifelong positions in these companies, and economics shake and technologies change, and the world turns and everything is different, and everything is just the same.

Someone asks if I am all right, and I don't understand why.

"You're breathing fast, sir. You're breathing very fast."

Am I?

Perhaps I am.

I close my eyes, breathe slowly. A player never shows their feelings, never reveals their hand. Only the board; only the game. The rest is distraction.

I counted up the pieces I had in play.

Thirty mercenaries in the trucks behind mine, dressed in police uniform. Another twenty armed men on their way, played through an arms dealer I'd won in Iwaki.

In my pocket, I rolled a coin round and round between my fingers. Flak jacket over my shirt, gun on my hip, we broke every speed limit, jumped every red light, and someone said, will it be a problem? and I supposed it might be so I phoned a policeman I'd won ... a long time ago ... and told him to ignore it, to seal the area around Ikedayama Park, nothing in, nothing out. Someone else said, will she run? so I phoned an arsonist I'd won in Nagoya, gave him the clear to bomb the air traffic control tower at Yokohama, grounding all flights, perhaps even— if we were lucky—sealing Japanese airspace. I let the Chinese secret service unleash the computer virus they'd been sitting on since I seized control of their agency, slicing servers in half across Japan and, eleven minutes after its execution, plunging Tokyo into darkness as it shut down relays in the power grid. I gave the go to every assassin who'd been waiting for the signal, every hitman and petty thug I'd kept in reserve, unleashing them on all of the Gamesmaster's pieces who'd been identified from Kyrgyzstan. No mercy. *Leave none alive.*

I tried saying the words out loud, tried matching the tone of her voice as she had spoken them, but nothing in my voice could make the words sound like her, make the words sound like me.

"Leave none alive," says a voice, and I find it suddenly impossible to imagine it is me.

Who spoke them, then?

That other fellow, the other man there, the one sitting with a gun at his hip, a coin in his hand, that man—what shall we call him? He lost his name so long ago, sold his heart, auctioned his soul and to become—here it is, here it comes ...

A player.

Not a person at all.

I rolled the coin between my fingers as we drove through the darkness of electrically broken streets until we came to the only building that still shone brightly in the night. Moriyoshi Tower, forty-nine floors of it, named for a heroic prince who fought valiantly and died betrayed. A glass spike to the sky: the pillar of wealth and vanity, it had its own generators, still shining bright, all the brighter for the darkness of the city that surrounded it. Looking up at it, I thought it was a very beautiful place to castle a king, and wondered if she liked the views.

A fixer gave me a quick rundown—shops for the first five floors, then offices, then restaurants, then more offices, then at the top a hotel so luxurious that it didn't even bother to have a website listing: you either knew about it or you weren't connected enough to afford it.

"Can you access their cameras?" I asked. "Can you see inside?"

She could not.

"That doesn't bode well," I sighed, unclipping the safety from my holster. "Even if it isn't a surprise."

We went inside.

Shops, still open. No one buying; faces pressed to the glass, looking out; people talking, pointing, marvelling at their suddenly black, suddenly silent city. We—thirty armed policemen, assault rifles and helmets—were almost unremarkable in the dead quiet of the sudden urban night, for if the power had failed, of course but of course it made sense that policemen had come.

We moved by, looking for a way up. Around, ads still blared to the uninterested eye, the newest phone, the latest computer, the smartest watch, the trendiest clothes, the most expensive glasses, the biggest films, the loudest books, the sweetest drinks, the richest foods.

Come buy come buy, said the walls.

You need the latest.

You need the best.

You need to be the latest, the best.
Hot hot, now now, more more!

I felt a prickling in the corner of my eyes and wondered what it was. At the unmarked lift to the hotel, a man in white gloves stepped forward exclaiming, "No! This is exclusive! You cannot come up here!"

One of the mercenaries hit him across the side of his face with a rifle, and five men piled into the lift. I stayed behind and when the bomb on top of the car detonated four floors up, I turned to the survivors and said, "We're taking the stairs."

On the twelfth floor my phone rang, announcing the arrival of reinforcements. I deployed them remotely, sealing off the ground floors of the building, putting a helicopter overhead to shoot down anyone who attempted to flee into the skies. On the fourteenth floor, another phone call alerted me to the bombing of Yokohama air traffic control. Seventeen people were missing, presumed dead; more information not yet forthcoming.

They started shooting at us on the twenty-third floor.

Initially I couldn't see who "they" were, as my mercenaries pushed me bodily out of the stairwell, already a killing ground. Only three corridors later, as we searched for an alternative route up and gunfire blared behind us, did I catch a glimpse of "them"—men in black suits, black ties, white shirts, who wielded sub-machine guns with a quiet professionalism and made no other sound as they blasted at us.

Their tactics were poor, their teamwork almost non-existent, but with a relentless force of numbers and a reckless disregard for their own safety, they kept coming—five dead, ten dead, fifteen dead or injured—and still they kept firing, kept pushing against us, until we were pressed between the killing ground of the stairwell and the bloodstained corridors of the tower ahead. I took the assault rifle off a man who fell by my side, a bullet to the femoral artery, dead in four minutes, and kept firing as the corridors filled with the stench of cordite and the thin, sickly traceries of smoke. My ears sang with the high shrill of cells dying from the volume of noise, and when someone threw a grenade at me, I was saved only by the weight of the dead man by my side, which absorbed most of the force of the blast. His blood ran down my face, stuck my hair together in clumps, stained my hands, and still the enemy kept coming.

"With me!" I grabbed four men, peeling away from the rest to make a break for the lift banks. One died when a door behind us opened to reveal a young man, barely seventeen years old, his face twisted with fear that he had forced to become rage, who leant out to spray us with bullets, and who died a few seconds later from a gunshot to the head. Another, less glamorously, pulled a muscle when he tripped over the body of a dead laundry woman, caught fleeing in a burst of wandering bullets that tore her stomach out and left her, nameless soul, sprawled across the field of battle.

We found a bank of lifts, and entering, climbed up through the access shaft in the ceiling to carefully remove the explosives wired up to the cable base, before pressing "up". As the doors closed, five men, alerted perhaps by some unseen controller, came running towards us and a bullet took out my limping soldier before the doors closed.

He didn't die quickly. He didn't groan or shout or scream, but sat on the floor of the elevator, one hand over the wound to his chest, breath coming pink from his lips, a look of surprise, more than pain on his face. We three, the three left standing, looked at each other uncertainly before one man squatted down to give his colleague the shot of morphine that hung from a chain round his neck. He said, "Thanks," and didn't seem to understand that he was dead and the lift was his coffin.

The lift stopped with a shudder between floors, two storeys short of its destination. We didn't wait for what would follow, but prised the doors open, wriggled out on our bellies onto the small box of floor above us. The last man pulled his feet free a moment before the explosive fired somewhere higher in the shaft, severing the cable of the car and plunging the elevator and its wounded prisoner forty-seven floors to their destruction.

I looked around the floor we'd crawled into. A reception area for a hotel. Glass fish-bowls held crystal stones and no fish. Clocks showed the hour in Moscow, New York, London, Beijing, Singapore, Cairo. TV screens down one wall blared out the news—crises here, disasters there, outbreak of disease, collapse of fortunes, broken, broken, broken, until the ads played, women with impossible smiles, men with impossible bodies, more, more, more, now, now, now, want, want, need.

A single receptionist stood behind a curving desk of crystal and aluminium. She was crying silently, back stiff and straight, a red silk scarf around her neck, a perfectly white cuff at the end of each sleeve. Were it not for the tears, she could still have looked like the perfect professional, waiting to meet guests. She stayed standing as we, bloodstained and armed, pass her by looking for stairs, and she bit back the sobs in the pit of her throat as we departed.

A black city outside, corridors of blue within. Doors were locked shut, nothing moved. A service trolley, soft towels and fragrant soap, sat in the middle of the corridor. In a corner, an ice machine spat white cubes onto the floor, something broken inside, the internal parts groaning, clunking with the strain. The sound of gunfire was distant now, men dying below.

We found stairs, started to climb. Two men with semi-automatic pistols burst from the floors above us, but we had come too far to die at the hands of amateurs and took them down before they could fire a single shot. Forty-seventh floor; forty-eighth; forty-ninth. A helicopter circled somewhere nearby, but the odds were high that it was mine, prowling the skies, waiting for someone to be foolish enough to cross its path. I pushed open the door to the highest floor with the muzzle of my gun, stepped into a corridor like any other, blue lights, potted plants, black marble floor. At the end of the corridor, a pair of double doors opened to a place unknown. White light shone beneath it, and then quickly went out. We moved forward. No one stopped us.

At the door, one man took a position to the left, the other to the right. I listened and heard nothing inside, threw a flashbang in anyway just in case, and the second after it burst, I was inside too.

A penthouse suite, a few lights burning, one above a desk strewn with papers, one next to a wall covered with screens. Three men on the floor, their eyes shut, their hands over their ears, guns at their feet—they died quickly, not knowing how.

Scenes of a life lived. A newspaper lay open on a sofa. A cup of coffee cooled on the crystal table, now flecked with bits of brain and blood. A white dressing-gown had fallen in a pile by the door, ready to be cleaned. A pair of high-heeled shoes, another of trainers, lay in a tatami-clad nook where visitors could remove their boots and put on slippers. There were no slippers to be seen. The wall of screens in one corner of the suite showed camera feeds, some from the hotel, some from other places: unknown walls, unknown corridors of power. I looked, and saw dead men filling the stairwells, frightened men—so few now—scurrying for shelter as the last of the bullets flew below.

Another pair of doors—black, metallic—stood a little ajar, leading from this room to another. We edged towards it, pushed the doors open, saw a room bigger than the first, couches and a low aluminium bar, a winter coat casually thrown across one of the stools, a chess-board set out on a table by the long glass window, the position halfway through a game, white winning. Not a soul in sight. Slowly, keeping to cover as we moved, we advanced, another set of doors ahead. I saw a shadow move across the line of light beneath the door and raised my hand to command a stop.

We froze, waited.

Waited.

Silence.

Even the helicopter outside was silent, an absence that frightened me more than any bullet.

I glanced at my two surviving men, and saw that they were afraid.

Saw that they sensed the thing we dare not name.

Silence.

393

Something behind us clicked.

The door we'd entered through, locking shut from behind.

The door ahead rolled a little ajar. I didn't see the hand that pushed the grenade through, but I guessed at it and ducked behind the bar, hands over my ears, eyes tightly shut. The blast rocked the bottles above my head, knocked a half-drunk cocktail from its perch, spilling peach juice and vodka across the floor in front of me. The second grenade was nearer and I heard one of my men scream, and someone start to fire and I peeped my head up long enough to see the men coming through the door—not aimless men in suits, but professionals in masks, body armour, steel-capped boots, assault rifles raised, centres of gravity low. One of my men got four shots off, taking down two of his attackers before a bullet caught him in the throat. The other was already dead, skin ripped from flesh by the concussive force of the explosions that greeted us.

I rolled up from behind the bar and started firing, happy now in the thought that the only people I could hit were enemies. Glass popped and burst, couches puffed their upholstery into the room, filling it with falling foam, and I think I killed two of them before a man I hadn't even seen, moving behind an overturned table which had once been adorned around the edges with the lacquered shape of dancing birds, got a shot off which slammed into the centre of my vest and knocked me to the ground.

Chapter 38

Bits and pieces.

I lay in bits on the ground, while pieces slotted into place around me.

They took my guns, my knife, my phone.

They pulled off my flak jacket, inspected their handiwork— the bullet embedded in the vest and the vast purple bruise already flowering above my heart. They picked me up and carried me through rooms of the hotel. Two men in body armour, helmets and boots, and a third who walked before, his face hidden by a balaclava, an assault rifle slung over his back.

They deposited me on a floor of clean tatami mats in a room smelling of incense. I rolled onto my back, turned my head either side, saw candles burning in long troughs of water that ran round the walls, a hundred little floating points of light, saw orchids in full bloom at the feet of a little shrine, no icons, no images except the flowers, the candlelight, a woman kneeling before it, head bowed like one in prayer. Her head was covered with a veil of white, her robes were white, white gloves covered her hands and she was silent, still.

I lay where I was and looked at the ceiling—faux wooden beams and panels—and listened to nothing at all.

The gunfire had stopped.

The city was dark and strangers were dead. How many had we slaughtered to come to this moment? How many lives had we destroyed?

I felt something in my pocket, a thing that my captors had not removed.

A tiny Roman coin.

Luck is sometimes merciful; the game never is.

I waited.

Then the woman said; "I'm very sorry it ends like this. I truly am. You were a great asset in the game, while it lasted, but even the best pieces must sometimes be sacrificed."

She didn't turn her head, didn't raise her voice, but stayed contemplating the candlelight. I looked up at the three armed men, too marked by death to be in this flower-scented place, and thought I recognised in one of them a certain bulk, a certain height, a certain aging about the eyes that reminded me of a man I'd once known. He pulled a gun from his holster, levelled it at my head and I, lying on the floor, started to laugh.

I laughed, and couldn't remember when laughter last had passed my lips.

I laughed at this moment and the way it was going to end. I laughed at the path that had brought us here, her and I, at the things which had then seemed so serious, and now meant so little. I laughed, and no one laughed with me, and caught by the solemnity of their silence I stopped laughing, tears rolling through the blood on my face, and looked up again into the masked features of the man who was going to kill me and wheezed, "Mercy."

Silence.

He did not move.

"Mercy."

He held the gun in a two-handed grip, pointed it at my head and did not move.

Then she spoke, my goddess, my lady all in white, my enemy, my love, she, the Gamesmaster, who still would not turn her head to look at me as I died, and she said, "The game is not merciful."

I half turned my head to see her better and, seeing that she would not move, I looked back again at my executioner, met his eyes, knew them, knew *him*, and said, "I know."

396

His finger tightened around the trigger, and he fired.

The first shot killed the soldier who stood to my left; the second killed the soldier to my right. They fell, too astonished to scream, but one of them was still breathing so he put two more shots into the man's head, kicking the rifle away from his crawling fingers. Now the Gamesmaster was on her feet, face still hidden, body thin and stiff, a rippling in her robes as they settled about her.

The man in the mask looked at her, and me, then pulled the ammo from his gun and threw it away. He unclipped the helmet from his head, tossed it across the room, pulled the mask from his face to reveal dark brown hair, a face that had lived too long, travelled too far, forgotten what it was to be itself. I could name that face, had met it a dozen times before, played a few friendly games with it, helped it once, saved it even, given it cause to doubt and reason to rejoice, and it was the face of Remy Burke, sometime player, piece in the Gameshouse's hand. How long had I fought to reduce her forces to that point where she would have to call on his? How many years had I spent positioning the board for just this moment, to be certain that his hand was on the gun?

Decades.

Centuries.

As long as he had been alive.

Remy Burke: a piece in my hand. The last piece I had to play; the last move I had to make.

He looked down at me and said, "My debt is paid."

I nodded, an effort from the floor.

He let the mask fall to the ground, looked once more at the Gamesmaster, did not look at me and walked away.

Silence in the house.

She stood; I lay. Groaning with effort, I rolled onto my belly, pulled the gun from the holster of the nearest dead man, held it close to me.

She did not move.

I crawled into a sitting position, levering my body backwards until it was propped against the wall. One of the corpses was bleeding slowly, a pool seeping into the mats of the room, sticking to the bottom of my thighs where I brushed the red liquor. Blood on my hands was drying to sticky brown streaks. Blood on my face was crisping to an itchy coat. I tried rubbing some of it away, but that only spread the crimson, didn't clear it.

In this state we remained, she and I, waiting.

I looked for words, and found none.

She waited.

I raised the gun to her, and nothing moved beneath the veil, not a shimmer, not a sound.

I lowered the gun again, letting it fall into my lap.

She waited.

At last I said, "Give her back to me."

A pause, a moment while she considered the question. Then: "No."

I raised the gun, two hands around it now, steadying the shot. "I have *won*," I breathed. "I won the game. The house is mine to command. Now give her back!"

Her head tilted gently to one side. "No," she repeated, confidence rising in her voice. "There are only two outcomes from this situation. You can kill me and the house will be yours to do with as you will. Or you can put on the white, take up my office and I will be free to go elsewhere, and the house will be yours still and you will belong to it. These are the only choices."

My arms were shaking, the gun gripped too tight. I looked inside for the laughter that had been there a moment ago, and it was gone.

"You must become the Gamesmaster." Her voice was soft, calm as she moved nearer, squatting down a little in front of me. I thought I saw the shape of her face through the veil, but perhaps I only imagined it, imposed some long-faded half-dream of what I thought she had once looked like on that empty white. "The Gameshouse shapes humanity. We are the soul of reason, the pinnacle of intellect; through the game we excel ourselves. You have excelled yourself, Silver. You have achieved an intelligence—and through that intelligence, a power—that exceeds that of the house itself. You must become the Gamesmaster; this is how the house grows, how humanity evolves."

"I don't want to be the Gamesmaster."

"Then kill me and burn the house—but know that there will always be a game, and there will always be those who play it. While the one called Bird is still alive, there must be a centre that fights him, a force to oppose his madness."

I lowered the gun, finding it now too heavy to hold, couldn't look at her white veil, turned my face away. "I just want her back," I said. "The house can do whatever the hell it wants."

"It cannot be love," she chided, so close now, her face level with mine. "Not after all this time."

"Can't it? Maybe you're right. After a few hundred years, after I'd walked round the world, slaughtered men, butchered kings, burned philosophers as heretics and made prophets out of madmen—after I lost my name—I think I began to forget the meaning of certain words. Guilt; grief; remorse; revenge; regret; happiness; joy; sorrow; love. They became merely... attributes... to be played on a piece to achieve a victory, and that victory was more powerful and more addictive than any opiate. To win—to be smarter than anyone else, and to *win*—that is the greatest joy a player has, truly, when all other joys are lost. Maybe that's the reason we're here now. To prove to you, who was always so much smarter than I, that now I'm a player worthy of your affection. Or maybe because playing you is the only victory worth achieving."

A sense of a smile behind her veil, her hands open wide for me, though her arms were pressed in tight, like a bird unsure if the offered morsel is food or poison. "Not the only victory," she breathed. "There is still one game greater than all the rest. This game we play now—it shapes the players of the next, prepares them to fight the adversary."

"Bird?"

"Bird," she agreed. "Take the Gameshouse, take the white, guide humanity to something better. You know him better than

399

most; you can see what he is, how... obscene... the world would be if he was allowed to roam free, Silver."

Her fingers reached out, brushed the side of my face. I flinched, drawing in breath, then grabbed her fingers tight before she could pull them away, held them to me, felt that strange, burning thing inside me that had lost its name, a thing that might have been grief, might have been something wonderful.

"Do you remember my name?" I asked.

"Yes."

"Will you tell me?"

"No," she replied, so soft, so very kind. "That is not the game we are playing."

I closed my eyes, unable now to look at that white nothing, the not-woman, not-human, not-thing that stood before me. Then I heard fabrics move and opened my eyes again, and she had lifted up her veil and was smiling. She smiled at me, and the tears fell across my face to see her, and I couldn't look away as salt dripped off the curves of my cheeks.

"Silver," she murmured, "when I defeated the Gamesmaster, when I made the house my own, I never thought of you as anything more than a piece. I want you to understand that, now that we are at the end."

I wept without noise. She smiled and I wept, and was all that there was between us for a little while.

I said, please...

But she lowered her veil, pulled her fingers from my hand, turned away.

Please, I said, and found that the rest of the words could not come with the sound. Please, my love, please, my wife, please, have mercy, have mercy.

(Luck is sometimes merciful; the game never is.)

But she was cold and white, unreachable, lost to me a long time ago.

"I love you!" I said, choking on the sound, kneeling at her feet with a gun in my hand. "Please: I love you!"

You love the game, she replied. That is all.

400

No, no, I love you, I love you, you, always you, all this I did for you, I did to set you free, to bring you back to me...

No. That isn't why you played. Perhaps once you played for love, but now you only play for the win. If you loved me, the choice would be easy. Take the white; set me free.

Silence.

I knelt at her feet and had no more words, no more sounds, no more feelings. Where had I been, and how had I come to this place? It seemed to me that memory was a distant thing, a film played about someone else's life, a stranger I did not know. I remembered the skin burning on my back as I half drowned in the Atlantic Ocean, could conjure up the taste of camel milk in my mouth, smell fish frying on a sandy beach, hear the laughter of children and the last breath of dying men, but in this moment, at this time, it was as if I watched these events, godlike, from far away, a ghost on a cloud witnessing the unfolding of other people's lives, impassive as the air. Only this; only this moment was real.

"Do you want to be free?" I asked, and she did not look at me. "Say it: say that you no longer want to be Gamesmaster and I'll take your deal. I'll wear the white, play the game, and you can go and live your life somewhere else, and die in some other place, and there will be no more games played by you or with your life. Say that's what you want and I'll do it. I will."

"You won the game," she replied. "You are what the white requires to further the game."

"Not you, dammit!" I shouted. "Not the Gamesmaster, not you! You, *you* my wife, you, the woman I married: if there is any piece of you left inside then tell me, tell me you want to be free and I'll do it, I'll be the Gamesmaster, *but you tell me!*"

Silence.

A silence heavier for the fact I had been screaming before.

Again, weaker now, I said, I love you.

I love you.

I love you.

The words died on my lips.

401

Silence.

I closed my eyes and tried to conjure up the picture of a man whose life I had once dreamed was my own. He was so young, lost so far in my memory, and he had sworn, before the game, that he loved his wife too. How had that love felt? Was it the love of a beautiful victory on a complicated board? Was it the ecstasy of snatching success from defeat? Was it the thrill of a heart pumping as you wait for your opponent to walk into your trap, to make the decisive to move? Was that love?

"I love you," I whispered, and even as I said the words, I realised I wasn't sure what they meant. Not now; not like this.

I pressed the gun against my own heart, finger against the trigger.

She—the Gamesmaster—turned and said, "No. You are too good a player for that to be your move."

And of course she was right.

My wife is dead, and I gave up on grief a long time ago. My friends faded, the world changed, the coin turned and only I remained. I lowered the gun.

Climbed to my feet.

Legs shaking, lungs hurting, gun at my side.

She waited.

"I lost my name," I said, "and am only a player. My wife is dead also: only the Gamesmaster remains."

So saying, I raised the gun, pointing towards her, and as I did, something small and metal slipped from my jacket, rolled to the ground. We stared at it, she and I, startled by the appearance of a thing so remarkably clean in this room coated in blood. Then slowly, keeping the gun still trained on her, I bent down and picked it up.

A little Roman coin.

(The coin turns, the coin turns. Everything changes and everything stays the same.)

My eyes went up and I imagined I felt her gaze meet my own from behind the veil.

"You wouldn't," she breathed. "Not like this."

I pressed the coin tighter in my fingers. "You tell me that the game goes on, no matter what I do. I could kill you and destroy the Gameshouse, and Bird will have won a victory—maybe not the war, maybe not that—but for a while, I imagine, the blood would flow and the fires would burn and the only word on men's tongues would be greed and war, until another Gamesmaster came, another figure all in white to restore the balance of things. Of course, by then, I'd probably be dead, my life run out without the Gameshouse's halls to play in, so maybe I wouldn't care. Maybe Bird would set his men on me and have them eat me whole, as they would have all those centuries ago, because flesh is rich and no one told them no. It is not a pleasant future that you present me, but at least you are dead and I am free."

She said nothing, eyes still fixed on the coin. I held it up between thumb and forefinger for her to see more closely, then crushed it back down into my fist, squeezed it until I thought skin might bleed. "Or I take the white," I went on. "Become the Gamesmaster, the guardian of reason, of logical outcomes and rational thought, the ultimate utilitarian for whom the death of millions is merely statistics, pieces on the board...and the old, unfamiliar words as truth, hope, justice, love...merely patterns of human behaviour to exploit for a more reasoned end. In theory the idea is appealing: I see why you took the offer. But you see,"—my finger tightened against the trigger—"the Gameshouse killed my wife. She was wonderful; she was simply wonderful. And the Gameshouse made her a monster, so in love with the game that she would rather die than be set free. I loved her. I loved her. But I find in this present circumstance, constrained as I am by the rules of the game, that I no longer know what mercy is."

I pinched the coin between thumb and index finger, balanced it on top of my closed fist.

"You wouldn't," she whispered. "You wouldn't."

"I see nothing but bad choices," I replied.

"You are a player: you choose between bad choices all the time."

403

"What would you have me choose now? To kill my wife? To kill myself? To let the game go on? What could you live with?"

"There is no guilt in the game, only the board..."

"There was me!" I screamed, voice cutting through her words, gun shaking in my hand. "There was me! You took the white and I was left behind; you read the board but you didn't see *me*!"

The coin wobbled on top of my fist, ready to fall; she raised her hands, steady, calm, spoke quickly. "I see you, Silver, I see exactly who you are. You are a player, a great player, there is no higher aim. The house, the game, *the game*, everything calculated, logic, reason, intellect, every move, every piece—we play the game, we calculate the vectors of the human soul and by playing, we make it better. We make *people* better."

"No," I replied. "We make them pieces or we make them players. That isn't better."

"It is—but it is. It is rational where rage isn't, logical where love is not; I never loved you." The words fell and I flinched, but the coin was still balanced on my hand, the gun still ready to fire. Her voice rose, higher, begging: "I never loved you; you were just a piece, so shoot me, shoot me, just shoot me but don't do it like this, don't decide on...on a whim! On *chance*!" She spat the word, veil billowing about her face with fury at the sound.

I smiled, remembered someone else's words. "Luck is sometimes merciful; the game never is."

Her hands were shaking but her voice, when she finally spoke, was stunned and cold. She said, "You won't do it. I never loved you; only the game. You are a player. You won't do it."

I smiled again, stared into the empty whiteness where a person should have been, and for a moment saw myself stood there, dressed in that same veil. The image seemed laughable: why did I need a veil, who had burned away every piece of my soul so long ago? What was there that is human about me left which I could possibly need to hide?

(A memory of the ferry to Saint-Malo. *Why are you crying? Why are you crying?*)

(A policeman, gunned down in the dark. *They are not my orders. They are not orders I recognise within the boundaries of the law.*)

(Thene, her black and white cat coiling around a stranger's legs, looking for attention. Who was that stranger, smiling at her there, eating omelettes with too much syrup? He had my face but no name, but if I concentrate it seems to me that I remember and...)

...there. There is he is. He reads a book on the beaches of Palmarin while children dance around him asking for money, money, American, money?

He crosses the Mongolian steppe with a family that knows itself to be the centre of the world,
listens to the mothers whisper stories of the stars.
There is a man fleeing from the fighting in Jammu
eating noodles with a pilot and her mother as he flies to Taipei
playing dominos with strangers in Russia
sat watching the waterfall in the mountains of Spain.

There he is, this man without a name, and as I look at him from this distant, cold place where now I have come, it seems for a moment that I am him, and he is me, and that after all, he does have a name.

"My name is Silver," I said, softly at first, then again, a little louder. "My name is Silver."

I raised my head again, looked straight into the whiteness where my wife's face should have been. "I am a player. I am also something else."

I slipped my thumb under the little coin, felt its weight on top of the nail.

"You won't do it," she breathed. "You won't."

I smiled, and was content. "My love," I replied, "how little you know about people."

I let the coin fly.

Chapter 39

The coin turns, the coin turns, the coin turns.

When it lands the world will change, and the house will fall or the house will stand, and she will live or she will die, and I will wear the white, or diminish and die of mortal old age.

Sometimes life deals a bad hand, and the prize was not worth the price you paid. Sometimes there is nothing in a choice.

The coin turns, the coin turns, the coin turns.

I am Silver, who played the Gameshouse and won. Did love, if love was a thing I felt, lessen or increase the odds of my success? Would a colder man have taken fewer risks, or sacrificed fewer lives, if he was not led by some nameless passion in his heart? Or is love only weakness, which reason shall erode, has eroded, has driven wholly from my heart?

I look inwards and I see only memories and deeds, and they too begin to fade.

A player has no need to be a person.

A player has no need for a name.

The coin turns.

There are greater games yet to be played, and the pieces we move across the board of this existence will not feel our white fingers touch them, will not know that their will was ours, their lives at our command, until maybe the very last, when they look back on their lives and wonder why. Why the currents of their lives pushed them left when they could have gone right.

They will call it chance, the people of this world, and for the most part they will be mistaken.

For the most part.

The coin turns; where it falls, nobody knows.

The coin turns, empires rise and empires fall, men live and men die, babies scream and dead men sigh; the world changes but people are always and are never the same.

The coin turns, the coin turns.

I am Silver.

I choose humanity.

The coin turns.

extras

orbit

meet the author

Photo credit: Siobhan Watts

CLAIRE NORTH is a pseudonym for Catherine Webb, who wrote several novels in various genres, before publishing her first major work as Claire North, *The First Fifteen Lives of Harry August*. It was a critically acclaimed success, receiving rave reviews and an Audie nomination, and was included in the *Washington Post*'s Best Books of the Year list. Her more recent novel *The Sudden Appearance of Hope* won the World Fantasy Award for Best Novel in 2017. Catherine currently works as a theatre lighting designer and is a fan of big cities, urban magic, Thai food and graffiti-spotting. She lives in London.

if you enjoyed
THE GAMESHOUSE

look out for

SOMEONE LIKE ME

by

M. R. Carey

From the author of the million-copy bestseller The Girl With All the Gifts *comes a heart-stopping Jekyll and Hyde–style modern thriller with a heroine you'll love but shouldn't trust.*

Liz Kendall wouldn't hurt a fly. Even when times get tough, she's devoted to bringing up her two kids in a loving home.

But there's another side to Liz—one that's dark and malicious. She will do anything to get her way, no matter how extreme.

And when this other side of her takes control, the consequences are devastating.

extras

Remember the tale of Dr. Jekyll and Mr Hyde? There are two sides to every story....

Maybe this is on me, Liz Kendall thought as she tried in vain to breathe. A little bit, anyway. For sure, it was mostly the fault of her ex-husband, Marc, and his terrifying temper, but she could see where there might be a corner of it left that she could claim for herself. Taking responsibility for your own mistakes was important.

It was Marc's weekend with the kids, and he had brought them back late. Except he hadn't really brought them back at all. He had left them outside, in his car, and had come inside to tell Liz that they were going to grab some dinner. You know, since it was already so late and all.

Hell, no.

Liz had surprised herself, speaking up for her rights and the kids' routine, reminding Marc (which he knew damn well) that tomorrow was a school day. She had been overconfident, was what it was. She had lost the habit of victimhood somewhere, or at least temporarily mislaid it. Forthright words had spilled out of her mouth, to her own astonishment as much as Marc's.

But Marc had some words of his own once he got over the surprise, and the argument had moved through its inevitable phases: recrimination, rage, ultimatum. Then when there was nowhere left for it to go in words alone, it had moved into actions, which speak louder. Marc had grabbed Liz by the throat and slammed her backward into the counter, sending the bags of groceries she had laid in for the kids' return cascading down onto the tiles.

"I'm going to fix you once and for all, you fucking bitch!" he roared into her dazed face.

Now she was down on the floor among the spilled foodstuffs and Marc was kneeling astride her, his teeth bared, his face flushed with effort, his wild eyes overflowing with hate. As Liz twisted in his grip, trying to open a passage from her windpipe to her lungs, she glimpsed a box of Lucky Charms on her left-hand side and a bottle of Heinz malt vinegar on her right.

Egyptian pharaohs sailed into the afterlife in reed boats piled with all the treasures they'd amassed in their lives. Gold. Jewels. Precious metals. In heaven, Liz would have condiments and breakfast cereal. Great, she thought. Wonderful.

Darkness welled up like tears in her eyes.

And that was when the iceberg hit.

Hard.

It hit her from the inside out, a bitter cold that expanded from the core of her body all the way to her skin, where it burned and stung.

She saw her hand, like a glove on someone else's hand, groping across the floor. Finding the vinegar bottle's curved side. Turning it with her fingertips until she could take hold of it.

Her arm jerked spasmodically, lifting from the ground only to fall back down. Then it repeated the motion. Why? What was she doing? No, what was this rogue part of her doing on its own behalf? Now that it had a weapon, why wasn't it even trying to use it?

A wave of glee and fierce amusement and anticipation flooded Liz's mind as though her brain had sprung a catastrophic leak and someone else's thoughts were pouring in. Stupid. Stupid question. She was *making* a weapon.

Three times is the charm. With the third impact, the bottle smashed on the hard tiles. The vinegar seeping into her lacerated skin made Liz's dulled nerves twitch and dance, but it was a dance with no real meaning to it, like that strange event she had seen once when she picked Zac up from his school's summer bop: a silent disco.

She drove what was left of the bottle into the side of Marc's face as hard as she could.

Marc gave a hoarse, startled grunt, flicking his head aside as though a fly or a moth had flown into his eye. Then he screamed out loud, reeling backward as he realized he was cut. His hands flew up to clutch his damaged cheek. Pieces of broken glass rained down onto the floor like melting icicles after a sudden thaw.

Some of them had blood on them. Liz's stomach turned over when she saw that, but it was as though some part of her had missed the memo: satisfaction and triumph rose, tingling like bubbles, through her nausea and panic.

That surge of alien emotion was terrifyingly intense, but in other ways normal service was being resumed. Liz's arms dropped to the floor on either side of her as though whatever had just taken her over had flung them down when it was done. The prickling cold folded in on itself and receded back into some hidden gulf whose existence she had never suspected.

Liz sucked in an agonizing sliver of breath, and then another. Her chest heaved and spasmed, but the sickness of realization filled her quicker than the urgent oxygen, quicker even than the overpowering smell and taste of vinegar.

What she had just done.

But it was more like what *someone else* had done, slipping inside her body and her mind and moving her like a puppet. She hadn't willed this; she had only watched it, her nervous system dragged along in the wake of decisions made (instantly, enthusiastically) elsewhere.

Liz tried to sit up. For a moment she couldn't move at all. It felt as if she had to fumble around inside herself to find where all her nerves attached. Her body was strange to her, too solid and too slow, like a massive automaton controlled by levers and pulleys.

Finally she was able to roll over on one elbow, her damaged hand pressed hard against her chest. She watched a ragged red halo form on the white cotton of her T-shirt as the blood soaked through, conforming sloppily and approximately to the outline of her fingers. A year-old memory surfaced: the time when Molly had painted around her hand for art homework with much more exuberance than accuracy.

Marc lunged at her again with a screamed obscenity, one hand groping for her throat while the other was still clamped to his own cheek. But he didn't touch her. Didn't get close. Pete and Parvesh Sethi from the apartment upstairs were suddenly there on either side of him, coming out of nowhere to grab him and haul him back. For a few seconds, the three men were a threshing tangle of too many limbs in too many places, a puzzle picture. Then Pete and Parvesh put Marc down hard.

Pete knelt across Marc's shoulders to pin his upper body to the ground, facedown, while Parvesh, sitting on his legs, took his phone out of his pocket to request—with astonishing calm—both a police visit and an ambulance. Marc was raving, calling them a couple of queer bastards and promising that when he came back to finish what he'd started with Liz he'd spend some time with them too.

"Lizzie," Parvesh shouted to her across the room. "Are you all right? Talk to me!" From the concern in his voice, she thought maybe he had asked her once already and she had missed it somehow in the general confusion.

"I'm fine," she said. Her voice was a little slurred, her mouth as sluggish and unwilling as the rest of her. "Just…cut my hand."

But there was a lot more wrong with her than that.

"Pete," Parvesh said, "have you got this?"

"I've got it," Pete grunted. "If he tries to get up, I'll dislocate his shoulder."

Parvesh stood and walked across to Liz. Marc struggled a little when he felt that his legs were free, but Pete tightened his grip and he subsided again.

"Fucking queer bastard," Marc repeated, his voice muffled because his mouth was right up against the tiles. "I'll fucking fix you."

"Well, you could fix your trash talk," Pete said. "Right now, it doesn't sound like you're even trying."

"Let me see," Parvesh said to Liz. He knelt down beside her and took her hand in both of his, unfolding it gently like an origami flower. There was a big gash across her palm, a smaller one at the base of her thumb. Parvesh winced when he saw the two deep cuts. "Well, I guess they're probably disinfected already," he said. "Vinegar's an acid. But we'd better make sure there's no glass in them. Have you got a first aid kit?"

Did she? For a second or two the answer wouldn't come. The room made no sense to her, though she'd lived in this house for the best part of two years. She had to force herself to focus, drag up the information in a clumsy swipe like someone groping in the dark for a ringing phone.

"Corner cupboard," she mumbled. "Next to the range, on the right."

It was still hard to make all her moving parts cooperate—hard even to talk without her tongue catching between her teeth. She thought she might be drooling a little, but when she tried to bring her good hand up to her mouth to wipe the spittle away her body refused to cooperate. The hand just drew a sketchy circle in the air.

When your own body doesn't do what you tell it to, Liz thought in sick dismay, that has to mean you're losing your mind.

Parvesh got her up on her feet, the muscles in her legs twanging like guitar strings, and led her across to the sink. He ran cold water across the cuts before probing them with a Q-tip soaked in Doctor's Choice. They were starting to hurt now. Hurt like hell, with no fuzz or interference. Liz welcomed the pain. At least it was something that was hers alone: nobody else was laying claim to it.

Marc was still cursing from the floor and Pete was still giving him soft answers while leaning down on him hard and not letting him move a muscle.

"The kids!" Liz mumbled. "Vesh, I've got to go get the kids."

"Zac and Moll? Where are they?"

"In Marc's car. Out on the driveway." Or more likely on the street, parked for a quick getaway. Marc wouldn't have had any expectation that he was going to lose this argument.

"Okay. But not bleeding like a pig, Lizzie. You'll scare them shitless."

Parvesh was right, she knew. She also knew that Zac must be getting desperate by now, only too aware that the long hiatus with both of his parents inside the house meant they were having a shouting match at the very least. But she had made him promise never to intervene, and she had made the promise stick. She hadn't wanted either of her children to come between her and Marc's temper. In the years leading up to the divorce, protecting them from that had been the rock bottom rationale for Liz's entire existence.

Whatever happens between him and me, Zac, you just stay with your sister. Keep her safe. Let it blow over.

Only this didn't seem like something that was going to blow over. Liz could hear sirens whooping a few streets away, getting louder: repercussions, arriving way before she was ready for them. When she still didn't even understand how any of this had happened.

The iceberg. The alien emotions. The puppet dance.

The room yawed and rolled a little. Liz went away and came back again, without moving from the spot where she stood. One of the places she went to—just for half a heartbeat or so—was the Perry Friendly Motel. A suspect mattress bounced under her ass as Marc bounced on top of her and she thrust from the hips with joyous abandon to meet him halfway.

Okay, that was weird. That was nearly twenty years ago. What was she going to hallucinate next? A guitar solo?

The next thing she was aware of was Parvesh applying a dressing to her hand, bending the pad carefully around her open wounds. "What did he do to you?" he asked her, keeping his voice low so the conversation was just between the two of them.

Liz shook her head. She didn't want to talk about it because that meant having to think about it.

"You've got bruises on your throat. Lizzie, did he attack you?"

"I've got to go out to the kids," she said. Had she already said that? How much time had passed? Could she make it to the street without fainting or falling over?

Parvesh tilted her head back very gently with one hand and leaned in close to examine her neck.

"He did. He tried to throttle you. Oh Lizzie, you poor thing!"

Liz flinched away from his pity as if it were contempt. She had tried hard not to let anyone see this. To be someone else, a little bit stronger and more self-sufficient than her current self. And since she had moved into the duplex, she had felt like it was working, like she had sloughed off an old skin and been reborn. But here she was again, where she had been so many times before (although something strong had moved through her briefly, like the ripples from a distant tidal wave).

"How did it happen?"

"It's his weekend. I was just . . . unhappy because he brought the kids back so late. I told him not to." The kids. She needed to make sure they were okay: everything else could wait. Liz headed for the door.

But she still wasn't as much in command of her own movements as she thought she was. She stumbled and almost fell. Parvesh caught her and sat her down on one of the chairs. She noticed that there was a dark streak of blood across the blue and yellow polka dots on its tie-on cushion.

The back of her head was throbbing. Putting a hand up to feel back there she found a lump like a boulder, its surface hot and tender. When Marc knocked her down she must have hit the tiles a lot harder than she thought. Another wave of nausea went through her but she fought against it and managed not to heave.

More talking. More moving around. The kitchen floor was still rising and falling like the deck of a ship. Liz lost track of events again, feeling around inside herself for any lingering traces of that presence. Her interior puppetmaster.

The outside world came back loudly and suddenly with the kitchen door banging open and then with Marc bellowing from the floor for someone to let him up because he was being assaulted and illegally restrained.

"So what happened here?" another voice asked. A female voice, calm and matter-of-fact. Liz looked up to find two uniformed cops in the kitchen, a woman and a man. She closed her eyes immediately, finding that the light and movement were making the nausea return.

Marc was talking again, or yelling rather, swearing that he was going to sue the Sethis for every penny they had. Pete told him to make sure he spelled their names right. "It's Mr. Queer Bastard and Dr. Queer Bastard. We don't hyphenate."

"Her husband attacked her," Parvesh said. "That guy over there. Him."

"Ex-husband," Liz muttered automatically. She opened her eyes again, as wide as she dared. "The kids. My kids are…"

"We've got an officer with them right now, ma'am," the lady cop said. "They're fine. Is it okay if we bring them around by the front of the house? We don't think it's a good idea for them to see this." She nodded her head to indicate the smears and spatters of blood all over the kitchen floor, on the side of the counter, on Liz and on Marc.

Marc was sitting up now, his back against the fridge. The Sethis had retired to the opposite corner of the room but the man cop, whose badge identified him as Lowenthal, was standing over Marc and a paramedic was kneeling beside him, holding a dressing pad to his face. Blood was oozing out from under the pad, running along its lower edge to a corner where it dripped down onto Marc's shirt. It didn't make much difference to the shirt: you couldn't even tell where the drops were landing on the blood-drenched fabric.

The lady cop talked on her radio for a few seconds. "Yeah. Bring them through the front door and find someplace where they can sit. Tell them their mom and dad are okay and someone's going to be with them soon." She slipped the radio back into the pouch on her belt and looked at everyone in turn. "Suppose we run through this from the beginning," she said. "What exactly happened here?"

"She ripped my face open with a bottle!" Marc snarled.

"A vinegar bottle," Liz added unnecessarily. The lady cop turned to Liz and gave her a hard, appraising look. Her badge read Brophy. A nice Irish name. She didn't look Irish. She was blonde and wide-faced like a Viking, with flint-gray eyes. Maybe cops got Irish surnames along with their badges. Except for Lowenthal.

"Are you saying this is true, ma'am?" Officer Brophy asked. "You assaulted him with a bottle?"

"Yes," Liz said.

"Okay, you want to tell me why?"

I can't, Liz thought bleakly. I don't even understand it myself.

"He was on top of me," she said. "Choking me." It was absolutely true. It was also irrelevant. That wasn't *why* she'd done what she did; it was only *when*.

"Can anyone corroborate that?"

"Yes, ma'am," Parvesh said. "We saw the whole thing. We live upstairs. We heard the noise through the floor and ran down. The kitchen door was open, so we let ourselves in, and we saw Lizzie on the floor with this man—" He nodded his head in Marc's direction. "—on top of her. She's Elizabeth Kendall and he's her ex-husband, Marc. Marc with a *c*. He had his hands around her throat. We were so amazed that for a moment we couldn't think of what to do. We just shouted at him to get off of her. But he didn't stop. He didn't even seem to hear us. Then Lizzie grabbed the bottle up off the floor and swung it, and that was when we stepped in. Am I missing anything, Pete?"

"That's how it went down," Pete agreed.

"Look at her neck," Parvesh told Officer Brophy, "if you don't believe us."

"I didn't touch her," Marc yelled. "They're lying. She just went for me!"

Officer Brophy ignored Marc while she took up Parvesh's invitation. She walked across to Liz and leaned in close to look at her bare throat. "Could you tilt your chin up a little, ma'am?" she asked politely. "If it doesn't hurt too much."

Liz obeyed. Officer Lowenthal whistled, short and low. "Nasty," he murmured.

"How's the gentleman looking?" Brophy asked the paramedic. She shot Marc a very brief glance.

"He'll need stitches," the paramedic said. "They both will."

"You just got the one ambulance?"

"Yeah. The other one is out in Wilkinsburg."

"Okay, then you take him. Officer Lowenthal will accompany you, and I'll follow on with Mrs. Kendall. Len, you ought to cuff him to a gurney in case he gets argumentative."

"I'll do that," Lowenthal said.

"This is insane!" Marc raged. "Look at me! I'm the one who's injured. I'm the one who was attacked." He swatted away the paramedic's hands and pulled the dressing pad away to display his wounds. The eye looked fine, if a little red. The semicircular gouge made by the bottle ringed it quite neatly, but there was a strip of loose flesh hanging down from his cheek as though Liz had tried to peel him.

"That does look pretty bad," Officer Lowenthal allowed. "You just hit him the once, ma'am?"

"Once," Liz agreed. "Yes." And hey, she thought but didn't say, that's a one in my column and a couple of hundred in his, so he'll probably still win the match on points even if he doesn't get a knockout.

She shook her head to clear it. It didn't clear. "Please," she tried again. "My children. I can't leave them on their own. I haven't even seen them yet. They don't know what's happening."

The two cops got into a murmured conversation that Liz couldn't catch.

"Well, you go on in and talk to them," Brophy said eventually. "While we get your husband's statement." *Ex-husband*, Liz amended in her mind. *Took the best part of two years to get that ex nailed on the front, and nobody ever uses it.* "They can ride with you to the hospital, if you want. Or if you've got friends who can look after them..."

"We'd be happy to do that," Parvesh said.

"...then they can stay here until you get back. Up to you. You go ahead and talk to them now while we finish up in here."

"I'm making a lasagna," Pete said to Liz, touching her arm as she went by. "If they haven't had supper, they can eat with us."

Liz gave him a weak smile, grateful but almost too far out of herself to show it. "Thanks, Pete."

"I was attacked with a bottle!" Marc said again, holding fast to this elemental truth. "She shoved a bottle in my face!"

"You told us that," Officer Lowenthal said. "But she missed the eye. You got lucky there."

"I'm filing charges. For criminal assault!"

"Okay," Brophy said. "We're listening, sir. Tell us what happened."

Liz got out of there. She didn't want to hear a version of the story where she was the monster and Marc was just in the wrong place at the wrong time.

The trouble was, if she told the truth she had to admit that there *had* been a monster in that kitchen. She had no idea where it had come from, or where it had gone when it left her.

If.

If it had left her.

if you enjoyed
THE GAMESHOUSE

look out for

THE TEN THOUSAND DOORS OF JANUARY

by

Alix E. Harrow

In a sprawling mansion filled with peculiar treasures, January Scaller is a curiosity herself. As the ward of the wealthy Mr. Locke, she feels little different from the artifacts that decorate the halls: carefully maintained, largely ignored, and utterly out of place.

Then she finds a strange book. A book that carries the scent of other worlds, and tells a tale of secret doors, of love, adventure and danger. Each page turn reveals impossible truths about the world and January discovers a story increasingly entwined with her own.

The Blue Door

When I was seven, I found a door. I suspect I should capitalize that word, so you understand I'm not talking about your
garden- or common-variety door that leads reliably to a white-
tiled kitchen or a bedroom closet.

When I was seven, I found a Door. There—look how tall
and proud the word stands on the page now, the belly of that
D like a black archway leading into white nothing. When you
see that word, I imagine a little prickle of familiarity makes
the hairs on the back of your neck stand up. You don't know
a thing about me; you can't see me sitting at this yellow-wood
desk, the salt-sweet breeze riffling these pages like a reader
looking for her bookmark. You can't see the scars that twist
and knot across my skin. You don't even know my name (it's
January Scaller; so now I suppose you do know a little something about me and I've ruined my point).

But you know what it means when you see the word Door.
Maybe you've even seen one for yourself, standing half-ajar and
rotted in an old church, or oiled and shining in a brick wall.
Maybe, if you're one of those fanciful persons who find their feet
running toward unexpected places, you've even walked through
one and found yourself in a very unexpected place indeed.

Or maybe you've never so much as glimpsed a Door in your
life. There aren't as many of them as there used to be.

But you still know about Doors, don't you? Because there
are ten thousand stories about ten thousand Doors, and we
know them as well as we know our names. They lead to Faerie,

to Valhalla, Atlantis and Lemuria, Heaven and Hell, to all the directions a compass could never take you, to *elsewhere*. My father—who is a true scholar and not just a young lady with an ink pen and a series of things she has to say—puts it much better: "If we address stories as archaeological sites, and dust through their layers with meticulous care, we find at some level there is always a doorway. A dividing point between *here* and *there*, us and them, mundane and magical. It is at the moments when the doors open, when things flow between the worlds, that stories happen."

He never capitalized doors. But perhaps scholars don't capitalize words just because of the shapes they make on the page.

It was the summer of 1901, although the arrangement of four numbers on a page didn't mean much to me then. I think of it now as a swaggering, full-of-itself sort of year, shining with the gold-plated promises of a new century. It had shed all the mess and fuss of the nineteenth century—all those wars and revolutions and uncertainties, all those imperial growing pains—and now there was nothing but promise and prosperity wherever one looked. Mr. J. P. Morgan had recently become the richest man in the entire history of the world; Queen Victoria had finally expired and left her vast empire to her kingly-looking son; those unruly Boxers had been subdued in China; and Cuba had been tucked neatly beneath America's civilized wing. Reason and rationality reigned supreme, and there was no room for magic or mystery.

There was no room, it turned out, for little girls who wandered off the edge of the map and told the truth about the mad, impossible things they found there.

I found it on the raggedy western edge of Kentucky, right where the state dips its toe into the Mississippi. It's not the kind of place you'd expect to find anything mysterious or even mildly interesting: it's flat and scrubby-looking, populated by flat, scrubby-looking people. The sun hangs twice as hot and three times as bright as it does in the rest of the country, even at the very end of August, and everything feels damp and sticky, like the soap scum left on your skin when you're the last one to use the bath.

But Doors, like murder suspects in cheap mysteries, are often where you least expect them.

I was only in Kentucky at all because Mr. Locke had taken me along on one of his business trips. He said it was a "real treat" and a "chance to see how things are done," but really it was because my nursemaid was teetering on the edge of hysteria and had threatened to quit at least four times in the last month. I was a difficult child, back then.

Or maybe it was because Mr. Locke was trying to cheer me up. A postcard had arrived last week from my father. It had a picture of a brown girl wearing a pointy gold hat and a resentful expression, with the words *AUTHENTIC BURMESE COS-TUME* stamped alongside her. On the back were three lines in tidy brown ink: *Extending my stay, back in October. Thinking of you. JS.* Mr. Locke had read it over my shoulder and patted my arm in a clumsy, keep-your-chin-up sort of way.

A week later I was stuffed in the velvet and wood-paneled coffin of a Pullman sleeper car reading *The Rover Boys in the Jungle* while Mr. Locke read the business section of the *Times* and Mr. Stirling stared into space with a valet's professional blankness.

I ought to introduce Mr. Locke properly; he'd hate to wander into the story in such a casual, slantwise way. Allow me to present Mr. William Cornelius Locke, self-made not-quite-billionaire, head of W. C. Locke & Co., owner of no less than three stately homes along the Eastern Seaboard, proponent of the virtues of Order and Propriety (words that he certainly would prefer to see capitalized—see that *P*, like a woman with her hand on her hip?), and chairman of the New England Archaeological Society, a sort of social club for rich, powerful men who were also amateur collectors. I say "amateur" only because it was fashionable for wealthy men to refer to their passions in this dismissive way, with a little flick of their fingers, as if admitting to a profession other than moneymaking might sully their reputations.

In truth, I sometimes suspected that all Locke's moneymaking was specifically designed to fuel his collecting hobby. His home in Vermont—the one we actually lived in, as opposed to the two other pristine structures intended mainly to impress his significance upon the world—was a vast, private Smithsonian packed so tightly it seemed to be constructed of artifacts rather than mortar and stones. There was little organization: limestone figures of wide-hipped women kept company with Indonesian screens carved like lace, and obsidian arrowheads shared a glass case with the taxidermied arm of an Edo warrior (I hated that arm but couldn't stop looking at it, wondering what it had looked like alive and muscled, how its owner would have felt about a little girl in America looking at his paper-dry flesh without even knowing his name).

My father was one of Mr. Locke's field agents, hired when I was nothing but an eggplant-sized bundle wrapped in an old traveling coat. "Your mother had just died, you know, very sad case," Mr. Locke liked to recite to me, "and there was your father—this odd-colored, scarecrow-looking fellow with God-help-him *tattoos* up and down his arms—in the absolute middle of nowhere with a baby. I said to myself: Cornelius, there's a man in need of a little charity!"

Father was hired before dusk. Now he gallivants around the world collecting objects "of particular unique value" and mailing them to Mr. Locke so he can put them in glass cases with brass plaques and shout at me when I touch them or play with them or steal the Aztec coins to re-create scenes from *Treasure Island*. And I stay in my little gray room in Locke House and harass the nursemaids Locke hires to civilize me and wait for Father to come home.

At seven, I'd spent considerably more time with Mr. Locke than with my own biological father and, insofar as it was possible to love someone so naturally comfortable in three-piece suits, I loved him.

As was his custom, Mr. Locke had taken rooms for us in the nicest establishment available; in Kentucky, that translated to a sprawling pinewood hotel on the edge of the Mississippi, clearly built by someone who wanted to open a grand hotel but hadn't ever met one in real life. There were candy-striped wallpaper and electric chandeliers, but a sour catfish smell seeped up from the floorboards.

Mr. Locke waved past the manager with a fly-swatting gesture, told him to "Keep an eye on the girl, that's a good fellow," and swept into the lobby with Mr. Stirling trailing like a man-shaped dog at his heels. Locke greeted a bow-tied man waiting on one of the flowery couches. "Governor Dockery, a pleasure! I read your last missive with greatest attention, I assure you—and how is your cranium collection coming?"

Ah. So that was why we came: Mr. Locke was meeting one of his Archaeological Society pals for an evening of drinking, cigar smoking, and boasting. They had an annual Society meeting every summer at Locke House—a fancy party followed by a stuffy, members-only affair that neither I nor my father was permitted to attend—but some of the real enthusiasts couldn't wait the full year and sought one another out wherever they could.

The manager smiled at me in that forced, panicky way of childless adults, and I smiled toothily back. "I'm going out," I told him confidently. He smiled a little harder, blinking with uncertainty. People are always uncertain about me: my skin is sort of coppery-red, as if it's covered all over with cedar sawdust, but my eyes are round and light and my clothes are expensive. Was I a pampered pet or a serving girl? Should the poor manager serve me tea or toss me in the kitchens with the maids? I was what Mr. Locke called "an in-between sort of thing."

I tipped over a tall vase of flowers, gasped an insincere "oh *dear*," and slunk away while the manager swore and mopped at the mess with his coat. I escaped outdoors (see how that word slips into even the most mundane of stories? Sometimes I feel there are doors lurking in the creases of every sentence, with periods for knobs and verbs for hinges).

The streets were nothing but sunbaked stripes crisscrossing themselves before they ended in the muddy river, but the people of Ninley, Kentucky, seemed inclined to stroll along them as if they were proper city streets. They stared and muttered as I went by.

An idle dockworker pointed and nudged his companion. "That's a little Chickasaw girl, I'll bet you." His workmate shook his head, citing his extensive personal experience with Indian girls, and speculated, "West Indian, maybe. Or a half-breed."

I kept walking. People were always guessing like that, categorizing me as one thing or another, but Mr. Locke assured me they were all equally incorrect. "A perfectly unique specimen," he called me. Once after a comment from one of the maids I'd asked him if I was colored and he'd snorted. "Odd-colored, perhaps, but hardly *colored*." I didn't really know what made

433

a person colored or not, but the way he said it made me glad I wasn't.

The speculating was worse when my father was with me. His skin is darker than mine, a lustrous red-black, and his eyes are so black even the whites are threaded with brown. Once you factor in the tattoos—ink spirals twisting up both wrists—and the shabby suit and the spectacles and the muddled-up accent and—well. People stared.

I still wished he were with me.

I was so busy walking and not looking back at all those white faces that I thudded into someone. "Sorry, ma'am, I—" An old woman, hunched and seamed like a pale walnut, glared down at me. It was a practiced, grandmotherly glare, especially made for children who moved too fast and knocked into her. "Sorry," I said again.

She didn't answer, but something shifted in her eyes like a chasm cleaving open. Her mouth hung open, and her filmy eyes went wide as shutters. "Who—just who the hell are you?" she hissed at me. People don't like in-between things, I suppose.

I should have scurried back to the catfish-smelling hotel and huddled in Mr. Locke's safe, moneyed shadow, where none of these damn people could reach me; it would have been the proper thing to do. But, as Mr. Locke so often complained, I could sometimes be quite improper, willful, and temerarious (a word I assumed was unflattering from the company it kept).

So I ran away.

I ran until my stick-thin legs shook and my chest heaved against the fine seams of my dress. I ran until the street turned to a winding lane and the buildings behind me were swallowed up by wisteria and honeysuckle. I ran and tried not to think about the old woman's eyes on my face, or how much trouble I would be in for disappearing.

My feet stopped their churning only once they realized the dirt beneath them had turned to laid-over grasses. I found myself in a lonely, overgrown field beneath a sky so blue it reminded me of the tiles my father brought back from Persia: a majestic, world-swallowing blue you could fall into. Tall, rust-colored grasses rolled beneath it, and a few scattered cedars spiraled up toward it.

Something in the shape of the scene—the rich smell of dry cedar in the sun, the grass swaying against the sky like a tigress in orange and blue—made me want to curl into the dry stems like a fawn waiting for her mother. I waded deeper, wandering, letting my hands trail through the frilled tops of wild grains.

I almost didn't notice the Door at all. All Doors are like that, half-shadowed and sideways until someone looks at them in just the right way.

This one was nothing but an old timber frame arranged in a shape like the start of a house of cards. Rust stains spotted the wood where hinges and nails had bled into nothing, and only a few brave planks remained of the door itself. Flaking paint still clung to it, the same royal blue as the sky.

Now, I didn't know about Doors at the time, and wouldn't have believed you even if you'd handed me an annotated three-volume collection of eyewitness reports. But when I saw that raggedy blue door standing so lonesome in the field, I wanted it to lead someplace else. Someplace other than Ninley, Kentucky, someplace new and unseen and so vast I would never come to the end of it.

I pushed my palm against the blue paint. The hinges groaned, just like the doors to haunted houses in all my penny papers and adventure stories. My heart pat-patted in my chest, and some naive corner of my soul was holding its breath in expectation, waiting for something magical to happen.

There was nothing on the other side of the Door, of course: just the cobalt and cinnamon colors of my own world, sky and field. And—God knows why—the sight of it broke my heart. I sat down in my nice linen dress and wept with the loss of it. What had I expected? One of those magical passages children are always stumbling across in my books?

If Samuel had been there, we could've at least played pretend. Samuel Zappia was my only nonfictional friend: a dark-eyed boy with a clinical addiction to pulpy story papers and the far-away expression of a sailor watching the horizon. He visited Locke House twice a week in a red wagon with *ZAPPIA FAMILY GROCERIES, INC.* painted on the side in curlicued gold lettering, and usually contrived to sneak me the latest issue of *The Argosy All-Story Weekly* or *The Halfpenny Marvel* along with the flour and onions. On weekends he escaped his family's shop to join me in elaborate games of make-believe involving ghosts and dragons on the lakeshore. *Sognatore*, his mother called him, which Samuel said was Italian for good-for-nothing-boy-who-breaks-his-mother's-heart-by-dreaming-all-the-time.

But Samuel wasn't with me that day in the field. So I pulled out my little pocket diary and wrote a story instead.

When I was seven, that diary was the most precious thing I had ever owned, although whether I technically owned it is legally questionable. I hadn't bought it, and no one had given it to me—I'd found it. I was playing in the Pharaoh Room just before I turned seven, opening and closing all the urns and trying on the jewelry, and I happened to open a pretty blue treasure chest (*Box with vaulted lid, decorated with ivory, ebony, blue faience, Egypt; originally matched pair*). And in the bottom of the chest was this diary: leather the color of burnt butter, creamy cotton pages as blank and inviting as fresh snow.

It seemed likely that Mr. Locke had left it for me to find, a secret gift he was too gruff to give directly, so I took it without hesitation. I wrote in it whenever I was lonely or lost-feeling, or when my father was away and Mr. Locke was busy and the nursemaid was being horrible. I wrote a lot.

Mostly I wrote stories like the ones I read in Samuel's copies of *The Argosy*, about brave little boys with blond hair and names like Jack or Dick or Buddy. I spent a lot of time thinking of bloodcurdling titles and copying them out with extra-swirly lines ("The Mystery of the Skeleton Key"; "The Golden Dagger Society"; "The Flying Orphan Girl"), and no time at all worrying about plot. That afternoon, sitting in that lonely field beside the Door that didn't lead anywhere, I wanted to write a different kind of story. A true kind of story, something I could crawl into if only I believed it hard enough.

Once there was a brave and temeraryous (sp?) girl who found a Door. It was a magic Door that's why it has a capital D. She opened the Door.

For a single second—a stretched-out slice of time that began on the sinuous curve of the *S* and ended when my pencil made its final swirl around the period—I believed it. Not in the half-pretending way that children believe in Santa Claus or fairies, but in the marrow-deep way you believe in gravity or rain.

Something in the world shifted. I know that's a shit description, pardon my unladylike language, but I don't know how else to say it. It was like an earthquake that didn't disturb a single blade of grass, an eclipse that didn't cast a single shadow, a vast but invisible change. A sudden breeze plucked the edge of the diary. It smelled of salt and warm stone and a dozen faraway scents that did not belong in a scrubby field beside the Mississippi.

I tucked my diary back in my skirts and stood. My legs

shivered beneath me like birch trees in the wind, shaking with exhaustion, but I ignored them because the Door seemed to be murmuring in a soft, clattering language made of wood rot and peeling paint. I reached toward it again, hesitated, and then—

I opened the Door, and stepped through.

I wasn't anywhere at all. An echoing in-betweenness pressed against my eardrums, as if I'd swum to the bottom of a vast lake. My reaching hand disappeared into the emptiness; my boot swung in an arc that never ended.

I call that in-between place the threshold now (Threshold, the line of the *T* splitting two empty spaces). Thresholds are dangerous places, neither here nor there, and walking across one is like stepping off the edge of a cliff in the naive faith that you'll sprout wings halfway down. You can't hesitate, or doubt. You can't fear the in-between.

My foot landed on the other side of the door. The cedar and sunlight smell was replaced by a coppery taste in my mouth. I opened my eyes.

It was a world made of salt water and stone. I stood on a high bluff surrounded on all sides by an endless silver sea. Far below me, cupped by the curving shore of the island like a pebble in a palm, was a city.

At least, I supposed it was a city. It didn't have any of the usual trappings of one: no streetcars hummed and buzzed through it, and no haze of coal smoke curtained above it. Instead, there were whitewashed stone buildings arranged in artful spirals, dotted with open windows like black eyes. A few towers raised their heads above the crowd and the masts of small ships made a tiny forest along the coast.

I was crying again. Without theater or flair, just—crying, as if there were something I badly wanted and couldn't have. As my father did sometimes when he thought he was alone.

"January! *January!*" My name sounded like it was coming from a cheap gramophone several miles away, but I recognized Mr. Locke's voice echoing after me through the doorway. I didn't know how he'd found me, but I knew I was in trouble.

Oh, I can't tell you how much I didn't want to go back. How the sea smelled so full of promise, how the coiling streets in the city below seemed to make a kind of script. If it hadn't been Mr. Locke calling me—the man who let me ride in fancy train cars and bought me nice linen dresses, the man who patted my arm when my father disappointed me and left pocket diaries for me to find—I might have stayed.

But I turned back to the Door. It looked different on this side, a tumbled-down arch of weathered basalt, without even the dignity of wooden planks to serve as a door. A gray curtain fluttered in the opening instead. I drew it aside.

Just before I stepped back through the arch, a glint of silver shimmered at my feet: a round coin lay half-buried in the soil, stamped with several words in a foreign language and the profile of a crowned woman. It felt warm in my palm. I slipped it into my dress pocket.

This time the threshold passed over me like the brief shadow of a bird's wing. The dry smell of grass and sun returned.

"Janua—oh, there you are." Mr. Locke stood in his shirt-sleeves and vest, huffing a little, his mustache bristling like the tail of a recently offended cat. "Where were you? Been out here shouting myself hoarse, had to interrupt my meeting with Alexander—what's this?" He was staring at the blue-flecked Door, his face gone slack.

"Nothing, sir."

His eyes snapped away from the Door and onto me, ice-sharp. "January. Tell me what you've been doing."

I should've lied. It would have saved so much heartache.

But you have to understand: when Mr. Locke looks at you in this particular way of his, with his moon-pale eyes, you mostly end up doing what he wants you to. I suspect it's the reason W. C. Locke & Co. is so profitable.

I swallowed. "I—I was just playing and I went through this door, see, and it leads to someplace else. There was a white city by the sea." If I'd been older, I might've said: *It smelled of salt and age and adventure. It smelled like another world, and I want to return right this minute and walk those strange streets.* Instead, I added articulately, "I liked it."

"Tell the *truth*." His eyes pressed me flat.

"I am, I swear!"

He stared for another long moment. I watched the muscles of his jaw roll and unroll. "And where did this door come from? Did you—did you build it? Stick it together out of this rubbish?" He gestured and I noticed the overgrown pile of rotted lumber behind the Door, the scattered bones of a house.

"No, sir. I just found it. And wrote a story about it."

"A story?" I could see him stumbling over each unlikely twist in our conversation and hating it; he liked to be in control of any given exchange.

I fumbled for my pocket diary and pressed it into his hands. "Look right there, see? I wrote a little story, and then the door was, was sort of open. It's true, I swear it's true."

His eyes flicked over the page many more times than was necessary to read a three-sentence story. Then he removed a cigar stub from his coat pocket and struck a match, puffing until the end glowed at me like the hot orange eye of a dragon.

He sighed, the way he sighed when he was forced to deliver some bad news to his investors, and closed my diary. "What fanciful nonsense, January. How often have I tried to cure you of it?"

He ran his thumb across the cover of my diary and then deliberately, almost mournfully, tossed it into the messy heap of lumber behind him.

"*No!* You can't—"

"I'm sorry, January. Truly." He met my eyes and made an abortive movement with his hand, as if he wanted to reach toward me. "But this is simply what must be done, for your sake. I'll expect you at dinner."

I wanted to fight him. To argue, to snatch my diary out of the dirt—but I couldn't.

I ran away, instead. Back across the field, back up winding dirt roads, back into the sour-smelling hotel lobby.

And so the very beginning of my story features a skinny-legged girl on the run twice in the space of a few hours. It's not a very heroic introduction, is it? But—if you're an in-between sort of creature with no family and no money, with nothing but your own two legs and a silver coin—sometimes running away is the only thing you can do.

And anyway, if I hadn't been the kind of girl who ran away, I wouldn't have found the blue Door. And there wouldn't be much of a story to tell.